FROM THE YONDER

A Collection of Horror from Around the World

Volume IV

War Monkey Publications, LLC
Orem, Utah

©2023 War Monkey Publications, LLC

First Print, 2023

Cover Art by Tracy Whiteside
www.tracywhiteside.com
Models: Sarah Prestage and Allison Samuels

ISBN 978-1-954043-09-1 (Paperback Cover)
ISBN 978-1-954043-11-4 (ePub)

www.warmonkeypublications.com

TABLE OF CONTENTS

A NOTE FROM THE EDITOR

It is always a challenge to know what to write once a project is coming to a close. Especially, when our offices are still occasionally being affected by the ongoing pandemic, and I have found myself working on the anthology in bursts of late nights (or since I am nocturnal, midday work).

Lately, I have been working with young schoolchildren on reading and writing. Youths for whom a well-crafted fart joke is the epitome of well written literature. For better or worse, this volume is not a treasure trove of fart jokes.

The stories, though, are well crafted. And it is my sincere desire that you, the reader, find them enjoyable, fart jokes or not.

Sincerely,

Joshua P. Sorensen

AUTHOR BIOS

ROSS BAXTER - After thirty years of naval service, Ross Baxter now concentrates on writing short stories. He has won a number of awards, and had a story included on the 2017 HWA Bram Stoker reading list. Married to a Norwegian and with two Anglo-Viking kids, he now lives in Derby, England.
Website: https://rossbaxter.wordpress.com/
Twitter: @rossbaxter1

DWAIN CAMPBELL - Dwain Campbell is originally from Sussex, New Brunswick, Canada. After a forty-year career as a teacher in Newfoundland, he retired in St. John's and studies folklore in his spare time. Contemporary fantasy is his genre of choice, and Atlantic Canada is a rich source of inspiration.

KEVIN MICHAEL CLARKE - Kevin Michael Clarke is 72 years of age and from Leeds. He became interested in writing when he retired. Kevin always preferred supernatural stories. His late mother hailed from Mayo, Ireland and regaled him with her superstitious tales of banshees and fairies over and over. She always wanted her ashes to be scattered in Ireland, so his inclusion in this anthology, "The Village of Carrowmore" is an homage to her.

ELIZABETH DAVIS - Elizabeth Davis is a second-generation writer living in Dayton, Ohio. They live there with their spouse and two cats - neither of which have been lost to ravenous corn mazes or sleeping serpent gods.

They can be found at deadfishbooks.com when they aren't busy creating beautiful nightmares and bizarre adventures. Their work can be found at Lolcraft, After the Fall, and Nightmare Sky.

MALINA DOUGLAS - Malina Douglas weaves stories that fuse the fantastic and the real. She was awarded Editor's Choice in the Hammond House International Literary Prize and was a finalist in the Four Palaces Fiction Anthology Contest. Publications include Because That's Where Your Heart Is by Sans Press, the National Flash Day Anthology, Wyldblood, Ellipsis Zine, Sanitarium IV, The Periodical Forlorn and Parabnormal. Anthologies include Underdogs Rise, Out of the Darkness by Wolfsinger Publications, The Monsters We Forgot Vol. II, and A Krampus Carol. She curated and edited the anthology Winter Enchantment and can be found on twitter @iridescentwords or at https://citrinesunstream.wixsite.com/iridescent.

GARRY ENGKENT - Garry Engkent is a Chinese-Canadian. He has co-authored three texts: *Groundwork: Writing Skills to Build On; Fiction/Non-Fiction: A Reader and Rhetoric*; and *Essay: Do's and Don'ts.* His fictional stories have appeared in *Exile, Many-Mouthed Birds, Emerge, Ricepaper Magazine, Savagerealmsgamebook, WTF,* and *Dark Winter Literary Magazine.* Most stories have a Chinese immigrant slant: "Why My Mother Can't Speak English", "Eggroll", and "Rabbit". His recent published forays into horror are "I, Zombie: A Different Point of View," "The Zombie and the Shedim," and "Swine."

MARK A. FISHER - Mark A. Fisher is a writer, poet, and playwright living in Tehachapi, CA. His poetry has appeared in: *Reliquiae, Silver Blade, Young Ravens Literary Review*, and many other places. His first chapbook, *drifter*, is available from Amazon. His poem "there are fossils" (originally published in *Silver Blade*) came in second in the 2020 Dwarf Stars Speculative Poetry Competition. His plays have appeared on California stages in Pine Mountain Club, Tehachapi, Bakersfield, and Hayward. He has also won cooking ribbons at the Kern County Fair.

LINDA KAY HARDIE- Linda Kay Hardie writes horror, crime, and fantasy stories for adults, as well as stories and books for children. She also writes recipes and is the reigning Spam champion for Nevada (yes, the tasty treat canned mystery meat). Linda's writing has won awards dating back to fifth grade, with first place for an essay on fire safety. Linda is a member of Horror Writers' Association, Short Mystery Fiction Society, Society of Children's Book Writers and Illustrators, and Cat Writers' Association, and has a master's degree in English from University of Nevada, Reno, where she teaches required courses to unwilling students.

RUSSELL HEMMELL - Russell Hemmell is a French-Italian transplant in Scotland, passionate about astrophysics, history, and speculative fiction. Recent/ forthcoming work in Aurealis, Cast of Wonders, Flame Tree Press, Lightspeed, Pseudopod, and others. SFWA & HWA. Find them online at their blog earthianhivemind.net and on Twitter @SPBianchini.

ANDREAS HORT - Andreas Hort is a multi-genre writer living in the Czech Republic. He's an omnivorous reader of fiction, comics, manga, poetry, and non-fiction. Whatever idea sprouts in his mind, speculative or grounded, wholesome or creepy, funny or serious—as long as it's interesting, he molds it into a tale. He's currently working on a novella to self-publish on Kindle in 2023.

LAURA G. KASCHAK - Laura G. Kaschak writes dark fiction for both adults and young teens, including the "Shadow Squad" book series. Her chilling short stories have been featured in many dark fiction anthologies. She grew up in the pine barrens with the constant companionship of the Jersey Devil and now lives in Virginia wine country, successfully fooling everyone into believing she's a grownup.

ZIAUL MOID KHAN - Born and raised in North India countryside Johri, Ziaul Moid Khan writes speculative fiction and philosophical poetry. He's fond of fiction books, pens, tea and coffee. Mostly self-taught in English, he loves creative isolation for exploration of his deeper being. Living in an idealism, someday he will decode life with all its mysteries. He says he's close enough to do so. Khan happily resides in Jaipur, Rajasthan with his wife Khushboo and their six-year-old young son, Brahmaand Cosmos. He has his work published in more than a dozen magazines, anthologies and journals. Email him at ziamoidkhan.b@gmail.com.

TOM LARSEN - Tom Larsen was born and raised in New Jersey and was awarded a degree in Civil Engineering from Rutgers University. He is the author of six novels in the crime genre.

Tom's short fiction has been published in "Alfred Hitchcock Mystery Magazine", "Mystery Tribune", Sherlock Holmes Mystery Magazine" and "Black Cat Mystery Magazine."

His non-fiction work has appeared in four volumes of the anthology series; "Best New True Crime Stories." Tom's short story, "Pobre Maria" will appear in the anthology, "Best Mystery Stories of the Year 2023" from Mysterious Press.

http://www.amazon.com/TOM-LARSEN/e/B00N00JLZM

Y. LEN - In 2020, Y. Len received an honorable mention from the Writers of the Future contest and, in 2021, saw the first story published on paper in the *Wight Christmas: Holiday Horror and Seasonal Subversion* collection. In 2022, another short story appeared in *The Bull* magazine. Two more stories are forthcoming in the *Down in the Dirt* magazine and *Trigger Warning: Cursed* anthology in 2023.

KEVIN PATRICK MCCANN - Kevin Patrick McCann has published eight collections of poems for adults, one for children (Diary of a Shapeshifter, Beul Aithris), a book of ghost stories (It's Gone Dark, The Otherside Books), Teach Yourself Self-Publishing (Hodder) co-written with the playwright Tom Green and Ov (Beul Aithris Publications) a fantasy novel for

children.
He writes regularly for International Times & most
weeks publishes a new poem there.

PHOENIX MCDONALD - Phoenix McDonald is a
disabled, non-binary, full-time writer living in
Oregon. They began writing in 2014 following a
brain cancer diagnosis, that apparently triggered a
writing bug in their brain. Since then, they have
published multiple short stories, written a YA
fantasy trilogy and are currently working on a new
adult fantasy novel.
Website: SynMcDonaldWrites.com
Twitter: @synphoenix72

SARA MARTINEZ - Sara Martinez is an author and
game designer. She is a passionate gamer and devoted
wife and mother living in the Denver, CO area. Sara
has a wide and eclectic variety of hobbies that she
occasionally finds time to pursue including cooking,
historical reenactment, needlepoint, painting, cosplay,
and karaoke. One of her life goals is to someday be on
the show Jeopardy.
Sara writes short fiction across several genres
including Horror, Science-Fiction, and Weird West.
She has a number of published gaming credits for
Deadlands, Call of Cthulhu and 5E among others. For
more information see saramartinezauthor.com.

KENT J. MOORE - Kent J. Moore is a Senior
Strategist for Physician Payment and contributing
editor to FPM, a peer-reviewed journal of the
American Academy of Family Physicians. In addition
to FPM, his work appears in Humanities, the National
Endowment for the Humanities' magazine, and Stories
from the Lockdown, an anthology to benefit
UNICEF's VaccinAid. Kent's short stories have won
local writing contests, and he has also written an
inverted mystery novel for which he's seeking
representation and publication.

DONNA J. W. MUNRO - Donna J. W. Munro's
pieces are published in Nothing's Sacred Magazine IV
and V, Corvid Queen, *Hazard Yet
Forward* (2012), *Enter the
Apocalypse* (2017), *Beautiful Lies, Painful Truths
II* (2018), *Terror Politico* (2019), *It Calls from the
Forest* (2020), *Gray Sisters Vol 1* (2020), *Borderlands
Vol 7 (2020), Pseudopod 752 (2021),* and others.
Check out her first novel, *Revelation: Poppet Cycle
Book 1*. Contact her
at https://www.donnajwmunro.com or
@DonnaJWMunro on Twitter.

SERGIO 'ENTE PER ENTE' PALUMBO - Sergio
'ente per ente' Palumbo is an Italian public servant
who graduated from Law School working in the public
real estate branch, who published a Fantasy

RolePlaying illustrated Manual, WarBlades, of more than 700 pages. Over 120 of his short stories have been published in publications throughout the World, with 18 more to follow in 2023/2024. He has been co-Editor, partnered with Mrs. Michele DUTCHER, of 5 different international anthologies.
He is also a scale modeler who likes to build mostly Science Fiction and Real Space models. The internet site of his Scale Model Club "**La Centuria**": www.lacenturia.it

STEPHEN PATMORE - Stephen Patmore is an early career short story fiction writer with a background in poetry.
Stephen has received accolades and awards from the likes of Bang Said the Gun at the Edinburgh Fringe Festival and has been published in the Big Bardaid Book, a Desert Hearts publication and initiative to bring contemporary poetry into schools. His spoken word album was released under the RRRants label, and his music is available in both digital and physical audio formats and has sold thousands of units to date.
Stephen lives in Sheffield England with his wife and their angry cat, Bones.

JOSHUA PETERSON - Joshua Peterson is an author with autism who currently lives in with his family in Normal, Illinois. His passion of writing began in early January 2014 when he wrote an original fantasy story on his laptop. Since then, he has written a few stories, including his first published short story, The Ghost who Haunts the Bathroom for War Monkey Publications. He continues writing to improve his writing skills and hopes to publish his first novella or novel in the future. Joshua Peterson is an Eagle Scout and a Heartland Community College graduate with an associate's degree of Digital Media Communication.

BECKA REX - Becka is an emerging author enjoying her very first publication in From The Yonder 4. Over the ~30 years she's been writing, she has amassed an artillery of original poetry and short stories. She is a game producer by trade but is currently working on her debut novel in the evenings and has high hopes of publishing more work in the future. Her favorite books are Wuthering Heights, War and Peace, and Post Office. She also enjoys gardening, sculpting, and spinning her fire hula hoop around from time to time.

CHARLES SARTORIUS - Charles Sartorius has one foot in the business world and the other tiptoeing into the literary one. An admitted project crunching MBA workaholic, he does make time to write both stories and music lyrics. Nordic Press has published his mystery crime short story, *The Missing Case of the Missing Case*, in its *Murder! Mystery! Mayhem! Anthology*. Another creation, *The Ancient Forest of Terror*, will be published in an upcoming horror anthology. Several songs appear on conventional venues (Amazon and Apple Music) like his comedic satire, *A Fart is the Best Response,* judged a finalist in the 2020 USA Songwriting Competition.

PHILLIP T. STEPHENS - Phillip T. Stephens attended the Michigan State writers' workshop. He taught writing and design at Austin Community College for 20 years. Phillip's writing and art appear in anthologies, literary publications, and peer-reviewed academic journals. His novels Doublemint Gumshoe and Seeing Jesus won multiple awards for independent fiction. He and Carol live in Oak Hill, Texas where they built a habitat in the shade of their oaks to house foster cats for austinsiameserescue.org. They found new homes for more than three hundred abandoned pets. You can find more of his work at https://medium.com/wind-eggs.

PETINA STROHMER - Petina Strohmer is a published novelist and writer of short horror stories (one of the most recent was bought by Alice Cooper!) She lives in the magical Welsh mountains with a raggle-taggle assortment of rescued animals. For more information, go to www.petinastrohmer.com

JAY SYKES - Jay Sykes is a non-binary creative and academic from Tasmania, Australia. They delight in birthing works that disturb whilst maintaining a sense of wonder and beauty. So far, they have had written pieces accepted by Sirens Call Publications, Science Write Now and The Last Girls Club, among others. They also sell their artwork and handmade jewelry in historic Salamanca Place, and assault the audiences of their hometown with their dark comedic observations. They hope to continue spreading a vague sense of unease far and wide!

MOLLY THYNES - Molly Thynes has been everything from a student at an all-girl's Catholic school to a nanny, a purveyor of haunted artifacts, and a mental health counselor, but she has been a writer before she even knew how to write. Her first love is the horror genre but has found inspiration in a few other genres too (just not romance). Currently, Molly lives in Saint Paul, MN with her husband, her son, and as many animals as their landlord will allow.

D.J. TYRER - DJ Tyrer is the person behind *Atlantean Publishing* and has been widely published in anthologies and magazines around the world, such as *Chilling Horror Short Stories* (Flame Tree), *All The Petty Myths* (18th Wall), *Steampunk Cthulhu* (Chaosium), *What Dwells Below* (Sirens Call), and *EOM:Equal Opportunity Madness* (Otter Libris), and issues of *Sirens Call*, *Hypnos*, *Occult Detective Magazine*, *parABnormal*, and *Weirdbook*, and in addition, has a novella available in paperback and on the Kindle, *The Yellow House* (Dunhams Manor).

DJ Tyrer's website is at https://djtyrer.blogspot.co.uk/

DJ Tyrer's Facebook page is
at https://www.facebook.com/DJTyrerwriter/

The Atlantean Publishing website is
at https://atlanteanpublishing.wordpress.com/

KATERYNA VOLOSHYNA - Kateryna Voloshyna is an author from Dnipro, Ukraine. She has M.A. in history and philosophy. She works as a content writer. Kateryna is fascinated by legends, fairy tales with a twist, and mysterious stories. Her first published story appeared back in 2012. Her stories were published in American and English magazines. Her first children's book was published in 2020.

<u>THE GHOST WHO HAUNTS THE BATHROOM</u>

by Joshua Peterson

The cafeteria, filled with six long tables with elongated benches attached was overcrowded by the students of Jefferson Elementary School as they ate well-cooked hamburgers and steaming French fries. At the third table, a young boy named Ronald told his friends, Jim, Henry, and Timmy, that he overheard a janitor calming to see a ghost in the abandoned girl's bathroom. The fourth grader's curiosity persuaded his pals to investigate themselves and all four discreetly ducked and crawled under the table. After stomping the hardened stairs, the young boys ran through hallways of art, frames of former students, closed classroom doors, and echoed footsteps. Two floors later, Ronald, Jim, Henry, and Timmy arrived at their destination as they took rapid, quick breaths in front of a rusty door with a "Do Not Enter" sign attached.

"Are you sure we should do this?" Henry questioned the mission. "We could get into a lot of trouble if we're caught."

"We have fifteen minutes until lunch is over," Ronald bragged. "With all the teachers eating lunch and the councilors clueless, we will find the ghost before recess starts. No one will suspect that we snuck away during lunch."

"What makes you sure that the janitor saw a ghost in the abandoned girl's bathroom?" Jim judged his pal's sources as he pointed a finger toward the door.

Ronald explained to his companions that his older brother once told him about a little girl named Sakura, who died in that same restroom years ago. The child was a Japanese-American citizen and a former student who was scolded and beaten by her young peers for being different. One day, the tormented tyke with tears pouring from her eyes ran from a group of mean girls and took refuge inside the girl's bathroom. As soon as recess was over, the same janitor entered the lavatory and found the student sitting on a toilet with her blood seeping from her lacerated wrists. The bathroom closed down since then, but people who entered the chamber claimed to see Sakura's spirting rising within the same toilet where she died.

"You know, it reminds me of an urban legend my grandfather told me about when he visited Japan one day," Timmy spoke. "Like Sakura's, it was about a ghost named Hanako-san who said to haunt the country's school bathrooms, but only the girl's bathrooms. He told me that if you go to the girl's bathroom on the third floor and then knock the toilet lid in the third stall three times, her ghost will appear and ask you to be friends with her. If you say, "no," she turns into a three-headed lizard and eats you. If you say, "yes," she'll drag you down through the toilet and spend the rest of your life in the underworld. No matter what answer you say, you'll die no matter what."

"That's a bunch of baloney," Ronald harshly critiqued. "It's just stories old geezers made up just to scare kids."

"Well, that's pretty scary if you ask me," Jim complimented.

"Are we going to hunt some ghosts or not?" Henry reminded his friends. "We now have ten minutes before the school bell rings."

"Yeah, you're right," Ronald agreed. And I think it's better if one of us goes into the bathroom to search for Sakura. That way, if one us is in trouble, the rest of us will help. One, two, three, not it!"

All four boys raced their fingers toward their noises while repeatedly yelling the same phrase. But Timmy was the slowest and therefore, he was chosen to go inside. The loser lad opened the door and reluctantly entered the abandoned girl's bathroom.

*****

As soon as he stepped inside and closed the door behind him, Timmy observed the entire emptied lavatory. The lonesome lad pinched his nose for corrosion spread all over the pink walls and ceiling with a non-operating fan. Toilets with no urinals in sight were stacked against the back wall and they were covered with brown and yellow stains. The place would have been cloaked in darkness if it hadn't been for a ray of light shining through a window. "A perfect place for a ghost to haunt," Timmy criticized for watching many ghost shows on tv.

"Sakura, are you here?" The boy called out the spirit's name. "My name is Timmy, and I'm here to see you. To prove that you're real." Silence came after the echoes stopped. "Hello?".

Silence returned and Timmy moaned as he massaged the back of his neck with his hand. Time was running out and the fourth grader needed to find the ghost, or he would return to his friends empty handed. But then the young boy remembered his grandfather's story and wheeled his enlightened eyes toward the third stall with the door open. He theorized that if he could summon Sakura like how Hanako-san is called in Japan, then maybe her spirit will appear. Timmy hurried himself until he stood in front of the same toilet to begin the ritual.

Timmy took a deep breath and said, "here goes nothing" before knocking the toilet lid three times.

"Are you here Sakura?" Timmy called out again.

"Yes," a spooky feminine voice answered, and Timmy jumped a little.

Lights flickered, turning darkness into light and vice versa that startled Timmy out of the stall, only to find the light switch downwards and untouched. All the remaining stall doors quaked on their own and roared louder than the lad's beating heart. Blood spewed from the toilet that over-flooded up to the boy's ankles. A laughing girl echoed, which jerked the trembling tyke's head towards the same stall. Then a paled girl in a black bob cut rose within the bloody fountain without staining her red dress.

"Are… are you the ghost of Sakura?" Timmy asked.

"Yes, I am," the ghost answered. "Want to be friends with me?"

Timmy swallowed and nodded.

"Then let's be friends forever and ever," the spirit grinned.

Sakura's arm extended until her hand gripped Timmy's wrist and he shrieked like a little girl. The ghost girl plummeted, yanking her new BFF along with her. If the crimson child hadn't grabbed the edge of the latrine, he would have fallen into the toilet. As his strength kept him from descending further, the crimson-soaked schoolboy looked down and spotted Sakura, laughing and surrounded by a vortex of flames. Timmy's eyes widen and urged his body to pull even harder to break himself free from the ghoul's grasp.

The struggle continued, but Timmy's fingers, damped from the seat, were losing their grip, bringing him close to the flaming whirlpool. The young boy called for help and his friends came barging into the red flooded chamber. All three boys spotted their companion in trouble and rush to his aid, stomping a trail of splashes. The strained schooler ultimately lost his grip and plunged into the toilet headfirst before Ronald, Henry, and Jim grabbed his legs. With just one pull, forged by the combined strength of three little boys, Sakura's hold on Timmy shattered and they yanked him out of the hellish portal.

After landing on his rescuers, Timmy got and ran out of the bathroom screaming.

"Get back here!" Sakura yelled with a demonic voice which spooked the three would-be-heroes.

The specter rose from the toilet, but its burning, red eyes turned brown after spotting the cowering boys.

"New friends!" Sakura exclaimed cheerfully. "Want to be friends with me?!"

All three shivering schoolers shook their heads.

"Then die!" Sakura's voice and eyes reverted to their malevolent form.

Ronald, Jim, and Henry screamed and ran.

As the shrieking boys headed toward the exit, Sakura morphed into a three headed lizard with charcoal grayed scales and white dorsal spikes and pursued them. The door slammed by itself before the schoolers grabbed and pulled the handle riotously. Even with their combined strength, the door refused to budge by the hysterical boys. Sakura eventually caught up to her prey and clamped the screaming boys with each gapping maw.

*****

Timmy ran through the hallway, leaving a trail of red footprints until he burst into the unoccupied but cleaned boy's bathroom. The crimson child hurried into the nearest stall, opened the door, which bumped into another one, and sat down on the sanitized toilet lid. As the traumatized tyke tried to regain control of his breathing, the image of Sakura and the torching tornado stuck on replay in his mind. A loud musical sound boomed through the speakers and the little boy jumped out of his seat. Then Timmy calmed down after he realized that the whimsical tone was the school bell.

As Timmy was about to leave, Sakura emerged from the toilet and grabbed him.

"Did you think you could just run away from me?" Sakura whispered into Timmy's ear. "Even hiding in the boy's bathroom, there is no escape. You agreed to be my friend, and as my friend, you and I will be together in the underworld forever."

Sakura and Timmy plunged into the toilet as the creaky door closed by itself.

THE END

<u>IT'S CALLED THE WENDIGO</u>

by Molly Thynes

December, 2020

"Are you telling me you would rather throw me and my money out the door, all over a piece of fabric?"

Hannah slunk backward, trying to make herself as small as possible, just behind the candy rack. In checkout number four, her mother stood screaming, spitting at the grocery store manager, who stood with his arms crossed over his black clip-on tie. Off to the side stood the teenage cashier Hannah's mother had finished cussing out, sniffing and rubbing her red eyes.

"Ma'am, the mask policy is the same across the state. Orders from the governor," the manager responded, impassive to the yelling. "It's not up to me to decide if your money is worth it or not."

"I forgot my mask at home!" Hannah's mother tried switching her tone to a more pleading treble, but too much of her residual anger still clung to her voice. "Couldn't you let it slide just this once, for the sake of getting some much-needed groceries?"

The manager didn't even try to stop himself from snorting out a laugh. First thing wrong with her story: her 'much needed groceries' consisted of a single party-sized tray of meat, cheese, and crackers from the deli. It didn't exactly paint a picture of feeding a starving family. Second: this was a small town, and this was hardly the first time Hannah's mother had gone grocery shopping since April. She had already had multiple allowances of 'just this once'. In fact, the employee her mother had pushed past when he prompted her to put on a mask before entering was watching them, sweeping the same square of tile over and over again.

And third…

The manager tilted his head in Hannah's direction. "You didn't remember when you saw your daughter walking out the door wearing one?"

Hannah's mother turned and shot her daughter a deathly glare, nearly baring her teeth. Hannah tried to cover as much of her mask as she could with her hand. The fabric pressing into her nostrils still carried the scent from fabric softener and mothballs from the sheet her grandmother had let her cut up to make as a supply for the family. Not that anyone other than Hannah wore them.

But pointing out Hannah's treacherous acts was the last thing the manager should have done if he wanted her mother to calm down.

"Regardless, ma'am, mask or not, I'm going to have to ask you to leave. Your behavior is becoming a disturbance to the other customers."

Hannah's mother turned her glare back to the manager, French-tipped nails flexing into her fists. "You think I'm the only one in this store who thinks these policies are a load of bull?" she shouted before turning her attention toward the back of the store, and the people wandering the aisles. "All of you! These 'laws' and 'policies' only have as much power as you let them have. If we all threw off our masks now, what would they be able to do about it?"

Whatever great stirring Hannah's mother hoped to rile up…it didn't happen. The people who did meet her eyes for the briefest fraction of a second just turned back to their shopping. *Honestly, Mom? It's been months!* The people who did throw tantrums like this at the beginning of the pandemic had long since been banned from the local grocery store and had to drive all the way to Duluth for their food.

And everyone who *was* wearing masks and still shopping at Jenson's Grocery…they just didn't care.

They certainly weren't going to drop their milk and eggs to take up arms against Manager Todd, who did not get paid enough for this.

When no one came to her mother's aid, it all snowballed. Hannah's mother glanced around frantically, nostrils flaring, until her eyes finally settled on two teenagers standing in the next aisle. An older boy with long black hair tied behind his head looked Hannah's mother up and down, while a younger girl with hair down and sweeping around her elbows held out a cellphone pointed in their direction. After all, these kinds of public meltdowns made for content gold on TikTok.

"What are you little papooses looking at?" Hannah's mother spat.

"Mom!" Hannah finally emerged from behind her hiding place. "What are you doing?"

Sure, Hannah's mother had never been the most "racially sensitive" person on the planet. None of Hannah's aunts, uncles, or adult family friends were. But up until now, it had just been little quips in whispered tones at parties. Never out-in-out slurs in the middle of the grocery store.

Hannah's mother glared at the teenagers with dark, flinty eyes. "The only reason the little parasites even wander off the reservation is to take food out of the mouths of people who actually live here! It's not my fault your GED course didn't teach you how to keep frybread and buffalo jerky on the gas station shelves!"

Jesus! Was her mother going to tell them "if they were hungry, they should eat grass" next?

"Mom, people are going to find out who you are and send that video to your boss!"

But neither of the two native teenagers tried to run or back away. They didn't even appear disgusted. The boy held his head tilted to the side, blinking slowly without looking away, while the girl watched them more through her phone, lip slightly parted as she twisted a loose end of her hair.

Finally, an older woman with streaks of grey rivering through her long braid leapt out from the aisle, a plastic bag hanging from the crook of her arm. "You two! Get away from her! We're going home!"

The woman – their mother? – rushed shuffling across the floor, pushing the two teenagers along as they struggled to look back, arguing to stay. The boy protested just a little too loud, "…whites going Wendigo."

Was that what he said? Wendigo? Was that just tongue-in-cheek Ojibwe for 'crazy white woman'?

"I'm not going to say it again, ma'am," the manager spoke up again. "You can leave on your own or I can call the sheriff. It's up to you."

Hannah's mother made a guttural almost-roar in the back of her through before locking eyes on her daughter. "Hannah, we're leaving! We're going to be late!"

Turning on her high-heeled shoes, Hannah's mother stormed across the grocery floor – *click, click, click* – toward the automatic doors. Hannah hurried to follow behind, clutching her purse against her side, keeping her eyes down. Hannah's mother remained silent, pushing the same strand of blond hair back behind her ear again and again. But this would absolutely not last, especially once they were out the door out of sight of witnesses.

"What exactly was that back there?" Hannah's mother growled as they stepped out into the blowing snow and the wind that found its way into every gap in Hannah's coat.

"What do you mean, Mom?" Hannah had to shout just to hear her own voice over the howling gusts of wind.

"Just hiding behind that candy while you let that manager disrespect your own mother!" she snapped as she strode across the ice-covered pavement, somehow keeping perfect footing. "Do you want to be a lion, or do you want to be a sheep?"

Hannah held out her arms to keep her balance as her own blond hair swirled in the wind and snowflakes caught in her eyelashes. This is something Hannah's mother had been talking about more and more in recent days: lions who are brave, fierce, and answer to no one, and sheep, weak and only able to follow the instructions of whoever was in charge, no matter how incompetent. Her mother had diligently categorized everyone they knew into being lions or being sheep. Hannah herself kept shifting back and forth as to what her mother considered her, but she always made sure to remind Hannah she could be part of the pride, or she could be eaten alive.

On and on, Hannah's mother strode effortlessly across the winter landscape while Hannah fought to keep her grip on the ground and to see through the coin-sized snowflakes. The seething rage her mother had unleashed in the grocery store seemed to give her a nearly inhuman ability to navigate through the vicious weather, more like a shark cutting through open ocean.

At least there wasn't far to go to reach their destination.

"I still can't believe I will be the only one showing up without a dish!" Hannah's mother grumbled as she stomped up the short staircase to the town's community center, which shared a parking lot with Jenson's Grocery – white-sided with four-paned framed windows.

Hannah took purposeful steps across the yet-to-be salted front porch until she joined her mother. Pushing through the rust-laced door, they entered the tiny one-story box of a building, with chipped plaster walls, old community posters no one had bothered to take down for twenty years, and the smell of hamburger and chicken stock lingering in the air. Hannah's mother tossed her coat onto a pile of massive, down-stuffed look-alikes. Hannah hung onto hers.

"Do you know if anyone else brought their kids with them?" Hannah asked, shutting the door behind them.

"I don't know, Hannah," her mother replied, tone clipped. "Just…go get something to eat. I need to go find out what the order is for addressing the meeting."

Yes, the meeting that, between the pandemic and the blizzard warning, probably should have been a Zoom meeting. But that would have defeated the entire point of this particular meeting, of "lions" meeting in their community den.

Her mother's hard-bottomed heels clacked against the cheap linoleum floor as she made her way to the small auditorium used by the community band and summer theater troops. Flanked on either side of the swinging double doors were a set of foldout tables, lined with bowls of chips, dessert bars cut and arranged into pyramids on plates, and countless other dishes of hotdish: tater tot, hamburger pie, chicken and wild rice.

Hannah leaned to glance through the still-swinging auditorium doors. Her mother had already managed to find her crowd of people. In a small town, the room was full of adults Hannah had known her whole life. There was Mr. Hagen who owned the gas station two blocks down from her house, Mr. Pederson, who owned Roger's Family Restaurant. There was Mrs. Larson, Hannah's seventh grade social studies teacher, and Pastor Schroeder, who ran the First Baptist Church (Hannah's family didn't go there, but a lot of his congregants were probably here).

"Sarah!" the pastor remarked, opening his arms to embrace her, his pointed chin spearing into her shoulder, grinning and showing his too-big teeth. After several of these town meetings, though, he and her mother had become good friends. "It's so good to see your smiling face!"

There were a *lot* of smiling faces in the auditorium. There was not a hand-sewn mask to be seen, and people kept intruding on one another's six-foot bubble of breathing space, governor's orders be damned. Orders like that had a hard time reaching that far north and that deep into the woods.

Once the doors finally closed, Hannah slipped her tablet out of her purse. Her mother would have been furious if she knew Hannah brought it with her, no matter how many times Hannah tried to explain that this was how school was done now. All it did was remind her mother of how life was different now and how well her own daughter had adapted to it.

Shaking it out of sleep mode, Hannah traced her fingers over the icons speckling the screen. Thank God, the WiFi was still on.

Snatching one of the chocolate-iced rice crispy bars off the table, Hannah ducked around the corner, tucking into a small alcove in the wall. Back against the wall, she slid down to sit cross-legged on the floor. Licking the melted chocolate from her fingertips, Hannah tapped the Internet icon, which opened directly to the distance learning homepage.

"Order, order!" came a booming voice from around the corner and behind the closed doors of the auditorium. "If everyone will take their seats, please, the meeting will commence."

But although whoever was heading the meeting called for order, there was still an almost-loud undercurrent of murmuring, like a nest of yellowjackets buried under the earth.

Hannah reached into her pocket for her earphones.

"We have all gathered here today…"

One earbud in.

"…to devise a collective strategy for how to stand against the massive government overreach that harmed everyone in this room and every family in this town."

Two earbuds in.

It was no wonder that there were no other kids here. And it wasn't just that they had been more adamant in their refusal to go out in the storm than

Hannah had been While every adult in this building –
and, for that matter, most of the adults in town – ranted
and railed against the pandemic restrictions, everyone
Hannah was friends with adapted to lockdown in the
way people said kittens and puppies could adapt to any
home environment. Kaylee managed to teach herself
how to knit, crochet, macrame, and embroider all in
the span of a few months. Sydney was on her way to
starting her own social media/comedy empire, all from
her phone. And Megan, Hannah's best friend in the
entire world, was in the midst of writing a fantasy
series set to rival the works of Tolkien, at least
according to Megan.

And Hannah, well… She texted her friends
every day, had regular Zoom calls with her cousins
who lived across the country, opened her first Reddit
account. Oh, and she had ended the semester with
straight A's for the first time in her life. That was
possibly her greatest crime of all in the eyes of her
mother. A sheep just survived under the yoke of
"governmental oppression", but what would you even
call someone who *thrived* under it?

Hannah opened to the video tab on her
American History page. One of the largest benefits of
online school was that the teachers had been able to get

a lot more creative in the guest speakers they were able to get to talk to the class. They could come from anywhere in the state – or anywhere in the country, really – and they didn't need to put on real clothes or even be awake during school hours. Anyone with a camera, an Internet connection, and a dream.

Ms. Swenson collected as many of these video lessons as she could: interviews with men in nursing homes who fought Nazis face to face, teenagers from South Minneapolis who snuck out of the house to go to the George Floyd protests, Indian boarding school survivors who didn't have near enough grey hairs to convince people that it was an event from long, long ago.

Hannah opened the tab to the newest video, which had actually been posted while Hannah had been in the car. It was an Ojibwe man named Rafael Sumner, not quite old enough to remember the residential school days. He didn't talk to them about history either. He was what Ms. Swenson called a 'folk storyteller.', and he would record himself telling them old stories the Ojibwe had been telling for centuries. There was no place where this fit into the curriculum of their twenty-year-old textbooks for this kind of thing, but Ms. Swenson told them the most valuable types of learning didn't always come from books provided by the state, and they should all take any opportunity they had to learn anything they could. What she meant was they should all be grateful he was willing to take time out his life to even tell these stories to the children of white Northwoods racists who made drunk Indian jokes in polite conversation.

Clicking on the video, it opened to Mr. Sumner – in his blue-button shirt with the beaded, bolo-like tie, hair slicked down with fine likes in the corners of his eyes – sitting in his living room with its orange-hued lights in the brown armchair, scuffed along the top.

"Hello, class," he said in that soft, relaxed, but resonating tone of his. "I'm glad to have another chance to talk today."

As he reached over to take a sip of his water, the noise of the meeting carried through Hannah's earphones.

"…supermarket had the God damned nerve to kick me out! I showed the manager my medical exemption card, and he tried to snatch it right out of my hand. I should have…"

"But anyway," Mr. Sumner's voice blocked out the noise, "You came here because you are looking for a story."

He glanced back over his shoulder, towards the back window. The wind was just picking up outside, and the pin-point snowflakes pinged more ice-like against the glass. "Winter nights like this, in particular, it makes me think of stories the older ones told about something that hunts in the cold." He turned back to the camera, the corners of his mouth pulling into a somewhat sly smile. "I hope everyone is in the mood for a scary story.

"This story is one you should all pay attention to, because it is about a creature that roams the whole of the northern half of the state, from the shores of Lake Superior all the way out into the densest woods. In fact, it's the woods that they prefer."

Hannah glanced up out the window, where the pine trees stood so packed together, they had no outlines independent of the other.

Yup, that's definitely us.

"The creature I am going to tell you about is called the Wendigo."

Hannah took a sharp intake of breath, tiny glass shards pinpricking their way down her throat on the way to her lungs. There was that word again. Wendigo. And this kind of buildup couldn't have been for something as simple as "crazy white women".

"And I feel it is especially relevant to talk about this creature in these days because it is a creature whose hunger is derived from its spiritual imbalance and, at heart, its selfishness."

In the pause between his breaths, someone in the auditorium shouted, "Big Pharma scam garbage!" Growling, snarling, deep.

"The Wendigo is not a creature that is secretive or one that hides. Its presence is usually preceded by winter storms or a foul smell in the air. It strikes people who are alone. And once they do make themselves known, they appear before the unfortunate soul, impossibly tall, lips chewed from their face, teeth and claws sharper than you could ever sharpen a blade.

"It moves faster than anything in the forest could hope to run, across land and over tree branches," Mr. Sumner said, trailing his fingers through the air. "It forever appears gaunt and starving, and it hungers for only one thing."

He leaned toward the camera and spoke in barely more than a whisper. "Human flesh."

Hannah gulped and reminded herself to breathe while the shouts in the auditorium bounced off one another.

"What the hell happened to the fourteenth amendment?"

"Live free or die!"

"Everyone's going to die someday. We can't let a bunch of maybes stop people from living their lives!"

The voices in the auditorium all snapped and bit at one another, one person's anger feeding off the other. And each new sentence arose to carry more rage in its tone than the one before.

"But what is most frightening about the Wendigo is that a Wendigo is not born a Wendigo. All Wendigos were once human." Mr. Sumner tapped his fingers on the side of his waterglass. "But how does one become a Wendigo? In most stories, it goes that once a person tastes human flesh for the first time, they find themselves craving it for the rest of their days, the hunger for human flesh consuming them.

"But as I said, that is the well-known way in which a Wendigo is created. And I did promise you that this creature would be tied to what we are seeing in the world today." "It is also said that one can become a Wendigo when they are in a state of profound inner turmoil, or when someone prioritizes their own selfishness above the needs of the community."

Hannah chewed at the inside of her lower lip and wedged herself further into the corner between the two meeting walls. Suddenly, it became clear why he had chosen *this* particular story to tell today.

"Academics who are a lot smarter than I have speculated that the Wendigo being linked with selfishness can be tied to the earliest days of the Great Lakes tribes. All of these tribes lived through long, cold winters, year after year. And the only way to survive them was to band together as a community. And those who refused to do so would be damned," Mr. Sumner spoke to the camera. "In a way, I suppose this could all be tied back to cannibalism too, for those of you familiar with the phrase 'eating their own'."

"Sarah Nelson now has the floor," a voice, hoarse and pained sounding, came from the auditorium. "Please come to the podium to speak."

Those sharp heels of hers clicked so loud, they even echoed through the walls, across to the opposite end of the building. Up the stairs, across the stage, then – *boom, boom, boom* – as someone tapped on the microphone.

"I'm so glad to see all of you who have come out tonight." Her mother's voice resonated in that sharp, clipped tone she had, even when she was happy about something. "We have all come out here tonight in opposition of a tyrannical government, and maybe even against the wishes of certain family members, to show the world that our voices matter!"

On the surface, a joyous cadence laced her mother's voice. After all, she was never happier than when she had an audience, especially one that already agreed with every word she said. But even still, she hadn't managed to shed the angry tone that tinged her voice in the grocery store. It still lurked there, just underneath the shiny surface.

"There is no denying how we have all suffered, both as a community and as individuals, in the last several months," her mother declared. "And suffering has a way of showing people's true colors. Some shut themselves up in their homes, cowering away. Then there are others – those who stand among us tonight – who stand up to meet the challenges of that suffering and then rise above it!"

These were just all the same things her mother had said at home, ever since lockdown started – when she wanted to go get her highlights done, when she complained that the mask was scratchy, when she couldn't yell at Hannah for being on the computer too much (because who could yell at their child for going to school?). But her voice didn't sound like the same old whining anymore. There was a cutting edge to her voice this time as though just on the verge of screaming.

Hannah reached up to cover the ear closest to her mother's voice and focused her best on the screen in her lap.

"I suppose the reason I am telling you this story in particular today is because of something my six-year-old said to me the other day," Mr. Sumner mused to the class. "I was doing some work on the computer, and I had the TV on in the background. The local news came on, and they were showing videos of an anti-mask protest out in Duluth."

Oh, yes. Hannah's mother had been there too. She'd left Hannah home alone, eating Fruity Pebbles and Kraft mac and cheese for two days. How many new friends had she met there and brought to *this* meeting?

"Anyway, when I turned around, my six-year-old was standing about five inches from the TV. When I told her to back up, she turned around and looked at me. She said, 'Daddy, what are those people doing?' And I have never been one to lie to my children, if I can avoid it, so I told her these people were protesting all the restrictions that were put in place because of the pandemic.

"Now, I've explained the pandemic as best I could to my child. She knows it's why she's not going to first grade in person this year, why she never got to go to the playground or the lake this summer, and why her and I always put on our masks that her grandma made us whenever we go out the door." Mr. Sumner said. "And knowing all this, my daughter then asks me, 'Why don't these people want to help the sick people?' I did not have an answer for her."

Mr. Sumner let out a deep sigh. "The best I could tell her is that some people are afflicted with a terrible disease of selfishness. It makes them unable to see past the noses on their own faces, and they cannot see that the good of their community is also what makes for the good of themselves." He then gave the very softest of laughs. "And that's when my daughter told me, "Daddy, I never want to go to Duluth. It's going to be full of Wendigos once winter comes."

From the other side of the wall, the crowd cheered at something Hannah's mother had said. What it was, who cared? It all sounded the same by now.

"And I could not stop thinking about that," Mr. Sumner continued. "At the risk of angering any of your parents who might be listening over your shoulders, what I keep seeing in all our community – great swaths of people unwilling to to help their neighbors, taking to the streets in protest of even the smallest inconvenience – it is something I have never seen in my life. At least, not in my community."

Hannah's mother attempted to speak once again, but the crowd inside had not stopped cheering, her mother's voice garbled between them and the wind fighting against the window glass.

"I wouldn't say the sense of togetherness I see from my own neighbors comes from a fear of the Wendigo." Mr. Sumner spoke these words somewhat wistfully. "Those communities that haven't embraced such an outlook…well, there are numerous things they have to fear as we head into the long winter."

The people in Hannah's community *did* have a sense of togetherness, in their selfishness. But that probably wasn't what Mr. Sumner meant.

As Mr. Sumner's voice trailed off, Hannah absent-mindedly reached for the rice crispy bar she had picked up ages ago. She took one bite…and immediately spit it out. Hannah gagged, wiping her tongue on her sleeve. The strong flavor filled her whole mouth, spreading thick over the sharp corners of the rice crispies – salty, metallic, not a shred of sweetness. Once she had spat out the last of it, Hannah cast her eyes down to the treat in her hand. The bottom was just ordinary rice crispies, held together with sugar and hardened syrup. But the frosting spread over the top of it, which was supposed to be chocolate was not.

It was dark brown, but as she trailed her finger across it, it smeared away deep red, fragments forming along the edges like clots. *Is this blood?* Hannah ran her tongue along the roof of her mouth. A penny-like taste spider-webbed its way down her tastebuds.

It was.

Throwing the dessert bar across the floor, Hannah pushed herself up to her feet, still clutching her tablet. She sprinted around the corner, sliding across the floor until she stood before the twin tables of food. Now that the heat of the food had wafted away, the lightness of the steam left nothing behind but the smell of the food. It was wet and heavy, like paper pulp.

Behind door, the noise of the crowd stopped sounding like the voices of anything human. Still angry, but softer, more rumbling, animalistic. Something that tapped into a more primal part of Hannah's brain, raising the tiny hairs on the back of her neck and curling her toes, preparing her to run.

Ignoring the animal instincts in favor of her human side, plate by plate, Hannah tore away the tin foil and the Saran Wrap as the smell grew chokingly thick. The center of a slivered chocolate cake oozed fresh red. As she broke the crust of the hamburger pie, long trails of grey intestines clung mucus-laced to the spoon. The pale chicken and wild rice were speckled with shiny, deep red chunks, like the beef livers small children would point and gag at in the grocery store.

From the tablet in her hand, Mr. Sumner's voice returned, resonating in the hall's entryway. "But in all the variations we have in the stories of the Wendigo, there is a consistency in it. Once they have been transformed, once they have developed that hunger to flesh, it is something they will never stop hungering for, no matter how much they consume."

Just then, something slammed full-bodied against the auditorium doors. Then again, and again. How was that ever possible? Those doors didn't even lock.

"Help me!" someone shouted from the other side of the door. "For the love of God, someone help me!"

In this voice, there was no anger, no rage. Just pure and primal fear. Soon, whoever it was at the opposite side of the locked door was joined by others, screaming, pleading for their very lives.

"Let us out!"

"Please!"

"They're going to kill us!"

The room on the other side filled with screams, and not just from those trying to get out. Soon, those pleading voices were drowned out by a chorus of much more otherworldly screaming. First, sounding of garbled, human speech sputtering nonsense. Then, becoming piercing cries, shifting between two octaves, reaching frequencies that shook the termites out of the old wood.

"OH, MY GOD! AAAAAHHHHHH!"

Now the door rattled, slamming in rapid jerks. The screams melted into a chorus of wet, ripping noises. Out from the wide crack where the doors met the floor, a tide of deep red seeped out, crested like the waves on Superior. That metallic smell that had lingered around the food table filled the air as though Hannah were standing in a foundry.

Hannah slowly backed away from the bleeding doors, hand clasped over her mouth to keep the disgust from spilling out. But once she was able to listen over the sound of the blood pouring in her ears did the new silence of the building truly reverberate. There was no more shouting from inside the auditorium, no stomping feet, no pounding fist, nor clapping to cheer it all on. Outside, the snow and the wind still shook the windows, but everything inside was still, quiet, and dead.

Except for a *click, click, click* moving across the floor.

"Mom?" Hannah stepped lightly toward the door, still shut tight, the way she left it. "Mom?"

Creeeeeak. The door pushed, barely an inch. And there it stayed, no one in the room making their way to venture back out into the entryway.

"Mom?" Hannah called out again.

Then, at the very top of the door, where the frame met the ceiling, a set of long, corpse-grey fingers curled their way around the edge of the wood, the dagger points of the nails tipped with painted white moon crescents.

"Hannah, sweetie," her mother's voice came. "Bring me something to eat. I'm hungry."

<u>DORY'S SACRIFICE</u>

by Phoenix McDonald

A curve in the path brought her small home into view. She sighed as she approached the front door; a shadow moved behind the window to the left. Her mother, Dory, watching for her return.

Warmth enveloped her as she stepped inside. A crackling fire filled the hearth set into the back wall. She pulled the bag from her shoulder and hung her cloak on a hook by the door.

Her mother grabbed her by the shoulders and spun her around.

"Mosha, where have you been? I've been waiting hours for you to return from the market. You should have been home hours ago!"

Mosha pulled away from her.

"Does it matter? I returned with everything on the list." She put the heavy bag on the table.

"I worry when you are so late," the older woman said. "Your father…" Dory choked on the words.

"Mother, Father died while cutting wood. I was just walking home. Nothing will happen to me."

"Then what took you so long?"

"I was visiting a friend," Mosha replied softly, thinking of Anya's soft blonde hair in her fingers, her bright blue eyes, and soft lips.

"A boy in town?" Dory's voice took on a hopeful tone.

"No, *Mother,*" Mosha replied. "I could care less about some *boy.*"

"Mosha, we talked about this obsession you have with other girls. If someone finds out, you could be hung for unnatural behavior. You must be careful."

Mosha's brow creased with anger. She pushed her mother away hard, sneering as the woman hit the floor and hitting her head on one of the table legs.

"I'm not sorry, Mother." Mosha spat, "You deserved that for the way you think about how I choose to love." Then she spun around and ran into her small room, slamming the door behind herself.

Dory slowly picked herself up from the floor where she had landed. She rubbed the lump on the back of her head, finding a small smear of blood on her fingers when she pulled them away. Mosha had gotten so strong. Her hip ached dreadfully from landing on the hard wooden floor, and her black hair hung in her eyes where it had escaped from the bun under her scarf. Dory pulled out the pins, her hair falling over her shoulders, then pulled it back into the tight bun, pushing the pins back into place.

She should not have mentioned Victor's death. It only brought back the memory of finding him lying in the woods; axe buried in his leg, blood pooled on the ground around. She could only imagine what Dory felt at the mention of the loss of her father. The memory sent searing pain cutting through Dory's chest as if she had just lost Victor yesterday.

"It just slipped," he had whispered to her as she sat with his head in her lap, stroking his hair. She had buried him behind the house herself, Mosha too young to help or understand.

A sudden thump against the door pulled her out of her reverie. Dory looked anxiously out the window first. As far out in the woods as she and her daughter lived, they did not get visitors often, so Dory was instantly on her guard. A large branch lay on the ground in front of the door. She looked up to see the treetops whipping madly back and forth; leaves swirled through the air and thunder rumbled overhead. As she watched, rain began to pour from the sky.

Gasping, Dory whirled around, leaning back against the wall, breathing hard. With a shiver, she pulled her heavy sweater more tightly around her body. She focused her dark eyes on the closed door behind which her daughter sulked.

Lips pressed firmly together, she walked to Mosha's bedroom door and tapped quickly. Then she opened it and stepped inside.

"Mother!" Mosha exclaimed at her mother's unbidden entrance, "I have asked you to respect my privacy. You didn't even knock"

Dory lowered her head and looked at her daughter sadly.

"There is no time for your whining, Mosha, and I have no concerns for your privacy right now. Baba Yaga is coming."

"Baba Yaga? Mother, really? Baba Yaga is a made-up story meant to scare small children into behaving."

"Do not speak of what you do not understand, daughter. Children's stories are often rooted in the truth." Mosha said quietly. "Listen to the storm outside."

Mosha could hear it, of course. Thunder crashed and rain pounded on the roof. The wind could be heard howling around the walls of the house.

"Yes, of course, but there are always storms this time of year, Mother."

"Not like this one."

Mosha sat down on the bed, her hands gripping the squares of a quilt she had sewn for her daughter's bed.

"She will arrive here, riding in her mortar, using her pestle to steer through the woods."

"Why? Why is she coming here?"

Dory stared at her daughter, dark brown eyes meeting bright green. Mosha had her father's eyes, an unusual color that had caught Dory's attention when first they met.

"Baba Yaga only leaves her cottage that stands on the legs of a chicken when she senses a child misbehaving. It is how she finds fresh meat upon which to feed."

"But… but how do you know she's coming here?"

Dory grimaced.

"The storm. A sudden storm that appears out of nowhere is a sure sign that Baba Yaga is coming to get her hands on the flesh of a child."

Mosha's eyes were wide and full of terror. Tears trembled on her bottom eyelids.

"What do we do, Mother?"

"That is why I will stay right here, Mosha. Baba Yaga will take no child of mine if I can stop it."

"No?" croaked a voice from the other room.

Footsteps clunked toward the bedroom door. Dory and Mosha stared at the figure that appeared in the doorway.

The woman facing them was buried in layers of filth. Her skin was nearly invisible beneath the dirt, except for her eyes, which twinkled merrily from between crinkled lids. Dirty gray hair hung over her face from within a hooded cloak, the color of which had long faded. Long, cracked fingernails extended like talons from her fingertips. Large black boots explained the clump of her footsteps. In her hands she held a long, oversized pestle.

"What crime has my daughter committed that Baba Yaga would leave her house to come all this way?"

The filthy woman smiled, revealing startlingly white teeth behind her cracked lips.

"Did she not push you, her own mother, to the floor just this very afternoon? The dishonoring of a parent is a serious violation."

Mosha swallowed hard.

"I thought you were here because of Anya."

Baba Yaga waved one long-nailed hand in the air.

"I care nothing for your choice of lovers. Lay with whomever you like. You must never put a hand on a parent, though. Come with me, child." A trickle of drool escaped the corner of her mouth, leaving a small clean streak behind it as it slid down her face.

She stepped forward, one filthy hand outstretched as if expecting Mosha to simply take it and follow obediently behind her.

Dory pushed herself to her feet and stepped between the crone and her daughter.

"Baba Yaga. I have already lost a husband. I will not stand by and lose my Mosha, too. She is all I have."

Baba Yaga stopped, bright eyes darting from Dory to Mosha.

Dory took a deep breath, pressing one shaking hand to her breast.

"What price? What will it take for Baba Yaga to give up her claim on my child?"

Baba Yaga appeared to ponder the question for a moment.

"Ten years," she croaked.

"Ten years?" Dory repeated.

"Of your life, woman." The crone said. "Give up ten years and I will leave you your daughter."

Dory closed her eyes.

"You may have my life, if you will spare my daughter."

"No!" Mosha cried out. "Take it from me! I will do it. I'm the one who dishonored her; it should be me!"

Baba Yaga's eyes shifted to Mosha.

"That is exactly why it cannot be you, child. Either you come with me, or the sacrifice is made to replace the child I give up. It is a lot to forsake on my part; I do not get to eat often.

"Are you ready?" she asked, looking back at Dory.

Dory nodded, sitting back down on Mosha's bed.

Baba Yaga placed one filthy hand over Dory's face.

As Mosha watched, the creases in the crone's face filled out, and the gray hair around her face returned to black. Her cracked lips healed, becoming full and smooth. The sagging skin beneath her eyes tightened. Years of accumulated dirt fell from her clothing and skin. Her long fingernails shrunk.

When the filthy woman withdrew her hand from Dory's face, Mosha gasped. Her mother had new wrinkles around her eyes and mouth. Dark circles sunk her eyes into her face. The hair pulled back so neatly into its bun was streaked with white.

Dory turned and gathered her daughter into her arms. Mosha burst into tears.

"Sshhhh, my love," Dory said, stroking Mosha's braids. "It was worth it, my love. For you."

Baba Yaga's eyes bored in Mosha's when she glared up at the witch.

"Remember, child, when you look at your mother, the price she has paid for your life. I am always waiting for a chance to feed. Next time, I will not be so willing to trade. Be very careful over the next two years. Anger is difficult to control."

She turned, hefted the pestle under her arm, and walked away. Her boots thumped across the floor. Mosha rushed to the window and watched as the crone flew off in her mortar, the pestle sticking out behind to act as a rudder.

Dory came out of Mosha's room and added some wood to the fire. Mosha felt sick, seeing the stoop in her mother's back as she moved about the room. In her mind, Mosha kept seeing her mother's face as Dory fell backward to the floor. She would give anything to take that moment back. It was too late; she knew deep inside her broken heart.

The price had been paid.

<u>CHINNY CHIN CHIN!</u>

by Y. Len

Without a single car to display my thumb to for the last couple hours, the desert highway appeared deserted. "SPRINGVILLE POP 411 ELEV 1,120—2 miles" read a faded road sign pointing to the left. As I crossed the highway and turned onto a side road, my stumbling feet picked up the pace in anticipation of a much-needed rest.

A full moon appeared in the darkening sky, bright, round-faced and big-eyed. Half an hour later, an unlit structure with black silhouettes of solar panels on the roof and heavy shutters on the second story windows came into view. A solid brick wall with concertina wire on top and evenly spaced searchlights and cameras seemed out of place in the middle of the Arizona desert. I kept going instead of asking for shelter there.

I was hardly a couple hundred yards from the compound, when a howl ahead slowed my steps. The howl repeated, closer. Muffled thumping on the ground, imagined or real, I wasn't sure, perked my ears. Was that a hungry predator or a whole pack of them, crazed by the full moon and ready to attack? A cold sweat ran behind my ears. I took a wobbly step back, turned around and ran. In less than a minute, out of breath and disgusted with myself, I banged on the low, iron clad door in the brick wall.

"Who's there?" asked a voice, "What do you want?"

"Help! Let me in, please! There are coyotes…"

"Not coyotes, that's a wolf!" interrupted the voice, "Anyway, do you want to stay overnight, or what?"

"Yes! I don't need much room, just to put a sleeping bag."

"Not a problem at all! What's your name, buddy?"

"Alex."

"And I'm Hogan," the voice said over the clunks and squeaks of the opening door. As the moon hid behind the clouds, a stocky silhouette shut the door behind me and secured it with numerous latches.

"So, what brings you here, Alex?"

"Hitchhiking, it's research for my next book."

As we walked toward the house by a parked Harley-Davidson, the wolf howled again. Hogan mumbled something raspy.

"I'm sorry, what was that?" I peered into the darkness.

"Never mind, Alex, let's get inside." He yanked the door open, let me into a dimly lit hallway that smelled of Pine-Sol, and dexterously repeated the locking down procedure.

"No, that's not a coyote. I know that daughter of a bitch very well," Hogan said in a low and throaty voice, as I followed him around the corner and up the narrow, poorly lit stairs. "She comes every full moon. Oh, watch your step, Alex, we're almost there. Now, have a seat. I'll be right back." He pointed to the couch barely discernible in the dark room.

"Where's the light?" I asked, "It's a little dark in here."

"Well, I'm off the grid here and right now all the juice that my genie makes is needed to protect the perimeter."

"So, that wire on the wall is electrified?"

"Yes. Five thousand volts in ten microsecond bursts! I wouldn't reco…" he was interrupted by another, this time very protracted, howl. Although muffled by the surrounding structure, it came from all directions at the same time.

"Not by the hairs on my chinny chin chiiiiiiin!" squealed Hogan. As if accepting a challenge, he shoved up his middle finger, stomped his foot, then turned toward me. My jaw dropped and my mouth went dry. I had a hard time deciding what was more unsettling: what I'd just heard or what I saw under a shabby baseball cap where Hogan's face was supposed to be. For it was hardly a face. Hell, it wasn't! It was much closer to a hog's snout. With no chin whatsoever to speak of.

"Oh yea, go ahead, scream your lungs out or run away if you wish. I'm used to it," uttered Hogan through clenched yellowish teeth, "Oh, wait a minute, there's nowhere to run."

"Ah, I, I'm, but…"

"No buts! Not everyone's got Brad Pitt's looks, that's all. End of story! Now, if you gonna stay, you better keep calm. I may need your help."

"Oh, okay. Yes. Sure, what do you want me to do?" I asked, taking a deep breath, still hesitant to look at my host.

"There," he motioned to the dark side of the room. My eyes adjusted enough to the scarce lighting to distinguish a big fireplace in the corner. "There's a pistol on the mantel. Not a real one, a tranquilizer. I want you to take it and keep an eye on the fireplace. I'm sure it won't come to that, but just in case, since I can't be in two places at once."

The pistol had a cool, comfortable ribbed handle and, despite an unusually long barrel, turned out to be well balanced and felt good in my hand.

"It's loaded, just point and squeeze the trigger," said Hogan from the opposite side of the room, clicking switches and pushing buttons. Three big computer screens came to life. After several keyboard strokes, black-and-white images appeared, showing brightly illuminated surroundings of the wall. Alternating between keyboard, mouse, and joystick, Hogan swapped, moved, zoomed, and focused images until one of them caught a big animal pacing back and forth in front of the wall. It was limping on its right foot and had a nasty whitish scar splitting the ear on its way from the forehead to the right shoulder.

"Here she is," Hogan said without taking his eyes from the screen, "You can relax now and make yourself comfortable. This may take a while." He pulled a gooseneck microphone closer to his mouth and flipped another switch.

"Good evening, Clarice," Hogan said, a faint nasal foreign accent replacing the raspiness in his voice, "Can't sleep again? I'll listen now."

"Aaaah-ooouuuuuuuuu"

"After your father's murder, you were orphaned. You were a couple of months old." He read from one of the screens, while two other screens tracked movement of the wolf from two different angles. "You went to live with cousins near a sheep and horse ranch in Montana."

"Aaaah-ooouuuuuuuuu, aaaaaaaaah-ooooouuuuuuuuuuuuuu, aaaah-ooouuuuuuuuu"

For the next hour or so, Hogan kept reading while the wolf paced outside the wall, occasionally interrupting with howls as if maintaining a conversation. With time, the gait slowed down and the responses became shorter, quieter, and less frequent. Finally, the wolf turned around in place several times and lay down.

*****

"I was born on a farm in Montana where my parents settled down after meeting each other at Woodstock," Hogan said, as we were washing down reheated leftovers of a homemade vegetable stew with a six-pack of Dos Equis. We sat in the brightly lit kitchen under a "HOLD ON TO YOUR DREAMS" poster featuring a winged pig. I was able to look at Hogan's face without flinching; he seemed pleased to have an attentive listener.

"It wasn't until the high school years, that my two brothers and I realized our, err, how should I put it? Our peculiarity. And I don't mean just the looks. We were comfortable with each other, but not with other people. With time, even among the three of us we socialized less and less, and it became obvious that each of us had grown to be a loner or, as some would say, a lone wolf. How ironic!"

The wall clock struck twice. Though tired, I was anxious to hear more.

"One day," Hogan continued, "my oldest brother went hunting and disappeared. We found his bow next to the demolished ground blind. The camouflage was spread around as if blown away by a blast. No body, no blood, no footprints. I didn't have a clue what had happened. All I knew was that in the middle of the night my brother, sprinkled with hog urine, had been hiding in a hole in the ground covered by straw.

"My other brother took it differently. Three days later he showed me a tiny wolf pelt, grumbling that the parents weren't in the den and one of the pups got away. He wanted to make a Davy Crockett style hat but was only able to get a pair of mittens out of it."

"Why would he think it was a wolf that attacked your oldest brother? I watched this documentary that said there's never been a case of a wild wolf attacking a human in North America."

"First, never say 'never'. Second, listen to this. Several months later," he paused to finish his beer, lifted his unkempt Lehigh Valley IronPigs baseball cap to scratch his forehead, and looked at me. "My brother went to fetch firewood and never came back. The back wall of the woodshed was blown to pieces. A mitten on the floor and a single set of wolf tracks in the snow gave me all the evidence I needed. Right then and there, I knew who would be next unless I did something about it. And I did.

"Not knowing how much time I had, I devoured books on wolf biology and behavior, firearms, self-defense, and home security. When the time came, I was ready. Not as ready as I'm now, but enough to survive the first encounter. The wolf couldn't get to me, locked inside the brick house, and after several hours of futile scurrying around, jumping, and howling, left with nothing. Although, not for long. Next time, he found the only unsecured entry to the house, the fireplace chimney. A clatter on the roof warned me in time, and I shot him dead as soon as he landed."

I sighed and took my eyes off Hogan's face. It was quarter after two on the clock, but he wasn't done yet.

"I thought that was the end of it, but boy oh boy, was I wrong! A week later, I found fresh footprints in the spring mud behind the house. One set was of an adult, although the size was smaller than I saw before, another could only belong to a pup. At sunset, they howled, circling the house in the distance.

"My fear and anger were tinted by empathy and even regret. Combing through the recent events again and again, I tried to find something, anything, I could've done differently, but there was nothing. I never intended to hurt anyone, but I did. I took another life to protect my own. It was just an animal, and my actions were justifiable by human morality, but on a deeper, basic level….

"One thing was for sure, I'd had enough! I wanted to leave all that behind, get on with my life and never see or hear another wolf again. Oh boy, was I naive!"

The wall clock struck three times. Recent excitement was being replaced by exhaustion, yet I couldn't decide what I craved more: getting some rest or hearing the rest of the story.

"To make a long story short," Hogan continued, "there and then I decided to disappear. A big city was out of the question, so instead I chose to put as many miles between me and the wolves as possible. I moved here.

"With my recently acquired knowledge, I was able to get a job as an online consultant and a sales rep for ADT. Business was good; I could not only support myself, but also start a family and have a very comfortable life. Instead, I invested all my time and money to design and build this house using the best construction materials and home security equipment available. It took her almost two years to find me."

"Her?!"

"Yes, her," he pointed in the direction of the door in the surrounding wall, "but all in good time, Alex, all in good time. The wall was finished, but there was no wire on top. As you might guess, she jumped over and headed straight for the roof. I saw everything over my surveillance system and was waiting for her, in front of the fireplace, with the tranquilizer pistol. That's, by the way, how I know it was 'she'. I kept her caged for three days and let her go only after the electric razor wire was installed on top of the wall."

"Let go? Why?" I asked, realizing that I would, most likely, do the same. There was also something else, something I needed to ask Hogan about, but couldn't put my finger on just yet.

"What was I supposed to do? Kill again? Yes, I knew what she came to do to me, but I also knew why. Besides, I was hoping she might stop coming."

"But she didn't, right?"

"You betcha," Hogan nodded.

"And?"

"It was a real mess. She got stuck in the wire and would have been burned to death if I hadn't switched the current off. She was knocked out and bleeding from multiple cuts and burns. It took a team of veterinarians several hours to revive and fix her up.

That was five years ago. After that disaster, I didn't see her for almost a year. It was a strange feeling. I almost, uh, missed her."

I looked at him and he quickly turned away, as if scrutinizing the "WHEN PIGS FLY!" wall clock behind him where the long hand was about to catch up with her squatter sister pointing at "3".

"Another beer?" Hogan asked after a minute of an awkward silence.

"No, thanks, I'm good."

"Okey dokey, then. So, she showed up again. Scarred, limping, but still determined. She didn't try to jump the fence anymore but ran around and howled all night. A human-like despair and grief coming from an animal! I felt pretty secure but couldn't simply ignore her and go to sleep. During one of those nights, I discovered how she reacted to the sound of my voice. At first, it would agitate her, but after an hour or so she would calm down and leave or fall asleep in front of the wall. I don't think it matters what I say but prefer something that fits."

His tone told me that the story was over. I was too tired to fully comprehend what I just heard, let alone to say anything appropriate for the occasion.

Suddenly, a question popped up in my mind and I knew I had to ask it there and then.

"You designed this house by yourself, right? Why did you need a fireplace here, in a desert?"

He thought for a while. "Nights can get chilly here," And, after a pause, "And lonely."

As he turned away, his eyes glinted wet.

WHEN DARKNESS COMES

by Laura G. Kaschak

"You have to be kidding me. The entire village closes down by 8 P.M.?"

The innkeeper silently scowls at me, offering no further explanation. I walk back to Quinn where he's waiting with both of our backpacks.

"They have a room for us tonight so we will wait out the storm here. But don't expect a late night at the local pub this time. The guy just told me it closes by 8 P.M. and so does everything else. We even have to be back here before 8 because he locks up and goes to bed by then."

Quinn's mouth falls open. "He's yanking your chain. No way that's true for the whole village. We've stayed in a dozen different backwards towns on this trip and never once have we heard of a place doing that."

I lift my shoulders, holding my hands up. "Well, true or not, let's drop our bags in the room and hit the pub while we can. Maybe someone there will speak enough English to explain."

*****

The temperature has dropped since we've been inside. The frozen remnants of the last snowstorm crunch under our feet as we walk to the pub. The storm coming tonight isn't supposed to be a particularly bad one for this region of Slovakia, but we've learned on this backpacking trip through eastern Europe not to take the temperature drops lightly. This nothing blip of a town wasn't a planned stop on our tour but it's better than freezing to death trying to get to the next closest town.

The tiny houses that line the street look like they've popped right out of a book of fairy tales. Not a single building appears to have been updated this century. The glow from their windows is the only light along the street.

Keeping my face buried down into my scarf, I bounce off Quinn as he stops short in front of me. He nods up towards a sign.

"Is this it, then?"

We've both been struggling with reading the language, but I spot a beer symbol in the window and point it out to him. We rush inside to relish in the warmth.

Low ceilings and an uneven pebble floor create the feeling that we've stepped into a cave rather than a bar. A handful of customers sit at heavy, wooden tables. All eyes turn to us as a hush falls over the room. We stand there in awkward silence until Quinn finally steps forward with a big grin and wave of his hand.

"Hello. Nice to meet all of you. Love the place. Mind if we sit down for a pint?"

A few eyes narrow with suspicion but most of the men quickly turn back to their own conversations, dismissing us with a shrug. At least the embarrassing rush of blood to my cheeks has helped them begin to thaw. I take a seat at the bar next to Quinn.

The bartender walks towards us, with an expression as welcoming as a pissed off honey badger. He looks to be either 40 or 80 years old, it's hard to tell if the leathery skin of his face was caused by time or sheer meanness. As soon as he speaks, I know his mother gave him cigarettes in the cradle. Probably without filters.

"Ok. What you want?" He grumbles at us.

"A couple of pints would be great. Whatever you have on tap. And if you serve food, we'd love a menu." I try to speak clear and not too fast since I don't know how fluent his English is. I also don't want any cracks in my voice to show how nervous I am speaking to a live man made of granite.

I'm sure he must have reverted to his natural stone form for a moment when there's no response, but finally a grunt is released from deep in his throat and he turns away without saying a word or changing his expression.

Quinn and I shoot a look at each other.

"Friendly sort of place, isn't it?"

"They're just not used to outsiders." A voice from the end of the bar calls down to us. His accent is thick but it's a relief to find an English-speaking local.

"We don't mean any harm and won't even be staying longer than one night. We just didn't want to get caught out in the snow coming tonight."

He seems pleased by that info,nods his head a few times and turns back to his beer.

"Good. Good. But if you are staying the night, just be sure to turn in no later than one hour after sundown."

The slam of a glass against wood makes us jump. Beer splashes my hand from the bartender pounding our glasses down in front of us. He's back to being an angry statue again.

"Uh, thanks. Food?" I make the eating gesture with my hand.

Never taking his eyes off us, his hand disappears under the bar and produces a small paper menu. He drops it onto the wet bar and skulks off.

"Excuse me." Quinn calls to the stranger at the end of the bar. "What was that you were saying about turning in so early? Does the village really shut down by 8?"

The man nods his head at his glass a few times before looking our way.

"Da. Don't be caught out too late. Don't even be out of your bed if you have any brains at all."

He must have read the confusion on our faces because he leans towards and explains with a hushed voice, "The babayka."

A chorus of murmurs spreads through the pub and we look around at all the customers nodding their agreement.

"What's a babayka?" I ask.

One of the women from a table stands and sits next to the man at the end of the bar.

"Did your mothers never warn you of the babayka?"

"Uh, no. We aren't from around here. I've never even heard of that before."

She sucks air in between her teeth and gives a sideways glance to the man while shaking her head. She mutters something to him in Slovak and returns to her table. He takes in a large breath and faces us.

"I'll tell you about the babayka. You need to know. Here, we are told as children that we must go to bed or the babayka will take you. Babayka looks for those out after dark. Those who dare to defy the darkness are never seen again."

He lifts the glass to his lips and downs half its contents in one gulp before continuing.

"Babayka comes from the darkness and is the darkness. Once the darkness has you, there is no stopping it. The covers of your bed are your only protection. Cloak yourself in their safety before it's too late."

Quinn smirks at me and rolls his eyes.

"Come on. You're telling me all the adults in this town are afraid of a story their mothers told them when they were kids? It's just a make-believe boogeyman. You do know that they only used that story to make you go to bed because kids will believe anything, right?"

I lay my hand on Quinn's arm to stop his mouth. He apparently didn't notice the bartender had moved in close to him and is now burning a hole into his head with a fiery evil eye. His meaty fist sits on the bar, knuckles turning white with strain.

Quinn glances down at the hand as if it's a rattlesnake about to strike at him.

"Uh, I mean yeah, yeah, ok. Makes sense. We'll call it a night early. We wouldn't want to cross paths with this baba-boogey-thingy. We'll put in our food order now so we can get to bed as soon as possible."

*****

The blast of icy wind slaps us in the face as we step into the street. The cold is an almost welcoming discomfort after choking down our meal while surrounded by angry stares and awkward silence occasionally interrupted by muttered, unknown Slovak curses.

Snow has begun to fall and the wind has picked up making it much harder to see the street than it was when we first came this way. Most of the windows in the old-fashioned houses have gone dark, leaving the street shrouded in shadows. I notice one window up ahead that's still glowing with warm light. It makes me think of a beacon of a lighthouse cutting through foggy sea air to rescue wayward ships on a stormy night.

As I stare at the window to guide me, I see a dark form move in front of it, blocking some of the light. Specks of icy frost assault my eyes, forcing me to us my hand as a shield. Even with the limited visibility, I can see that the silhouette is that of a man.

I'm about to say something about it to Quinn when the silhouette moves to place a hand against the glass. We've gotten close enough now for me to spot that the fingers are much too long. They extend almost to the top of the window, tapering into sharp points at the end.

"Is that guy looking into people's windows?" Quinn asks.

The elongated fingers slide down the glass with a loud squeak. A shiver runs down my spine that has nothing to do with the temperature.

"Something's not right, Quinn."

"Hey!" Quinn shouts to the man.

The head whips towards us while the body stays facing the window. Eventually, the rest of its form follows the head with strange, disjointed movements that fill the air with popping sounds, like when knuckles are being cracked. It shutters to a stop.

Being backlit by the only light on the street makes it impossible to make out any distinct features. But I catch a flash of yellow reflecting off its eyes for a split second. The cracking sound starts again as he tilts his head from side to side, as if sizing us up. This small gesture is done as jerky and unnatural as everything else.

My heart drops into my stomach when it goes into motion again but thankfully, I realize it's moving backwards instead of towards us. The creature edges away from the light of the window and melts into the shadows.

"What the…." Quinn's sentence falls away.

"Let's just get back to our room. Now."

*****

No matter how warm I am now, I still can't stop shivering. I climb into the twin bed on my side of the room.

"Are you actually going to bed?" Quinn asks as I pull the blankets up with shaking hands that suddenly remind me of the grotesque twitching mannerisms we witnessed out there in the dark. A fresh wave of nausea washes over me. "You're really gonna just lie there, awake for hours? Those yokels really got to you back there, huh?"

"What got to me is that thing we saw on the way home. I don't know what it was or if it even has anything to do with what the locals were telling us. But the sooner I get to sleep, the sooner morning gets here. I'm not messing around finding out anything else about this place."

"You mean that creeper we saw? I can't believe some perv peeking into windows is going to shake you up this much. We aren't even on the first floor so it's not like he's able to look in here."

I shake my head as I click off the lamp next to my bed.

"You didn't look close enough. That was no man. I don't know what it was. And I'm not taking any chances."

Quinn blows out a puff of air and slaps the sides of his thighs with his hands.

"This is just crazy. What am I going to do the rest of the night with everything closed and you hiding under the covers from the boogey man like a toddler pissing his diapers?"

"I think you should get under your covers, too. You heard what the man said about them giving you protection." My words sound insane and foolish even to my own ears and yet I feel the truth of them down into my bones.

Quinn stands next to his bed, gaping at me with disbelief. A movement by his feet catches my eye. It looks as though the darkness beneath his bed begins extending forward. It forms into long, pointed fingers. There's a brief glint of light reflecting off two yellow eyes.

My brain searches for words of warning just as a sinister chuckle fills the room. Quinn's head turns to the door, assuming the sound must be coming from someone in the hallway.

I force my throat to squeak out, "Quinn?..."

The fingers curl like smoke around Quinn's ankles and yank him off his feet. He lets out a grunt as his elbows slam onto the floor. I reach my hand to him and he looks up at me. We lock eyes, his confusion and terror on full display. His hand lifts, reaching towards me. Before we connect, he's swept backwards, under the bed.

He slips into the darkness effortlessly, leaving nothing behind but the echo of his last small yelp.

I throw back the covers, ready to run across the room and search under his bed. Before my foot touches the floor, I hear a soft chuckle from beneath me. I lift my foot back onto the bed and pull the covers over my head.

They are my only protection from the darkness.

PEARCED

by Jay Sykes

"Alexander Pe-arce,

Appetite so fi-erce,

Raise your head,

From the dead,

Dare you to come and eat us!"

The childish tune repeated, echoing through the trees in a seemingly endless, infuriating loop. I'm sure the happy campers had performed that ditty many a time before, to no effect. This time, however, they had the misfortune of singing it not one hundred feet from the bones of one of my unlucky companions.

My remains scattered following my dissection, I have no real resting place. Parts of me swarm around the places I had impacted the most when I was alive, around the bones that still bare scars from my gnawing. The day I heard that tune, every part of me was called together, back to one place again. I was no longer made up of whispers on zephyrs, tumbling stones in the path of streams, and leaves ripped from trees with no cause. I was almost human once more.

I couldn't see, but I could sense the presence of the little troupe. Five newly-minted adults formed a whirlwind of bustling energy around a campfire. They were preparing their evening meal; I could tell from the hunger and anticipation that followed them like yapping pups. A stabbing nostalgia took painful shape inside of me. Food and eating were the two great loves of my life, and I had missed them both dearly. I longed to feel the pull of meat torn by my teeth, the drip of blood against my chin, the swelling satisfaction of a full belly. I could, I would feel it all again. I just had to wait for them to go to sleep.

It took longer than I hoped; these individuals seemed determined not to obey the suggestion of the sun. They were savouring their new-found freedom, celebrating it with late, aimless nights. Everything was so interesting to them, and they were all so interesting to each other. They tried my patience mercilessly.

Hours of strange, thumping music, cackling, and fondling later, they all managed to make their way into one shelter or other. Yet another hour of attempted experimental intercourse, and they all drifted into post- (or pre-) orgasmic slumber.

I dipped into their dreams, hoping to find someone susceptible to the seduction of indulgence, someone for whom morality was made up of grey areas. Only one who saw the world the right way would be able to help me regain everything I had lost when that noose was placed around my neck.

I found myself drinking in a cocktail of the nauseatingly whimsical and morosely mundane. Fear of judgement, ridiculous fantasies and depraved desires threatened to overwhelm me completely. One individual was trying to explain his plummeting academic performance to his parents, another was somehow winning millions of dollars in a sports competition simply by besting their schoolhouse rival, a third was engaging in what he thought was sex with three different but almost identical women. I saw no potential in these dullards; even their weirdest wishes were directed towards all the wrong sensations! Pride, envy, lust; Why would one focus on such mediocre siblings of the greatest, the most primal sin of all?

The other two seemed promising at first; their nocturnal imaginings were less literal and more conceptual, and disturbing even to me. Their subconscious minds were determined to bathe them in the fears they were most desperate to avoid. One was caught in an endless cycle of labour, her imagined child crowning and receding, fire possessing her sex. The other was fumbling through a dreamscape of utter blindness, despairing at the lost of their artistic career. I tried to provide them each with an alternative to their suffering in the form of that hedonistic pleasure most dear to me, but their minds rejected all of my attempts to distract them from their terror.

As I was loosening my grip, resigned to another couple of centuries of near-oblivion, I felt a flicker of hope. The failing student's desperate attempts to explain things had become more aggressive. His dream-self had his father by the throat, and was screaming obscenities, pulling every thread of his own inadequacies and finding paternal abuse at the end of the line.

I sunk myself into the poor boy, and made a suggestion. I thought it would take more convincing, but his subconscious was surprisingly content to ram his teeth into his father's flesh. I seized my chance, flooding his brain with everything I could remember of consuming the body of man: the thrill of the ultimate taboo, the all-too-inviting flavour, the buttery, smooth texture of a creature that barely works its muscles. His mouth was watering; a drop of drool escaped and meandered down his jowls.

He choked on his own saliva and rocketed towards consciousness, trying to evict me from his brain. My very being sank as he opened his eyes, but then I realised: I could finally see! I still had a hold on him. I didn't know how long it would last, so I grabbed control of his arms and flung them around the neck of his tent-mate.

At first he couldn't believe what he was doing, he fought me constantly, as did the body beneath my borrowed form. It was all I could do to keep them from crying out and keep him from bucking me off of his mind. But then, something about the challenge beckoned to the young man, and he followed, nervously at first, but with growing confidence. He didn't really want to kill them. He just wanted to see if he could.

Only when it was too late did he pause to take in the enormity of what his body had done. Shock froze him, he had no idea what to do next. I made another suggestion. After all, they couldn't become more dead, could they? Waste not want not…

As he was wiping his mouth, he whispered, as if knowing I was there:

"Man's flesh is delicious. It tastes far better than fish or pork."

KONGAMATO RAIN

by Petina Strohmer

An agonised scream rang through the canopy.

Vast wings blotted out the equatorial sun blazing into the jungle clearing. Talons with razor-sharp tips dropped their cargo, the figure of a man who caught on every branch and thorn on his way down.

Finally, he crashed onto the forest floor and the villagers hurried over. Lying face down in a pool of his own blood, he had huge lumps of flesh gouged out of his back, through layers of muscle, exposing the pale bone beneath. His fingers fell open and released a small rock, speckled with bright particles.

With the last of the life left in him, he raised his head and managed three words:

"Kongamato has returned."

*****

It had been raining all day.

And all of yesterday.

And the day before that.

In fact, it had been raining solidly since Sarah and Jonathan had arrived in Equatorial Guinea.

"Does it ever stop?" Jonathan grumbled.

In the relative shelter of their tent, the water still managed to seep through from somewhere and drip off the brim of his hat. Incessantly.

Sarah ignored him, analysing the data they had collected so far.

"If it goes on for much longer," Jonathan said, "I'm going to grow gills." He shook his head and droplets of water splashed everywhere.

Sarah shielded her laptop. "It's a rainforest," she muttered, her eyes never leaving the screen. "The clue's in the name."

"It's a hell hole, that's what it is," Jonathan declared.

"One that's going to make ECon in general, and us in particular, very wealthy."

"You hope."

Sarah spared him a cursory glance. "So why are you here?"

"The same reason as you."

"Hmmm, but it appears that only one of us has the courage of their convictions." She rolled her feline green eyes.

"I-"

"Look," she said over him, "it's not what comes out of the sky here, it's what comes out of the ground."

"Again, you hope."

"The data so far suggests that my hope is well-founded. We already know this country is rich in both oil and gas. ECon is the largest mining company in America and has been taking full advantage of that, but look at this."

She turned the screen to show her colleague several areas outlined in yellow. "Gold," she said with hushed reverence. "If it's here, Jonathan, and I believe it is, we're going to find it. In fact, I'm not going back to the company without, at the very least, conclusive evidence." She stroked the gleaming chain around her neck.

Jonathan yawned. "What time are the elephants arriving in the morning?"

"Dawn."

He groaned and stretched out his long, thin legs. "I mean, *elephants*? Seriously?"

Sarah shrugged. "The Land Rovers can only go this far. If we want to go any further, we have to do as the natives do."

"Personally, I can't wait until ECon bulldoze a proper road through this God-forsaken wilderness."

"As soon as we find gold," she smiled, "they will."

"I'll see you in the morning." Jonathan crawled out of the central tent and sloshed back to his own. Far above him, a dark shadow crossed the moon.

*****

The next day, it was raining. Hard.

The elephants stood impassively in the downpour while their handlers attempted to load the two Americans and all their equipment onto the beasts' broad backs.

Sarah was checking and re-checking the scientific instruments then making sure that they were properly protected from the weather. The rain ran from her uncovered head, down her long red hair and soaked her clothes. Absorbed in her work, she didn't seem to notice.

Jonathan, on the other hand, sat morosely on one elephant's back, his hat pulled down, his collar pulled up and his face looking like a smacked ass.

"Cheer up!" Sarah laughed as she scrambled up in front of him. "Today, we hunt for treasure."

Jonathan peered into the trees above. "Yeah, but what's hunting us?"

Sarah frowned. "What do you mean?"

"Well, I only have a rudimentary memory of Spanish from high school but while you've been otherwise engaged, the villagers have been talking about 'death from the sky.'"

"What?"

"I think that's what I heard. Anyway, they seem pretty jittery about it."

Sarah stopped what she was doing and, for the first time that morning, actually looked at the people around her. They moved quickly and efficiently but as Jonathan said, kept stealing furtive, frightened looks at the sky. She shook her head. "Probably some ancient superstition. Nothing for us to worry about. We are scientists, Jonathan. I told you, I'm much more interested in what comes out of the *earth* here, rather than the air. Right," she said briskly. "Let's go."

The ECon party lumbered its way through the jungle. Birds squawked and monkeys chattered but neither the villagers nor the elephants seemed perturbed by the noise. Sarah studied her map and Jonathan complained about the midges. Reaching the first survey site, the equipment was unloaded and while the scientists set everything up, the guides and the animals settled themselves to rest.

The day wore on, hot and humid, as photographs, notes and samples were taken. Curious antelope watched from a distance and from high in the canopy, birds studied the intruders.

"OH MY GOD!!!"

At the sound of Jonathan's outburst, the whole place exploded into action. The antelope leapt away, the birds screamed warning calls as they took to the air and even the elephants stamped their feet. The first thing every villager did was look upwards, terror etched across each of their faces.

"What? What?" Sarah cried, running to her colleague.

Jonathan raised his hands into the air. "Can't you feel it?"

"Feel what?"

"It's stopped raining!"

Sarah stared at him. "Seriously, you dumb ass?" She waved her hands in a calming motion at the terrified guides. "It's okay. It's all right. Erm – er --, Está bien," she said, using the only scrap of Spanish she could recall.

They stared at her, eyes wide.

She pointed to Jonathan then crossed her eyes and made a circular motion at her temple with her forefinger. "Idiota!"

There was a little nervous laughter and the elephants were settled with pats and strokes but the sense of unease was now palpable.

"Jerk," Sarah growled at Jonathan as she went back to work. "You pull another stunt like that and I'll give you something to be *really* scared of."

*****

The early evening light cast long, distorted shadows over the forest floor and the nocturnal creatures began to call.

An exhausted but satisfied Sarah collected up her findings and chivvied the guides into action. They were still on edge, peering into the darkness of the canopy. "Está bien, está bien," she tried to reassure them. "Come on, Jonathan, these people don't want to be out here when it gets dark."

"Neither do I," he replied and climbed onto his seat. The scientists slipped into silence as they plodded their ponderous way back towards camp.

It came out of nowhere; all jagged teeth and barbed claws.

Dropping onto the first elephant, it slashed and ripped and tore, slicing the flesh of the mount and its riders. The blood of both poured in a scarlet torrent onto the earth. Rearing up, the elephant struck the attacker with a heavy trunk, sending it crashing into the people below.

Sarah wiped the blood out of her eyes and grabbed her gun. Below her swirled a storm of eyes and teeth and flapping flesh. She waited until the creature was broadside and pulled the trigger.

In the midst of the explosion, a dark shape rose from the chaos and disappeared into the trees while all else was total madness.

*****

Due to Sarah's quick thinking, the assailant had been chased away before anyone was killed. However, there were some serious injuries. Sarah and

Jonathan had both sustained deep scratches and puncture wounds that resembled bites as had many of the guides on the ground. Some of the wounds had penetrated to the bone and in one man's case, severed an artery. An emergency tourniquet was all that had prevented him from bleeding out completely. He was driven overnight to the nearest hospital but was expected to lose the leg.

First light revealed further the extent of the havoc.

Carefully packed, most of the scientific equipment had survived unscathed and was still attached to one of the panicked elephants recovered the next day. "Good God," Sarah breathed as she traced the deep scrapes in the animal's hide. "What on earth could do that kind of damage?"

"I don't know and I don't care but I'm not hanging around to find out," Jonathan cried, putting his slender hand to the bandage around his head.

"You are," Sarah told him. "You're contracted in, buddy. I can't do this alone and I'm not hanging around for your replacement."

"You can't-"

"I would say good morning but under the circumstances…" The bulky figure of Oumar, the local chief of police, blocked the door to the barn.

"You got that right," Jonathan huffed.

"So," Sarah asked him "what do you think happened last night?"

Oumar produced a notepad from his voluminous jacket pocket. "That's what I was going to ask you?"

Jonathan held up his hands. "We don't know. We don't have animals in Central Park that try to rip your head off."

"So?" Sarah asked again.

The policeman chewed the inside of his cheek while considering his answer. "Probably a leopard," he said at last.

"A leopard?" Jonathan said.

"Yeah, big cat. Strong, solid animal, with spots."

"I know what a leopard is," Jonathan snapped.

"Yeah but I s'pect you ain't been up close and personal with one before. Least not in Central Park."

Despite her sore face, Sarah smirked.

"But it came from above," Jonathan protested, "like a giant bird."

"Leopards don't fly" Oumar pointed out.

"I mean…"

"And birds don't have teeth," he added.

Sarah snorted with laughter. Jonathan glared at her.

"But leopards do climb trees," Oumar went on in his slow, deliberate tone, "and can then drop down onto their prey."

"And do these attacks happen regularly?" Jonathan asked, the colour rising on his high cheekbones.

Oumar shrugged. "Leopards gotta eat, just like the rest of the rest of us." He eyed Jonathan's tall, skinny frame. "Tho' there ain't much meat on you… sir."

Sarah stepped forward. She wasn't a big woman, all lean muscle and sinew, but looking at her, Oumar was sure she was much more of a challenge to their attacker than Jonathan was. "The locals are talking," she began and noticed a sudden change in the police officer's face. She could almost see the shutters coming down.

"Don't do much else," he said tightly.

"About death from the sky."

Even in the equatorial sun, Oumar's gaze took on an arctic quality. "Gossip. Folklore. That's all." His tone was dismissive, but his eyes told a different tale. "Simple people, simple beliefs."

Sarah wasn't convinced but realised that she wasn't going to get much further with this. At least not yet. "Well," she said casually, "I guess I'm just lucky I had my gun. Perhaps the guides will take their weapons next time."

"Next time?" Oumar muttered under his breath before turning and walking away.

*****

It was several days before Sarah and Jonathan had consolidated their data from the first site and were ready to travel again. However, they were going nowhere without elephants and guides. The villagers sat impassively by their animals as Jonathan shouted and swore at them.

"Enough!" Sarah commanded.

"Huh!" Jonathan said, throwing his hands in the air. "Let's see if you can talk some sense into them."

"Well," said Sarah, standing aside to reveal a woman behind her, "an interpreter would probably be a good start. I don't think our pidgin Spanish is up to this negotiation, do you? This is Mariame from the city of Malabo."

The woman nodded at Jonathan and then at the guides.

"Probably better than Google translate, don't you think?" Sarah said.

The scowl lines on Jonathan's long face were growing deeper by the day.

"Mariame," Sarah addressed the woman. "Could you please ask our guides why they are refusing to work. They have been paid a whole month in advance."

There was a burst of rapid talk, some of which was obviously heated.

Then Mariame turned to Sarah. "They say their lives are worth more than the money."

"It's a pay dispute?" Sarah asked.

"No," Mariame replied. In a hushed tone, she uttered a single word. "Kongamato."

This, in itself, set off concerned chatter between the native people.

"Excuse me?" Sarah said. "What is Kongamato?"

"The death from the sky."

Jonathan rolled his eyes.

"Meaning what, exactly?" Sarah asked patiently.

"The Kongamato is like a giant bird with a wingspan of several metres. It can fly but it has no feathers. However, it does have the talons of an eagle and a long beak full of sharp teeth."

"A bird with teeth but no feathers?" Sarah echoed.

"Now hang on a minute," Jonathan interrupted. "What you're describing is a-a pterodactyl – and they've been extinct for millions of years."

"So you say," Mariame's face held no hint of humour.

"So science says," Jonathan snapped, shaking his head.

"Tell me," Mariame said, maintaining her composure, "what are you looking for in the jungle?"

"Gold," Sarah replied.

"And you're sure it's there?"

"Our data suggests that it is highly probable."

"Probable." Miriame let the word hang for a moment. "But you're not 100% sure."

"No," Sarah admitted.

"However, you *are* sure that the Kongamato aren't in there? Despite the fact that these people think so, enough to refuse a significant amount of money, and they've lived here all their lives. The Kongamato guard the river but they will protect the whole of the rainforest if they need to."

"This is getting nowhere fast," Jonathan interjected. "What do these people want to get them to do the work they've already been paid for?"

Mariame turned back to the villagers and a long conversation ensued. Eventually, she returned her attention to the scientists. "They will accept double pay-" she began.

"Well, there's a surprise," Jonathan huffed.

Mariame raised her eyebrows at him then continued. "They also want double the workforce for protection, all armed with guns."

"Done," Sarah agreed. "How soon can we head out again?"

*****

"ECon is not going to like this," Jonathan told Sarah later than evening.

"They're one of the biggest mining companies in the world," Sarah reminded him, "they can afford a few extra expenses. They'll think it's worth paying for a few more people and their guns when we discover rich seams of unmined gold for them."

"You really think they'll buy the idea of a dinosaur defending the treasure?"

"It doesn't matter so long as we can steal it from him."

"They'll-" Jonathan began but was cut off by a loud screech from the darkness above their heads.

"Come, noble dragon," Sarah laughed. "Let's have at thee."

*****

It took over a fortnight to meet the villagers' demands in which time, there had been a lot of commotion in the treetops but no further attacks.

"Strange, isn't it?" Jonathan remarked, collecting up their equipment, "as soon as the guides get what they want, a) the trouble stops and b) they're all happy to venture back into the dragon's lair."

"I don't think they're exactly happy," Sarah said, watching the men. They loaded the elephants but all had eyes everywhere and the slightest noise had them reaching for their guns. "However, they're keeping their word. But, Jonathan…"

"What?"

"Just don't pull another scare stunt like last time or you won't have to worry about the dragon anymore."

"Why?"

"Because you'll be shot dead."

*****

The mist rose from the tops of the wet trees, flamingos and herons waded through the river and the mosquitoes were eating Jonathan alive – or so he complained, over and over.

Sarah had long since tuned him out as well as ignoring how jittery the guides remained. She did notice, however, that the one time the party spotted a leopard high in the trees, not only did the guides seem untroubled by it but despite the creature's formidable teeth and claws, she didn't believe it could have inflicted the kind of damage they had sustained.

Several trips had now passed without incident and today they were ready to really dig. Sarah smiled. She was sure she would have all the evidence she needed now; gold ore in her hands by the end of the day.

The party reached the excavation site, set up the equipment and began digging. The day was long and the work was hard but the scientists finally found what they were looking for. Sarah was ecstatic, holding the rocks up to the light and examining their golden veins.

As usual, Jonathan burst the bubble. "It's late and it's starting to rain. Again. Let's call it a day and return tomorrow.

"No," Sarah replied, her eyes never leaving the prize. "Let's collect just a little more before we go. You never know what tomorrow may bring."

"More rain?" Jonathan suggested. "The guides are getting restless and the last thing we need is another strike."

The natives were, indeed, troubled. They listened to screeches in the air and stared at the black clouds overhead.

"Honestly," Jonathan went on, "you think they'd be glad of the work. And once the gold mining begins here-"

One moment he was speaking, the next he disappeared. Sarah followed his scream upwards to see him in the clutches of a giant winged creature.

"Kongamato!" the guides screamed, dropped their packages and grappled with their guns as they ran for cover. The elephants reared up, trumpeting loudly amid the sound of shrieks and gunfire. and charged off into the trees.

"Wait, no wait…" Sarah cried but was silenced by something landing heavily beside her.

It was Jonathan. Or what was left of him.

His face was sliced cleanly in two. One eye was missing. The other sat on his cheek, the optic nerve still attached to the dark, empty socket. His throat was ripped open, exposing the rough tube of the trachea, beneath which his torso had been shredded. There was nothing below the waist except for the base of the spine, the glistening bone hanging like a grotesque tail.

Sarah tightened her grip on her precious rocks and raced into the undergrowth, screeches and screams echoing in her ears.

*****

Oumar appeared at the door of the hospital waiting room. "It will come as no surprise to you, Sarah," he said quietly, "that after that onslaught, nobody will be returning to the jungle."

Sarah sat, still clutching her rock like a comfort blanket, trying to make sense of what had happened.

Five of the guards were dead, their bodies ripped to pieces and many of the others had sustained serious injuries. Limbs had been ripped from their sockets, skulls punctured, chests and bellies sliced open. Three of the survivors were fighting for what was left of their lives in intensive care.

"They did try to warn you about Kongamato," Oumar went on. Mariame, sitting sadly in the chair opposite, nodded in agreement. Nobody bothered with the ruse of leopard attack any longer.

"But-but why?" Sarah managed, her wide eyes staring through Oumar into the middle distance.

"What would you do to defend your home?" Mariame asked.

Sarah thought for a moment. "When ECon found oil in this country during the 1970s," she said, "it was a complete game-changer. The economy boomed virtually overnight, and the people went from being poor peasants to a political power to be reckoned with. Gold will do the same; not the dregs discovered before but the rich seams that I have unearthed."

"Oil did change the area," Mariame agreed, "but not in the way you describe, the way that rich foreigners imagine. Look at these people." Mariame gestured through the window to the guides who were being patched up in the surgery next door. "Do they look rich and powerful to you?"

Sarah could only shake her head.

"The profit from our natural resources goes to the government, not the people. That's why they agreed to return to the rainforest even though they knew the risks. They couldn't afford not to. Even so, they know how dangerous it is to try to steal from Kongamato. As soon as you return to America with your tales of buried treasure, your company will want to just rip up the jungle to get to the gold."

Sarah opened her mouth to protest.

"You've seen what happened to the Amazon rain forest. The Kongamato will not let that happen to their home. And there's something else you should all know; Kongamato have supernatural regenerative power. The harder you cut them back, the stronger they will return. Not necessarily as individuals but certainly as a species. They are relentless. You could win a battle but you'll never win the war. Nobody will dare return to this rainforest."

Sarah stroked the rock, thinking, *ECon will.*

*****

Within weeks, squads of heavily armed ECon miners and their machines arrived in Equatorial Guinea. Their sights were set on the gold and nothing was going to get in their way.

The villagers watched them and shook their heads. Even if these people succeeded, very little of the money would trickle all the way down to them. The Kongamato had slept peacefully for years, and village life carried on quietly around them, but now they had been disturbed, they would defend their homelands to the death.

The bloodshed was only just beginning.

*****

Bulldozers gouged great scars across the virgin rainforest, its inhabitants fleeing in fear. The river was dammed to provide more power, dirt roads were established and the machines dug deeply into the earth.

Electric generators rattled, diesel engines roared and hundreds of workers shouted over the din, drowning what was left of the rainforest's natural rhythm.

ECon took the stories of dinosaur defenders with a shovel load of salt but, nevertheless, had provided heavy armoury for their workforce. More than enough to deter any indigenous interference.

Lights were strung up and a small village of Portacabins erected to house the ECon army.

People of the jungle saw oil seep into their water and plastic waste clutter the forest floor. They turned their faces to the sky.

*****

ECon had been in the area for just under three months when it happened.

Midnight is the hour of monsters, silently observing from the treetops as the miners did their evening checks. The Kongamato were said to be solitary hunters but now there was a whole host of these dark creatures, high in the canopy, watching and waiting.

As the last lights were being turned out, they swooped.

Shouting and screaming was punctuated by rapid rifle fire, the bright flashes briefly illuminating knife-edged teeth and claws. Under the cover of darkness, the creatures rained down upon the invaders, tearing muscle and crushing bone.

Arms, legs, heads and intestines dropped, bounced and slopped onto the ground as their owners were dismembered in flight.

The men thought that the spotlights would give them the advantage, but even experienced guards froze in fear at their first sight of these fiends. Scaly wings, spanning many meters, blocked out the moon. Red raw teeth hung with tatters of skin and bloody barbed talons clutched huge chunks of flesh.

And they screamed. Long jaws opened to emit loud, high-pitched screeching like nails drawn down a chalkboard. The air was coppery to the taste and blood fell in heavy showers.

Huge guns, mounted on armoured vehicles, fired into the overhead storm. Bullets, grenades and shells whizzed, thudded, and exploded in the air, bringing down wings and beaks and claws. Like fireworks, the ammunition lit up the sky and blew the creatures apart. Burning and bleeding, their bodies fell to the forest floor.

Before the humans could congratulate themselves, reinforcements arrived. The dark sky was full of hundreds of winged devils maddened by the smell of blood. The miners were forced to retreat, the cries of their dying comrades and the screams of the Kongamato ringing in their ears.

*****

Enraged, ECon flew their specialist attack team in at first light. The soldiers listened to the insane babbling of the men who had survived last night's battle but weren't sure they believed them. However, whatever was out there, they were determined to kill it. Nothing and no-one was going to prevent their employers' extraction of gold, the most precious commodity on earth.

The villagers watched the soldiers arm themselves and their vehicles and disappear into the trees.

As expected, the daylight hours were quiet, and the soldiers collected up the remains of the creatures' bodies to be returned to base and burned. The ecologists would be up in arms if they knew about this but what the eye didn't see…

Night came and so did the Kongamato.

Automatic gunfire punctuated the air, and the sky was lit up by flamethrowers. From the village, the natives saw the Kongamato torn apart by bullets and their bodies drop from the sky on flaming wings.

Yet still they came.

The ancient and the modern, the natural and the manmade, the Kongato and the humans, battled all through the night. Explosions blew the earth into the sky and forest fires raged.

It was complete carnage.

By dawn, the soldiers were the only things left standing – at least, a few of them were. Most of their comrades lay dead and dying alongside the bodies of hundreds of Kongamato. Blood, both human and animal, soaked into the bare ground and the black tree stumps sent smoke rising into the empty air.

*****

ECon were ordered to pay millions of dollars in compensation for the damage they had done. The ecologists raged against the destruction of a huge area of virgin rainforest although they would be incandescent about the extinction of a species as yet unknown to science if they ever learned of it. ECon spun stories of regular wild animal attacks and forest fires, knowing that the fees they had to pay were peanuts compared to profits from the gold. All evidence of the Kongamato had been destroyed to protect gold mining in the conveniently cleared jungle and nobody took much notice of the natives' superstitions.

As the heavy machinery roared in the distance, high in the surviving canopy, mothers tended their nests. They watched as the large green eggs started to crack and legions of long, sharp-toothed beaks emerged.

BOO HAG

by Charles Sartorius

Was it possible? Intellectually, he knew it couldn't be, but falling rapidly into slumber, he could still sense her red glow hovering above his prone body, sucking precious breath from his lungs. His mother's cousin had warned him yesterday about the ghostly hag; told him to check daily for even the smallest of cracks in the walls of his guest hut – that's where she'd enter. He had forgotten of course, thought it was some kind of local jocularity conjured up to frighten mainlanders, even kin – not the innocuous folklore he planned to study academically. Scholarly interests did not include hocus-pocus. But this brief state of absolute horror was real…damn real. Then blessed sleep conquered him in the shadow of flickering candlelight. When he awakened the next morning short of breath and exhausted beyond comprehension, a gut-wrenching trepidation began to fester inside.

It had begun as a research project on Gullah culture in the winter of 1891 during his sophomore year at South Carolina's Claflin University. Frederick Jackson convinced his favorite professor that spending the winter semester on Saint Helena Island off the coast was a worthwhile project. An endeavor he promised would significantly enhance his educational pursuits in folklore studies, from a sociological perspective, of this Sea Island's culture. Because his mother was a native Saint Helena Islander, family members agreed to provide requisite room and board; ergo, cost would not be a prohibitive factor in his stay.

After reviewing his written proposal, Professor Williams gave the academic green light only after Frederick made assurances communication with the locals would not be a barrier. Although not fluent in Gullah Creole, exposure to it in his childhood would most likely suffice. Additionally, if communication roadblocks arose, his mother's cousin, James, would provide translation as needed. James had spent many years on the mainland in his youth and could easily toggle between the two forms of oral discourse.

As far as Frederick knew, he was the first member of his maternal side of the family to be born on the mainland. His mother, Mary, had moved to the Charleston area with her parents and younger sister prior to her tenth birthday. Apparently, the move was made for economic reasons although the explanation was ambiguous. Even with many prying queries by a maturing Frederick, no details were provided. Mama had met and married a native Charleston man shortly after her twentieth birthday, immersing her adult self in the local lifestyle; exposure to his mother's native culture was piecemeal at best. Visiting kin venturing to the mainland provided a few relevant scraps here and there; as far as Frederick could recall, Mama never returned to her island birthplace even after the passing of her beloved grandmother.

The young Mr. Jackson was the first in his family to attend college. As he grew up, Mama continually reinforced the benefits of academic pursuits. Obtaining a postsecondary degree was not optional in her determined mind. She was a self-educated woman; her son would be formally so. Although notoriously limited, emancipation a few decades earlier offered greater opportunities for her son's generation. After Mama learned that two of the first five females of African heritage to ever receive a college degree were Claflin University alums, there was no doubt where he'd be pursuing his post secondary education. Undoubtedly, she'd be living vicariously through her only child's academic pursuits…and Frederick wasn't about to cross Mama. At least in that regard.

The young man made no mention of his research or travel intentions during his return home over the holidays. As far as his mother was concerned, he'd be heading back to campus in January. A strangely remote feeling reinforced what he'd already surmised - Mama would not approve; when he arrived on the island, only then he'd send her an explanatory letter. If antagonized, at least Mama's wrath would be from a distance, something he'd prepared himself to deal with.

So far it'd been a mild winter on the mainland, the climate no different when the young man arrived by boat to Saint Helen's Island in the mid-January afternoon. With belongings in tow, he'd stepped off the dock into the smiling embrace of James who he'd written previously advising of his pending arrival (and request not to mention it to Mama).

"My, my you grown, "a beaming James said. "The last time I was on the mainland you was no more than knee high to a toadstool."

"You look exactly the same," Frederick lied. James was a lot grayer and thinner than he remembered, almost emaciated. "The only thing different is your smile – it's grown a lot bigger," the young man added chuckling. Even before college

Frederick had become a bit of a grammar snob thanks to Mama; he'd soon realize that James would occasionally speak proper English (peppered by Southern slang), but most times not. He frequently rattled off a generous helping of Gullah Creole, forgetting himself. It was a mixed bag of communication – something Frederick thoroughly enjoyed. His mama always told him that if not in an educational context, correcting someone's grammar was just showing off. Frederick anticipated he'd be biting his tongue frequently during the upcoming weeks.

"I can already tell by the way you speak you mama made sure you became an educated college man; the family's most proud."

"I haven't graduated yet, a few more years to go, but no plans to let Mama down."

"You best not – there'd be hell to pay if you disappoint her. Hawa's always had dat fire in her belly. Anyway, let's get you settled." James grabbed Frederick's baggage and turned toward town, briskly walking off the weathered dock with the young man following closely behind.

"Hawa is Mama's basket name, right?" Frederick vaguely remembered some visiting relatives calling her that although she discouraged it, preferring to use her given name, Mary, on the mainland.

"Right; what we called her on the island. Call me Tamba, everyone else here does."

"I'm still Frederick no matter where I go," the young man replied.

"Named after Frederick Douglas; Hawa decided on the name long ago if she ever had a son – he a hero to her."

"To all of us," the namesake replied. Not far from the dock, a horse and wagon awaited; Tamba threw the young man's baggage behind the seat and they took off down the dusty road. After about a half mile, Tamba pulled up on the reins and stopped suddenly in front of a faded blue shack.

"We here, son." The small structure was a modified A-frame with a tiny porch and an outhouse in the rear. Tamba retrieved Frederick's bags and they both stepped onto the porch and through the only door.

"Not much, but it's comfortable; be an oil lamp and candles on the table and a fireplace to keep you warm. Logs out back." Sparsely furnished, the hut also had a bed and another small table with a water basin, cups, pitcher, and a few necessities for dining.

"It'll do; since I'll be devoting a majority of my time speaking with the locals, I won't be here much other than sleeping and consolidating my notes."

"Take a bit for the local folk to warm up to you even if you Hawa's son. My house is just down the road; you'll have dinner tonight with me and my wife. Tomorrow, we start in on dat project – make a plan, ease in slow."

"Okay, I appreciate the room and board, but I'm determined to earn my keep. On the weekends, I'm available for any odd jobs you might have. I could start by painting this faded hut, maybe a nice rust brown."

"No brown, Frederick; if you gonna paint, it be the same color, haint blue. No other color'll do; help keeps the bad haints away, even Boo Hag, but not as much."

"Boo Hag?" asked Frederick halfheartedly. He had little interest in these matters.

By Tamba's expression, Frederick could tell he was dead serious – he vaguely recalled haints was a local term for ghosts and other supernatural entities. "Check for cracks and holes, inside and outside, every night, you hear? Boo Hag fit through those easy cuz she leaves her skin behind; there's some patch material around back if needed. I know you educated and all, but that don't stop no Boo Hag, you on the island now – don't let the hag ride ya. She feeds off breath."

Frederick nodded in agreement; when researching the locals, it was best to humor them – good for building those critical personal relationships. He'd be doing a lot of nodding in the following weeks he reckoned.

The evening passed quickly; Tamba's wife, Anyika, was a joy, her cooking just as Tamba described - swit (delicious). Frederick, feeling the effects of his journey, had excused himself early, returning to the hut for what he anticipated to be a restful night.

Come daybreak, he couldn't catch his breath. His first attempt at rising out of bed failed; he'd need to muster up more energy – energy he didn't seem to possess. Tired as he was, he finally managed to raise himself off the mattress, attempt number three. Just as he balanced on wobbly feet, Tamba knocked on the door.

"Come out, young Frederick; lots doin' today."

Frederick stumbled across the room, undid the latch, and let Mama's cousin in. Immediately, Tamba's expression turned somber. "You look bad; you sick?"

"No, just really, really tired. Maybe I haven't yet recovered from the journey."

"You no foolin' me, son. You gotta visitor last night; I was afraid this happen." He then grabbed Frederick, escorting him outside into the fresh air and plopped him down on the porch steps. "You mainlanders don't listen to nothin' - you not check last night?"

"Check what?"

"For cracks and holes. You sit here while I look 'round the hut; check the roof too. Take some deep breaths until I finish."

Frederick embraced Tamba's advice and after a couple of minutes was feeling a little better, his energy gradually returning. He could hear Tamba's footsteps on the roof. "Damn, a big one. This crack need patching immediately; you stay put, I fix it." Tamba patched the roof in less than fifteen minutes; double-checking for any other cracks or holes. Satisfied, he returned to the front porch.

"No college work for you today, young man; need to rest and regain some strength."

"But…"

"But nothin'- I stay with you all day, we gotta talk anyway – my house." Knowing that without Tamba's assistance his project would be significantly impacted, Frederick reluctantly complied. Tamba headed home to pick up his horse and wagon, returning to fetch his woozy kin.

"Drink some of Anyika's special brew, it be good for what ails ya." They sat on chairs surrounding a tattered rectangular table beneath a large shade tree in Tamba's backyard sipping hot sweet tea. "I not mention to you mama about her son's plans cuz I thought you be smart enough to let her know before leaving. Knew when you showed, you didn't say nothin' to her. One of my wife's kinfolk travelin' to the mainland today, so Anyika asked her to visit Hawa soon as she get off dat boat. We shoulda put you up last night, but knowing you Hawa's boy and her past with the hag, we afraid. Thought it be okay as long as you look for cracks and fix 'em; my fault for not mentioning a roof check…not dat it mattered. You not gonna listen."

"Mama's going to know? I was planning to write her a letter today explaining everything."

"If I know you mama, when told, she come here even though she swore to never return. Hawa and family run away long ago on account of dat hag; had to or die."

"What?" Frederick felt his gut tighten, butterflies frantic to escape.

There was cosmic fear in Tamba's eyes. "For some reason Boo Hag attracted to Hawa, the child. And she be the only one who could see dat ting at night when the hag came visitin' her mama, your grandma. With everyone sleepin' in the only room of theirs, Hawa would somehow sense it and wake up when dat hag come to ride her mama, sucking breath for sustenance. Hag wanted you mama I tink, but she too young to get much energy from; even so Boo Hag stare at Hawa with blazin' red eyes as she ride. At first, Hawa too scared to scream, but when she finally did, Boo Hag leave fast. Happened over and over even though the house was checked every day for cracks, holes. Her parents believed Boo Hag use Hawa's sensitivity somehow to sneak in; knew dat ting getting frustrated when Hawa screamed – if her mama wake up while bein' ridden, dat hag take her skin and you grandma die. Hawa's family needed to escape the island. Might been an enemy put some bad mout on 'em – a curse, maybe help guide and strengthen Boo Hag."

Frederick was speechless; cognitively he wouldn't ordinarily believe the nonsense spewing out of Tamba's mouth, but last night was unexplainable. Still, Frederick was determined to continue his research project; he'd put in too much time and effort getting it approved and would not be deterred. Finally, he composed himself enough to utter, "I'm staying, Tamba, and need your help as we agreed."

"Tings different now, Frederick. I tink dat hag knows you Hawa's boy. Be bad for you, son."

"Not as bad for me as the university if I don't continue. I'm heading back to the hut, enhance my research outline, and start early tomorrow with or without you."

A slight smile parted Tamba's lips. "You just like Hawa, got the belly fire; Anyika will prepare some food and drink to take back to the hut. I have to tink on still helping. Remember one ting – if dat Boo Hag rides ya again tonight and you awake, don't struggle, pretend like you still sleepin' - fight her and Boo Hag takes you young skin. You not immune; got Sierra Leone blood runnin' through those veins."

Frederick returned to the hut, his mind swirling from Tamba's boggling input; still, he must forge ahead. He wasn't sure how his professor would respond, but maybe he'd write a separate paper on the island's hocus-pocus folklore, specifically the Boo Hag. If encouraged, he could continue that research back in South Carolina – there were plenty of people immersed in Gullah culture (or some semblance of it) throughout the Lowcountry.

The young researcher burned the midnight oil, writing ceaselessly, breaking only for a brief dinner and a few journeys to the outhouse. Finally, he could continue no more. Exhausted, he fell into bed fully clothed. A dark sleep enveloped him almost immediately; lucid dreams battered his synapses with visions of skinless red luminescent hags pursuing him throughout the cosmos – no place to hide from their horror. He fought to awaken but their subconscious grip was too strong. It seemed to go on for hours.

He awoke abruptly to the sight of the hideous red glowing Boo Hag floating prone above him, hungrily extracting breaths from his lungs. He lay still for a moment, remembering Tamba's warning about resistance. But like his mama, he was a fighter and that urge overwhelmed him.

Suddenly, the hut's door burst open with one savage kick; Mama stood there, eyes ablaze. "You're not gonna ride my boy, bitch!" The hag turned, separating from the young man; she stared intently at the intruder. "Up and out now, Frederick. There's a boat ready to leave at the dock. Run! I'll meet you back home – go."

Frederick knew better than to argue; he rolled from the bed, grabbed his notebooks and scrambled out the door. Even though exhausted from the hag's dirty work, he managed to stumble into Tamba's wagon that Mama must have borrowed, took the reins, and made a beeline to the dock.

When he got there, Tamba was waiting with the boat's captain. "Get in – now! I promised Hawa to come along, see you safely home."

During the ride to the mainland, Tamba explained that once Hawa learned about her son's research project, she scoured the docks frantically for a boat, eventually finding one for hire. Arriving on the island in the hush of night, she went straight to Tamba's home; he filled her in on the details.

"I never seen you mama so mad. Ever. It snuff out any long time fear she have; reminding her of the danger be a waste of time."

"She said she'd be back home." Frederick tried his best to believe his own words.

"Hawa not comin' back. If dat ting in the hut, Hawa's plan was to distract it as best she could; maybe stall her until sunrise where Boo Hag could no longer take a skin – be trapped like dat for eternity."

"Then there's still a chance."

"Chance, nothin'- as special as you mama is, no mortal can defeat dat hag in the end. No sir. Hawa's lost her covering – it be the Boo Hag's now. When morning comes I know dat hut be empty – never find her. You can never go back, son; if there be a bad mout on you family, it just got worse." Tears streamed down Frederick's face, his lungs gasping for air. The ride back to the mainland took an eternity.

Mama had sacrificed her own skin to save her son's. Before setting foot on the mainland, Tamba made him swear to never tread on that island again. Frederick swore, knowing it was contrived. He'd turn his academic focus to the dark folklore of the island, discover a methodology to vanquish the hag, even travel across the ocean to Sierra Leone for further research if necessary – there had to be a means to destroy that monstrosity.

Frederick would avenge Mama's demise … even if it took a lifetime or his life. Like her, his belly burned.

IF LOOKS COULD KILL

by Kent J. Moore

I'd seen corpses with more life.

G. Clayton Kaiser, Public Relations Director for Kansas City's Nelson-Atkins Museum of Art, had all the liveliness of an anemic sloth and all the color of a faded dish rag in his white dress shirt and charcoal gray bow tie. We sat on opposite sides of his desk in the museum's Bloch Building. Kaiser's girth suggested a lack of self-restraint also evident in his office decor. Replicas of famous artwork cluttered every flat surface, vertical and horizontal, with no discernible theme or organization. Maybe it was the "busy" appearance of his office that made Kaiser seem torpid by comparison.

As he peered at me over the half-moon glasses perched on the end of his nose, I had the feeling he was looking down on me in multiple ways. Maybe it had something to do with the green, knit tie I kept hoping would return to fashion or the worn, chambray cuffs protruding from my rumpled, navy blazer's sleeves.

"What did you say your name was again, Mr…?"

I handed him my business card. "K'Burg. Charles K'Burg."

"How unusual."

"Yeah. When my ancestors first arrived from Prussia, it was 'von Krutchenburg.' Somewhere along the way, one of 'em figured it was just simpler to shorten it to 'K'Burg'."

"How may I help you today?" He spoke more through his nose than his mouth.

"Doing a story on Madame Roggon and hoping you can set me up with an interview. Her agent won't return my calls, texts, or emails." I leaned forward and gave him my best "work with me here" look. "Thought you might have more luck, especially since the story will promote interest in her exhibit."

Kaiser shook his head, his jowls wobbling longer than his head did. "I am afraid that is quite impossible, Mr. Burger."

"K'Burg."

"K'Burg. Thank you. Anyway, I fear it is just impossible. Madame Roggon has a strict policy of no media interviews. Thus, no reporters were invited to the opening gala on Friday evening."

"How am I supposed to do my story on her without speaking to her?" My voice's pitch and volume rose with my blood pressure.

My desire to finish the story had more to do with getting paid than getting the facts. Truth was, I had no interest in some fluff piece on a so-called renowned sculptor few folks outside the Nelson had ever heard of. I'd much rather have been covering a homicide or the latest scandal in city government. However, Kansas City's murder rate had taken a nosedive lately, and the metro's political powers had been keeping their noses clean heading into the November elections, a month away. So, the Allied News Service assigned me to write about Madame Laureey Roggon and her exhibition at the Nelson. Wanting to keep my job more than my dignity, I found myself stuck in Kaiser's office on a Monday afternoon. I stifled a yawn and watched a police car go by the lone window, its lights flashing. It took everything I had not to run down to the museum's parking garage and go tearing after it.

Kaiser pointed to the press packet he'd handed me upon my arrival. "I have provided you with everything you might possibly need to write a wonderful story about the museum, Madame, and her work. I would write it for you myself, but I have too many details associated with the gala to which I must attend to spare the time. Besides, I imagine doing so would violate journalistic ethics, although that phrase often seems like an oxymoron these days."

I tried a different tack. "You know, Mr. Kaiser, I bet a big, important man like you has talked with the artist." I placed more emphasis on "big" than I probably should have, but the subtle jibe went straight over Kaiser's almost bald pate with room to spare.

"Oh yes, I had a lovely conversation with her. She is in town for a few days, for the gala and opening of the exhibit, you know."

"Yeah? So, what'd you think?"

"Well, she has a definite continental flair to her. Of course, she is a French national originally from Greece. As such, she has a savoir faire unusual for one apparently so young."

"How old is she?"

"Oh, I could not say for sure. One does not ask a woman such things, you know. However, were I to guess, I should say she is in her late twenties or early thirties."

I grabbed a pen and made a note of that on the back of the press kit. "And what's she look like?" The photos in the press packet showed only a woman in a black niqab and robe that covered everything but her eyes and hands.

"I really do not know. I will say she is an extremely modest woman. She wore a niqab the whole time we were together. I think it must be a religious thing."

I wondered if it was really a "didn't want to be seen by Kaiser" thing but kept that to myself. Getting nowhere fast, I circled back to where we'd begun.

"You said there's a gala Friday night. I'm sure my readers would love to hear about that. What can you tell me?"

Kaiser rubbed his fat little hands together with a gleeful smile. "We are hosting it here in the Noguchi Sculpture Court, just outside the galleries where the exhibit is housed. The caterer is famous for their Mediterranean food and wine, apropos to Madame's Greek heritage."

"Sounds swank. Black tie, I assume?"

"Oh, absolutely. Invitations have been sent only to Society of Fellows members at the Patron level and above. The event is extraordinarily exclusive."

"Maybe I could do a story on the gala. Hype up the value of museum membership, that sort of thing."

"Now, there is an idea worth consideration. We always seek ways to encourage membership growth at that level."

"Terrific! What time should I be there?"

"Well, the gala begins at seven, so …." Kaiser shook his head and wagged a finger in my face. "Oh, Mr. K'Dog…"

"K'Burg."

"Right, Mr. K'Burg, you are a sly one, are you not? You just want to cover the gala so you may speak with Madame. Shame on you." He chuckled and wagged his finger in my face, again. "I cannot have that, you know." I forced myself to smile back even as I shrugged in resignation.

Kaiser pushed himself back from his desk and heaved his bulk upright. "Well, I think we have covered the necessary ground here. If you follow me, I will give you an expeditious tour of Madame's exhibit. You can see for yourself what exquisite work she produces."

I followed Kaiser from the executive offices to the Noguchi Sculpture Court. Kaiser showed his identification to the security guard at the entrance to the featured exhibition space, and we entered.

Our footsteps echoed in the cavernous hall devoid of life except for Kaiser and me, not that Kaiser was all that lively. The dim, ambient lighting, cool temperature, and sterile, dehumidified air reminded me of many morgues I'd visited over the years. Track lighting, aimed at highlighting, made each of the stone sculptures stand out against the stark white walls behind them.

The first sculpture was labeled "Jim, Boston, August 2016." Kaiser stopped and extended his arm toward the statue, as if introducing me to an old friend. "This piece, often referred to as 'Gentleman Jim,' is a classic example of Madame's work. The subject is an unknown, unexceptional man. He appears out of context. As such, the viewer has no concept regarding his identity, occupation, or anything else of relevance about him beyond his name, his town, and his attire. He is, for all intents and purposes, unremarkable." Kaiser paused and admired the statue with a smile. "And yet, Madame has rendered him in such detail as to make his appearance simply astounding. This celebration of the common man is what has set her and her work apart."

As Kaiser delivered his mini lecture, I observed "Jim" was decked out in a pair of tasseled penny loafers, cuffed and pleated slacks, and a sport coat over a shirt and tie. Kaiser's statement about the detail was, if anything, an understatement. Each piece of the tassels' fringe was readily distinguished, and there was a paper-thin gap between the cuff and pant leg on each side. The jacket's herringbone design was flawless as was the tie's paisley print. The wrinkles and liver spots on his hands mirrored my own mid-life skin.

But it was the face that really captured my attention. Eyes wide open, almost bulging. Nose pinched. Lips pulled back in a rictus of repulsion revealing an open mouth in silent scream. I'd seen that look before, among the living and the dead in Afghanistan and Iraq and not in any museum.

"What's with this guy's expression?" I asked.

"Ah yes, 'the look.' You will find all of Madame's work has some variation on this expression. Some people find it a bit off putting. I think of it as an ironic juxtaposition or nonconformity to her sculptures' otherwise traditional poses and aesthetics."

"Mind if I take a few pictures for my story?"

"Actually, I do mind. Strictly no photography is permitted in the exhibit hall. However, you will find select photos of her work in your press packet along with a complete list of all sculptures featured in the exhibition."

Kaiser continued to guide me around the exhibit, throwing in bits of trivia about how heavy the statues were and the equipment needed to move them into the gallery. As with "Jim," each one featured a life-sized man chiseled from gray stone in exquisite detail. Whether it was Hal from Seattle in his hiking gear, Gabriel from Paris in his beret, or Konstantinos from Athens sporting nothing but swim trunks, they were all rendered in such detail you would swear the stone appearance was a fraud. However, the one I touched when Kaiser turned his back for a moment was rock solid. Like "Jim," each featured a disconcerting look of terror demanding further investigation.

*****

A few days later, as the aroma of cheap coffee and a half-eaten breakfast sandwich permeated my studio apartment's kitchen, which also served as my office, a pop-up window on my laptop announced an incoming video call from my boss. Antonia "Toni" Castillo graduated from an Ivy League journalism program. Her shoulder-length black hair framed brown eyes, an aquiline nose, thin lips, and a perfect set of teeth. In her early thirties and born about the time I was collecting my journalism degree from Ohio State, she was the youngest bureau chief in the news service's history and worked out of the Midwest bureau's offices in Chicago. She made it clear her current position was just a steppingstone to bigger and better things at the New York headquarters. Early in our professional relationship, we'd reached an understanding. She understood I was a dinosaur who could still write a story others would pay to read, and I understood she knew how to sell the news, even if she didn't really know how to write it. Thus, we tolerated each other more than we would have otherwise, which wasn't saying much.

The coffee and breakfast sandwich started a war in my stomach as I tried to get comfortable on my molded plastic chair and used my mouse to click on "Connect."

"Hello, Charles. How is your profile of Madame Roggon progressing?" Toni's high-pitched voice had a smooth, silky quality that belied her often fiery temper and left me picturing a rich, dark chocolate covering a habanero pepper.

"Great. Just great."

"So, you will submit it on time?"

"Sure, Toni. Just need to talk with the artist and—"

"You have not interviewed her yet?"

"Her agent won't return my calls, and the Nelson's PR guy isn't helping either. But I've got a lead on an opportunity. The Nelson's hosting an opening gala for the exhibit Friday evening, and Roggon's the guest of honor."

"And you have an invitation?"

"Not yet, but I'm working on it."

"Will this involve another call from the Kansas City Police Department, Charles?"

"Absolutely not, Toni."

"It does not matter. I need that piece by the end of the day on Friday. The gala Friday night will be too late. Just do what you can with what you have and send me the story by the deadline."

"Sure, Toni, whatever you say." I paused before launching my next salvo. "You know, I think there's more to this artist than meets the eye. Her bio says she's a French national of Greek origin, but I can't find any records for her as a student, apprentice, or artist in residence in either France or Greece."

"That is why I assigned you to do a profile on her. If we already knew what there is to know, there would be no point in writing about her."

"Yeah, but I mean there may be even more to her than that."

Toni frowned. "What are you talking about?"

"Well, the Nelson's PR guy thinks she's in her twenties or thirties, but the dates on some of her work suggest she's much older than that. I haven't found anything to confirm just how old she is."

"You think this woman is hiding her age? Well, I have news for you. She would not be the first."

"I know, but between that, the lack of records in France and Greece, and the niqab she wears, there's this literal and figurative veil of mystery I can't seem to crack." I grabbed a quick mouthful from the stained mug next to my laptop. "Since I've been having trouble connecting with the artist, thought I'd see if I could track down some of the models she's used – I assume she uses models – and get their perspectives. So, I took the names, cities, and dates from her statue titles and started searching the Web."

Toni's attention drifted as her eyes shifted to something offscreen, so I cut to the chase. "Let me show you something." I displayed a picture from the press packet. "This is a Roggon sculpture labeled 'Len, Baltimore, February 2016'." I pulled up another picture and shared it with Toni, "Now, this is a photo of Leonard Case."

Toni leaned in to look at the images on the screen on her end. "It looks like the same guy."

"I thought so, too. Mr. Case is also from Baltimore."

"You found the model for her sculpture. So what?"

"Mr. Case went missing in February 2016, during the period Madame Roggon's exhibit was on display at the Baltimore Museum of Art. He's still missing. And he's not the only one. I crosschecked the names, cities, and dates listed on the titles of Madame Roggon's sculptures with missing person's reports in the corresponding cities on the corresponding dates. I can connect at least half the sculptures in the exhibit."

"Do you have any other visual connections like Mr. Case?"

"No, the press packet didn't have any other close ups like this one, and I was effectively prohibited from taking pictures while I was there the other day."

"Let me see the list of sculptures." I pulled up the list and shared it with Toni. She reviewed it then shook her head. "Charles, most of these guys have common first names, like Jim, John, Robert, and Michael."

"I know, but—."

"Are you suggesting she's a serial killer based on one visual match between a sculpture of hers and a photo of a missing person in Baltimore? She may have never met Leonard Case and simply sculpted his likeness using the same picture you just showed me."

"Yeah, but—."

"Besides, from the pictures of her I have seen, she is even more petite than me. How did she kill and dispose of all those men? I have no doubt she could take you. Hell, my abuela could take you, but I doubt Madame Roggon has overpowered multiple fully functional men. Have you shared your suspicions with the police?"

"Well, no, but—."

"If you do, let me know. I want to be there when you tell them an internationally known artist who looks like she would blow away in a good wind has been killing well-built men after sculpting their likeness from stone and getting away with it for years. I want to watch when they laugh you out the door."

Toni had a point, but it didn't satisfy my curiosity. "But Toni, I really want to talk with Madame Roggon. I want to ask her about Len from Baltimore and the other sculptures whose titles align with missing persons. There's more than a coincidence here. I want to follow my hunch as far as I can. That's what a good investigative journalist does. If you could get me access—"

"Listen, Charles. Not every story involves murder, scandal, or corruption."

I came out of my chair, pointing a finger at her through the computer. "But what if this one does? What if this woman is secretly killing men in every city where she exhibits then flaunts her ability to do it by displaying statues of them, like…like trophies?"

Toni grabbed her head as if trying to keep it from exploding. "Dios mio, K'Burg! Do you hear yourself? I did not assign you to investigate this woman. I assigned you to write an engaging profile of her. You are lucky to get any assignment at all. Most subjects do not want to speak with you, because your reputation precedes you, and it is not a flattering one. Just write the damn profile, do it on time, and leave the conspiracy theories to less reputable sources on the internet. If you cannot, I will find someone who can."

After a moment of silence, she continued in a more deliberate manner, her glare no less intimidating just because it was virtual. "You will write the story I assigned you. You will write only what you can substantiate about this woman. You will not subject our news service to legal action we do not want and cannot afford. Do you understand?"

I threw up my hands in mock surrender. "Yeah, I understand." I clicked "Disconnect," and Toni disappeared from my screen. I understood, but that didn't mean I would do as I was told.

*****

The rich are typically served by people who are not, so a well-placed Benjamin among the catering staff gained me back door access to Friday night's gala. I had excavated my lone suit from the recesses of my closet for the occasion. A charcoal gray two-piece that I only wore to wakes, weddings, and other depressing occasions, the suit had seemed a good investment when I'd started work for the news service. However, I ended up wearing it only a handful of times. Now, like me, it was dated and out of style. I thought it would help me blend in at the gala. Amid the tuxedos and designer evening gowns, all it did was get me confused with the docents and the catering staff circulating with trays of drinks and hors d'oeuvres.

The guests who weren't in the adjacent exhibit hall mingled in the Noguchi Sculpture Court to music from a classical string quartet in one corner. The contemporary art in the court, especially the six-foot cube of granite labeled "Ends," looked like it belonged in a rock quarry or construction site more than an art museum, but it provided convenient cover as I stalked Madame Roggon in vain and tried to avoid G. Clayton Kaiser. The latter waddled around in his black tuxedo and white dress shirt, reminding me of a pretentious penguin with a bad combover as he gladhanded the museum's patrons.

Eventually, I spotted Madame Roggon amid a throng of admirers in the exhibit hall. As in her photo, she wore a black niqab and gown that covered all but her eyes and hands. She was every bit as diminutive as her press packet suggested, making her difficult to spot even though her outfit was unique among the other women's evening dresses.

The thought she could somehow overpower grown men everywhere she went suddenly seemed as ludicrous as Toni had thought. I was tempted to set the drink I was holding on top of "Ends" and slip away before anyone could expose me for the non-patron that I was. Then, a pair of elderly ladies wandered by, and I remembered a woman doesn't need to be big and powerful to kill a man. She just needs the right tools, like a bit of arsenic in elderberry wine.

I looked at a couple of statues in the hall. Bob from Chicago wore a Bears sweatshirt above sagging jeans and had a middle age spread that prompted me to suck in my own gut. Meanwhile, Darnell in Phoenix was young, nude, and possessing a well-toned physique I could only dream of. The only thing they had in common was a facial expression that told me something was wrong here. I owed it to my readers and Len in Baltimore, assuming Len was still somewhere in Baltimore and among the living, to get some answers from Madame. Besides, I hoped to gather enough evidence to justify continuing my investigation and getting back to writing stories worthy of my talent, despite Toni's warning to drop it. If I failed and Toni found out what I did, I could lose my job.

Of course, I could lose it anyway. She'd said she wanted the profile of Madame Roggon by the end of the day. Literally, I wasn't late. Practically, I knew she'd wanted it by close of business. So, I'd texted her earlier about having internet and computer problems and then sent her a file that alternated between intelligent prose and gibberish, hoping it would substantiate my excuse and buy time to attend the gala before filing my real story.

The rich and famous avoid taxes, menial labor, and many other things that vex me and the other 99 percent. One thing they can't avoid is using the restroom. Eventually, Madame Roggon drifted away from the crowd toward the short hallway at the end of Noguchi Court. I followed and got there in time to see her step into the ladies' room at the opposite end.

I ambled into the hallway and used one of the drinking fountains between the men's and women's restroom doors.

Having not been on a date or in a genuine relationship for a while, I'd forgotten how long women can take. Thankfully, no one else lingered at the water fountains, preferring the gala's complimentary champagne to the city's water supply. I tuned out the buzz of conversation accompanied by chamber music and listened for toilets flushing beyond the bathroom door, wondering which one would herald Madame's reappearance.

When I was afraid the sounds of running water and what I'd already drunk might necessitate my own use of the restroom, Madame Roggon exited the ladies' room accompanied by a well-endowed grande dame of Kansas City society stuffed into a sequined evening gown.

I straightened up and stepped in front of Madame, leaving room for the other woman to pass if she chose. Instead, she stopped next to Madame and appraised me and my suit, wrinkling her nose and frowning as if confronted by a foul odor.

I focused on my target. "Madame Roggon?" I asked.

"Yes. And you are?" Her voice had a lush, smoldering quality to it like a cat's purr or Eartha Kitt in her prime. But even more arresting were the green eyes that gazed out from the thin strip of olive skin revealed by her niqab and her exotic, intoxicating fragrance with its hint of honeysuckle.

"I…I'm Charles K'Burg. Big fan of your work."

The grande dame rolled her eyes and muttered, "Some people…" in a haughty tone that left no doubt what she thought of "some people." With a rustle of fabric and the click of high heels, she returned to the gala, leaving Madame and me behind. I gave her a mock salute behind her back then returned my attention to Madame.

Her eyes suggested a hidden smile beneath the niqab. "I do not think Mrs. Van Doren approves of you."

"Yeah, well, I don't think much of her either, but whatcha gonna do?" I shrugged.

"You said something about being a fan?" Madame asked.

"Yes, huge fan. Love what you've done. Your attention to detail is amazing. May I ask you a question?"

"I believe you just did."

I chuckled. "Guess I did. Okay, here's another. Where do you find your models?"

"What makes you think I use models?"

Her question in response to mine reminded me of every evasive politician I'd interviewed over the years. "You saying you don't use models?"

She gave a dismissive wave of the hand. "No, I just wonder why you think I do." Her eyes narrowed as she looked beyond me a moment, then redirected her attention to me. "I will return to the party now."

She started to step around me, and I shifted so I was between her and the sculpture court, again. "It's Len from Baltimore."

"I beg your pardon?"

"Your statue of Len from Baltimore. That's what makes me think you use models." I pulled my smartphone from my jacket and retrieved the headshot of the statue in question. "Here's a picture of your statue." I swiped that picture away and showed her one of the missing Leonard Case. "And this is the real Len – or Leonard – from Baltimore." I toggled back and forth between the pictures. "They're clearly the same person."

When I looked back up from the phone, Madame Roggon's arms were crossed, and she was focused on me. The eyes had narrowed with a slight crease in the bridge of her nose. "Yes, there is a remarkable resemblance." She made another unsuccessful attempt to get past me.

"When's the last time you saw the real Len from Baltimore?"

"I never said I did. You ask many questions for an art aficionado. You do not happen to be a reporter by chance?"

"Me? Nah, I'm just interested in where you get your inspiration. I noticed your statue bears an uncanny likeness to a man who went missing in Baltimore when you exhibited there." I pulled out the list of statues Kaiser had given me. "In fact, quite a few of your works seem connected to missing persons."

Now, instead of trying to circumvent me, Madame Roggon moved toward me, shoulders back, head erect, and unblinking eyes boring into me from beneath the niqab. I instinctively retreated as she walked me backwards toward the gala. The smooth purr of her voice took on a harder edge.

"Mr… K'Burg, is it?

I nodded.

"Mr. K'Burg, I thank you for your interest in my work. I get my inspiration from many places, such as movies, magazines, and even conversations with adoring fans such as yourself." She stopped long enough to eye me from head to toe. "It would bring me great pleasure to immortalize you in stone, Mr. K'Burg. But right now, I see your presence is desired elsewhere."

She pointed behind me, and I turned to find G. Clayton Kaiser standing in the doorway that led from the hallway to the sculpture court. A step behind and to either side of him were two men who looked like they might play on the Chiefs' offensive line. Along with dark suits, they sported earpieces that all-but-announced they were in the security business.

Kaiser shook his head. "Mr. K'Ville…"

"K'Burg," I corrected.

"Mr. K'Burg, right. Your name is not on the guest list, and I believe I told you in no uncertain terms that members of the press are strictly prohibited this evening. And yet, here you are."

Madame Roggon moved to Kaiser's side, the purr returning to her voice. "He informed me he was not a reporter. I see now he is one and a dishonest one at that. Thank you for your intervention." She laid a hand on Kaiser's arm as a twinkle in her eyes hinted at the smirk I suspected hid beneath the niqab.

Kaiser patted her hand. "Mrs. Van Doren said someone was accosting you outside the ladies' room. I thought she might be exaggerating, but I see she was not." He glared at me. "I am very disappointed in you."

"Yeah, well, that's me. Just one big disappointment. You do throw a lovely party though. Any chance you could arrange my nephew's bar mitzvah?"

Kaiser shook his head and frowned. "I cannot have you upsetting Madame with who knows what kind of questions." He gave an almost imperceptible nod, and the two gorillas stepped forward to escort me from the premises. Each grabbed one of my elbows with a grip I felt certain would leave a mark. My shoulders slumped, and I gave Madame a parting shot. "The next time you're in Baltimore, tell Len I said 'Hello'…if he's still around."

Once we cleared the sculpture court and were out of sight of the guests, the Bruise Brothers hustled me out the nearest exit and onto the sidewalk beyond. When they were gone, I picked myself up and started walking west. The party was over for me, but my night was just beginning.

*****

A benefit of being a crime reporter is you learn tricks of the criminal trade, like breaking and entering, also bribery. Thus, thirty minutes after being thrown out of the Nelson, I slipped into the condo near the Country Club Plaza my sources said Madame Roggon was using, thanks to another well-placed Benjamin and some tools that were only illegal if I got caught.

The heat hit me as soon as I stepped inside, as if I'd gone directly from Kansas City to Phoenix. If

Madame Roggon was a killer, she must be a cold-blooded one.

I turned on my phone's flashlight and entered the kitchen. Among its contents was a knife set with a wicked looking cleaver that gleamed in my flashlight's beam. I examined each piece and saw no traces of blood or other evidence to suggest they'd been used for carving anything more than salad. A search of the adjoining dining room yielded even less of interest.

I turned my attention to the living room. Light from the full moon streamed through a bank of windows along the outer wall, illuminating a room devoid of furnishings. Instead of carpet, a canvas tarp covered most of the floor. To one side, a six-foot folding table held an array of fascinating tools.

I stepped over to the table and added my flashlight to the moonlight. Among the implements were mallets, a set of chisels and points, and a rotary power tool with multiple accessories that looked like they could drill or cut anything. In short, the table held everything one needed to cut and shape a block of stone into a terrorized man or to terrorize a man to death before cutting him down to more easily disposable pieces. My mouth went dry.

Examining the tools, I heard an erratic series of squeaks from the hallway off the living room. I fought the urge to bolt and instead crept to the doorway connecting the living room and hallway. The squeaks persisted, and there was another sound, a scratching or gnawing that came from behind a door at the end of the short hallway. Taking a step toward the door, I saw someone else staring back at me. I gasped. Then I stuck my light in the stranger's face and saw my reflection in a wall mirror at the opposite end.

Shaking my head and smiling at my own stupidity, I walked to the end of the hall and put my hand on the knob of the closed door. The squeaking continued, as did the scratching and gnawing, and now, I could also hear the rustling of movement. I took a deep breath, turned the knob, and opened the door, sweeping the room with my flashlight as I did.

Atop a dresser, a wire cage held a dozen or more white mice moving among the wood shavings that lined the bottom, playing on hamster wheels that squeaked as they spun along with the squeaks of the mice themselves, some of whom were gnawing on rawhide chews and wooden block toys. I stared down at the beady-eyed rodents as they went about their business.

What the hell was Madame Roggon doing with a cage full of mice? I'd heard of emotional support animals, but I didn't recall mice making the list. I'd also heard of people having rats and mice for pets, but usually, it was one or two, not a dozen or more.

I scratched my head and searched the rest of the bedroom and adjoining master bath. The clothing in the closet and dressers was consistent with what one would expect of a young woman always seen in a niqab and gown that covered everything but her hands. No jewelry besides a few rings of gold and silver, some with Greek symbols, which again fit with Madame Roggon's bio.

I wandered back to the living room, pondering my next move. My brief, unofficial interview with Madame had reaffirmed my suspicion she was hiding something but gave me no leads as to what or how to prove it. The search of the condo was equally fruitless. I sighed. Maybe Toni was right. Maybe I just needed to write the assigned story and move on.

That's when I heard footsteps and voices at the condo's door and a key in the lock. I scrambled for the dining room and hid behind the well-stocked bar separating it from the living room. A moment later, the front door opened and closed, and the voices became distinct.

Madame spoke first. "Welcome to my abode." I heard her walk onto the tarp in the living room.

A heavier set of footsteps followed hers, and a deep bass voice asked, "You want I should turn on a light or something?"

"No, I prefer to work by moonlight."

Curious to see her guest and what they were doing, I turned on my phone's camera and extended the end of the phone past the edge of the bar. The camera revealed Madame's guest was one of the goons who threw me out of the Nelson. He stood with his back to the bank of windows that formed the living room's outer wall. Facing him, Madame was illuminated by the Plaza's bright lights and the moon. They were both dressed as I'd seen them at the Nelson.

"Would you strike a pose for me?" Madame asked.

The security guy squared his shoulders, crossed his arms across his broad chest, and stuck out his chin at a slightly elevated level. Madame approached him and used her hands and arms to gently turn his top-heavy body toward the windows while keeping his head turned toward the center of the room.

"Perfect," Madame said. "Now, hold that pose and look at me."

With that, she removed her niqab. Whether it was the phone's camera, the lighting, or a combination of the two, her skin had a glow that highlighted the pert nose and full lips painted a garish shade of red. Her black hair was laid back in cornrows.

Her model gave a strangled gasp but remained rooted to the spot as Madame's cornrows began to move. I couldn't feel a breeze and didn't think cornrows were subject to drafts anyway. Then, one of them hissed. That's when a cold shiver ran up my spine while something warm ran down my leg.

Madame approached the security guy as the color drained from his face and hands and his dark suit faded to a marbled gray. She reached out and stroked a hand across his features while the snakes on her head slithered to their full length and hissed, tongues darting out between fangs.

My mind raced back to Mrs. Baltzley's high school English class. Perseus cutting off the snake-covered head of Medusa, who could turn people to stone with just a look. So why wasn't I turning to stone like the security guy? Then it hit me. I wasn't looking directly at her. I was seeing an image reflected in my phone, just as Perseus had with his shield.

I watched transfixed as Madame Roggon admired her latest creation a bit longer then disappeared through the doorway on the opposite side of the living room. I heard the door to her bedroom open and close, followed by sounds of movement and running water, as if she were getting ready for bed.

I was afraid to move and equally afraid to stay. My mind raced. Should I call the cops? Yeah, that conversation would go well. 'Hello, police? I'd like to report a woman with snakes for hair turning men to stone.' Should I try to kill her while she slept? Would the snakes sleep, and what if they woke her before I could kill her? Maybe, I should just get the hell out and be thankful it wasn't me petrified in the living room.

I stayed where I was until there had been a solid 30 minutes of no sound from down the hall except the occasional squeak I'd heard earlier. Then, I straightened up and paused while my creaky joints adjusted to the fact I was moving again. I crept into the living room and touched the statue on the tarp. Where once stood a man of flesh and blood now stood a statue of a man who'd died a horrible, agonizing, albeit silent death, if the look on his face was any indication.

As I raised my phone to snap a picture or two, it began to blare "Darth Vader's Theme." Toni was calling. In my scramble to silence the phone, I accidentally accepted her call.

"K'Burg! Where the hell is that story? When I said 'end of day' on Friday, I did not mean—"

I killed the call and the sound simultaneously. A voice behind me said, "Mr. K'Burg, how nice of you to grace me with your presence."

I flipped the phone to selfie mode and used it to look over my shoulder. Madame Roggon stood there wearing nothing but a gossamer white nightgown that left little to the imagination. But I was only interested in the snakes that bobbed and weaved about her head. The tail end of a white mouse protruded from one's mouth.

"Do not be bashful, Mr. K'Burg. Turn around, so we may continue our conversation from earlier this evening. I imagine you must have many more questions now."

"You…you're Medusa." I moved away from her and tried to put the statue between us, although not so much that I lost sight of her in my phone.

"Not quite. I am a Gorgon. Medusa was my sister. My name is Euryale. My sister was raped by

Poseidon in the Temple of Athena. Finding no fault in Poseidon, Athena unleashed her fury and punishment on Medusa, transforming my sister into a monster. Talk about blaming the victim. For the crime of standing with Medusa in this travesty, I suffered the same fate."

She grabbed a tool from the nearby table and used it to smooth part of the statue. "The curse of Athena was not without its silver lining. As you see, I can change anyone who looks upon me as I really am into stone. Over the millennia, I have used my gift to finance the lifestyle to which I have become accustomed and to exact a certain amount of revenge on the male of the species." Standing in front of the statue, she caressed it like some long-lost lover. "I typically only add one specimen to my collection in each city, but in this instance, I will gladly make an exception."

I closed my eyes and pressed the button on my phone to snap a picture. In the dim light of the condo, the flash activated, and I heard Euryale shriek with what I hoped was momentary blindness. I opened my eyes long enough for my phone to confirm she was still in front of the statue. Then I closed them again, turned, and tackled the top-heavy sculpture, driving it down on top of the Gorgon in hopes it would crush her. Her screams told me I'd hit but not killed my target.

During the fall, I lost my grip on my phone and heard it drop to the tarp-covered floor somewhere in front of me. I scrambled from the pile of myself, Gorgon, and statue and crawled around in search of my phone, my eyes closed to avoid an inadvertent glimpse of the Gorgon. In the background, Euryale bellowed in anger, yelling what I imagined were Greek expletives while her snakes hissed. I prayed I got to the phone before Euryale got to me.

My right hand touched the phone. I put the screen in front of my face and opened one eye. Behind me, Euryale was pinned prone beneath the statue, which formed an "X" with her on the bottom. She kicked her legs, and her arms clawed the floor as she struggled to move the weight atop her. The statue shifted a bit. Given her petite build and how much the sculpture must weigh, I wondered whether she'd be able move it enough to escape or how long it would take her if she could. The statue shifted some more.

I jumped up and headed for the front door. Euryale's roars of frustration had turned to grunts of exertion, and a look back via my phone showed she was making slow but steady progress toward freedom. I took a detour into the kitchen.

As I walked backward toward Euryale, she redoubled her efforts. Her movements became more frantic, less coordinated. I sat on the end of the statue closest to her head, my eyes still riveted to my phone rather than the reality it reflected.

The warm, seductive voice was gone, replaced by a high-pitched shrieking. "No! Stay away from me! Do not dare—"

The scream that followed the cleaver's first whack across her neck caused my entire body to shudder. I closed my eyes to block out the sight while I retched. Then I opened them and finished what I'd started, Euryale screaming until the last blow severed her head from her body. The snakes continued to hiss and squirm for a few moments afterwards, thrusting their forked tongues in a wild, last gasp and then dying one at a time.

The ensuing silence was almost more unnerving than what preceded it. I draped my blood splattered jacket over the lifeless head of the Gorgon. Then, I walked into the dining room, poured myself a glass of ouzo from the bar, and dialed 9-1-1.

*****

When the KCPD arrived, I warned them not to directly look at what was under my jacket. The petrification of one unfortunate detective convinced them to listen to me. They took my statement, confiscated my cell phone, and sent me away with a warning to keep my mouth shut. They didn't have to worry. I hardly believed it myself, and without my phone or any other proof, I knew no one else would either.

Thankfully, the police didn't call Toni. Her anger at being cut off and her plans to "can your sorry ass" evaporated when I scooped every media outlet in the country by reporting Madame Roggon had disappeared. The official police report listed her as a missing person. I have no idea what became of her after Kansas City's finest escorted me from her condo. I do know Len from Baltimore and the others showcased in her exhibit are not missing. In fact, they're safely interred in the archives of the Nelson-Atkins Museum of Art, monuments to what can happen if looks could kill.

END

THE RIVER'S WHIM

by Malina Douglas

A sense of foreboding rippled through Dash as he gazed into the black, impenetrable water. The Griboedov Canal carried the faint whiff of algae, cigarette smoke and something he could not place.

As he walked along the ledge, golden orbs gleamed like trapped souls. From the sky, he could tell nothing. It was swathed in the perpetual pale gloom of the White Nights.

He checked his instructions. *Find the gold-winged gryphons on the Bank Bridge. At 21:21 you will meet Konstantin Radionovich Vratushkin. He will assist you on your assignment.*

Dash doubted he needed assistance. He was certain that rationality could overcome nature's oddities, that every strange occurrence could be explained.

*****

As he walked along a pale pink building, gold wings rose from the gloom. A pair of gryphons guarded a narrow footbridge. Dash stepped between them, along a railing like the ribbing of a butterfly's wings.

A man walked towards him, stopped in front of Dash and said, "The jellybean stew is congealing." The code phase.

Dash nodded. "Konstantin?"

"Yes." As he stuck out a pale hand, Dash observed a strong straight nose, a chiselled jaw and grey eyes with a steady gaze.

Though he'd been sent as a translator, Konstantin made it clear that he was a philosophy student, that he was writing a thesis on Kantian ethics and it was within eighteen pages of completion.

"So where are we going?" interrupted Dash.

"To a riverside dacha not far away."

"How far?"

Ninety-four kilometres. Here's your train ticket. We depart tomorrow morning, eight-thirty sharp.

*****

As concrete sprawl gave way to wide fields, Dash turned to Konstantin.

"What do you think is causing the disappearances?"

"The villagers say it's a vodyanoi, resembling an old man dwelling on the river-bottom. That he must be appeased."

"Do you believe them?"

"I grew up on the stories, but we shall have to—"

Their conversation broke off when a woman stepped aboard and took a seat across from them.

Like a flower turning towards the sun, Konstantin's attention shifted, and he launched into a rapid conversation with the woman, who introduced herself as Masha. She reminded Dash in nearly all ways of a sunflower, from her cropped sun-yellow hair to her beaming face to her long slender body in a jaunty green top and short skirt.

She had a clear, light voice that to him was not clear at all because he didn't understand her. His translator became so absorbed in the conversation, punctuated with frequent laughter, that he ignored Dash's questions completely.

He closed his eyes and let their conversation wash over him like a gushing mountain stream.

*****

When Dash woke, the conversation was still going, and it continued till their stop, out the doors of the train, across the station, into a taxi, down a bumpy dirt road and all the way to a blue metal gate, where Masha departed.

They arrived to a house with a broad, shaded terrace and peeling white paint.

On the table was a note in a cursive scrawl:

Disappearance of Larissa Melkina,

last night, 22:44.

Take the raft and find the source of the disturbance before the river claims its next victim.

"Let's go," said Konstantin as he hurried down the hall.

Moored amongst the river-reeds was the raft. It was nothing like the curvaceous, inflatable thing that Dash had imagined, but more like a pile of logs lashed together with rope.

Konstantin disappeared and Dash found himself sitting on the bank, tapping his foot and glaring at the river. He had left his trenchcoat and boots in the house and wore a black singlet with slacks rolled to mid-calf.

He looked up to see Konstantin walking towards him with Masha.

Dash stood and brushed off his slacks. *"You invited the girl from the train aboard our raft?"*

"Hello, Dash!" Masha beamed at him. Her short dress of buttercream cotton revealed long tanned legs and high heeled sandals. Entirely inappropriate for the mission yet Dash could find no fault with her.

"This is not a summer boating excursion," he hissed at Konstantin.

"You mean we're not supposed to enjoy it?"

"It's not a question of enjoyment. We're going on a mission."

"So, we're supposed to be serious all the time?"

Dash expelled a sigh. "Just get on the raft."

Konstantin murmured something to Masha, and she erupted into squeals of laughter.

"What did you say?" demanded Dash.

"Oh, I just said it's lovely weather for boating."

Dash frowned, quite certain that he had said something different.

Dash helped Masha onto the raft, and she giggled as it swayed beneath her sandals.

From a canvas bag, Konstantin withdrew a belt, brown leather with a copper buckle. "I have a feeling I should give you this."

"Thanks, but I already have a belt."

"Not like this one."

Dash examined the buckle. The copper oval was embossed with a fluid, curving script. "Do you know what it says?"

"It's a dedication from Czar Alexander. A rare collector's item."

"Thank you." Dash slipped off his old belt and replaced it with the new one. He pushed off from the shore with a wooden paddle and used it to row while Konstantin rowed from the other side. Masha stretched her legs out and tanned in the mild summer sun.

The river was wide, the current sluggish. On the smooth, grassy bank, cows grazed on fields fringed by trees.

A few minutes later, Konstantin complained his arm was hurting and passed his paddle to Dash.

Dash paddled as the sun rose and sweat trickled down his back.

He heard a peal of laughter and shot a glance behind him. Konstantin was tickling Masha as she giggled and squirmed. The raft shook.

"Please stop that."

Konstantin's smile vanished. "Oh right. We're supposed to be serious." He murmured an aside to Masha and she burst into laughter.

"I said, stop it!"

Masha fell silent. Konstantin gazed at the landscape with tight lips and narrowed eyes. The bank rose and fields gave way to dense pine forest.

The river narrowed and the current grew swifter. Dash used the paddles to steer them around boulders. Ahead he saw the water flow swift and white.

"Hold on!"

The raft took a sharp dip and Dash heard shrieks followed by laughter.

A boulder rose ahead, and he steered around it.

Dash heard a high, sudden yelp and a splash. He turned. Masha was in the river, treading water to her chin.

"We've got to do something!" wailed Kostya.

Dash peeled off his shirt and dove in.

*****

The shock of the cold shot through him as he hurtled with the current. He dove, till the water darkened to murk and the jellyfish flutter of Masha's dress stirred before him. As his fingertips brushed her ankle, he felt a tug on his foot and jerked it back.   He reached down and felt hands, slimy fingers holding on like a vise, pulling him deeper as the pressure built in his lungs. He kicked but could not break free.

Dash felt a pop and he landed on his feet in an air pocket.

Pebbles shifted beneath him as he stood. Seated on a stout stone chair was a green-skinned creature with a flat nose, a moustache that drooped past his wide, froglike mouth and a beard tangled with river-reeds.

The vodyanoi.

On the ground beside him hunched Masha, small lips clenched together, and sodden dress plastered to her shivering body. Around them, river reeds trembled in the murk.

"Release her," ordered Dash.

The vodyanoi spoke in a deep, guttural voice. Dash could understand nothing.

"Masha, can you translate for me?"

"*Nyet*," she said.

Dash's shoulders sank. "What can I do then?"

Dash felt himself sinking. If he could not bargain with the vodyanoi, he would be stuck there, as the river reeds swayed, and life rushed on above him but he could not reach it.

The vodyanoi's round yellow eyes gazed unblinking.

"I can understand you," said a clear female voice.

From between the reeds stepped a rusalka. White lace clung to her porcelain skin and wet green hair fell to her hips. She stepped forward and stroked the side of Dash's face. He shivered.

"Who are you?"

"Larissa," she whispered, and her voice came out as a hiss.

"Ask him to release Masha, and I'll ensure the river is protected."

She spoke to the vodyanoi. His replied in a low grumble.

"Promises are insufficient. What can you give him?"

"I don't know." Dash looked down. The copper of the belt-buckle glinted. He slid off the belt. Keeping hold of the leather end, he held out the buckle to the vodyanoi.

Webbed fingers brushed the surface. Thick brows bunched together.

"It's a rare collector's item."

Larissa translated and the vodyanoi grunted. He snatched the buckle but Dash pulled it out of his reach.

"One more thing. You must promise to stop stealing people into your realm."

When Larissa translated, the vodyanoi let out a booming laugh.

His yellow eyes flickered from the buckle to Dash and back again. He gave a curt nod.

Dash held out the buckle and the vodyanoi took it, with no change in his gruff expression.

He spoke to Larissa and she nodded. "He says to return you to the surface, but.." She slid a hand along Dash's shoulder and tilted his chin up. "Won't you stay a while?"

"I can't," said Dash between clenched teeth.

Larissa's mouth curved like a fishhook.

"You're awfully pink," she said, pinching Masha's cheek. "Why don't you join us? You'll make a lovely rusalka once your flesh becomes paler."

"No," said Masha, her face forming an expression as if she'd swallowed something disgusting.

"Go!" said the vodyanoi with a flick of his webbed hand.

Larissa took the hands of Masha and Dash, surged upwards and pierced the membrane of the air pocket. As she swam, Dash felt an odd sensation and looked behind him.

The vodyanoi was holding the buckle in one hand and peering down at it. He brought it to his lips and spoke.

The symbols glowed and began to move. He laughed, a deep booming sound that chilled Dash's bones. Dash felt the urge to turn back but the rusalka's grip was tight, his air too little. As his lungs burned, he gazed at the light on the water's surface, till the longing for air took over his sensations, they crested the water, and he breathed sweet relief.

He found himself washed up on the riverbank, Masha beside him. With a flicker of white feet, the rusalka disappeared into the deep.

Masha turned to him.

"*Spasibo*," she said, and her embrace transmitted a feeling much deeper than words.

Before Dash could reply, she turned to the side and drew a sharp breath.

Dash followed her gaze to large brooding boulders and saw the wreckage of the raft.

"Kostya!" she yelled and broke into a run.

Konstantin stepped out from the rocks, clothing soaked but intact. He ran to Masha and embraced her as if they had been parted for a century. His lips locked onto hers and Dash turned away.

Kostya clapped him on the back as if they were old friends.

"We've done it! A triumph of man over the forces of nature."

"I suppose so."

"Let's drink to our success!" Konstantin drew a flask from his pocket, unscrewed the lid, tilted it back and passed it to Dash.

Dash took a swig. Spiced liquor coursed down his throat and he coughed. For the first time since his arrival, his muscles relaxed.

"Care to join us, Masha?"

She was standing on the riverbank, her body unnaturally still. Without looking back, she stepped into the water.

"Masha!" Kostya ran to her, Dash on his heels.

She spoke in a strange, far-off tone.

"What did she say?"

Konsantin scowled. "That the vodyanoi is calling her. And the music of the river is... more beautiful than anything else."

She dove into the water.

As Konstantin dove after her, Dash had an odd knowing that she was already gone, too far to return to the mortal world, that Konstantin would come back without her.

*****

"The river's whim," said Konstantin as he hunched on the shore afterwards, "cannot be tamed or even understood."

Bubbles rose to the surface and Dash realised the vodyanoi was laughing.

THE WALKER HOUSE

by Becka Rex

The front door to the Walker House was pushed open with great force, splintering the quiet stillness of a Monday afternoon. A series of sharp heel clicks tapped across the lobby floor. The proprietor of the inn was leaning upon his desk wrinkling his forehead over an open ledger book. He recognized the footnote even before glancing up.

"Mr. Walker," said the voice, echoing the sharpness of the shoes. In evenings passed, he had referred to his friend and toasting companion as A.B. and answered to Alonso. But today's business was clearly between Mr. Walker and Mr. Scribner, one a hotelier with waning vivacity, the other a creditor left too long unpaid.

A.B. wedged a smile into the corners of his countenance as he looked up from his books. "Mr. Scribner," he said. "Won't you follow me into the office?" There were no guests in the lobby – sadly, there were few anywhere on the grounds – but he would not risk discoloring any patron's stay with tense and embarrassing conversation. Mr. Scribner's terse footsteps followed Mr. Walker's fluid gait into the room behind his desk, and Mr. Scribner was hardly across the threshold before his assault began again.

"There will be no more deferrals, Mr. Walker," he said with the same acidity as before.

"One more moment," A.B. said softly, motioning toward an easy chair at the far corner of the room. It housed his mother, who had recently been dozing there, and was now pretending to still be doing so. Her son touched her gently upon the shoulder, and she showed all the signs of awakening unawares. She promptly gathered up the knitting that had fallen across her lap and rose toward the door, smiling sheepishly at her son and his rigid visitor. Mr. Scribner was at least so kind as to remove his top hat and offer a "Good afternoon, madam," as she made her departure.

It was a typical June day in Perry, New York, and the windowless room of their meeting was stifling. Mr. Scribner seated himself without reinstating his hat. A.B. closed the door, silently praying the temperature of the room would hasten the close of the forthcoming discussion. Hannah Walker lingered on the other side of the door for a moment, and heard their conversation begin once more.

"It has been too long since your last payment," Mr. Scribner said. Her son's voice was inaudible. Hannah might have stayed there straining to eavesdrop, but a flurry of footsteps clomping down the stairs made her flinch away from the door.

"Ada Walker!" she called to the girl who was barreling down the stairway carrying a small crate in her arms. Two boys from a neighboring farm followed her closely, faces red with excitement. All of them stopped upon the step they had under them when Ada's grandmother spoke.

Hannah said no more, only cast a questioning eye at the lot. "We've captured a snake in the barn!" Ada instantly confessed. "We're going to keep him awhile. In *this*." She tipped her head toward the wooden box.

Hannah noted the voices rising in the room behind her. "Have done with it then," she said to the children. "Before the vile thing gets loose again." She followed them outside, seating herself upon the veranda. She held her needles ready but did not resume her project, consumed by a heavy thought blanketed by blank stare.

Whether due to the temperature of the room or the conversation, Misters Scribner and Walker emerged from the office and the hotel a short time later. The visitor paid no cordialities to his elder during his exit. He swept by, not even noting her through the cloud of consternation which followed him into his carriage and promptly up the road.

A.B. offered no information to Hannah, though he suspected she knew something of its nature. He sat upon the veranda and smoked in silence, listening to the peals of laughter rising from the barn.

*****

That evening another visitor came to call, though this one was both anticipated and pleasant. "Ready to be off?" he said, hopping down from his vehicle.

A.B. met him where he stood, turning to gaze at the Walker House. "Is it not enchanting tonight?" he said, admiring the hotel he'd built a decade before. "Perhaps tonight I ought to stay within."

These last words were hardly ever uttered by A.B., the town's chief backslapper. There was never an event he heard about after its occurrence, nor an invitation he willingly declined. Those who kept his company could not imagine equal festivity in his absence, nor were they frequently forced to attempt it.

Edgar and A.B. had a weekly ritual of joining a few other men at the nearest tavern. As A.B.'s closest friend, Edgar knew there must be a reason for his wanting to refrain from their usual evening of light talk and heavy drink. "Perhaps I ought to join you for a pint here," he said. "Won't be any good at the pub tonight anyway."

A.B. smiled with sincere gratitude and led Edgar inside where Mrs. Abigail Walker served them each a pint and retired for the night. The light talk acquired weight as the evening unwound and the ale was consumed.

"I don't know how we can continue," said the host, his voice cracking over the words. "I was certain the roads would bring more guests, not carry them to other destinations. I tell Abby not to worry, for success is so nearly upon us if we can be patient. I keep waiting, keep telling her to wait, and now Alonso is making threats, saying that he for one is finished waiting." A.B.'s head drooped as his eyes wettened. "But what have I got to give him? Nothing. I'll be forced to sell the Walker House – and there's little certainty of even finding a buyer."

"Nevermind that, old friend," said Edgar. "Everything will work itself out, you will see that. The right way always presents itself eventually."

Hannah Walker, a restless nighttime sleeper, was hovering once more at the limits of earshot, a skill she sharpened almost daily.

"It's June," her son croaked. "Our busiest time of the year should have started, but the house is nearly empty. I have failed at this business."

"The door isn't barred up yet," Edgar said. "Perhaps we can speak with Truman about running an advertisement–"

"Anyone reading that paper is already familiar with Silver Lake," he said. "It seems everyone prefers to make their holidays farther from home these days."

"I imagine that will be short-lived," Edgar said.

"And there's more of course. Abby's desperate for another baby. Ever since William…" this time A.B.'s voice broke apart completely, unable to speak of the son who had not survived his infancy in the previous year. "But I can hardly provide a home to the three women that already rely upon me."

With a hard pebble of guilt rising in her heart, Hannah moved silently away, her suspicions confirmed. Again, she returned to the veranda, but found herself too agitated to sit there long. As the moon was full and the evening bright, she walked the path that led to Silver Lake, which her son kept perfectly maintained.

When she reached the waterline, she was surprised to find that she was not alone there. "My apologies," she said to the person resting in half-darkness, and she turned back toward the inn.

"You are not disturbing me," said a woman's voice. "I would relish the company." Such an invitation was unusual for Hannah, and she could not resist. In the three years since her husband's death, she had lived at the Walker House as an unneeded ward, often shuffled around like the child. Though Abigail paid her mother-in-law no resentment, she had a particular way of running The Walker House, and Hannah did her best not to interfere.

She joined the stranger on the bench where she was seated. On her approach, she noticed the woman's unusual dress, with colorful beads attached to an ornate dress of foreign fabric.

"What a lovely cloth your dress is made from," she admired.

"I believe its origin is Greece," replied the woman. "Though I found it in Versailles." Hannah's mouth opened with disbelief.

"What adventures you must have known," she said, looking back toward the lake and finding the moonlight in the waters. "Are you a sort of gypsy?"

"Something of that sort," said the other. She had a way of speaking that made one word flow into the next, which Hannah found very pleasing. They exchanged abbreviated recountings of their lives' works. The widow's was much more easily told. But once she'd started talking, she felt a great urge to continue, and soon this unusual stranger knew all the troubles of her mind.

"Perhaps this Edgar is right," said the gypsy when Hannah had finished. "Perhaps there is something yet to be done."

Hannah, whose slender face was shining with tears, looked hopefully at her confidant. "You've traversed the world healing wounds with unknown magic," she said. "Please tell me that you have some means of healing mine."

"I am no magician," said the gypsy. "I have merely given myself over as an instrument for the powers that surround our world. I am no masterful cook, only a spoon. I have no control of how the ingredients are mixed."

"But you *can* stir them."

"Oftenest with unintended outcomes, and never without sacrifice," the gypsy warned.

"I would give anything – *anything* – to help A.B. keep hold of his dream." She dried her cheeks against a sleeve and gazed at her new acquaintance.

The gypsy checked Hannah's eyes and found the sign of desperation that was so familiar in her profession. "Very well," she said. "But I am to continue onward in the morning, so it must be done tonight. The ritual will not be a pleasant experience, such things never are. That is the only promise I can give you. I have no control of the potency of the spell. It could well be that nothing changes at all."

Hannah nodded, ready to obey any instruction that followed. Her commitment was tested by the very first that was dispensed.

"It will be necessary to claim the life of an animal, I'm afraid," said the gypsy. Hannah squirmed upon the bench but said nothing. "I noticed a litter of kittens…"

"No, no!" Hannah cried. "We mustn't. Not them. Those are Ada's precious pets. She would be too distraught in losing even one. And should we fail, she will need every comfort."

The gypsy interpreted these words as the first sign of refusal, and Hannah could see it. "However," she added hastily, "I do know the whereabouts of a captive snake, if that would suffice. I would feel no guilt in ending the life of such a creature as that."

"A serpent will do perfectly," said the gypsy. "Better than all the little cats combined, in fact."

Hannah went to fetch the crate and a few other household necessities. Meanwhile, the gypsy went first to collect ingredients from around the lake, and then back to her lodgings for some mystical powder and other agents of enchantment that such people are known to travel with.

Both women returned to their original meeting place ready to begin the ritual. "I must repeat once more that the remainder of this evening may be difficult for you, and that we are not guaranteed anything will come of it." Hannah reiterated her firmness of will.

"You brought the bucket of water?" the gypsy asked.

"I have the bucket," Hannah said. "Though it was so burdened by the water, I thought I'd collect some here." She took a few moments to draw some silvery water from the lake. Clearly this aroused some private thought in the mind of the gypsy, but afraid of a reprimand for not carefully following her instructions at the onset of their discourse, she did not request elaboration.

The bucket filled halfway, it was replaced upon a level piece of ground next to the crate. The gypsy added first the crushed leaves and berries she'd collected, and then dashes of various powders, each with a unique and vibrant hue. Lastly Hannah was instructed to pour in the handful of salt she'd collected from the house.

The gypsy then produced a little bundle of red silk, unfolding it to reveal a dagger with three interwoven metallic loops formed upon the pommel. The weapon was handed to Hannah who only had a moment to admire it.

"This is the instrument you will use to sacrifice the serpent," said the gypsy. Hannah instinctively recoiled but nodded just after the quake passed over her. "I am determined," she assured the other.

"I will help you as much as I'm able," the gypsy said softly, her heart sincerely touched by the mother's love for her son. She quickly lifted the box's lid and snatched the black snake from it in the same motion, holding it by the neck above the bucket. "Now," she said, steadying the animal by the tail with her other hand.

With a wince, Hannah plunged the blade into the snake's belly. Blood drained in dark red lines down the body and into the vessel below it. Once the water absorbed the reddish hue, the gypsy tossed the carcass into the lake to become the midnight snack of some lucky water scavenger.

Without wiping the blood from her hands, the gypsy added one more ingredient to the gruesome concoction: a silvery drop that sparkled in the moonlight on its descent.

Hannah's face had been tensed in mortification since the gutting of the snake. She scarcely breathed, terrified that the woman would soon inform her she must drink from the bucket. To her greatest dismay, that is exactly what the gypsy commanded next.

"I don't know if I can," she said feebly, her stomach roiling at the thought.

"You must. Only a sip is needed if you're able to keep it in your belly. If you become sick, you'll need to drink again." She swirled the ladle around the bucket of blood and water and salt and mystery, filled it, and handed it to Hannah to taste.

Hannah was shaking so fiercely that she spilled the first ladleful and had to dip it again. She shut her eyes and drew a tiny sip of the revolting liquid. Though she coughed violently and raked the fingertips of her unbloodied hand over her tongue, she swallowed the drink and kept it down.

She felt immediately feverish. The gypsy laid her hand over the clammy forehead, rasping wildly in foreign tongues unknown to Hannah or anyone else who resided in the town of Perry.

Hannah fainted, but as she was a very small woman, the other ably moved her to a bench before she fell all the way to the ground. There she rested uneasily, and when she woke, the wanderer and all her strange equipment had vanished. The bucket and ladle remained, both perfectly clean and ready for use in the kitchen. The frail woman sat up with effort, the pain in her stomach growing steadily as she resumed consciousness. What relief it would be to let go of the poison within her, but she sat with her hands guarding her mouth like sentinels for half an hour, rubbing the dried blood away as soon as she was able. She then rose timidly and stumbled slowly back to the Walker House.

Edgar's carriage had long since departed, and everyone staying there was far into their dreamland journeys by the time Hannah reentered the lobby. She dragged herself up the stairs and into her little room with the last scrapings of energy and fell upon her bed as her sweating body finally gave up its struggle to remain erect.

*****

The next morning, Ada quickly noted the disappearance of her captive reptile, but several passed hours before anyone realized Hannah had not left her bed.

In the afternoon, Abigail rapt softly upon Hannah's bedroom door. Hearing no reply, she entered to her mother-in-law, pale and clammy, strewn across her bed like unfolded washing, still clothed in her daytime finery. She knelt next to the woman, relieved to find her still breathing.

"Artemus!" she screamed. "Come at once! Your mother—"

A.B. was below, attending to the registry of a guest who was making his first visit to Silver Lake. He pushed a set of keys across the desk. "Room five, just down the corridor to your left," he said, already hurrying up the stairs.

In the next moment he'd replaced Abby at Hannah's side. "Get some salts," he instructed her, slapping his mother's pallid cheeks in attempt to revive her. "Mother!" he cried. "Mother, can you hear me?"

It was the salts that brought her to again, opening her eyes to the three worried faces of her family members surrounding her.

"What's happened to you, Grandmother?" Ada cried.

Hannah hardly remembered her journey back, but the bucket and ladle lying nearby proved to her that she'd made it.

"I went to the lake last night," she said, her voice as weak as her ruined body. "I was there a long time, and I grew thirsty. I knew if I went all the way back to the well, I would not return. And the night was so peaceful, the lake was so beautiful, I drank of it, and now I fear I have injured myself."

A.B. groaned at her insensible decision to consume water from the lake. "You'll be sick," he said, glancing around the room. He snatched up the bucket and set it at her side. "Use this," he instructed.

Her fingers shielded her mouth as she heaved a little, her body desperate to obey this order, her mind determined not to. "No," she said. "Bring me water. Fresh water is what I need most." They brought her water, and she drank it off, requesting more. Every member of the family made at least two trips up and down the stairs bringing it by the pitcher before her thirst was satisfied. Then she fell fitfully back to sleep.

As soon as she was out again, A.B. was riding his horse toward the town physician. He found only the physician's wife and returned with the news that the doctor would call in the evening.

By the time the sun set, he'd still not arrived. Another dubious round of hydration attempts occurred, this time requiring more than double the water as before.

"Where's it going to?" Ada wondered. She poked at the sheets in search of dampness, but they were dry. Hannah's skin had stopped perspiring as well; it was now as arid as a Bible page in full sun. As the hours passed and the well bucket was continually raised, Hannah seemed somehow only to lose water, as if it were evaporating from her the instant she drank it.

Her hands and arms chafed red, and she scratched at them whenever she was awake, though mostly she stayed bent at the stomach with her arms wrapped around her middle.

The doctor's cart was met by the entire family in the front yard. "Thank heaven," Abigail said, taking his arm and hurrying him toward the house. "She seems to be in agony."

A.B. informed the physician of her symptoms and their cause (as he knew it) while they ascended toward her bedroom. Inside they found her still doubled over, eyes pressed painfully closed but not asleep.

"Good evening, Mrs. Walker," said the physician, who knew her from a previous visit when Ada had sprained her ankle. Hannah made no response.

He took up her wrist to feel for the pulse, but first turned it over in his hands to study the condition of the skin. "Very unusual," he said, returning his attention to the heartbeat. When he found it, he found it was very weak. He set down her hand and addressed A.B.

"It seems her body is of inadequate hydration," he stated. "But you say you've brought her barrels of water today?" A.B. nodded solemnly. "And the cause is known to be ingesting water from Silver Lake?" Another affirmative reply.

"It's curious," the doctor continued, "because I enjoyed the same lake with my wife and daughters only a few days ago. Little Mattie, bless her, must have swallowed gallons of it before we could stop her, and she was completely unaffected. Naturally, a young body is more capable of fighting ailment, but something this distressing for your mother must certainly have had *some* effect on a young child." He pinched the bottom of his chin as his musings went silent.

"What are you saying?" asked A.B.

"I only wonder if it is possible this illness was achieved through another means. Has your mother been known to do anything *irrational* in the past?"

"Never," said A.B., crossing his arms across his chest.

"Never tried to harm herself in any way, I assume?" A.B. repeated his last word. "I see," the doctor mumbled, words again trailing into thought.

Before leaving, he advised the Walkers to keep close watch on her and bring the water any time she requested it. He promised to consult his medical library in search of possible causes and cures and arranged to return the following day.

After a long night of study, Dr. Murphy was convinced Hannah had contracted some sort of parasite which was sucking her dry and demanding more and more, ruining her frail body in its course.

He commenced an attempt to kill this parasite by means of bitter coffee, and then strong brandy, both of which proved no effect. His last attempt was to heat her water and mix in a large quantity of salt, which Hannah at first drank greedily as any other water she was given. But before she finished the glass, it fell from her hand as she commenced writhing brutally against her mattress amidst shrieks of suffering. She tore at herself, skin and scalp, as both doctor and son fought to restrain her. Her mouth foamed, her eyes rolled up into her head, and then her body went still again. Resettling her into her bed, the doctor pressed his ear to her chest and confirmed that she lived. Her breathing was more pained than ever.

The next day, they placed Hannah, barely conscious, into the nearest bathtub, which seemed to bring her more comfort than she'd known since the onset of her condition. There she remained, the water frequently changed as it continually grew cloudy by the particles of skin that were detaching from her body. She assured everyone that she was recovering and needed no further doctor's visits, preferring quietude and privacy. She would be fine with a bit more fresh drinking water, and perhaps a bit more to follow.

But several days into her bath, A.B. insisted upon closer inspection of her, now seeing that the water's opaqueness had mostly cleared off. He found his mother greatly changed from her state a week prior.

Her delicate skin was now completely washed away. In its place were something more akin to lizard's scales with a greenish color and sharp points that each overlapped the top of the next. Dragging one's palm against those points would leave the hand with tiny lacerations. This epidermal transformation spread across her arms, legs, and hands, and was progressing up her neck and into her reddened face.

Though such a development would be peculiar alone, it was overshadowed by another that was far more worrisome. The woman in the tub had a face unlike his mother's, twisted and stretched as if her very bone structure was changing. And so it was. Within another week, the sides of her head had moved further apart, with a distinct flattening effect toward the top.

Her midsection, too, was becoming wider and longer, though the shape of her arms and legs went presently unaffected. Soon she was unable to fit into the bath. At her request, she was moved into a muddy pond on the hotel grounds.

The doctor called many more times, and though he read everything he could on every possible related condition and consulted every other physician in his acquaintance, he could find no trace of beneficial information.

Hannah found it necessary to confess her secret to her son before she lost the ability to speak. Like the rest of her body, her tongue had become misshapen, and she required considerable effort to verbalize her thoughts. As he was sitting next to the pond, his forehead pressed to his knees, she struggled to say, "I am sorry."

"Oh, Mother," A.B. sobbed. "It is I who should be sorry. I should have provided a better home for you, away from this cursed lake."

"I did this," she said with great exertion.

A.B.'s head lifted with a jerk as he brought the organism she was becoming back into his view. "So the doctor was right! You poisoned yourself? Oh, why Mother? I know we haven't been the most fortunate.

But no matter. Simply tell me what you took so that Dr. Murphy can find a way to mend it."

Though it took over an hour and lacked many details, Hannah the pond creature explained to her son what she and the stranger had done.

When A.B. told the doctor this information about the snake's blood and untold ingredients of nature and witchcraft, the latter responded with a knowing nod. "Yes," he said. "I suspected there was more to it than that. Unfortunately, we are still unable to treat her without knowing of those especial additives she consumed. The snake you described is not venomous. Unless it was carrying some sort of illness itself, that was probably not the source of her ailment."

A.B. scoured the hotel registry for unusual names and found nothing. There was no record of a lone woman staying there in the last month, only businessmen and families. He did the same at every other local lodging with no better result. He started to suspect his mother might have started losing her sensibilities in conjunction with her physical affliction.

Yet it hardly mattered, for there was no longer hope of reversing Hannah's transformation. She had grown so large as to find the pond constricting, though her human appendages remained still unchanged in size. They did darken in color, however, and eventually she was unable to move them. They dangled lifelessly from her new body, which was no longer recognizable as having ever been human.

Her hunger had returned and become its own issue. After devouring the small fish in the pond, A.B. brought them in for her, a new expense he could not afford. He found it cheaper to purchase crates of dead rodents and discarded parts from the butcher and the tanners, and his ravenous mother seemed not to care what was fed to her.

As she ate, she continued her enlargement. As she expanded, so did her appetite. About a month after she drank the blood of the snake, her arms finally fell off her, and she ate them as well. She purposely detached her own legs afterward and consumed them too.

Ada, Abby, and all the animals now stayed as far as they could from that pond. Disgusted as he was, A.B. vowed never to quit her, though part of him was relieved that she could no longer speak. It was clear that she would soon outgrow the pond, which was already more monster than water, and he would not be able to remove her by himself.

He'd not been away from his home since Hannah fell ill. When Edgar stopped over on his way to the tavern each Monday evening, A.B. sent him away, unable to confide anything further than that his mother was unwell. The next time Edgar visited, he was shown inside, where his friend handed him a whole bottle of brandy as he took a whiskey for himself. He drank as heartily as his mother had done in the first days of her ailment, and it wasn't long before he was recounting the whole story for the disbelief of his closest friend.

Edgar listened with great concern and little reply. The tale was told through sobs under a bent head. When A.B. raised his eyes to Edgar's, he could see pity intermingled with incredulity. He hauled Edgar off his stool and out of the Walker House, his friend fighting to take back control of his arm. "I'll go anywhere you say," he told A.B. "Only calm yourself. You are worrying me."

A.B. loosened his grip but did not slow his pace or entirely release his hold upon Edgar. They reached the pond quickly. Upon his first glance, Edgar saw nothing out of the ordinary, but upon the second he noted a strange fin rising from the water as they approached. The fin was attached to a long spine, still rising, that ultimately revealed a monster's reptilian head.

His captured arm tensed, his feet reversed their direction, and he struggled against A.B. to retreat. But A.B. was the larger man and insisted upon Edgar's seeing what Hannah had become.

When her head cleared the water, she hissed, as a way of expressing her aching hunger. Then she plunged petulantly back into the pond as far as its shallow depths could manage to take her hulking body, which stuck out of the water at all times.

Then, A.B. let go of Edgar, who made a speedy line to his vehicle. But when he reached it, he did not get in. A.B. did not pursue him. For a moment, he stood looking regretfully at the waters then meandered back to the front door of the Walker House. There, Edgar rejoined him, quite ready to believe his story now. They went back inside and finished their bottles, after which they spoke easier.

They devised a plan to move her, utilizing their strength, plus that of their good friend Truman Gillette, editor of the Wyoming County newspaper and owner of the largest transport cart they knew of.

Edgar paid Truman a visit later in the week, and at first, Truman was certain that Edgar was playing a trick on him. But Edgar soon convinced him by the same means that he was convinced, first extracting the promise that Truman *would* help them *if* it turned out to be an accurate account.

As a newspaper man, it was not in Truman's nature to keep quiet about a good story, but as a loyal friend and decent man, he resolved to do so, and to help get A.B.'s mother moved into Silver Lake. The three men first inspected the wheel bearings and axles on the cart to ensure it could handle Hannah's newly acquired weight. From there the task was surprisingly simplistic, the most effort spent in convincing the two non-relatives that the creature was still A.B.'s mother and would not attempt to eat them.

That as nearly achieved as it was going to be, the creature moved as far out of the water as she could squirm, and the three men strained to hoist her onto the cart, which was not achieved on the first attempt. Once done, however, the procedure was much like launching a boat into water, and it went easily and without major incident.

The three men returned to the Walker House, bodies exasperated but spirits full and fresh. They drank to their victory and chattered the evening away.

A.B. shared with them everything his mother had expressed about how her condition came upon her.

"I don't understand," Edgar said. "Let's say that she really has become transfigured at the hand of some ancient gypsy spell. How could that be of benefit to your establishment?"

Truman's eyes shone brightly as the answer clicked on within his mind. "I might know of a way," he said. The other two expressed their intrigue. "Let's say I printed up a story on this in the *Wyoming*," he said. "Chances are, firstly, that every reader in Wyoming County would be suddenly struck by an urge to go peek at the lake."

"Indeed," A.B. agreed. "But that would be of little help."

"Sure," Truman continued. "But as the word spread, perhaps other papers pick it up. Suddenly, travelers are stopping by for a gander as well."

"And passing the night at the Walker House," Edgar finished.

"Precisely," said Truman with a confident nod and a swig.

"Though you're likely correct," A.B. said, "I couldn't bear to make my mother a public spectacle."

"No one would have any idea it was ever your mother," Truman said.

"The point is that it – *she* – is my mother still, and I think it's best to keep her secret as long as it will keep. I'll hold a funeral service for her. I'm sure Dr. Murphy will corroborate some falsehood of her death. She'll have to keep herself out of the way, for her part."

"The lake is much larger than the pond. Unless she never ceases to grow, it will conceal her," Edgar said. Internally he wondered how long it would be before she was discovered.

It wasn't long at all.

*****

Within two weeks' time, a fanatical tale swept over the small town of Perry. Six witnesses, four men and two boys, were pursued in their fishing boat by a greenish sea monster. Alonso Scribner and his two sons made up half of the observers. It followed them at proximity, snapping hungry jaws toward terrified oarsmen. (One was a target of particular interest, though the party was never aware of that detail.) Most of the townsfolk dismissed the story as fabrication, particularly as the night was moonless and dark as it ever was. But the account varied little between its tellers, who eventually signed an affidavit swearing to its truth. The telling spread throughout the county and outward, and Truman again suggested to A.B. they make mutual use of the unfortunate situation.

A.B. then agreed, for after much consideration, he realized that it was always his mother's wish to benefit the Walker House by her sacrifice. Truman printed the article under a pseudonym, which other newspapers indeed reprinted, and by August the hotel was occupied to capacity. A.B. was even forced to transform Hannah's bedroom back into lodging, though he packed her things away neatly. He was yet unable to release the fantasy that she might someday retake her human form.

With all eyes cast toward the lake, she was spotted several more times by tourists and locals alike. Still, only the Walker family, Edgar, Truman, and Dr. Murphy knew the true origins of what was now being called the Silver Lake Sea Serpent. At the height of her fame, she was seen flailing around from seven unique vantage points, ten people all describing the same occurrence. It was then that Dr. Murphy paid another visit to the Walker House.

"It seems your mother is experiencing a state of distress," he said as plainly as if he were dispensing any other, ordinary diagnosis.

"I should say," said A.B. tilting his brandy glass. Though he remained at home, he was infrequently seen without such a beverage in hand. Mostly it was assumed to be due to the stress of an overbooked hotel. But that difficulty had never been so easy. He had nearly repaid his debt to Scribner and was on course to have done by season's close.

"I mean to say that she seems further troubled. Hungry, most likely."

A.B. exhaled thickly. "I'm certain she is."

"And I may know of a temporary solution," he said, looking around to confirm their isolation. "Old Mrs. Brown passed on this morning. She is to be buried in a few days." A.B. looked at him with renewed interest.

"There's no family, no friends to speak of."

"You're not suggesting…"

"She chewed off her own limbs, did she not, Artemus?" A.B. rehung his head upon the peak of his spine. "Then I cannot say that I view this as such a great leap into darkness unknown. Anyway, Mrs. Walker's sure not to mind." Reluctantly and with a wave of repugnance for what had once been his mother, A.B. agreed to feed her Mrs. Brown's cadaver.

Days later, she devoured it in three bites, barely surfacing during her feast. Fresh bodies were hard to find in such a small town. A.B. never admitted to anyone that he twice unearthed a deceased person that had not yet had the chance to fully decompose, refilling the grave and then dragging the corpse into the lake.

*****

By September, a new type of attention came upon the lake, as Daniel Smith joined the scene, a famed harpooner and hunter of deep-sea monstrosities. He vowed to capture the Silver Lake Sea Serpent still breathing and bring light to what was troubling the suddenly booming town of Perry.

His initial efforts unsuccessful, the town, fueled chiefly by ridiculed witnesses, formed a watch party for the animal, declaring open season upon its scaley hide. A.B. was more distressed than ever, constantly dreading the moment of their success.

"We must call it off!" he begged of his three conspirators within the private confines of his barn.

"How could we?" Truman said, experiencing both guilt and pride for the effect his printed words had made upon the town.

"We'll say that we made it all up!" A.B. said. "Tell them it was just a rouse to drum up new business for a floundering inn."

"That would be fine," Edgar said, "Except that they'll continue seeing her."

"What if we could get them to stop coming, stop searching for her? We could make some sort of rubber model and spread the word that it was all a hoax. Many of the papers have been saying that anyhow, and at least one has pointed suspicion at me. I would take full blame. I'll not name any of you. Only help me make the thing."

They agreed, but never believed it would hinder the search, especially for the locals who had already spotted the creature. At the onset of the project,

A.B. insisted the false proof was all that would be needed, but through the gentle patience of his friends, he began to understand this was unlikely a final solution and could do even further damage once others started to question why he'd tried to disprove it. On the one night when the company broke from constructing the hoax monster, he made his way to Silver Lake to appeal to his mother.

He rowed out to the middle of the water. The night was clear and serene, and she rose quietly beside his boat as soon as it reached a depth that was comfortable to her.

Her head emerged from the silvery water, and her enlarged, reddened eyes inspected him with what he supposed to be pity and regret. "I have failed you, Mother. In seeking to rectify my mistakes, you have ruined yourself."

She placed her head gently upon the side of his boat, careful not to apply so much weight as to upturn it. Though he'd rowed out unsure if she'd be able to understand him, or that she'd even appear to him, he was certain now that she was fixed upon his words and taking them in with much consideration. Inside her monstrous serpentine skull, she was still the parent that had comforted him when he skinned his knee, still the same person who remembered the recipes for his favorite meals, still the mother that loved him without end or resistance.

"You have to leave," he said. A quiver ran down her beastly neck, causing the boat to rock. "They'll hunt you until they've killed you," he said. "And I won't have it." She continued gazing up at him and issued what he interpreted as a sigh. "Be comforted, at least, that though you have transfigured yourself into this," he was going to add the word "monster," but instead left it at "this". "Your hex was successful. The Walker House has never been busier. They come from across the world to see you here." Her head rose up into the air again. "My debt to Scribner is resolved." He sensed that she was pleased by this news. "I wish that meant the curse was broken," he said dejectedly. But he knew that, having "chewed off her limbs" as Dr. Murphy described it, she would never exist as a human again.

There were two small rivers that fed from Silver Lake, and A.B. encouraged his mother to make an exit by one of them. The longer was favorable, as it had the ocean at its other end, but he never saw which one she took. All he knew was that she was no longer truly sighted in that lake again, and the hoax snake they concocted in her likeness was never needed.

Two years later, when the Walker House fell to flames, that giant rubber serpent was discovered among the wreckage. A.B. Walker told the press and the townsfolk that he'd made it all up for its value to his ledger. The newspapers reminded their public that they had never trusted the stunt, and townsfolk mostly forgave him because they too saw the value in his supposed lie.

Historians have recorded the entire account as a hoax. Over a century later, Hannah Walker, though known by many other names now, is still spotted sometimes in Lake Ontario or upon the eastern coast where Canada and America meet, but she has never since been seen at close range nor allowed herself to be photographed.

UKRAINIAN COSSACK WEREWOLF

by Kateryna Voloshyna

1628, Ukraine

"Run! Run!" the fear was spreading from one experienced Tatar soldier to another. One by one they were turning their heads towards the hill with the dark shadow rising upon it.

Airat, a young Tatar, pressed his palm close to his mouth and cried, "Hey! What's going on?"

He asked his elder friend, "Why are they screaming? We are winning here, not these Cossack bastards."

"Hurry up! Run… I'll explain to you later when we are safe," his friend, who was already running, shouted back. He pulled the young soldier in the opposite direction from the battlefield.

All they could hear now were screams. At first, the screams contained fear, then only wails of despair. Something was coming closer. The young Tatar soldier, who could barely carry all the armor he received from his leaders, desperately wanted to close his eyes, fall down, and pretend that he was back in his small village, playing with a cat and helping his father at home. His older friend dragged him mercilessly, hurting his arm. They stopped somewhere back in the deep and dark forest, while screams of his fellows continue to reach his ears, tearing the once calm and warm night air with thunder-like roars.

"What is going on? Mehmed, stop, please, I can't." He just couldn't run any longer.

"If you want to live, run," Mehmed looked at him with the face of complete terror. "The Devil is here!"

He finally understood. He's heard about him! Oh, he knew everything about the devil, Shaitan, who turned into the wolf every full moon and could stop any bullet with his teeth. And who did not? Everyone knew about Ivan Sirko, the scariest warlock, and the chief of Ukrainian Cossacks. The young boy did not need any other words to speed him up. His father was living proof of the devil's supernatural powers possessed by Sirko. His father met Sirko once on the battlefield when the Cossack hetman was only 15 years old and was still learning how to turn into a wolf and other magic tricks. Back then, Tatars decided to loot a Ukrainian village but were met by several Cossacks.

It looked like an easy win for the Tatars at first. They had at least fifty men, all strong, well-trained, with a sword and gun in each hand. There were only three Cossacks on their way, but it looked like only one of them was planning to fight them. It was a young boy, younger than Airat now, in a simple white shirt and dark oversized pants fixated with a big scarf as a belt. Watching his two fellows move aside, the Tatar men began to laugh. They offered a quick death to him, and one of the best shooters among them pulled the trigger.

Airat's father later recalled that at that very moment everything stopped. They felt the shiver, and some of them even turned their heads back to the road they came from. The strange youngster was holding the bullet in his teeth. Slowly he spat it in his palm, and talked in a low melodic voice, in their native language:

"Did you think a bullet could stop me? Why do they always think that they can kill me?" He turned his head to his fellows who were laughing, enjoying the situation. "Do you know who I am?" He turned his head back to the enemy.

The Tatar troop was confused and no one knew what to say. The leader of the troop finally asked "So, who are you?"

"My name is Ivan Sirko, and I am a leader of this people. My whole life everyone was trying to kill me, from a midwife, who thought that I am a monster, just because I was born with a full set of teeth to the uneducated villagers, who were scared of seeing a boy, born under the full moon, who could speak since he was born," the youth smiled, "Only recently the devil showed up at my training place, bothering my fellow Cossacks who trained with me. He challenged us to fight him. I caught him by the tail, swirled him in the air, and threw him into the river."

"Oh, what a splash it was!" said one of Ivan's two fellows from the side of the hetman. "I wish you could see this fall! We had to rename this place into Chortomlyk. And since you don't know Ukrainian, I translate for you as Devil's Splash."

The Cossacks laughed heartily.

"Well, don't worry, my brothers, I have prepared another show for them as well," winked Ivan.

Feeling that something awful coming upon them, Airat's father, who stood in the last line, thought that he did not need to wait any longer and started to run. He heard screams, the very same screams filled with pure terror his son heard these many years later. Airat's father turned his head around, seeing the big black wolf, huge enough to reach the moon, with lightning in the eyes, chewing upon his fellow Tatars. It looked like he killed them all at once. His father had ran faster, but the monster caught him, tore off his left hand, and threw it in the bushes.

"I will spare your life, miserable man, don't worry," said the big wolf with Ivan's own voice, "but you need to tell the others what you saw today. Remember me, remember that you all must stop hurting my people, my country. I will not give you any other chances." Perhaps the monster said more, but the soldier fainted. Two days later he woke up in his home, without one hand, with a clear memory of everything that happened.

No matter how hard the soldier had tried to warn his fellows, no one listened to him until it was too late. One by one, Tatar generals sent the best armies to kill Cossacks and destroy the Ukrainian people. One by one, they were killed. Only a few survivors ever returned with tales of a shapeshifter, a devil, who can turn into wolf. Now, Airat was trying to hide deeper in the forest to escape the horrible destiny of his army.

"Did you know that this devil, Sirko, ordered his Cossacks to cut his right hand after his death and take it with them on the battlefield?" Mehmed ran next to him, breathing heavily.

"Why?" Airat was desperately trying not to turn his head back to check out whether there was huge wolf rushing toward them.

"He said that his hand will help anyone who holds it to crush the enemies, no matter how many of them come to Ukraine, or what weapon they use. He told them that his hand can stop even the devi…" Mehmed did not finish the sentence. Airat felt fiery breath on his neck.

2022, Ukraine

"Orest, come here! Quickly," the young soldier, Andriy, called to his friend, the one-time professor of archeology in a more peaceful time. The sound came from the trench they dug to hide from Russian shelling "Come here! I think I have found some weirdly looking mummified hand. It looks like a right hand! Check it out!"

<u>THE LAGAHOO</u>

by Tom Larsen

Authors note: The Lagahoo is a creature from Caribbean folklore. Related to the French Loup Garou, The Lagahoo can take many forms, human or animal, but when the moon is full it becomes a werewolf.

The Lagahoo, having taken the form of a crow, watched from the shade of the conch shack as the cruise ship doors opened and the passengers emerged. It reminded him of the way the triggerfish laid her eggs in the shallows, thousands of tiny white organisms squirting out of her underbelly and forming into a quivering gelatinous mass.

Tour guides, taxi drivers, trinket vendors, and ganja sellers darted into the amorphous blob, preying on the weakest, spiriting them away singly or in small groups.

The Lagahoo pecked at the crumbs of bread scattered about in the sand, because that's what crows do, but mostly as an outlet for his anxiety. It was dangerous enough to be out and abroad in the daylight, but to stalk and kill a white man?

If an islander disappeared on his way home from an evening of rum-soaked tomfoolery, well that was one thing.

"The Lagahoo got him," his family would say. They'd mourn his passing, and life would go on. But a white man? There would surely be an investigation.

The Lagahoo laughed involuntarily, the sound coming out as a harsh *caw*. After all, he bore the power of Loup Garou, the wolf. He had nothing to fear from any man, black or white.

*****

In his heart, though, he knew that he was not the Loup Garou of his younger days. Centuries of roaming the wooded expanse of the island had made him weary and a bit fearful. Each time that he took on his true form, his coat of stiff black fur was a bit thinner, and more gray showed around his muzzle. He ate listlessly these days, sometimes no more than a small goat or a couple of island rats, even though he fed only once a month, when the full moon shone.

He knew instinctively that his time was coming to an end, something he had never contemplated, or even thought a possibility. He had been sure of his own immortality, but gradually the realization had taken root. Along with this realization had come an obsession. Before he left this plane of existence, he would taste the flesh and drink the blood of a white man, something his instincts told him no other Lagahoo had ever done, certainly not on this island.

*****

The crowd dwindled as the sunburned tourists went off to do whatever they did with their precious few hours on the island. A young couple lagged at the edge of the dock as if undecided what to do or where to go. The Lagahoo flew up and lit in a breadfruit tree to get a closer look.

The woman was angry, or frustrated. He couldn't be sure. If he were in human form, he would be more in tune with her body language and facial expressions, and the words she spoke would be clear to him, rather than the jumble of angry squawks that he heard with his tiny crow ears. Lately it had become increasingly difficult for him to take human form, which he took as another sign of his impending demise.

The man was angry, a certainty even to his crow brain. He stood in sullen detachment, his arms folded across his chest. Finally, the woman threw up her hands and stalked off in the direction of town. The man stood watching her go with his hands on his hips and then turned and headed off toward one of the beachfront bars.

Perfect. He would have killed the woman as well, if he had to, but he thirsted for the blood of the man.. The blood of the islanders had always satisfied him, but a white man's blood might be different, somehow stronger and more vital. The blood of the islanders tasted sluggish and weak, from generations spent in the oppressive heat. And anger might make *this* white man's blood stronger still.

He would need to take a different shape to lure the man into the woods; but what shape? *Rastamon*? No. This man was young, so he probably smoked the herb, but a smelly dreadlocked bum approaching him from out of nowhere would only frighten him.

The Lagahoo watched for a moment longer and then took flight with a raucous cry.

*****

The young white man watched the bartender place a shot of rum and a bottle of Red Stripe in front of him. He would have preferred tequila and a Corona, but "When in Rome…" The fight with his wife had been so silly. He couldn't even remember how it started. Maybe it was from being confined together in their tiny cabin, which was all they could afford. Well, it would do them good to be apart for a few hours. He'd have a couple of drinks; she'd buy some souvenirs, and they would patch it all up tonight.

Conversation in the bar stopped. The young man looked up to see a beautiful woman enter the bar. Her skin flaunted the color of strong cappuccino. She had white, perfectly even teeth. Her iridescent blue-green dress clung to her body like plastic wrap.

"Why the long face, Mister Mon?" she purred, taking the stool next to him.

*****

Those in the bar that day would talk about it for years, back in Duluth or Chicago or Toronto, but their accounts would differ. Some said the island woman turned into a snarling rat when the young man's wife entered the bar screaming and threatening. Others swore they saw a coral snake slithering away. The bartender, born and raised on the island, refused to talk about it. He hurried his customers out and pulled down the storm shutters behind them.

*****

The sun had begun its rapid descent into the ocean. The Lagahoo, now having taken the shape of a frigate bird, soared above the cruise ship dock. Its slender body tensed rigidly from anger and frustration as he watched the young couple, now reconciled, waiting to board. They stood arm in arm, whispering to each other like the young lovers that they were. He banked into the wind, descending for a closer look, and his frustration intensified. He had been elated when the young couple had separated earlier, confident that in the form of the beautiful island woman he could lure the man into the forest and immobilize him. Then, when the sun fully set, and the moon rose, The Lagahoo would feast. But with the two of them now having made up, the task's difficulty doubled.

Giving up was not an option. The Lagahoo was a proud creature and having set his sights on the young white man he could not rest until he had tasted the man's flesh and drank of his blood. He would have to use his cunning. He landed behind a clump of tall grass, quickly shed his avian body, and emerged in the form of a common street dog, skinny, with one deformed leg, its fur matted and dirty, and ridden with fleas.

Showing its teeth and laying back its ears, the dog approached the young couple. The Lagahoo felt a jolt of satisfaction as the woman turned and clung tightly to the man. The young man's face showed at first fear, then a sort of false bravado as he stepped in front of the woman. As if his puny pale-skinned body could protect her from Loup Garou! Remembering that he was appearing in the guise of a street dog, not the fearsome entity that he would become at moonrise, the Lagahoo darted forward baring his teeth, preparing to sink them into the woman's ankle.

Age had weakened him so much that he came up short. Decrepitude left him unprepared for the vicious kick that the young man delivered to his ribs. Howling with pain, the Lagahoo rolled away and struggled to regain his footing. He gathered all the force in his hind legs and launched himself through the air, going for the man's throat. Not in the form of Loup Garou, just a filthy crippled street dog, his leap ended in humiliation as the man easily fended him off and pushed him back to the ground.

In a fit of fury and desperation, the Lagahoo attacked again, tearing into the man's calf. The man yelped and shook his leg to disengage the snarling cur, then kicked it solidly once more. The Lagahoo ran a few feet away, bared his teeth, and growled low in his throat.

The young man, rather than running away to seek medical attention, advanced toward the skinny brown dog, picking up a small sharp-edged rock as he came. The assembled crowd of tourists stood by in stunned silence. Something had changed in the young man, that much was clear. Something beyond the crowd's comprehension.

The Lagahoo, with the wisdom that comes only from having lived several hundred years, recognized the look on the man's face. He had experienced a moment of victory when he kicked the dog in the ribs, and he thirsted for more. The Lagahoo would use the man's sense of pride against him. Snarling and growling, he feinted toward the man and then turned and ran off, staying out of rock-throwing range. Alternately advancing and retreating, he led the young man further and further from the crowd.

The two policemen who had been assigned to keep order at the docking area stood by idly, amused at the antics of the silly white man and the filthy cur. But the crowd of tourists, as if awakening from a communal slumber, began to stir. Pulsing and swelling like an amoeba, the crowd lurched forward as one. Startled by the change in circumstances, one of the policemen spoke rapidly into his radio, possibly summoning reinforcements, more likely calling his friends to witness this phenomenon.

The Lagahoo retreated. Once he reached the edge of the forest, he took shelter beneath the spreading leaves of a small *bwa mang* tree. The young man, blood streaming down his wounded leg, dropped the rock he had been carrying and turned to face the crowd. When he raised his hand, the crowd stopped its advance and stood uncertainly, as if awaiting further instructions. The young man approached his wife, at the front of the crowd. He took her in his arms and kissed her deeply and then turned and advanced toward the Lagahoo while she stood in stunned silence, her hands clasped in front of her and a look of terror on her face.

Something was happening that he couldn't understand, at least not consciously. Still, he kept to his plan, darting forward and then retreating. With each advance and retreat, though, he felt his strength ebbing further. It no longer felt as if he were drawing the man into his realm, but as if the man were pursuing him and pushing him into the forest.

The Lagahoo decided to stop the charade. He turned and trotted down the narrow path toward a familiar clearing, one of his favorite killing sites. The man would follow him; of that he had no doubt.

Reaching the clearing, The Lagahoo stopped and turned to face the rising moon. Still in the form of the street dog, he sat back on his haunches waiting for the transformation into Loup Garou. Soon, the beast would feast on the silly white man who dared to think that he could best him.

The transformation occurred more slowly and painfully than ever. The Lagahoo had become some strange hybrid, part ferocious wolf- part flea-bitten street dog, when the young man entered the clearing.

The Lagahoo was an instinctive creature, not a reasoning one, but now for the first time in his life, he experienced conscious thought. He had roamed these forests for centuries, while generations of humans and animals were born, lived, and died. And no matter how many of them died there were always new ones to take their place.

So, it followed, didn't it? Surely, he was not the first Lagahoo, nor would he be the last. He wasn't immortal, after all. His species just enjoyed a longer life span than the others. That explained his constant weariness, his diminished appetite, his increasing difficulty in changing forms. The Lagahoo was dying, and on some level, he welcomed it.

The young man entered the clearing and stood erect, looking directly at the full moon. Somehow, it did not surprise the creature when the man's pasty white skin began to turn dark, or when the stiff black hair began to sprout, first on the man's arms and legs and then his face. Apparently, the bite on the man's leg had been sufficient to transfer the power of Loup Garou into this skinny white body. Although, he found it surprising how swiftly the power transferred.

The Lagahoo licked his lips, imagining the taste of the man's flesh and blood. He gathered himself for another attack, but he was too weak. The one thing that he wanted to experience before he died had been denied him. Were he human, he would have cried.

The Lagahoo watched as the man grew taller and broader, his clothes tearing and falling away as his body swelled. The new Lagahoo threw back his head and howled at the moon, a sound that would terrify the islanders and the tourists.

The sound also frightened the Lagahoo, but when the new Loup Garou focused his fiery red eyes in his direction, the fear melted away, replaced by a feeling of peace. He became aware that his own transformation had not only stopped but reversed. The Lagahoo, once again in the form of the filthy street dog, turned his neck to face the fearsome creature. When the razor-sharp fangs tore into his body, he felt his life force being drawn into the new Loup Garou, and the warm embrace of death take its place.

THE GHOST OF ST. HILDEGARD'S CENTER FOR MYSTIC ARTS

by Linda Kay Hardie

Karen climbed the steps to the porch of St. Hildegard's Center on a brisk late September afternoon in a last-ditch effort to discover the truth. She'd had enough of the family legend that put her branch in the wrong. Charlene, her half-second-cousin, wouldn't let go of the argument that Karen was descended from a murderer. And what did that make her, if her veins carried the blood of a woman so insane as to want to die in flames while killing a nun?

After years of research in library newspaper files and too many rabbit-holes on the internet, Karen decided the direct approach was her best bet. Just go into the historic former hospital in Virginia City, Nevada, where her great-grandmother had been locked up for insanity.

Opening the door and stepping inside the arts and literary foundation, she saw an office to the right with a woman sitting at a desk. Karen tapped on the open door with a knuckle, and said, "Knock, knock."

The woman looked up. "What can I do for you?"

"I'm Karen Sutter. I'm here to find out if I can talk to one of your ghosts."

"Sister Mary Michael?"

"She's the one."

"What's your interest? Are you a journalist?"

"A relative. My great-grandmother is the one who is supposed to have killed your nun. I want to find out the truth and clear her name if possible."

"We've had thousands of ghost hunters over the years, but you're a first. I didn't realize that the mental patient's name was even known, let alone that the fire might have been set on purpose." The woman nodded. "But we've never had anyone ever report talking to the sister or hearing her speak or make any noises at all."

"I'd like to try. It has to do with finding peace for the two branches of my family. Mine is descended from Beth Sutter, who was the patient here. The other branch comes down from Beth's husband Charles, who remarried after her death. They've hated us and called us murderers for 134 years."

*****

Janet Andrews, manager of the Hildegard Center, led Karen on a tour. The historic four-story building had been a Catholic hospital from 1879 to 1897, run by the Sisters of Service. Right before the turn of the century they donated the building to Storey County, which operated it during the decline of Virginia City as the silver boom slowed down, until the 1940s. Once the hospital closed, the building sat vacant until 1964 when local artists teamed up to turn it into an arts center.

They renamed it after the patron saint of creativity, St. Hildegard von Bingen, who was known for writing letters, books, music, and medical dissertations, all without a formal education. And because Hildegard was also known for her psychic visions, and the fact that the building was haunted, they added mystic to the name.

Fine arts and literary arts groups held retreats, classes, and other projects there. Ghost hunters studied the building and held events there, too. But since it was mid-September and schools were back in session and it was too early for the Halloween-themed spooky affairs by supernaturalists, Janet was able to give Karen a full tour.

"Besides galleries for art exhibits and classrooms for activities, we have 17 guest rooms that we rent out," Janet said. "Eight are located on this floor, which is the second, one is downstairs on our accessible level, and five are up on the third. Most of these rooms were patient rooms, and the two guest rooms on the fourth floor were quarters for the nuns."

"Which room burned down, killing Sister Mary Michael and my great-grandmother?"

"We don't know."

"Don't you have records of renovations to the burned room?"

"No. Those were the Catholic hospital's records, and Storey County didn't get them. Or maybe they were lost in the 24 years that the building was empty before our foundation was formed."

Janet stopped in front of a door marked eight. She unlocked it, opened it, and gestured for Karen to walk in.

She saw a beautifully-furnished room. A turquoise chest of drawers with mirror, queen bed with beautiful six-pointed star quilt, comfy brown chair, and hardwood floor. Ahead and to the left were two tall windows with old-fashioned pull-down shades and sheer curtains. There was a turquoise end table with a lamp next to a rag throw-rug by the bed.

"It's lovely," Karen said.

"This could possibly be the room you're looking for, because people have seen Sister Mary Michael peering out these two windows, although no one has said she looked frightened or in pain. But we've also had visions of her at the bottom of the staircase up to the third floor, trying to help a small boy ghost with iron braces on his legs. Obviously, a polio patient who died in the hospital. And her ghost is often seen floating down the hallways, checking in on patients long gone."

Karen walked to the west-facing window and looked out over Virginia City. She'd thought she might perceive some vibration or feeling here. But there was nothing.

"Have your psychics ever pinpointed which rooms are haunted?"

"Ghost hunters we've worked with say they've found signs of ghosts all over this building," Janet said.

"I'm not sensitive, myself, so I have no idea. Some of our overnight guests have experiences and others don't. There's a local writers' group from Reno, part of an international children's book-writing association, that's held numerous retreats, and many of them have had ghost encounters."

"My biggest worry is that I'm too practical and facts-based to ever see a ghost," Karen said with a wry smile. Sometimes she thought she'd become an accountant to prove she wasn't overly emotional or mentally unstable. Numbers could always be counted on to do what they were supposed to do.

Janet smiled back and shrugged. "That's my problem. But if I were sensitive, I probably wouldn't be able to work here, so I guess it's a benefit. Let's check out some more rooms and see if you get any vibrations."

Karen found the rest of the second-floor rooms, some with pairs of smaller beds, to be as darling as the first one they visited and just as empty of ghosts. Then they reached the third floor.

"Room 10 used to be the chapel for the hospital," Janet said, unlocking the door.

Karen stepped into the room and shivered. "Woo, it's cold in here! Is the window open?"

Janet followed her. "It feels fine to me. And the window is closed." She shook the handle of the west-facing window. It was locked.

"Now it feels fine." Karen paced around the room. It was small for a chapel, slightly smaller than room eight and similarly decorated, with old-fashioned chests of drawers, although these were dark stained wood instead of painted. Same gorgeous hardwood floor, but no rag rug. Queen-sized bed with a deep blue duvet and matching pillow covers. No more chills, but she did have a sense of serenity.

They looked at the rest of the rooms, more of the same with single queen beds or pairs of full- or twin-sized beds. Karen didn't feel anything unusual in them. Same with the two rooms on the fourth floor. Janet took Karen down to the first floor, where there were galleries for art exhibits, the kitchens, a dining room, and other rooms, including the final guest room. No more vibrations or anything.

Along the way, Janet shared other ghost stories, like the one about the phantom horse-drawn hearse that was often seen at the south side of the former hospital, waiting to transport those who didn't survive their stay. A spectacle conducted in complete silence: No jangle of harnesses, no crack of the whip, no whinnies from horses, no crunch of gravel under wooden wagon wheels. All the way up to Virginia City's Silver Terrace Cemetery on a hilltop north of town.

Back at Janet's office on the second floor, Karen asked how she could rent a room to stay a night or two.

"We only rent out to groups, artists, or wedding parties," Janet replied. "Except for members of our foundation."

"What does that cost?"

"Regular memberships start at $50 and go up from there."

Karen whipped out her debit card. "One membership and two nights in room 10, please."

*****

Back home down in Reno, Karen packed a bag. She boxed up groceries, too, although she might go out for dinner at one of Virginia City's many good restaurants or bars. She didn't have to worry about her husband, Jim Smith, because he was off at a convention of the Jim Smith Society, a national club for people with that name, and wouldn't be back for several more days.

Someone banged at the front door. Must be Charlene because everyone else was civilized and used the doorbell.

"Come in, Char!" Karen called.

Charlene burst into the living room, slamming the door behind her.

"What's all this bullshit," she declared, hands on hips.

Besides a permanent scowl, Charlene had eyes the color of dogshit, Karen always thought. Brown was too nice a description of them. Charlene was proud of her pronounced resemblance to their shared great-grandfather, Charles Sutter. She had his strong chin and blond hair, while Karen's face was rounder and her hair brown with auburn highlights.

Charles abandoned his four children when he married his second wife. The three younger ones were raised by their 18-year-old brother, Donald. Karen's grandfather was the younger brother Samuel. It was no wonder there was antipathy between the two branches of the family. The only thing that puzzled Karen was why the step-great-grandmother's side was so angry at her side, when that side's relatives were the interlopers.

Karen focused back on her half-second-cousin, who'd been talking all this time. She picked up the thread of Charlene's latest complaint, which was that Karen was poking her nose into things better left unpoked with this latest attempt to find the truth of what happened to Beth Sutter. There was no need to spend the night at St. Hildegard's.

"It's completely obvious what happened back then. She was a killer. You're just wasting your time," Charlene lectured.

"It's my time," Karen said quietly. She often wondered why she put up with Char, but that's how she'd been raised. Family was important, and you stayed in touch, even if you didn't much like them.

She shooed Charlene out the door, then locked it.

*****

Many people Karen knew complained about the drive from Reno up Geiger Grade, the steep and winding road up to Virginia City, but she loved the views and the off-the-beaten-path-promise. She always stopped at the historical marker that pointed out the old wagon train trail down in one valley, left from all those settlers with their dreams. (Not to mention the nightmares of the people who already lived in those "unsettled lands," but that was another story, Karen knew.)

Friday was the full moon, and Karen hoped that one of the two nights would wake up the ghosts in the old hospital. Two nights was to give her twice the chances of seeing a ghost, especially Sister Mary Michael.

Settling into room 10, Karen noticed a small band of wild horses grazing on the Hildegard Center's front lawn. There was a stallion, dun with black dappled over grey, three sorrel mares, and one frisky, creamy palomino colt. Except for her car in the gravel parking lot, Karen could believe she'd gone back in time.

After that, she unpacked and put her clothes away in the chest of drawers, then carried her box of food to the kitchen and put the cold items in the fridge and others in a cupboard.

Time to look around. Karen walked the half-mile up Union Street to the Bucket of Blood Saloon, owned by McBride & Sons, and in business since 1876. The interior was dusky but welcoming. A woman wiped down the long, old-fashioned bar. Karen sat at the bar and ordered a glass of zinfandel.

"White or red?" the bartender asked.

"Red, of course." Karen wiped the sneer off her face. "Sorry. I'm sure you get plenty of the white-zin tourists up here. I'm a snob; I drink real wine. Whoops. There I go again."

The bartender smiled. "Coming right up." She opened a fresh bottle, poured a glass, then left the bottle on the counter next to Karen.

"I'm Sam," she said, leaning across the bar to bump elbows.

"Karen." She slid her credit card across the smooth wood. "That was my grandfather's name, Sam."

The bartender smiled and tucked the card in her shirt pocket. "What are you in town for?"

"Chasing ghosts." Karen took a generous taste of her zin. "Mmm, nice."

"Thanks. Which ghosts?"

"Sister Mary Michael down at the Hildegard Center."

"Cool."

"My great-grandmother was accused of the nun's death. I'm here to clear her."

Sam pulled an open energy drink out from under the counter. "Here's to your success."

Karen lifted her wine glass and tapped the can. "Thanks."

"If you don't mind my asking, why is it important to you? It's gotta be more than a century ago."

Karen gulped the last of her wine, nodded at the bottle, and Sam poured another glass.

"The whole situation broke my family apart. My great-grandfather married again right away, and he left his four kids from the first marriage to fend for themselves. My great-uncle Donald was 18 and raised his siblings. My grandfather was the youngest at six, and the two girls were 10 and 11. Donald married them off when they each turned 15."

"What happened to them?" Sam asked.

"I don't know. I looked for them on all of the genealogy websites, and I even checked out the cemetery here. No luck. I know that most families don't stay that close in touch after 100 years, but it still bothers me."

Sam shrugged. "I'm sorry, but it's just another example of the erasure of women in history."

"Yes!" Karen drank. "That's what it is, that's why it gets under my skin."

Sam lifted the wine bottle, as well as an eyebrow. Karen nodded and set down her empty glass. Sam poured.

"Where's a good place to eat?" Karen asked.

"Down in Reno," Sam said. "No, there are a couple of restaurants still open around here, but most closed a little while ago at four o'clock. Covid's been brutal up here."

Karen downed her wine and held out the glass. "Well, damn. I'm sorry to hear that. I'll have to start coming up here more often and spend more money."

Sam held up her energy drink again. They tapped another toast.

"Good thing I brought a small casserole of homemade lasagna," Karen said. "Plus, my own bottle of wine to go with it."

*****

Karen climbed the stairs from the first floor to the third, carrying an open bottle of wine, an empty glass, and the novel she'd read during dinner. She had heated her lasagna in the large oven and tossed a salad with a homemade gorgonzola dressing, topped with the last of the season's grape tomatoes. It was almost nine o'clock, because she was a late and leisurely eater.

Juggling everything to get her room key out of her pocket, she finally unlocked the door and stepped inside. She felt a chill as she stepped over the threshold.

"Hello, ghost," Karen said. "Are you Sister Mary Michael?"

No reply. The chill faded. She set the wine bottle and glass on the chest of drawers to her left and tossed the paperback onto the bed.

*****

A chill woke Karen. "Ghost, I'm tired of this."

Bright light shone through the window shade. Karen sat up in bed. Was it the moon? Tomorrow was the full moon, so it would be bright now. Or technically tonight was full moon. What time was it? Her phone said 3:13.

And was that an oil lamp she smelled? Decorative old-fashioned lamps were in style when she was a girl, and her parents had several they carefully used around the house. But she was distracted by the light, which shimmered and formed into a ball, then zoomed around the room like a lunatic cat. A flying one. The ghost, about the size of a cat, suddenly turned and aimed itself at her face. Karen fell backwards onto her pillow and watched the light zip overhead and disappear into the wall.

She closed her eyes, and when she opened them again, the room was bright again. This time it was 7:30 a.m. and the sun was up. Did she see a ghost? Or did she dream the whole thing?

A chill passed through her. "Stop that, you damned ghost!"

*****

Karen explored Virginia City on what turned out to be a glorious fall day, unseasonably warm with a temperature in the high 60s, after breakfast at the Comstock Cafe. She still mourned the loss of the Mark Twain Bookstore, even though it had closed about a decade ago. And she was saddened to see the loss of many other newly-closed businesses up and down the main drag due to covid. She spent hours walking up and down C Street, as well as exploring the lesser-known areas of the historic town. She had lunch at the Red Dog Saloon before heading back to the arts center.

Back in her sometimes-chilly room, Karen took out her laptop and wrote about her time in Virginia City in her journal. She described the rooms in the arts center, in case she wanted to use some of her experiences, fictionalized, in a novel. Despite being a self-described cynic about ghosts, she did have an imagination.

She wrote about her experience or dream during the night. Was this all going to be a waste of time and money, as Char had accused? She explored what she'd thought she'd seen. Her memories were clearer than dreams usually were for her. She remembered the time on her phone. She remembered the chill that woke her. She remembered the fear she'd felt when the ghost aimed itself right at her face.

But what did it all mean? Was it trying to tell her to leave? Or was she supposed to have followed it? Damn. Numbers were so much more reliable!

The sun set over the hill that loomed over town and dusk settled in. Karen walked back to the main part of town to have an early-for-her dinner at Cafe

Del Rio at seven o'clock. She finally headed back around 8:30 after chatting with the people there, the customers and staff. It was a lovely evening.

She had just opened the door to her room when she heard a sarcastic voice behind her.

"So, you're doing it." Charlene stood in the hallway, her face in its usual frown.

"Why the hell did you come up here?" *There goes my relaxing evening*, she thought.

"Aren't you going to invite me in?"

"No." Karen stepped out and locked the door. "What do you want?"

Charlene sniffed the air. "Did you leave a pan on the stove? Smells like smoke. That would be just like you, to burn this place down like your great-grandmother."

Karen started to count to 10, then she remembered the lamp-oil smell from the ghost during the night. But this was more than that.

"Shit." She rushed down the stairs and stopped on the second floor when she heard women's screams to the left. She ran down the hall. The shrieking came from inside room eight. Smoke seeped out from under the door.

"Don't bother. They're as good as dead already." Charlene grabbed her arm.

Karen pulled away and pushed open the door. An oil lamp on the floor was burning the rag carpet. A nun was struggling to free a woman who was chained to the brass bedstead.

"Sister Mary Michael?" Karen asked.

The nun and the woman on the bed turned their heads toward Karen.

"Great-grandmother?" Karen took a step into the room.

The woman in the bed stared. "You're the spit and image of me at age 33. Who are you?"

"I'm your great-granddaughter. I came from the future to find out what happened here."

"Charles had me declared insane and committed here," Beth Sutter said.

"What did you do?"

Beth laughed, her blue eyes sparkling in the flickering light. "I wore trousers, drank whiskey, and cussed. I read books. And since Charles was having a dalliance with young Miss Rose Carson, he wanted me out of the way. You just missed him. He's the one who dropped the lamp."

Karen, who'd been mesmerized by Beth, noticed that the fire was burning rather slowly.

"Dammit, Karen! What are you up to?" Charlene's voice broke the spell. The fire flamed up, and Karen took a step back away from the heat.

"Charles, you son of a bitch!" Beth cried. "I would recognize you anywhere."

Karen turned to look at Charlene in the doorway. She noticed her cousin's face looked very masculine in the firelight. The usual grumpy look was quickly replaced by pure hatred. Charlene was the "spit and image," as Great-Grandmother had said, of Great-Grandfather Charles. Karen had seen him in a tintype photograph with his first wife and family. The ones he cast off to be with his young lover. Was Charlene the reincarnation of Charles?

Char turned to glare at Karen, loathing in her eyes.

"When is this?"Karen asked.

"It's 1888," Sister Mary Michael snapped. "Enough of this family reunion. We need to get out of here." She continued to work at the lock on the chain with a long hatpin.

"No, save my grandchild," Beth said, pointing to Karen. "Please."

Sister Mary Michael looked from Beth to Charlene to Karen. She dropped the hatpin and shoved with brutal strength, and Karen staggered back and fell on her butt in the hallway. *Good thing I'm well-padded,* she thought incongruously.

"I want Charles, that adulterer and murderer!" Beth shouted.

The nun grabbed Charlene and slammed the door. Smoke billowed out from under it.

Karen, alone in the hallway, scrambled up and grabbed the knob. Despite the heat, she turned it and found the door wouldn't open. Locked. She pounded on the hot wood, hearing screams inside. She coughed from the smoke.

Suddenly the only noise was Karen's fists banging on the door of room eight. The screaming had stopped. The door was cold. There was no smoke at all. What happened to everyone? Especially Charlene, who turned out to be the reincarnation of Great-

Grandfather Charles, who also turned out to be a murderer? And what could Karen do?

She reached for the knob with her left hand. The door opened easily.

Charlene lay in a pile on the floor. The room was perfectly normal again, a charming guest room in an historic building with moonlight streaming in through the west-facing window.

She helped Charlene up and looked her in the eyes.

Her face looks strange, Karen thought.

She realized the face wasn't pinched in a scowl. Charlene's eyes looked warm and friendly. And bright blue, just like her great-grandmother's.

Karen stared at the blisters forming on her right hand. She heard Beth's voice, "Let's go home, my dear. You need some butter or lard for your burns."

END

MY FAMILY'S REDCAP

by Elizabeth Davis

All families carried something with them from the Old World; a rare few brought treasures, the merely lucky brought faded photographs, and most brought only thread-worn stories. My family brought a hole.

It was a family secret, of sorts. We all knew instinctively, my siblings and I, without any hushed orders or oaths of secrecy. The neighbors never asked about it, always in the shadow of the great oak in the backyard. Not even on the moonless night each month that my father would march us out, wordlessly, and we would all gather around, looking down into the darkness where two red eyes leered out, while my father dumped a bucket of raw meat down the hole.

Then, he would leave and we would always follow.

We never asked and they never explained. Not until my 13th birthday.

Years later, I had forgotten about the hole until I returned back to my family's home for one last visit.

My father's dementia meant he was moved to a care home, the best my siblings could pay for. My mom had died two years previously from lung cancer, having given up cigarettes too late.

No horror movie had ever captured how haunting your family home becomes when all the family is gone. Even with my sister and brother constantly texting me questions and comments, pictures of old family pictures brought back memories that we couldn't stop sharing. Even with no texts from an unknown number letting me know that my new number was compromised. Even with the oldies station playing, disco pounding through the boxes. Some ghosts just can't be shaken.

But still, it was my job. I was the oldest, my siblings argued. It's traditional to do this sort of thing.

What they didn't say was that they had jobs and I didn't. I still wondered what Mikey had sent my former boss, causing him to call me red faced into the back office. I wasn't even given enough time to learn via work gossip He had let me know via text that he was so sorry that I got fired, from a new number I promptly blocked.

That they had safe homes, and I was still camped out on a friend's bed, my few boxes around me. Technically apartment-sitting for her, but her girlfriend had just scored a nice loft at a rate that meant it had to be cursed. She didn't want to break her lease, costing more than just finishing out the last three months, so she let me live there. I offered to pay, but she dismissed it out of hand, saying that she had her share of crazy Exs and bad breakups. Amanda was always too generous.

Or that I had no problem giving up how much time was needed to get the job done properly. Which was better than staring at the walls and reassuring myself that I was making the right decision, that eventually Mickey would lose interest in wooing me back. I suspect my siblings were hoping that I would stay, find a job, find a nice man, and be happy again.

I didn't think of my 13th birthday until I pulled out an old stack of carefully preserved report cards, with my 7th grade card on top.

My parents had sat me down on the couch with all the solemnity of genuflecting before the church altar, and my father explained that back in history, at my age, I would have been considered an adult man. I was gripping my knees with sweaty palms before my parents arrived at the main point. They would be gone for the whole weekend to spend time with my Aunt. (There must have been a family crisis of some sort, but they never let us really know. We only ever caught the edge of hushed phone calls, even after we left for college). Meals were in the freezer, I just needed to pull them out and put them in the stove. Emergency numbers were neatly written on a post-it note, stuck to the fridge. I just needed to make sure that Mary and David stayed out of trouble.

Just as I daydreamed about taking my parents' blockbuster membership card for a weekend-long movie marathon, my dad cleared his throat. The words that came out were different from the roaring bluster that had started the conversation, shrinking down to a mouse whisper. "There's meat in the fridge, in the crisper drawer. Don't forget about Saturday night." I nodded, going back to my daydreams. That had been on Monday. Saturday was a whole world away.

I frowned down at the record cards as I tried to remember what my father meant by that. As I dumped them into the to-be-scanned pile (It was really junk, but junk that was a touch too sentimental to simply toss without making an electronic file that would probably never be opened,) I tried to remember that weekend. I remembered the arguments at Blockbuster over the movies we picked, with David complaining that I didn't pick any scary movies. I remember Mary being sick on Saturday morning after a breakfast of ice cream. The cleaning rush that happened Sunday evening, as we realized our parents were only hours away, wanting to hide any smidge of misbehavior.

I did not remember for two days.

I had successfully cleaned out my father's study, laboriously sorting his books into keep and give-away piles, hauling out the broken recliner, and moderating a light-hearted debate about who got his singing bass. The next day I was going to have to set up the shredder and fill the air with paper dust. I debated shredding the letter I had received that day in the mail.

I hadn't opened it yet. But I knew the handwriting on the address in the back. I knew that I should open it. But if I didn't, then I didn't have to know if Mikey knew I was here. That he was just throwing a Hail Mary to keep tabs on me through my befuddled father. That it would be useless as evidence, that he never said anything threatening in writing.

I looked longingly at my father's nearly empty bottle of scotch as the sun went down. But I was a clumsy drunk, and while I could entertain my college dates by rattling off original couplets without a slur before nearly tripping while getting up, it didn't amuse Mikey. I absentmindedly rubbed the scar on my arm, which I thought maybe I got the night that I learned that Mikey didn't like me drinking, when I finally remembered what my father had said about that Saturday night and how I had forgotten until we were cleaning up the Sunday morning afterwards..

I had been desperately cleaning the kitchen. I opened the fridge, a mop of paper towels clutched in my hands, wiping up droplets of spilled ice cream, when I saw the brown butcher's bag sitting in the crisper drawer. As I pulled the soggy bag out, the stench of rotting meat hit me and then I remembered.

Panicking, I ran out the back door, leaving the fridge door hanging open. I stumbled into the darkening backyard, able to find the hole by the glowing red eyes. In those last shadows of day, I shakily pulled out the bag, emptying it all down the hole. Before the meat had fallen far, the red eyes darted up. I stared at the figure of a spider climbing out, all bony limbs and teeth taken from my mother's knife block. Even in the color-drained dusk, dull red light permeated everything around him. His hair bristled like an angry tarantula's, hiding what little clothes he had.

I tried to pull my arm away, but he had it in his grip before I blinked. No matter how hard I pulled, even as my shoulder whined in its socket, he wouldn't let go.

"You're late." He growled, sounding exactly like my neighbor's unfriendly dog. "We have a bargain, your kin and I. Haven't I always protected your family from their numerous enemies? I did not leave my castle to be ignored."

"I'm sorry!" I blurted out, panicking, as he pulled himself to my height. This close, I couldn't see more of his face than the burning red eyes, the sharp teeth and bristling beard, smeared with dirt and meat. I rested my eyes on the least threatening part of him, the dark red cap pulled down, a few stiff hairs poking out. Far better than the torn leather jerkin, hair sticking out like porcupine quills, or the metal boots with small bones sticking out of the joints.

"I need something fresh, and you're late."

I screamed, and I would've thought the quiet night would have been broken by curious neighbors and my panicked siblings; yet nothing stirred as his teeth sunk into my arm.

I shook my head, reducing the memory to vivid childhood nightmares that mangled memory and dream into a Frankenstein monster. To further reassure myself, I went outside with my flashlight. I walked past the battered swing set, my mom's smoking lawn chair that still smelled despite the years of wind and rain. I looked for the stump of the great oak, taken out by Oak Wilt. No hole swallowed the light, no red eyes looked back at me. A childhood fear vanquished, like all the other monsters in the closet.

I slept soundly until the second letter arrived.

This one was different. Same handwriting, but heavier. Different enough for the unraveling anxiety inside my chest to force my hands to tear open the envelope.

The first page was pleading that his place was no longer his home without me. The second page was different. It was a blown up picture of Amanda's apartment, with my struggling spider plant in the window. On the back of it, his handwriting continued. "This doesn't look like a home either. Is that why you've been out? Maybe I should ask Amanda, since it's supposed to be her place. I hope to see you soon. Love Mikey. PS. Do I need to stop by your Dad's?"

My heart beat in my throat and I stared down at the letter. There was a decision to make. As the older brother I had to be responsible.

I haphazardly packed my few belongings. This house was a precious place of memories for my siblings and I. But I could not do a thing to protect it if Mikey knew I was here. Calling the police was out. No one would take me seriously, not when I outweighed him by 60 pounds and three inches. They would laugh if I told them how hard it was to bring yourself to hurt someone who just wanted the best for you, and loved you more than everyone else, even if they had a temper and it wouldn't be an issue if I didn't keep making him angry.

I had seen him angry. I didn't want to see him desperate. Not here.

The drive was long, hours stretched by nerves as I left behind the idea of escape. I was going to have to face Mikey, and then what? I looked through my options, finding dead ends. Moving across the country, living in hotels wasn't going to last long with what was left of my bank account, even if my siblings helped. I couldn't stay with them. They were my younger siblings, and David had children, small and fragile. I could try to fight back, to finally raise my hand, and then face DV charges, because I was bigger and who would believe that Mikey was a threat to me? The jury would see me and just see a brute.

Maybe this is the way it was meant to be. Maybe it would be better this time. Maybe I would be better.

My jittery path to Amanda's apartment was interrupted when I saw the door ajar. He was here already.

I opened the door, expecting to see him looking at me with that deep inhale of disappointment. But there was just silence as the radiator chugged away. The only thing out of place in the living room was a single red drop on the pinkish-greyish carpet. A drop that pointed into the kitchen.

I stepped inside, the copper smell assaulting me. I felt bile raise up as my eyes made sense of the splatter. A table was overturned, the cheap plastic vase cracked on the floor, the fake flowers trampled. I could still see the outline of a red handprint trailing down. Scratches marred the fake wood of the cabinets below the sink. Mindlessly I dipped down to pick up the glittering gold in the middle of one of the puddles of blood.

Fairmont High school 2001, sized for hands barely smaller than mine. Whose band had felt warm as we held hands.

I instinctively pushed my fist into my mouth, ignoring the blood caught on it, forcing myself to breathe slowly through my nose. A flicker of movement behind the table caught my attention, and adrenaline sprung me there just in time to see gangly arms retreat back into a hole, a hole that wouldn't be normally noticed in the shadows of the corner. The burning red eyes looked at me between a bright red cap, still dripping blood to the teeth below.

"I told you we had a bargain."

OLD WIVES' TALES

by Sara Martinez

In the year of our Lord 1858, gold was found in the foothills of the Rocky Mountains, near what would become the city of Denver. I was 15 years old at the time and I distinctly remember the effect the news had on my father. Ever since I was little, we'd moved from place to place, trying to find a home safe for colored folks, so I knew the look my father got when he was fixing to move out of town. But this time, there was something else there, too: an obsession with the idea of striking it rich. The notion of finding gold put a manic gleam in his eye, and I knew it wouldn't be long before we'd be leaving town again.

After some months' time, the gold fever still had a firm hold on my father; my mama teased him gently about it each night as she tended to the washing up after dinner. Eventually, we packed our belongings into a small wagon and set out West. My father's foster mother, Grammy June, rode inside the wagon with our gear, but there wasn't much room for anyone else, so most of the time we walked alongside our old mule, Molly. Molly trotted slowly, but the 'Pikes Peak or

Bust' sign that hung on the back of our wagon stood testament to Papa's optimism.

This was hardly the first gold rush out west, but California and Nevada were as distant as a foreign land, while the eastern side of the Rockies must have felt attainable to my father. We travelled slowly; Mama and Papa tried to be gentle on Grammy June's aching bones as much as they could. We traveled alongside several different groups, but often we'd stop to rest for longer than our companions, opting to either catch up with them or fall back with another set of wagons.

One morning partway through the journey, I walked alongside the wagon, lost in thought, contemplating our nomadic lifestyle. My father noticed my far-off look and inquired, "What's on your mind, boy?"

"Papa, when we reach Denver City, will we stay there for good?"

Papa sighed. "I hope so, Thomas. It would be nice to set down roots, but you know how it be. If the rent gets too high, or folks are too unfriendly to our kind, we have to move on." He cleared his throat. "If the stories of gold be true, I can dig enough up so we can build a real life for us all."

From the other side of Molly, Mama spoke up. "It would be nice to own our own house. And it would be easier on Grammy, too." She glanced back in the wagon where Grammy June sat nestled on top of Papa's carpentry tools and our other meager belongings. "You holdin' up in there?"

"I's fine, child," Grammy answered, though she shifted in a way that led me to believe she lied. Though she would never let on if it was, I feared the journey from the rail town in Kansas Territory where we had been living proved too hard on her. Grammy June may not have been blood, but she was surely kin. She had traveled along with my parents as they moved from place to place, trying to find a home safe for colored folks. After I was born, she tended to me while Mama and Papa worked, and I spent many a night on her knee as she regaled me with stories. Sometimes they were about our family and how life had been on the plantations. Others were more fantastical, full of African princes, voodoo priestesses, and monsters that preyed on men. I loved Grammy's stories; they made me shiver and long for a world where such wonders existed. Grammy had been a healer for the other slaves when the master would refuse care, blending herbal medicine and what she called her hoodoo magic. She retained that helpful, albeit superstitious, nature and instilled in me a duty to care for others as I grew.

As the shadows started to lengthen, we stopped to make camp on the side of the road. The mountains were just visible in the distance, dark peaks against a riot of color in the sky. I helped Papa with the tent while Mama started the fire to cook supper. After we had eaten, I sat on the ground, leaning against the wagon. "Will you tell me a story, Grammy?"

She shifted stiffly on her blanket seat. "Just one, then Grammy needs her some sleep. Le'see," she contemplated for a moment. "I think it's time you hear how your Mama and Papa met." My mother and father glanced at each other for a moment, then nodded their approval. "You know your Papa's mama died when he was a baby and his papa was sold to another farm, so I took him in. He learned to make furniture from my late beau, and he got good real quick. Your mama worked in the big house on account of how good she cook." Grammy took a sip from the canteen before continuing. "The master wanted a new cabinet for the kitchen and had Papa make it. When he took it inside and them two saw each other, they knew they belong together. They would sneak off to meet after dark, until one night a guard found them and gave your Papa a whuppin'. That very night, he come to me and ask for help to escape."

"Grammy June is a better schemer than I could ever be," chuckled Papa.

Grammy waved a hand at him dismissively. "Hush, you interruptin' my story. Anyhow, we waited until a night wit' a big storm, when the wind was howlin', then set fire to the barn, letting all the horses run free. The master's men was so busy putting out the fire before it spread and trying to catch them horses, they didn't know until too late we had run into the woods. The wind meant the dogs couldn't track us all, neither. We got as far out from Louisiana as we could, movin' until we found a place where the slave catchers couldn't take us back." She stifled a yawn. "Now, it time for me to get my rest. Good night, child."

With that, I helped her to her feet and she toddled off to the tent. My parents turned in shortly after that; I stayed up for a bit to stare at the starry sky. I felt truly lucky for all my parents had risked building a life for us. And as we got closer to our destination, I hoped they could finally reap the reward for all that work. I whispered a prayer for good fortune on the rest of our journey before going to bed.

*****

We arrived in Denver City in early July of 1859 and found dirt roads, jumbled tents, and slapdash wooden structures surrounding the somewhat stouter brick buildings downtown. New tents went up by the day, so it was no trouble to pick a spot to claim as our own. I helped Papa build a wooden base to pitch our two-room tent over and then we broke down the wagon to build workbenches. As soon as the shop was complete, Papa set out a shingle advertising his services. He worked next to the road, shaping furniture for our home. His care and craftsmanship were enough to catch the eye of passersby and find his first customers.

One day not long after we had settled in, four men came to the shop. One was a Negro like us, another white, while the other two had long black hair and ruddy skin, so I took them to be Indians. They spoke to my father in hushed tones that I could not fully make out, occasionally glancing my way. He laughed at their request, but the men impressed their sincerity upon him, and the money they paid him silenced any lingering doubts.

When they left, I asked my father what they'd wanted. "Now, son, never you mind about that," he said. "They're paying good money and that's all we need to know. I don't understand it, but it don't matter none and it ain't my business." And he would not tell me what they wanted nor let me assist in the work.

The quality of my father's work was plain and the men became regular customers, though I learned next to nothing about them; not even their names. Their generous payments soon allowed my father to purchase mining gear and a pack horse to carry it while still keeping our living basically comfortable.

Once he had the necessary equipment, my father began to set out in search of gold. When he was gone, the carpentry work fell to me; though I didn't have the skill he had, I could do the basics. He still handled all the work for the four men, though, and refused to allow me to help. My mother would fret, and Grammy would mutter while he was away, but he paid it no mind.

At first, he was only gone a day or two a week, but before long, he was setting out most days. He would come home every night, but later and later as time went on. The carpentry work was steady and money continued to come in, but Papa's patience started wearing thin as again and again, he came back with nothing more than a few tiny nuggets of gold or nothing at all. When I was younger, he had been a kind and gentle man, but something seemed to weigh on him now. His shoulders became stooped, and he was much quicker to anger, even sometimes getting short with Grammy June. I hardly recognized him.

Papa was in a foul mood at the lack of success of his latest mining excursion when the four regulars came by one day. He was unusually curt to them as he negotiated their latest order, and I worried he would drive them off. This time they carried large packs laden with trinkets, unidentified boxes, and rolled-up maps. There were several tools I didn't recognize, but I spied at least one pickaxe lashed to a pack.

Abruptly, my father strode to the back of the shop, something he did more often now when he was feeling frustrated about something. Trying to make up for my father's ill temper, I broke the silence with conversation. "Are you prospectors, too?"

The taller of the Indians glanced at his compatriots before replying, "No, son, we're more like ... hunters."

"Oh! Like for deer, or a catamount or bears?"

The white man chortled. "We definitely go after dangerous predators," he replied with a twinkle of amusement in his eyes.

The Negro man shot his companion a warning look, then announced, "It's time to move along. Let these fine men go about their work." Each one tipped his hat, then they left.

After they had gone, my father wheeled on me. "What are you running your mouth for, boy? Those men pay us good money and I won't have you bothering them."

"I'm sorry, Papa," I stammered. "I didn't mean no harm. I thought I was making them feel welcome."

His hand raised as if to strike me, but then he lowered it slowly. Through gritted teeth he seethed, "You ain't here to think. You do what I tell you and you keep your head down."

The ensuing silence was broken by Mama calling us for supper. Anger warred with sorrow in my father's eyes, but he turned and stalked away without another word.

I stood quivering, fighting back tears. I had never known my father to be so cruel. I slowly followed to the table. Papa sullenly took food to eat at his workbench, leaving me with Mama and Grammy June. When Mama asked why I was so quiet, the words came tumbling out, "I'm worried about Papa.

He's gone so much now and angry when he gets back. I wish we'd never come here!"

Grammy sighed, leaning back in her chair. "I fear dis gold fever is twisting his mind. It almost like he under a curse." She fiddled absent-mindedly with the gris-gris around her neck.

Mama glanced at her, frowning. "All I know is, if he don't find gold soon, he might not be fit to live with us no more."

*****

Papa worked in the shop until late then left at dawn the next morning. I did as much work as I could, based on what I recalled of the jobs left undone. Mid-afternoon, the group of men returned, inquiring after my father. When I told them he was gone, a look of concern passed between them.

"He made a special order for us and we need it today. Look for a burlap sack," said the short Indian. The wood shop had grown cluttered with my father's repeated absence but eventually I found the sack tucked under a bench. It had been pushed so far back I nearly missed it. Wooden pieces jostled against each other inside as I handed the bag over, but I didn't dare open it. The Negro man hefted it in his hands a moment, then pulled the drawstring apart enough to peek inside before closing it up.

"Excellent," he said. "Be sure to thank your father for us." The white man took out a small pouch that jangled as he pressed it into my hand. I watched as they walked down the road to a group of hitched horses. They hefted the packs on the animals' backs then unhitched and mounted them and rode off.

When they were out of sight, I opened the pouch and found more gold coins than I had ever seen in one place before. I excitedly took it back to our tent and placed it in the tobacco tin my father hid under a floor board, where I knew he kept our money.

Having finished my work, I kept Grammy company until Mama came home from her laundry job. We ate supper in tense silence, all keeping watch on the door. But Papa never came home that night.

The next morning came and there was still no sign of my father. Mama paced nervously for a time, pausing sometimes to press her knuckles to her mouth as she did when deep in thought. Grammy mended some clothes while humming to herself and periodically dozing in her chair.

Finally, around midday, my mother broke her silence. "Thomas, you have to go out and look for your father. He could be hurt or trapped, or God knows what." She knelt beside their bed and pulled out a dog-eared map. Unfolding it on the table, she beckoned me over. "Here." she pointed to a spot in the near foothills. There were circles dotted up and down the map, but all save one had been slashed through with an X. The circle under my mother's finger was centered in a gulch ending above Clear Creek.

"I can't leave you and Grammy alone," I protested as I grasped her meaning.

Mama shook her head. "You have to go; I need to stay here with Grammy, but someone has to find Papa and I don't trust no one else." She turned to the cabinet and began pulling out a few tins of food, then bent over to Grammy's basket of cures and picked out a few bottles as well as some bandages. To that, she added a flint and a compass before tying it all up in a sack.

As my mother worked, Grammy June called me over. "I gots a bad feeling 'bout dis. You need protection." She pulled the gris-gris over her head and placed it on me, tucking the bag under my shirt. "Keep this close; it help keep you safe."

Bewildered, I accepted the sack from Mama and followed her outside as she laid a blanket over

Molly's back. She handed me the sack and a small oil lantern, as well as a sack of oats. Pulling me into an embrace, she held me for a time before whispering, "Bring him back to us," before letting go.

A lump formed in my throat, but I did my best to appear stoic as I nodded and climbed on the mule. Mama hugged herself after waving goodbye and Grammy June sung a soft prayer as I rode off.

It was about 10 miles from town to the spot marked on the map. I urged Molly on as best I could along the trails, but it was late in the day before I approached my destination. As the mule picked her way alongside the creek, we finally came to the bottom of the gulch. I let her drink from the creek before tying her lead to a stout-looking tree, then surveyed my surroundings. The sun was already touching the peaks high above me and my heart sank as I realized it would soon be too dark to search. "Looks like we'll be spending the night here, girl," I groaned to Molly.

I made camp as best I could, starting a small fire and laying the blanket out on the ground. Warming a tin of beans over the fire, I listened and watched as I was plunged into darkness the moment the sun dipped behind the mountains. The rushing of the creek was music as I ate, broken only by the sound of Molly crunching her oats.

Studying the map by firelight proved too difficult, so not long after I finished eating, I wrapped the blanket around me to try to sleep. The music of the water proved most relaxing as I drifted off.

*****

A lilting voice invaded my dreams. It was feminine and comely, but strive as I might, I could not make out the words. Soon, it was joined by other voices, weaving an eerie harmony with each other. The voices seemed to be calling me and I awoke in a daze.

The fire had burned down to embers, casting precious little light in the surrounding darkness. Molly snored softly nearby and the only other sound I heard was the creek. The moon was largely obscured by clouds and shadows from the fire danced all around me.

Then, I heard it again, so soft I had to strain to make it out: voices, beckoning from somewhere. The sound sent a shiver down my spine and raised all the hairs on the back of my neck. Around me, shadows danced and pressed closer, threatening to surround me. I had the intense sensation of being watched, though no soul appeared to be around.

I heard another voice, calling for help. I could swear it was my father! "Papa!" I cried, "Where are you!" but I heard no reply. Gathering and lighting my lantern, I set off from camp to try to follow his cry. The wind began to whip as I struggled to find my footing in the inky dark. After a bit, I cut up the rocky side trying desperately to locate my father's voice.

Heavy rain began to pour, the driving wet soaked me to the bone. My heart sank as I realized I had no idea where my camp was. I could no longer hear my father's voice over the storm. As I stumbled in search of respite, I still could not shake the feeling I was being watched. Then, I saw a faint yellow light in the distance that soon became the outline of a house.

Salvation! As desperate as I was to find Papa, I could do no more in the storm. I needed shelter. In my haste to approach the light, I misstepped and turned my ankle on the wet rocks. Crying out, I fell down an embankment, smashing my lantern against a stone, striking my knee upon another, and my head upon a third. Lying in a blearied state, I thought I felt a figure loom over me, but I could not be sure as the darkness overtook me.

*****

I awoke to warmth and soft lamplight. Was this the hereafter? Had my head cracked open and sent me to the Great Beyond? My vision slowly resolved to find myself in a small bedroom, plain and unadorned. I was tucked into a narrow bed, covered in a worn and faded quilt, the darkness held at bay by a single oil lamp on the dresser. A kindly looking white man comfortably in middle age sat on the foot of the bed. He gave me a pleasant, if perhaps a bit weary, smile and patted the quilt.

"Glad to see you're still with us," he gently rumbled.

"Where am I, sir?" I rasped, fighting against the dizzying feeling in my head as I sat up in the bed.

"In my home. Well, mine and my wives'," he replied with a strange tone to his voice. He handed me a cup of water as he spoke.

I gulped the water deeply, gasping, "And who are you?" between mouthfuls.

"Name's Daniel Jensen. I was out tracking a stray calf that had wandered off. The storm hit, and if I hadn't come across you, you mighta never been found." He stood, gently easing off the bed. "Now you should rest up. You took a nasty blow to the head and your knee is mighty swollen. You'll need some time to recover."

My eyes were starting to feel heavy, so I handed the cup back to Mr. Jensen and settled my head against the pillow. "Thank you, for saving me," I said, exhaustion already overcoming me. He gave me another small smile as he opened the door.

"We'll see tomorrow if you truly were saved," I thought I heard him whisper after he turned to go, but I decided I must have misheard as I fell asleep.

*****

Eventually I awoke; I thought it was daytime, but it was impossible to say exactly when. A heavy curtain was pulled across the small window, letting in only faint light. I tried to sit up in the bed, but my head swam and there was a blinding pain in my knee, forcing me to fall back with a gasp.

A mere moment later, I heard the doorknob rattle and open, and a stunningly beautiful woman walked in. She was tall and lithe, with strong features and wavy black hair cascading down her back. The only thing to mar her perfection was the almost sickly pale tone of her skin.

"Awake at last, I see," she purred in a low voice.

I struggled for a moment to find my voice. "Y—yes, Ma'am," I finally stammered.

She smiled, but it didn't quite seem to reach her eyes. "Good, it's just about supper time."

"I slept all day?"

She sat on the edge of the bed and touched my leg. "Yes, my dear. You took quite a bump to the head and we wanted to make sure you got your rest." Something odd shone in her eyes as she continued, "You must be starving after all that, though. We will eat soon."

Standing, she pointed to the pitcher and basin now on the dresser and instructed, "Wash up for supper, now, and come join us when you're ready." With that, she turned and left the room.

Slowly, I pulled back the covers and swung my legs off the bed. Pain blossomed in my knee, but not so terrible that I couldn't stand up. I quickly washed my face and hands before hobbling out of the room.

The door opened to a larger room where I saw the stove and kitchen off to the far left, with a large table in the center and a settee and several chairs to the right. Mr. Jensen sat in one of the chairs, reading, while three slightly younger women were clustered around the stove with the woman I saw earlier standing nearby to direct them. As the door closed behind me, every head in the room turned to look. The women's faces were inscrutable, but Mr. Jensen put down his book and walked over to me.

"Glad to see you're up and about," he intoned, as he laid a hand on my shoulder. He steered me to the table, pulling out a chair on one of the long sides for me to sit, then lowering himself to the chair on the end next to me. "Isabel, are we about set?" he asked.

"Just about," the woman from earlier replied, before sitting at the other end from him.

As if on cue, the three other women turned from the stove and approached the table; one placed a dish in front of Mr. Jensen, the second gave one to me, and the third set glasses down for him and me. The three then sat on the opposite side of the table from me. They were all lovely as well, though not quite as much as Isabel, but they also shared the same peculiarly pale skin. Mr. Jensen smiled at me, then gestured across the table. "This is my first wife, Isabel," he introduced. Sweeping his hand to the other side, he continued, "And these are my other wives, Ada, Eden, and Tabitha."

My brow furrowed in shock; four wives? What kind of a house was this? Sensing my surprise, he said,

"You see, we are Latter-Day Saints; we follow the principle of our biblical forebears in taking on multiple wives to welcome more souls into the kingdom of Heaven."

I racked my brain for a half-forgotten memory. "You mean Mormons?" I asked. "I thought you all lived in Utah territory."

Isabel's face darkened slightly. "We used to, for a long time. But we found ourselves no longer welcome, so we had to move away."

"A peddler came into town one evening and we offered up a room to stay. He repaid that kindness by attacking Isabel and fleeing into the night." Mr. Jensen added, with regret in his voice. "After that, she became sick; so severely we thought she had died and we were ready to bury her. But then she suddenly recovered and it seemed a miracle. Some of our neighbors said it was unnatural, though, and drove us out. So, we ventured east and settled here, where we wouldn't be bothered. We're close enough to the city to get supplies when we need, but mostly we keep to ourselves." He seemed uncomfortable now, so I decided not to press the issue further.

"I'm sorry to hear of your troubles, but glad you were here to find me in that storm," I said gratefully.

"We're glad to have you," Isabel interrupted, her voice impatient. "But, enough conversation, it's time to eat." She gestured to the food.

I looked down at my bowl. It was some sort of stew, with chunks of unidentifiable meat covered in thick gravy alongside a few potatoes and carrots mixed in. Something about it smelled a bit odd, but I couldn't guess what. Mr. Jensen was tucking in beside me, so I picked up my spoon. As I lifted it up, I realized something; none of the women had food in front of them. "I'm sorry," I stammered. "I didn't mean to start before everyone was ready."

Across from me, Eden grinned. "Oh, don't worry, we'll eat later."

Ada tittered. "We always wait for the menfolk to eat first!"

"Yes, there will be plenty for us to eat after," Tabitha added.

Isabel glared at them for a moment before turning to me with a smile. "We'll be fine, just eat up."

I shrugged and turned back to the plate. The taste was even stranger than the smell, but I ate a few mouthfuls to try to be polite to my hosts. As I ate, I looked around the room a bit more. Something about it had struck me as odd before, but I couldn't quite place it at the time; now I noticed that there were no windows anywhere. There was light enough from the lamps inside, but it was nearly impossible to tell the time of day.

A prickling sensation crept up the back of my neck and I turned my attention back to the table to see that the women were watching me intently. Something wasn't right; the taste of the stew coated my mouth, and I was starting to feel a mite lightheaded.

"I'm sorry," I mumbled. "I think I need to lie back down ..." I tried to stand but struggled to find my feet.

"There, there," soothed Isabel. "You need to recover your strength. Why don't you eat some more?"

I stared down at the stew. Memories of some of Grammy's tales bubbled to the surface, reminding me of poisoned meals for unwary travelers. "No, I'm quite full."

"Enough!" screeched Ada, interrupting.

"No more games," growled Tabitha.

Eden eyed me hungrily. "I'm starving."

Isabel rose from her chair, "Fine. If he won't eat the sleeping powder, we'll do this the hard way." Advancing on me, her mouth fell open and for the first time I saw her teeth. Even against her pale face, they shone bright white, two of them extending long past the others and ending in unbelievably sharp points. I scrambled to get out of the chair, but my leaden reflexes caused my feet to tangle with the chair legs and I fell sprawling on my back. Isabel loomed above me, and I was certain I was a goner when I finally heard Mr. Jensen speak.

"No. I can't do this anymore." He rose and stood over me, as if to try to shield me from her. "I've been silent for too long; He's barely more than a boy and I won't let you hurt him."

Isabel laughed throatily. "You think you can stop me, you weak man?" She backhanded him across the face and he went flying across the room. Her strength was incredible. Mr. Jensen crashed into a wall and slid down in a heap. In the blink of an eye, she was on him, raising a hand high. Her fingers now ended in vicious claws and she slashed down at him, opening up long wounds across his chest and belly. "I'll deal with you later," she growled, then stalked her way back to me.

In the meantime, Ada, Eden, and Tabitha lifted me with no more effort than it would take to hold a rag doll. I struggled feebly in their iron grips as Isabel approached.

"My sister-wives and I are hungry," she purred. "Usually, we have to hunt for our meals, but you heard our song and came practically to our doorstep."

Taking one of her impossibly long nails, Isabel flicked it down my neck, opening a cut that welled up with blood. She licked her talon and shuddered in delight. Her mouth opened wide, and I swear her fangs lengthened. "Time to feast," Isabel declared, looming as the others' grips on me tightened.

Suddenly, there was a loud thud and the front door smashed in.

"Drop him, you undead harlots!" thundered a voice.

I looked past Isabel to see the hunters entering the house, polished wooden stakes brandished in their hands. Isabel spun around and shrieked, while the others hissed and dropped me unceremoniously to the floor. The men charged in, stakes raised, each singling out a woman and attacking with coordinated precision.

The women rushed to meet them with extraordinary speed and grappled the interlopers with freakish strength. Something pricked the back of my mind; I recalled another one of Grammy's stories about creatures with pale skin, unnatural strength and speed, and a lust for blood.

Vampires!

The tall Indian fought with Tabitha, while Ada slashed at the white man, who narrowly dodged the attack. The shorter Indian had Eden pinned to a wall, and right in front of me, Isabel struggled with the Negro man. He lifted the stake high, but Isabel grabbed his wrist and wrenched it sideways. With her other hand, she circled the man's throat and lifted him off the floor. She laughed evilly as her hand tightened to choke the life out of him. The other men were still occupied; no one else could help him. I had to do something!

I racked my brain. What had been the weakness of these creatures in those stories? In a flash, I recalled it: symbols of faith could harm a vampire.

I leapt to my feet, pulling the gris-gris out from under my shirt, and lunged at Isabel's back. As I pressed the bag against her neck, it sizzled on her skin as if I had touched her with a poker from the fire.

Isabel's scream was ear-splitting, and everyone else froze as I stepped back. Her hands pawed at her neck, and she spun to face me, mouth gaping. As she moved to strike me, the point of a wooden stake pushed its way out of her chest. The Negro man had recovered and struck true once her back was turned. She tried to speak, but no sound came out as she collapsed to the ground.

Ada, Eden, and Tabitha all wailed in anguish, and the hunters took advantage of their distraction to thrust a stake into each of them.

The battle was over as suddenly as it began. The men collected themselves for a moment before piling the bodies in the center of the room. One went out the door and came back with a metal canister. He sloshed some liquid over the vampires. The scent of kerosene assaulted my nostrils.

In the comparative quiet that followed, punctuated only by the sloshing of the canister, I heard a muted sobbing and ragged breathing from against the wall. Mr. Jensen was still crumpled where he had fallen, his long, jagged wounds oozing blood and some of his guts spilling to the floor. His pale face was tight with pain as he weakly beckoned me over. I knelt beside him, unsure of any way I could help.

"I'm sorry, boy," he panted. "I never should have brought you here. I thought I could protect you, but I was wrong."

I gingerly took his hand in mine, trying to give some minor comfort. "Way I see it, after hitting my head, I would have died out in the wilderness if you hadn't found me. At least here I had a fighting chance."

Mr. Jensen nodded slightly, tears streaming from his eyes. "I really did love them, all of them. And I think they loved me, at least before…" he paused, gasping in pain. "When that stranger attacked Isabel and she took ill, I was terrified of losing her. When she sat up from the coffin at the funeral, I thought it was a miracle. I was too blind to see the truth, though our neighbors did and cast us out for it. Even after it was obvious what she became, I thought I could still save her soul. Instead, she made my other wives like her; monsters who craved blood."

He coughed, and it was a horrid, rattling sound. Blood trickled down from the corner of his mouth and I sensed he was not long for this world. "At first, I tried to keep them sated with animal blood," he whispered hoarsely, "but eventually they wanted more. They began to pick off stragglers from the trails, or lost miners. I pretended to myself that they only chose wicked men, but in truth I don't know if that was so. When I found you out there, I couldn't leave you to die, but I also feared what would happen when I brought you here. I was right to be concerned." His eyes fell shut and he coughed again; it was heavy and wet. His strength seemed just about to fail him.

Finished with their grisly work, the other men had gathered silently behind me. The Negro man cleared his throat and said, "We're almost finished, son; time to go."

"Isn't there something you can do for him?" I pleaded, gesturing to the dying man.

"'Fraid not," he replied gently. "He's too far gone, and we can't risk him turning as well."

"It's alright," Mr. Jensen said weakly. "If I can beg a boon: please lay me with my wives. I could not save their lives, but at least let me be with them in death."

The hunters looked at each other for a moment, and each nodded slightly in assent. They lifted Mr. Jensen up with surprising care and gently carried him to the piled bodies, laying him on the floor beside them. The dying man whispered, "Thank you," and then went still.

The shorter Indian pulled a large box of matches from a pocket and shook a few out. He passed one to each of his compatriots. My eyes went wide as I understood what they were about to do.

"You mean to burn them?" I cried.

The taller Indian nodded gravely. "Fire has great cleansing power. It will purify any remaining evil that may linger in this place."

Each man struck his match in turn and tossed it on the bodies. The kerosene blossomed immediately into flames, which quickly spread. The Negro man steered me towards the open door, with the rest of the men close behind. We were barely outside before the fire reached the roof and the entire house was ablaze.

Mesmerized by the conflagration, I stared, trying to make sense of all that had happened. The white man pulled a flask out of a wagon, which had been pulled up nearby, and took a sip before passing it around to his companions. When it came back to him, he held it out to me. "It's been your lucky night," he commented. "Want a sasp?"

I stared at him a moment, then took the flask and drank deep. Immediately, I regretted it, as fiery liquid threatened to close my throat. I spluttered, then gasped for breath. The men chuckled with paternal amusement.

When I could finally speak again, I asked, "How did you find me?"

"We saw your mule tied up at your camp by the creek while looking for our quarry," the short Indian explained. I glanced over and saw Molly tethered to the far side of their wagon. "It didn't take long to track you here. We soon realized you had been taken to the very lair of the monsters we were hunting, so we knew we had to act quickly."

I took a deep breath as tears began to fill my eyes. "You have already done so much for me, but I need to ask more." Word spilled out as I described my father's foray into mining and his failure to return home, as well as my certainty I had heard him cry for help in the nearby hills. "I tried to look for him, but I don't think I can do it alone."

The shorter Indian pulled a stake out of the burlap sack, tossing it in his hand. "The boy's father makes the best hunting gear I've seen," he said. "We can't just leave him lost."

As the men all nodded in agreement, the Negro clapped his hand on my shoulder. "Let's go find your father."

THE WATER MAN

by Dwain Campbell

Psychiatrists are scarce as whiskers on a frog along this Newfoundland shore. Just as well, or I would be chugging Thorazine in my Maxwell House coffee.

It is that damned Tsunami Dream. Upgrade dream to night terror, 9.9 on the Edgar Allan Poe Scale.

It begins with sickening anxiety, experienced by my astral Self as I write lesson plans at the kitchen table. Then follows a building thunder, a relentless, palpable whoosh, and as I rise in panic the old house suddenly shakes as though hit by a Howitzer shell. Boards shatter and splinter, and my dream self is certain the woodshed has given way. Wresting open the kitchen door, I am knocked over by sea water violently frothing over the doorsill. Cod heads, rotten seaweed, and severed squid tentacles are flotsam in the slime green torrent. Instantly, the wave is chest high, and lethal, preternatural cold shoots through me. Cardiac arrest is instant, and I choke my last.

I thrash awake in the upstairs bedroom. Anemic sunbeams slant through the seaward window, doing little to warm my icebox sleeping chamber.

Bloody hell. I am a basket case.

I want to stay in bed. I don't want to get up. God help me.

However, it is Monday morning, and my sick days are gone. Migraine headaches have chewed them up.

I swing legs out of bed, gasping at the sharp chill. Despite two pairs of wool socks, my feet are icicles. Is that the answer, Dr. Freud? My subconscious registers frozen feet, and texts a wacko nightmare to alert me of the fact? Pop psychologist I am not. I shuffle into seal skin slippers and make for the bathroom and warmth. Poor as a church mouse, I can only afford to heat rooms with water pipes. Still, a Saudi sheik couldn't heat this rattle trap house. Bird nests have more insulation.

My breath hangs in the air. Lovely.

Indifferent shower. Cup of tepid coffee. Egg sandwich, yolk dripping everywhere. The sum of my life.

Well, not quite. I teach history and geography, plus a slew of boring veg courses, at Bear Harbor Collegiate. Add academic grade 11 math, because I am the only free teacher in that schedule slot. Honestly, I don't know the ratio Pi from pumpkin pie, but that is not the point. *A teacher is a teacher, and if I assign you brain surgery, you'll teach it.* So threatens my principal, an unthinking bureaucrat who would have been happy counting heads at Auschwitz,

I exit the ancient, paint peeling house at the end of Pippy Lane. Ice crunches under LL Beans as I gingerly mince to my aging Ford Ranger, crossing fingers that the fickle heater will work this morning. It does, and the defrost wheezes as I laboriously chip thick ice from the windshield.

Atlantic waters heave onto a nearby beach, and I see shore boulders are banded with ice. This, in early May. And you wonder why I am a depressed? Back home in the Maritimes girls are wearing sundresses, cows graze on lush green pastures, and the trees have actual bloody leaves. Here spring is two months late, if it decides to come at all.

A school bus stop is at the end of my driveway, and I survey the scene to make sure kindergarteners are clear of the road. They are, most out in the field intently stomping ice-covered tussocks of grass. The older ones are shivering beside the wooden Lion's Club bus shelter while hypnotically studying cellphones. I wait a sec to crank a few more blessed British Thermal Units out of the engine before I literally get in gear.

One munchkin totters close to a rickety, derelict fishing shed that juts from a seaside overhang. I roll down my window to bellow a warning, but an unlikely rescuer appears to grab the lost lamb by the scruff of her coat and bodily drag her back to the roadside. Unlikely, for it is the reprobate Cody Hennessey, voted by teachers as Most Likely to be Busted for Dealing Drugs. He looks the part: white hoodie patterned by rolling dice, jeans that are belted bellow his rump, a dome hat complete with hologram on the rim, and a gold chain that Tupac would envy. It is a damning indictment on Canadian culture that most of our teenagers aspire to be South Philly gangsta hoodlums.

The teacher in me instinctively thinks he should be praised. I stop by the bus shelter and call out. "Hey Cody. Good job getting the mite away from the drop off." I add a cordial thumbs up for emphasis.

Manifestly bored, he merely shrugs and mutters, "Whatever, Bro. Don't feed the Water Man. Everybody knows that, sure." Eyes, hidden by funky sunglasses, immediately return to his phone.

Water Man? After last night, any mention of water jangles my nerves. I dismiss the cryptic comment as usual teenage gibberish.

It is a steep climb out of the cove and onto the South Shore highway. It is a fifteen-minute drive south to school, time enough for a couple of tunes on the Classic Rock station. CCR is running through the jungle, *at least they are warm*, and the Rolling Stones want an emotional rescue. If they get one, I hope they send it on to me next.

Self-pity deepens when I arrive at the Collegiate and remember I am on supervision. *Monday, Monday, can't trust that day.*

With busses rolling in, I position myself on the crumbling sidewalk between parking lot and school. Good thing I am switched on, because my duty partner is busily collecting gobs of ice-snow in a mason jar.

"What's up with the jar, Miss?" In Newfoundland, all female teachers, however old, are 'Miss'.

Mrs. O'Malley, high school English teacher and guru of all local wisdom and gossip, rises from her stoop with much effort. "May snow, grand for eye ailments. You Come From Aways are lore deficient."

"Bubble, bubble, toil and trouble, add a dash of May snow?" With her wild, iron gray curls and ruddy Irish face, she could pass for a Macbeth witch quite handily.

O'Malley grins, but her eyes follow a file of lethargic middle schoolers as they sleepily shuffle off Bus Six. Mondays are usually sedate until recess.

Font of local knowledge, is she? "Miss, who is the Water Man?"

"Whoa. Where did that come from this morning?" Plain to see she is nonplussed, for a moment at least.

"Cody Hennessey said, "Don't feed the Water Man."

She grunts. "Cody lives in Tea Cove, yeah? You too?"

I nod affirmative. "Live in the rambling old Pippy House, at the end of Pippy Lane."

"They did tell of a Water Man there, decades ago. These are creatures of lore and legend, shuffling anthropomorphic aquamen who lurk beneath fishing stages. They snatch unsuspecting children and carry them off beneath the sea." Bus Eight kids are a bit more raucous, but we scowl in tandem, and they settle before entering the school. "Undoubtedly an old wives' tale, to keep youngsters off unsafe fishing stages."

"Right," I say, absurdly relieved at this prosaic explanation.

"Still, some say it was a Water Man that drove the Chance Cove people away. They suddenly packed up *en masse*, went to St. John's, and booked passage to Boston. Not a soul returned, so the story goes."

"Some say," I observe dubiously,

"So the story goes," she repeats a tad stubbornly.

That does nothing to cheer my glum mood. The Water Man. Great.

The last bus pulls away, the 8:50 a.m., bell rings, and it is time to earn my pay. The day passes in usual ho-hum fashion, with not a hint of color or excitement to commend it. Even my lesson on the Holocaust fails to excite interest beyond morbid questions on SS execution techniques which, sad to say, fall far short of the gore-shock kids watch on *Saw*,

Hostel, and *Hannibal* movies. We live in a sick world. The only bright spot is the persistent drip-drop of melting ice as May sun takes feeble hold.

The last bell rings. No teams to coach, no program planning meetings, no Social Studies Department conclaves. I'm out of there like a shot.

One stop on the way to Pippy Lane. I pick up a humongous bottle of white wine at the Ferryland Liquor Express. The young female clerk eyes me, probably thinking I should man up and get a case of beer like 99 percent of Baymen would. I mutter about being invited out to dinner, to protect my fragile masculinity, but the truth is I am self-medicating vino style. I will answer the wave in the Tsunami Dream with a counter-wave of Gallo Family wine, and if the Water Man shows up, I'll clock him over the head with the empty bottle.

There are hours of daylight left when I make Pippy Lane. The whine of chainsaws come from several backyards, so there are men about. This puts a little steel in my spine, and instead of directly entering the house, I impulsively cross the narrow field, mostly gone to rose bushes and young dogberry trees, and inspect the ramshackle fishing shed. From a discreet distance, of course.

The abandoned, tottering shed is in complete disrepair. Only a few flakes of rust-red paint have survived the decades, and the windows are boarded up with mildewed plywood. Moss grows slime green on the shingles, the remnants of a stove pipe is holed with rust, and the rickety wooden pier itself, held aloft by a wildly canting log scaffold, is missing half its slats. The vicinity is redolent with the scents of tar, rotting nets, and thick mats of kelp that have collected under the stage. This place is an accident waiting to happen, and it is a wonder no Halloween arsonist has torched it.

My imagination is obscene. For the Water Man to stand beneath the stage and snatch a child on the pier, he would have to be eight feet tall.

Chainsaws cease wailing. I look up to see three men intently watching me. Their posture is tense, pure fight or flight. Such scrutiny freaks me out. *Take a picture, why don't you?* I pretend not to notice them and sashay to my house with forced nonchalance.

First chore on my evening agenda is to get the parlor woodstove going. The pipes are cleaned regularly, so I use cotton balls soaked in Vaseline and birch bark to flash start a fire of thick poplar branches. Fire crackles madly, and I will nurse the mini-inferno throughout the evening.

I get three electric kettles boiling. If the Pentagon knew of the WMD biohazard fermenting in my dirty underwear basket, it would call in a preemptive airstrike. So, for half an hour I run steaming kettles into the woodshed attached to the kitchen and fill up a porcelain wash basin. By and by I dump smelly underclothes into the sink and add Sunlight dish soap since I am too bloody lazy to buy detergent. I stir the lot with a sawed-off broom handle until the water looks positively murky, then hang each offending garment on a twine clothesline, there to drip onto the dirt floor.

Work done. Time for proper boozing. Dressed in two pairs of pajama pants, umpteen pairs of wool socks, and a bulky St. Mary's University hoodie, I flop into an ancient armchair that could easily be a prop on *Downton Abbey*. That thought prompts me toward Netflix. I settle on a mindless martial arts movie with subtitles.

At first, I take the yipping to be the wailing of Kung Fu masters on the screen. Then I realize the barking, if I can call it that, comes from outside. I mute the TV, and yes, by God, it sounds like an orca choking on a bone.

I cautiously peer out the living room window, rapidly deducing that the noise is coming from the ominous fishing shed. It is twilight, and a feeble purple-yellow glow bruises the western horizon. This chancy light silhouettes the shed and decrepit pier. I see no yodeling dogs, or coyotes, which is the next possibility that comes to mind.

There is a godawful splash, but I see nothing. A seal in distress?

Down the lane a screen door bangs open. The walls are paper thin, I hear everything. "Git, you goddamn thing. I'll shoot your effing head off, you gets up over that bank. You took me Great Aunt Sally in the Big War, and you'll nab no more of us." It's Mrs. Clancy, three sheets into the wind, not unusual. However, she usually drinks at her kitchen table and never says boo. This is a tirade, a scene right out of *Cops*. I kill the lights and rush to a window that affords a view of the Clancy yard, not a scenic landscape given the several cannibalized snowmobiles strewn about. Holy jeez, Mrs. Clancy is violently waving a 12 gauge, and menfolk are sensibly well back as they try to coax the weapon off her.

Eventually she surrenders her ordnance, and is clearly weeping as they lead her inside, out of the dank twilight.

I listen hard for several minutes. Nothing more from the shoreline.

Freaked out and scared sober, I double check all doors and windows. Pippy House secured, I beat a retreat upstairs to my bedroom, which I stock with a baseball bat, a butcher knife, and my wine bottle. Once I wrestle my steamer trunk full of books across the door, I quick-glance under the bed to make sure the chamber pot is in place. Not much of a fortress, and I brood on this and the oppressive patter of cold rain that troubles the shingles above me.

I'm not stupid. Is there a connection between the Tsunami Dream and the Water Man? Good God, I'm talking about them like they are real. Maybe the only commonality is my psychotic brain.

Anxiety wars with ethanol, but I make darned good and sure ethanol wins. My last coherent though is that I'm going to be facing a hundred youngsters tomorrow with the Mother of All Hangovers.

At some point in my sleep, I find myself standing on the shore, quite near the old fishing stage. At first, I am buoyed, for the Tsunami Dream never starts like this. In fact, it's a sunny day, and the Royal Blue cove is placid. As a matter of fact, the cove is pristine and idyllic, and I now see that the shed is not a junk heap any longer. In this dream, it is in full repair, sound in every respect.

"I'm the tiniest Billy Goat Gruff, that's who I am!"

A little girl in a red gingham dress has materialized on the now solid, well-maintained pier. Definitely a preschooler, she is on her tummy, looking down beneath the stage. "You won't get me, Mister Troll," she giggles.

From afar, seventy years distant, I hear "Sally. Supper is ready, you comes the once. Saaaaallly!"

Now I feel fear. Like an axe buried in my gut. I try to move, or cry out, but sometimes one can't do squat in dreams.

Sally lifts her head. She makes it to her hands and knees. Then a great limb —tentacle? —sweeps her off the stage. A fraction of a second and Sally is gone. She didn't even cry out.

I'm stunned. Yet I am instantly by the fishing shed, desperately looking under the pier. Nothing.

Not even salt water.

I blink, and the water level in the cove drops a meter. The water is receding toward the ocean, leaving fish to helplessly flounder on suddenly exposed mudflats and slimy boulders.

I've taught enough geography to know what is happening. Sure enough, three miles out there is a curling wave as tall and solid as the Great Wall of China. My gibbering dream-mind knows I have but minutes.

Tidal wave. Tsunami.

I sprint, but in nightmares one simply runs on the spot. Or wildly falls, as I do countless times trying to make Pippy House, a mere 100 meters away. The wave-thunder grows, as does my abject terror, but I am no closer to the house. The rumble reaches a horrible crescendo, and then, quite suddenly, I am in the house and frantically scrambling up the stairs on all fours. I do not make the landing.

A Hiroshima blast wracks the house, tears it off the stone foundation. Windows implode, and putrid, briny sewage roils into the lower floors. It is a sea witch's brew of detached gull wings, seal entrails, and malformed, eyeless crabs. The skull of some long-drowned sailor, carried on the brackish flood, careens off rose-print wallpaper and snags on a brass coat hook. A half-rotted ship's figurehead of a Saracen maid, breasts covered in barnacles, wedges in the gaping front door. The stench is grotesque, like the offal bin of a fish plant left out in the hot sun, and I want to vomit…

…onto the bedroom floor. In groggy half-sleep I scramble to find the chamber pot. I retch in absolute misery, and only afterward do I realize my brain is figuratively dribbling out of my ears.

God, I am running grossly late. Wash out mouth with Listerine. Run a fork through hair, can't find a comb. And throw on yesterday's rumpled clothes. Guzzle three Extra Strength Motrin—better make that four. Crawl into the Ranger and pray I do not have enough alcohol in my system for a DUI.

With that frightening thought in mind, I creep extra slow past the bus stop. Unusually, there are about ten grim-faced mothers in attendance, each tightly gripping the hand of a youngster.

Don't feed the Water Man.

I reach the coastal highway. For a second, I contemplate turning right and running for the Nova Scotia ferry and home. However, if I burn the School District like that I will never teach again. I wheel left for Bear Harbor Collegiate.

Welcome to the worst day of my life. Not only do I look like an extra from *The Walking Dead*, but I can't even talk without my head pounding. I show Youtube videos all day.

Humiliation is icing on the cake. Before I can slink from my classroom at 3:15 p.m., Mrs. O'Malley breezes in. "A word, if I may?

"Well, I'm kind of in a…"

"Mess. The buzz never made it to the guidance counsellor or principal, but I caught it. The kids smelled booze on you."

"Ouch."

"And frankly, your pallor is whiter than a trout's belly. You know, we do have an Employee Assistance Program." Forward though she is, O'Malley neglects to name me an alcoholic, head case, or both at once. However, the implication hangs in the air. Truth to tell, I've pondered my sanity without her prompting.

"Right," I sigh heavily, having no energy for protest or pretense. "I'll do up some lesson plans for a substitute and take a sick day with doctor's note." She nods but doesn't move. "And phone the EAP Coordinator."

Suddenly brighter, she observes, "It's what we pay union dues for". I think that is the end, but she continues. "I grew up on this shore. The Tea Cove people are nervous. It's not a great spot to be for someone with, you know, low voltage mental health issues. Maybe you should spend the night in a St. John's hotel."

"Maybe," I grunt noncommittally. What a rotten day. At least O'Malley can hold her tongue. If my students tell tales over the supper table, there may be several angry moms banging on my classroom door tomorrow. That's a huge incentive to book off sick.

In a half hour, I am back in Tea Cove. If tumbleweeds were blowing up the lanes, I would call it a ghost town. The yards are empty, though one or two curtains part to allow furtive observation as I idle through to Pippy Lane. Oddly, horseshoes have sprouted on gates which are also adorned with hexing dogberry branches that sport frozen, wizened berries.

Welcome to *The Blair Witch Project*, Newfoundland edition.

The Tsunami Dream and Water Man are clearly linked and accelerating. It's all psychological. The weird actions of my neighbors have been registered by my primordial subconscious. which is now serving up horror stories at night.

The ol' credit card is maxed out. My bank account is empty as a root cellar in March. Still, I do have a VISA Gift card from my grandparents, which is my Zombie Apocalypse getaway fund. The Tsunami Dream and the mythic Water Man superstition are no apocalypse, but ah hell, maybe they're worse. Best bet is I clean up, dart into St. John's for a cheapo room in an airport hotel, and get my head examined in the morning.

So, I get all the kettles boiling, to prime the bath for the lukewarm trickle from the ancient water heater. At Christmas someone put some cheesy-girly bath salts in my stocking, and I sprinkle them in the tub because I feel as scuzzy as I look. The foam is an evergreen color, and the scent is minty. I lock all the doors, put on some light Jazz, and light a few candles. Ready at last, I ease into the blessed scalding bath water, one 'Oh yeah' at a time.

Once fully immersed, last night's sleeplessness catches up with me. Utterly relaxed, my breathing slows to a contented whisper, and a slow track by Natalie Cole has me somnolent, nodding. Candle flames dance like faraway angels.

In this state I must have kicked out the plug. A liquid gurgle alerts me, but my body feels like a million kilograms of deadweight. It's like some old hag is sitting on my chest. The water level in the tub drops several centimeters, and now I can make out the beginnings of a whirlpool over the drain. And in the swirl, face down, are the figures of children no larger than finger puppets. One wears a red gingham dress.

One horrified gasp, one panicked heave, and I managed to slosh into a sitting position. The bath suds have turned to cloying algae, thick with eels winding about my legs.

I cry out, but Pippy House is a long way from any help.

Now the drain whirlpool is rapidly growing. The hypnotic, Kaleidoscopic maelstrom starts to suck me under. I flail at the sides of the tub, but the metal is soft like sea bottom mud.

And then, a webbed, clawed hand lunges from the whirlpool eye, and catches my ankle like a shark bite. I scream, but dirty, foul seawater clogs my mouth and nostrils.

*****

"He drowned in his own bathtub? Just like that? No explanation."

"That's what my sister said." O'Malley's sister, a secretary in the Medical Examiner's office, did not have confidentiality in her vocabulary. "No drugs, no brain tumors, no foul play, according to the Mounties."

The principal sourly shook his balding head. "Well, all I know is we have Public Examinations in a month, and an emergency social studies teacher who doesn't know Albania from Argentina. We're doomed."

Your blunt soul is doomed. O'Malley stepped to the corner office window and surveyed the dark Atlantic. She pursed lips.

There is more in Heaven, Earth, and the Deeps than is dreamt of in your philosophy, Mr. Principal.

<u>HER PIECES AND PARTS</u>

by Donna J. W. Munro

Back in the early 1800s, Molly Crenshaw sold spells, bits of hair knotted around willow bark and salves to sooth a bad tooth, out of her clabber shack on the edge of French Town in Saint Charles. Her dark skin and black eyes didn't frighten the mostly white customers. Her religion did.

"Molly," one man said, clutching his love potion to his vested chest, pale face hectic with red splotches on his cheeks, "you gon' get y'self hung one day."

She wore the white of voodoo priesthood to serve them, dress miraculously clean though she'd just cut the head off a chicken and danced with the spirit of an Orisha to make his vial of love vital enough to catch the pretty widow woman on Bayard Street. All her customers said the same and Molly Crenshaw nodded when they did, but she kept at it. She'd come from Haiti, escaped slavery, and settled in the village that hugged the Missouri River, making her trade all she could. Wasn't much else for a freed woman without means or a master to do. Besides, she liked that they needed her to bless their crops or protect their barges with chicken foot charms.

"I gon' pray, sife, for you and the widow," Molly said, bowing her head and waiting for the man to leave.

She'd seen her death and knew it was coming, but she'd be damned if she wouldn't be herself right through the end. The Orishas made a promise to Molly as she spun in the sifted dirt, feet stamping to a tune only she could hear.

"Lemme stay me," she'd pray around the spirits riding her as she worked, "make me stay powerful, and make me rise again."

The Orishas, unable to save her, promised her those, each one.

When the spring floods came with tornadoes and hailstones, the crops of Saint Charles drowned and splintered in the muddy fields. Folks cast about, praying at church, wringing their hands, but nothing could be done to save the harvest. Worry turns to anger and anger to hate like a diamond in your belly. Hate like that has to go somewhere or it cuts you to pieces.

The people of Saint Charles turned on poor Molly Crenshaw, marching up in her yard with a rope already tied in the thirteen loops of a hangman's noose made for witches like her. In the yard, her crooked catalpa tree clinked with hanging duppy bottles going "clank-clink" in the winds' breath.

"Clank-clink" as they throw the rope over the branch.

"I didn't curse no crops, Mazora. I did nought but good for you folk," Molly said, creole lilt strained in fear as they dragged her out of her clabber-sided house into her yard.

But the lynch mob heard nothing of her true words. They just wanted her blood to quench the hate in their bellies.

"String her up."

"Stretch her witch neck!"

"Clank-clink" as they cinch it tight around her neck.

None but her death would satisfy them.

As they put the rope around her neck, she grit down her teeth and lifted her arms, just as the Orisha taught her. "I rise again if you kill me. The Orishas promise me rise."

A woman in the back fainted away and a man cursed the name of the Redeemer. The sky lit with a bolt of truth, making the dogs howl and horses twitch and whinny. Was a sign, sure as anything.

"Cover her mouth," they said, "so she'll not curse us."

But the cursing didn't need saying.

Molly didn't scream when the rope went taunt and her feet kicked looking for the ground. She struggled and her bottles clashed, singing their sad song loud. As they clattered, her eyes made promises to all the folks. They knew she'd rise if she could. Once the bottles' "clank-clink" only sounded because of the wind, the mob cut her down. They knew she'd rise if she could, so they cut her into little pieces and shoved them into the duppy bottles from the crooked tree. They buried the biggest part of her right there under the tree, then took the bottles home to bury in yards, far away from each other.

They say the bottles didn't stay put. That they move each night, under the ground, making their way to the crooked tree.

Molly's still Molly. Molly is powerful. Molly's gonna rise again.

*****

In the fullness of time, Molly's murder faded to a story that older brothers told to scare their twerpy kid sisters or annoying baby brothers too stupid to deal with.

"Molly," they'd say with brutal leers on their faces, "is burrowing through the black dirt back to the crooked catalpa tree," they all knew still leaned on the iron crutches the town had given.

"Molly's grave didn't need any headstone," they'd say, "because the tree weeps her name in the wind and the bottles "clank-clink" still echoes through the branches."

Local teens rode bikes to the fenced in tree and on a dare, they chanted Molly's name.

"Molly Crenshaw, Molly Crenshaw!" But they'd never climb over the pointed iron fence. Something about the space, the air around the tree, steamed with warning that no little kid can ignore. But older kids always wound up on the bad side of Molly Crenshaw.

*****

Jake and Will took their girlfriends to Molly's grave one night to scare the girls into their arms. But the girls just seemed bored.

"Jake, this is dumb. Take me home," Lily said, pushing her long hair out of her face. The wind whipped fluttering threads into her mouth. They'd been staring at the crooked tree for a half hour with the boys telling Molly's story in voices that echoed between them.

Kimmy rolled her eyes in annoyance. "Yeah, I'm cold."

Will, not ready to let the girls win this, hopped over the fence into the overgrown grass skirting the crooked tree. The wind puffed up around him and wind chimes tinkled in the distance, but Will sneered at them still safe on the other side of the fence.

"Come on, Jake. I dare you!" He said, backing into the mist, words weaving with the foggy breath of the night.

"Don't do it." Lily grabbed Jake's arm and pulled him back, wide eyes watching Will fade into the fog.

Kimmy clung to the fence. "Will!" She whispered loudly, but the "clack-clink" noise drowned out her call. Jake shook off Lily's hand.

He jumped over the fence and turned to Kimmy and Lily, "We'll be back." Then he walked into the fog chasing after Will's echoing call.

"Clack-clink, clack-clink, clack-clink" filled the air in his wake, ringing in Kimmy and Lily's ears so loud they covered them and shrank to the ground, clutching each other. Around them the air swirled with Molly's name, Jake's pained grunts, and Will's gurgling screams.

*****

The next morning, a pair of kids on bikes came by wanting to scare themselves silly calling Molly's name at the crooked tree. They found the girls there, hugged together with eyes squeezed shut, blue skin, mouths hanging open, scared to death. And on either side of them, the boys lay folded on the fence points, flapping sheets on a line.

END

According to local legend, Molly Crenshaw, voodoo priestess and freed slave of Caribbean descent, lived in St. Charles, Missouri. For a time, the town came to Crenshaw for her charms and spells. Severe weather ruined the harvest, so the people of St. Charles blamed Molly. An angry mob lynched Molly, and to prevent her from rising, cut her into pieces and buried them war apart from each other. Old timers say anyone who stands on her grave and calls her name will wind up dead.

<u>PICTURE THIS...</u>

by Kevin Patrick McCann

It was a soft morning. There'd been a light drizzle first thing but then that had blown inland and now there was a breeze, a few clouds and the beginnings of a warming sun. The sand dunes were deserted. Joseph took off his knapsack, sat down amongst the clumps of marram grass, lit a cigarette and looked out to sea. The tide was going out and dozens of seagulls were swooping and screeching along the tideline. There were plenty of pickings. Small crabs trapped in suddenly sand locked pools, starfish, lugworms. As a child he'd found the thought of all those little deaths would reduce him to a sobbing flailing mess. Now he watched with detached indifference; during the eighteen months he'd survived in France before getting the whiff of mustard gas that saw him eventually Honourably Discharged, he'd seen far, far worse and felt little or nothing.

Unlike so many of the others he'd shared a ward with during his time in hospital, he was never troubled with nightmares. He just found he couldn't speak. They'd tried giving him electric shocks and he'd endured session after session until they finally gave up. His lungs were damaged anyway so he was discharged and advised to live on the coast.

"The sea air will help," they'd said before thanking him for his service and packing him off to civvie street.

He finished his cigarette, stubbed it out in the sand, stood up and stretched. He listened to the seagulls' wailings. When he was a child his Grandad had told him seagulls carried the souls of drowned sailors keening for dry land so every night when he knelt down to say his prayers, he would ask the Holy Virgin to set them free and let them go home.

He took out his pocket watch. Six-thirty a.m. The Grocer's would be open by now and he needed tea and milk. He set off back through the dunes until he reached the road back into Mere Ends. It led to the Mermaid Inn and a row of shops. He went into the Grocer's and as he got to the counter, produced a small slate and a piece of chalk from his knapsack.

The Grocer smiled and said, "Morning Mr. Toomes. What can I get you?"

Joseph wrote QUARTER TEA PINT MILK PLEASE on his slate and passed it across the counter.

The Grocer smiled again and as he weighed out the tea said, "Nice morning." Joseph nodded, smiled back, got his milk and tea, paid and left as quickly as possible. On the way back to his cottage he met several locals. They all wished him a *Good Morning* and he nodded and managed a smile in return but nobody attempted to engage him in conversation. They were all far too tactful for that.

Once he was back at the cottage, he'd opened the living-room window, made a pot of tea, half-filled a glass jar with water and then sat down at the desk in the corner of his living-room and stared down at the blank sheet of paper that stared back up at him. He opened his case of watercolours, selected a brush, took a sip of his tea and leaned back into silence. An hour went by and his tea (forgotten) when he finally moved again and took a sip, was cold. He drank it anyway.

Outside the morning drifted by. He could still hear (faintly) the seagulls calling and below that (even more faintly) somebody singing. He couldn't make out any words but the melody was maddeningly familiar. It was a simple enough tune and after he'd heard it repeated just three times, began whistling softly in harmony. It got louder. He responded by whistling louder. A breeze gusted in through his open living-room window and blew his still blank sheet of paper onto the floor. As he bent down to pick it up, an even stronger gust followed and the room darkened. He went over to close the window and could see it was clearly clouding over.

There was a flash of lightning and he began counting. He'd got as far as seven when there was a clap of thunder. He waited. There was another flash of lightning and he began counting again. This time he only got as far as three. Big storm and moving in fast. The wind was getting stronger too. His living room was now as dark as twilight and the thunder clapped again as rain began hammering down. It was so heavy that the spinney at the end of a field opposite his house faded as if enveloped by fog.

It rained for the rest of the day but he was inside and dry so really didn't mind. He'd planned to take the ferry over to Fleeton and visit the Bank but that could wait until tomorrow. The rain gradually eased to a light drizzle and about ten that night finally stopped altogether.

Next morning was bright and fair. He'd slept deeply the night before and only had the vaguest recollection of dreaming…something about the sea and somebody singing.

He made tea and toast but then found the toast was dry in his mouth and he couldn't swallow. The tea tasted vaguely salty so he left that too and decided to head down to the landing stage and get an early ferry across the bay. There were only three other passengers. They all nodded, wished him a *Good Morning* and then went back to their own studied silences. He paid, boarded, and went over to the Port bow and leaned against the rail. There was a light breeze, a clear sky, and a calm sea so once they set off, the crossing was smooth. A dozen seagulls hovered and swooped just a few yards off their bow; they were close enough for him to catch a glimpse of silver every time one of them caught some of the mackerel that'd come in with the tide to feed.

But then as one of them swooped down, something white that moved at the speed of a blur pulled it under. The rest of the seagulls scattered screeching as the tail and fin of some huge fish curved above the surface and then disappeared just as quickly.

Nature red in tooth and claw, he thought to himself as the ferry docked. He disembarked, made his way to the bank, drew out some cash and then wandered up to the twice weekly market. He bought himself some local potatoes, half a pound of cheese and some eggs. He was about to head back to the ferry when he noted a new stall selling bric-a-brac: second hand books, phonograph records, "as new" plates and cutlery. A bored looking man (who was clearly the stall holder) glanced across at him and said, "Feel free to browse sir; no obligation."

Joseph nodded and was about to walk on when he noticed a small framed picture of about six inches by six, behind some mugs. He lifted it out for a closer look. It was a watercolour of a young woman; or rather the head and shoulders of a young woman. Her hair was blonde, her lips extraordinarily red and her eyes a very bright shade of blue. It was a long way from being good; on the other hand, it wasn't bad either. He could maybe copy it or better still, take it as a starting point for a new series of pictures of his own.

He turned it over to see if there was a price tag on the back. Nothing so he got out his slate, wrote *how much?* and then held it up for the stallholder.

The man made a great show of thinking about it so Joseph shrugged, put the picture back and half-turned turned as if to walk away.

"All right," said the man, "to you, sir, just two pounds."

Joseph shook his head and wrote *Ten shillings* on his slate.

The man affected an expression of outrage and said, "Fifteen and not a farthing less!"

Joseph shook his head and pointed back to the ten shillings written on his slate.

"You drive hard bargain. Tell you what, let's split the difference and call it twelve bob."

Joseph shook his head and under the ten shillings on his slate wrote *war veteran*.

The stall holder nodded thoughtfully. "Same here," he said. "Boer War." He paused again, scratched his head and finally said, "Oh all right then. Ten shillings it is."

By the time he got back to the ferry, the weather had really turned. The sea was getting rougher by the minute, the sky was black and there were waves crashing right over the jetty. He decided to get the bus back. It was a longer journey, half an hour as opposed to a five-minute ferry ride but he was in no rush.

He was the only passenger on the bus. It had begun raining and was getting very windy. So much so that the driver was forced to slow down as a crosswind was buffeting them and his visibility was down to only a few yards. He half turned in his seat and said, "This is only going to get worse. Do you mind if we pull in at The Black Horse until it's passed over?"

After they'd parked under some trees, the driver turned again and said, "Fancy going in for a wet? I'm buying." He paused before adding, "The name's David by the way."

Joseph pulled out his slate and wrote JOSEPH and then pointing to his throat, shook his head. David nodded and said, "Was you born like that?" Joseph shook his head. "War, was it?" Joseph nodded again.

The pub was surprisingly busy but there was an empty table over in the far corner. David got them a pint each and after he'd taken a long swig said,

"My brother," he began then paused and looked away for a few seconds, "my brother was killed in that lot." He drained the last of his pint and half stood, looked down at Joseph's untouched beer and said, "I'll get meself another if you don't mind."

Outside the rain had turned to hail and it was so overcast the landlord turned on the lights as a fusillade hit the windows. As David stood up go to the bar he said, "Some bugger's been whistling up the wind all right. Two hours ago, not a cloud in the sky and now we're getting bloody hail."

David came back with another pint for himself and two whiskeys. He pushed one across to Joseph who shook his head and pushed it back.

"Ah well," said David, "waste not, want not," and drained both glasses. He then sank half of his pint in one swig. "You know what I think," he began and Joseph noticed a slight slur in his speech, "that whole bloody war was kept going because there's money in munitions. Russians had the right idea. Shot their officers and went home. If our lads had done that my brother…my brother…" Suddenly, words failed him and he stared angrily at the table top.

The silence grew and Joseph was aware of a growing silence rippling out from their table. Every pair of eyes in the room were focussed on them. David picked up his glass and drained the rest of it and then looked at Joseph's virtually untouched pint.

"You not want that?"

Joseph shook his head but as David reached across to take it an old man at the next table pointed at him and said, "Do you not think you'd best go easy on the ale while yer drivin' that bus?"

David went red and said angrily, "I'm all right. I can hold me drink…and what's it got to do with you anyway? I paid for it and I'll sup it."

"All right," said the old man, "in that case I'll buy it off yer. Save me havin' to go up for a refill…save me legs."

David seemed to suddenly deflate. Joseph could see the anger in him being rapidly replaced by shame. "All right Mr. Gosney. I wouldn't take yer money." He turned to Joseph. "Looks like it's clearing a bit now. I'll just nip tut Gents and we'll be on our way."

The hail had stopped and the room was getting lighter. David put the pint down in front of Mr. Gosney and made his way to the toilets. As soon as he was out of earshot Mr. Gosney turned to Joseph. "Him and his brother were close. He was turned down by the army. Bad heart but his brother went. Killed a month later only there was talk as how he'd done himself in. As if that wasn't bad enough, Spanish Flu took his Mam and Dad."

The sun was coming out when they got back onto the bus and set off back to Mere Ends. Before he started the engine David said quietly, "Look I'm sorry about that. It's been eight years now so you'd think…" His voice trailed off and a few seconds later he started the engine. The rest of the journey back normally only took about twenty minutes but the road was wet and there was shallow flooding in places so David took it slowly. Joseph sat back in his seat, got the picture out of his knapsack and stared at it.

It was a much better picture than he'd realised at first viewing. The hair was textured and he could make out highlights. The eyes were a cold blue like ice in the moonlight; and as he stared into them, he felt himself getting drowsy. His own eyes fell shut and he could see vague swirling patterns of colour. There was a faint singing in his ears but he couldn't quite make out the words and he woke up with a jerk. The picture had been perched on his lap and as they pulled in and parked by the shops, it tumbled onto the bus aisle and slid along to by the driver's seat. David reached down and picked it up.

He looked at it and then said quietly, "Where'd you get this?"

Joseph got out his slate and wrote BOUGHT IT IN MARKET. WHY?

"Because my brother had this picture with him when he went to France. I know he did because he showed it me. Only it wasn't in his belongings that the army sent back to us after."

Joseph wiped his slate and wrote MAYBE MORE THAN ONE?

David handed him back the picture. "I doubt that seeing as how it was my brother that drew the damn thing. He said he'd dreamt about her. He had this mad idea that she was somehow real."

Joseph cleaned his slate and then wrote WOULD YOU LIKE PICTURE?

David shook his head, "No thanks. Some folk might think she's a beauty but I don't like the looks of her. My brother was obsessed with her in the end. She was all he ever bloody talked about." He paused, "If I were you, I'd chuck the thing onto the back of the fire. It's bad luck. She's bad luck."

As Joseph walked back up the lane and home, he thought, *Obviously David's wrong. His brother might have drawn it but he couldn't have taken it to*

France with him otherwise it would never have ended up on the market stall. Unless someone stole it off him, survived, came back to England and then sold it to a market trader who in turn, sold it to me.

That didn't seem very likely though. Far too many coincidences. No, David's brother must have copied the original or else what he drew was a similar picture. It was a common enough subject. He'd seen that image in just about every art gallery he'd ever visited.

He smelt the damp as soon as he walked into his cottage. The stone floor was shiny with wet and there was a shallow puddle just inside the threshold where the floor had been worn down by generations of previous tenants. He shuddered with the sudden cold.

Get a fire going, he thought, *take the chill off.*

The coal scuttle was full of coal but it was all soaked as well. The driftwood he'd collected and chopped up for kindling glistened with damp. When he pressed the flat of his hand against the armchair, water rose up between his fingers. He felt his stomach swoop in sudden panic as he thought, *What the hell's going on?* and as he went through the rest of the cottage, his panic grew.

Everywhere was soaked. His bed, the clothes in his wardrobe and chest-of-drawers, the rugs, curtains, even the loose tea in the tea caddy which seemed to be rusted to the kitchen table. His oil paints (unopened) were fine though and so were his watercolours, sketch pad, watercolour papers and canvas.

It was obvious he couldn't stay here. True enough, he'd slept in worse places in France but then, there'd been no choice. Now there was. What with his War Pension and the allowance from his father, he could afford to stay temporarily at the Mermaid Inn. He knew he couldn't stay there indefinitely. He'd taken a twelve months lease on the cottage so would still have to pay the rent and couldn't afford the cost of staying at the Inn as well. It must have been all that rain. Obviously, there was a hole in the roof or the window frames were loose or some such thing.

A sudden strong memory came back to him.

He had still been at school. He'd hated the place. The food was terrible, a lot of the Masters and older boys were sadistic bullies and he found most of the work boring beyond belief. He was frequently caned on the flimsiest of pretexts and his only escape was into books. There was one Master, Mr. Turner, who wasn't quite like the others. He did use the cane but only as a last resort and frequently read poetry and stories to the boys.

One day, the heating in school broke down. It was early December and already bitterly cold. The headmaster had sent the word round that lessons would continue as normal and added that if any boy was feeling too cold, he could soon remedy that with his cane.

Mr. Turner announced that that afternoon they would be learning the "art of listening", told them to put on gloves, scarves and outdoor coats before settling down to listen whilst he read to them. Joseph couldn't recall anything that he'd read to them except for one story. It was about the ghost of a young girl who'd drowned herself and every Christmas Eve she'd materialise and, because she was made of water, drench whatever room *(just like my cottage)* and occupant she appeared to. It was supposed to be humorous and ended with the ghost being lured into a giant ice-house and frozen solid. Most of the other boys had laughed when the story reached its punchline. He didn't. Mr. Turner noticed he wasn't laughing and asked him what was wrong.

"I thought it was sad Sir," he'd said and there was a catch in his voice.

Turner had nodded and said, "It wasn't true you know. It was just a joke."

He'd nodded back and said, "I know that Sir. I just felt sorry for her that's all."

He'd heard a few sniggers as he said this and that night when he went to get into bed, he found his sheets and blankets were soaked and there was a note on his pillow which read *Love from the Water Ghost.* He'd wrapped himself in his coat and slept on the floor and next morning when the Housemaster discovered him, he was caned for wetting the bed.

How long ago was that now? Nearly twenty years and yet it still stung.

There was plenty of room at the Inn for him. He'd bought writing paper from the shop and so was able, with some help from the Landlord, Jim Dyson, to hire a couple of men to air and dry out his cottage. He'd brought some of his wet clothes with him and Mrs. Dyson washed them and hung them out to dry.

"They'll be ready for you by tomorrow," she'd said.

He'd arranged for his meals to be brought up to his room but when his first meal was brought up to him, he found he couldn't eat and, in the end, slipped along the landing to the bathroom and flushed it down the toilet.

He had a good view of the bay from his bedroom window. The sky was clear so at least his cottage couldn't get any wetter. He'd write to the landlord, tell him the place was leaky and damp and demand he do some repairs. He didn't want to leave the cottage though. He liked the place; liked the solitude, the sea, and the silence.

That evening he went out for a walk along the dunes. The mares tail clouds were underlit a deep scarlet which augured well. A fine sunny day tomorrow would help dry out his cottage all the quicker. He sat down on one of the sand-dunes and looked out to sea. It was calm and there were a few seagulls weaving patterns across the sky.

He wondered again about the cottage. Was he being haunted? No! Of course not. He no more believed in ghosts than he did in fairies or mermaids. He had once though, well, he'd wanted to. Wanted to believe there was more to the world than cold dormitories and Latin Grammar.

He'd actually thought that adult life would be better. It wasn't. France had stripped away the last of his illusions along with his voice. Now, he was here, alone and (at the suggestion of a psychiatrist who said it would be good therapy) trying to paint again and somehow go back to being the man he was before France.

He slept well that night. No dreams as far as he could remember and he woke up early. Early enough to watch the sun come up and go for another walk along the dunes. When he got back to the Mermaid, he went up to his room, got out the watercolour he'd bought yesterday, sat on his bed and studied it. There was a subtle change in the facial expression. Yesterday it had looked almost bland but to-day there was something about the mouth. A half-smile that made her look as if she had a secret that she was intending to share. The eyes were warmer. Her skin was beaded here and there with water. There was even discernible muscle tone.

The background yesterday seemed to be featureless off-white greying watercolour paper but now it looked more like a sea-fog and as he stared, he was sure he could see the vague outline of a headland.

It was clearly a much better picture than he'd first thought. He wanted to copy it. No, better, he wanted to make a bigger version. In oils maybe.

When he got back up to the cottage, he found most of his furniture had been taken out into the open air. He'd hired a father and son, George and Arthur, to make the place habitable and it was George who greeted him with, "Not as bad as it looked. We got some dry kindling and coal so there's a fire going for starters. We've opened all the windows to air the place and my missus has taken away your bedding to wash and dry."

Joseph nodded then got out his slate and wrote HOW LONG?

George scratched his chin and made a great show of thinking about it. "We thought we might have to do some repainting but the water damage isn't so bad. I'd say a couple more days at the most. We'll leave the paint in your outhouse if that's okay? The place will need re-doing inside and out come the Spring but there's no rush." He got out his tobacco tin and papers and began rolling a cigarette. "You must have holes in the roof but we've found nowt." He finished rolling, licked the edge of the paper, lit the finished cigarette and took a long drag. "My old Grandad would have said you'd had a visit from the mermaid's ghost."

Joseph looked at him and wrote WHO? on his slate.

George scratched his neck and said, "Oh, just some old tale." He took out his pocket watch and turned to Arthur, "Half-ten lad. Time for a brew I'm thinking." He then turned back to Joseph. "Time for our tea break, sir. You're welcome to join us and if you're interested, I can tell you the tale. Might be useful for you what with you being an artist and all. Give you an idea for a picture I shouldn't wonder."

After Arthur had made tea, they sat down on three old chairs that had been brought out of the kitchen and wiped dry. George smiled and offered Joseph a cigarette and for a while they sat sharing tea, tobacco and silence.

"Story goes," George began, "as there were a mermaid lived in the sea round here. From time to time, people saw her swimming just off the headland. Sensible folk let her be but there was one fella were obsessed with her. Went out in his boat all the time looking for her. One day he got lucky and caught her in his net. So, he brings her back to land and puts her in a pond and plans to keep her.

Only the pond was fresh water and she needed to be in salt to live so she died. Story goes that before she died, she cursed him and said that…"

His son Arthur cut across him with, "She'd be revenged or woken with a kiss by some handsome Prince I'll bet!" He began laughing. "Honestly Dad, s'just some old kid's tale!"

George glared at him for a moment and then continued, "…even then, if he put her body back in the sea, he'd be forgiven. Only he didn't. Instead, he buried her and planted a tree on her grave to hold her in."

Arthur interrupted again with, "Why'd he need to do that? She was dead!"

This time George ignored him and went on, "Anyway, the pond goes stagnant and, in the end, they filled it in. They say her ghost hangs around here and when she gets lonely, she swims unseen into people's houses just to be near the living again; and that you'll know she's visited you because when you wake up in the morning you'll find everywhere soaked."

He took a last drag on his cigarette, dropped the butt and ground it under the sole of his boot and then stared at his feet. The silence was broken by Arthur. "Yes, either that or they just had leaky rooves. Besides which, I heard as she was one of them seal people. The ones who shed their sealskins and look human. Or maybe she comes back as a vampire and drains the life out of men she's made fall in love with her."

"I didn't say it was true now did I! I was merely telling this gent the tale." George looked at his watch. "Besides which, that's a different story altogether. Anyway, we'd best be getting on."

It was unusually warm even for late August and his cottage was ready to move back into three days later. He bought a few basics in the village shop on his way back to the cottage. The place was spotless and there was no feel of damp in the air so it had been aired properly as well; but there was something. A faint smell that seemed to get stronger by the minute and it was familiar. It was like the stench that drifted across No-Man's Land when the dead that lay abandoned began to bloat. He wondered if it was an hallucination. When he was in hospital, there was an officer in the next bed to him who swore blind he could smell mustard gas. He would wake everyone up in the middle of the night screaming, "Gas! Gas, boys, gas! Get your masks on!"

Joseph opened every window in the cottage but that made it worse. It soon became obvious that it was drifting in from outside. He went into the back garden to see if he could pinpoint the exact source and noted it was strongest around the apple tree.

And no wonder, he thought to himself as he noted that the apples on the tree were discoloured and the windfalls rotting on the ground. He stepped off the path, (noted the grass was waterlogged) reached up, picked one and gently squeezed it in the palm of his hand. The result was a thick brown pulp that oozed between his fingers and gave off a stench that left him gagging. For a moment, he had a vision of men at Mons falling off the duckboards and being gulped down by the mud; and then he remembered the one who'd done it deliberately; the one who'd smiled and waved to him before sidestepping onto the mud and vanishing in seconds. Hodges. Yes, that was the name. Hodges. Only been with the Platoon a month. Quiet sort.

He went back inside, set to and laid a fire in the grate: he began with small pieces of driftwood which flared blue when he lit them (the same blue as the woman in the picture's eyes) before carefully placing on lumps of coal. It took a while but eventually he had a decent blaze going. That seemed to drive the smell back; well, either that or he was just getting used to it.

The smell was one thing; the possibility of being flooded out every time it rained was quite another. He decided to write to the Landlord, terminate his tenancy, refuse to pay another penny in rent, and look for another cottage.

He got his easel and canvas set up, propped the watercolour up on his mantlepiece, went back to his canvas and sketched a rough outline in pencil of her head and shoulders.

He paused, stepped back and stared at the canvas. His arms felt heavy and he wondered if he should get something to eat but decided to leave it. The thought of food made him feel queasy.

He picked up his pencil and blocked-in eyes, nose, mouth, and the rough outline of hair. He decided to begin with her eyes so mixed some blue then selected his most delicate brush and began blocking in the irises and instead of white, he painted the eyeballs gold.

Mouth next, he thought but when he mixed the red for her lips, it just didn't seem red enough. What he wanted was the exact shade of blood so picked up his penknife (the one he used for sharpening pencils), sliced into his thumb and squeezed out a few drops onto his palette. He added some red oil paint then more of his own blood and kept on mixing until he got the exact shade he was after.

Now the lips shone with life. He stepped back and considered. Skin next maybe…no, the hair! He mixed a golden shade of yellow and again added a few drops of his own blood. The effect was even better than he could have hoped. Her hair had depth and texture. Skin next. In the watercolour, her skin was chalk white but he knew that wouldn't do. He put some zinc white onto his palette, added some yellow but still wasn't convinced so added a few more drops of his own blood and then tentatively applied a few strokes to the canvas. It looked okay so he applied more. The skin went from the bloodless white of a corpse to the white of snow…no that wasn't it. More the white of whitecaps on waves, clover, or apple blossom.

Time went by; much more time than he'd realised until he noticed how dark the room had become. He glanced at his watch. It was almost nine o'clock at night. He went over to the window and looked outside. It was a clear night and he could see the full moon peering over the treetops.

He was about to light some lamps but decided against it. The moon would give him all the light he needed.

Early next morning Mrs. Dyson looked out of her bedroom window at The Mermaid and saw Joseph carrying a sack and walking along the tide line. Every now and again he paused to pick up driftwood, strands of kelp and what she assumed were shells. She saw him again the next morning and every morning after that for the rest of the week. After that, she didn't see him again. Close to a month went by and one evening in the bar of the Mermaid she got talking to David, the village bus driver. "Have you seen anything of that artist recently?"

"No," said David, "as a matter of fact, I haven't." He took another swig of his pint. "Tell you what. It's my day off tomorrow. I'll go up to his cottage and check on him."

The first thing David noticed was that the cottage door was ajar so after gently knocking, he went inside. There was an almost overwhelming smell of paint. He found Joseph collapsed on the living room floor. One glance at his emaciated body was enough for him to realise that Joseph was dead. That and the smell of decay that was almost but not completely masked by the smell of paint. A canvas was set up on an easel that was leaning back onto the wall. In the centre was the pencilled in outline of a human head and shoulders, but as yet, no figure had been painted in. The background was an undersea landscape of coral and kelp and this landscape had been continued on the wall as if it was pouring out of the canvas' edges. In addition to that every surface, the table, the mantlepiece even the floor had been painted over and then littered with shells, pieces of driftwood and drying kelp. A bedsheet had been nailed over the window and more seascape painted over it.

The watercolour that had been painted by his brother was still propped upon the mantlepiece.

The door into the kitchen was wide open and the back kitchen door, the one that opened out onto the garden, was smashed off its hinges. He stepped through and saw the apple tree uprooted. He went closer and could see the tree was clearly diseased so assumed that Joseph had dug it out. He'd also dug out far more soil than was necessary and, in the process, had flung it wildly all round the edge of what was clearly a small but deep pit. No sign of the spade though. He glanced back round at the cottage. The upstairs windows were dark and he wondered if they'd been painted over with seascapes as well.

When he got upstairs, he found they had; as had the walls, doors and floors. There were half a dozen empty paint tins and a discarded brush lying on the landing floor.

He went slowly back downstairs. He was about to leave and go down to the village police station, when he paused, stepped back, took down the watercolour off the mantlepiece and slipped it under his jacket. His brother had painted it so he reasoned that by rights it was his now.

As he pulled the front door of the cottage closed behind him, he heard faint singing off in the distance somewhere.

<u>EVER AFTER</u>

by Mark A. Fisher

Ella struggled to keep her eyes open. She hadn't slept the night before. She'd been too apprehensive to sleep. After their argument, Dale had gone quiet, instead of his typical kind of angry.

And while Ella had laid sleeplessly in their bed, trying not to stir, worried that he'd wake up. She came to a decision. She had to leave. After he left for work, she'd pack up whatever she could and head south. She'd make herself scarce in Los Angeles. She'd be able to hide, and he'd never find her down there.

And so she did. Though Dale had taken longer than usual to get himself out the door. Yet he had eventually left. As soon as he had turned the corner out onto the main street out of their Redding neighborhood. Ella grabbed a suitcase and filled it with some essentials. Then she grabbed her stash of cash and climbed into her old car intended only for going shopping around town and set herself in motion.

For six, or was it seven, hours adrenaline and traffic kept her awake through Sacramento and then on to past the East Bay. She wasn't even going to take the most direct route. Why make it any easier for Dale than she had to.

But now, down past Big Sur, all the adrenaline was gone. It was late in the afternoon and she'd been awake over twenty four hours. Ella glanced at the GPS on her phone, up ahead there was a state park. Julia Pfeiffer Burns. She'd stop and rest for a bit before she'd move on.

Ella pulled into the parking lot and turned off the car. Then she stopped fighting and was asleep in an instant.

Ella jumped and looked around anxiously. It took her a moment, but she remembered where she was, and the tapping came at the window once again. Ella looked to see a young man peering in at her with a look of concern on his face.

"Are you OK?" The young man asked. Ella nodded, not trusting herself to speak. "You're sure?" The young man's concern was clear.

"I'm… Fine. I'm fine." Ella stretched a bit then opened her door. Her legs were unsteady from anxiety and exhaustion.

The young man put on his hat, and Ella saw he was some sort of park ranger. "I'm sorry," Ella said, "I was just so tired I needed a moment to shut my eyes."

"No big deal," the ranger said, "but this is kind of a lonely spot here, and you never know when someone might stop by." The ranger looked out and gazed into the distance. "You know, if you've got time…" The ranger paused. When did park rangers get to be so young? Ella wondered to herself. The ranger continued, "Right now would be a good time to take a hike and see if you could spot the Dark Watchers."

"The what?" Ella asked.

"The Dark Watchers," the ranger repeated. "Legends say there are human like creatures that are sometimes seen out in these hills overlooking the ocean."

"Umm. Creatures?" Ella looked nervously past him to the overlook.

"Frankly, I think they're an atmospheric phenomenon." The ranger studied the sky around them. "Low sunlight casting shadows onto very thin fog or clouds, or whatever it is that forms at this time of day." He paused then stared into Ella's eyes. "But the legends go way back to the Native Americans. John Steinbeck's supposed to have mentioned them in one of his books." He scrunched up his face. "I can't remember which one off the top of my head."

Ella glanced anxiouslyy around the parking lot. "But they're nothing to be afraid of," the ranger said reassuringly. "They're called Dark Watchers, and that's all they ever do. So even if you see one, there's nothing to worry about."

"Oh," Ella tentatively smiled. "I might could use a walk before I get on the road again."

"Hey, if you need a place to stay, we've got a campground just another couple miles further down the road. I'm not supposed to let folks sleep in their cars, but I think you could use a bit more sleep."

"I… Thanks, I might just take you up on that." Ella looked at the young man. "And I think I will take a little walk and see if I can spot your Dark Watchers."

"If you decide to stay, just head up the Pacific Coast Highway here and turn left after a couple miles. The ranger cabin is just a little ways in." The ranger pointed back down the road.

"Thank you," Ella said, then waited for him to climb in his truck and turn back out onto the highway.

Ella stood wondering what to do. She was in no condition to try to drive much more today. And the day would soon turn to night. The park ranger's invitation seemed to be her best course. But… She wasn't ready to go and settle for the night just yet.

She looked around and spotted a path heading in the direction of the ocean. It had been years since she'd had a chance to just look at the ocean. Watch the waves. Dale had never wanted to go. She was sure she could spare a few minutes and maybe she'd see a 'Dark Watcher'. Ella laughed to herself for the first time in a long time.

With a lighter heart Ella walked down the tree lined trail towards the ocean. She couldn't hear it yet, but the smell of the salty air made her smile. After just a couple minutes the trees ended and she could see a cliff and a view of the ocean beyond. Walking up to the edge she looked out on the vista for a few minutes.

Ella sighed and closed her eyes. As she opened them, she thought she saw something out of the corner of her eye. She turned. And there it was. It was a shadowy human shape, tall, maybe ten feet. Maybe more. And it kind of shimmered with the breeze. It was wearing a broad brimmed hat, or was it some kind of old-fashioned hair style? Ella wasn't sure.

And she felt it was watching her. Dark Watcher was an incredibly accurate name for whatever it was.

For a moment, Ella thought she could see its eyes. Then it turned and looked up the trail back towards the parking lot. Then it faded away.

Ella turned towards where the Watcher had glanced and coming out of the trees was a form. A man. As he came out of the trees, she could see him clearly. It was Dale. How?!

Ella stood frozen, unable to move, as Dale walked up to her.

"I'm disappointed Ella," Dale said, the anger only showing in his eyes. The way she'd seen it so often over way too many years. "You should have known I couldn't let you leave."

"How?" Ella asked.

"A while back, I put a 'find-your-phone' app, on your phone. Just in case." Dale stepped towards her. "I knew exactly what you were thinking last night. So, after I got to work, I decided to do a check. And guess what, there you were, already on the I-5."

"Dale, please, just let me go." Ella pleaded as he took another step towards her.

"Oh, no, Ella. You have to remember, this, us, it was forever after. Just like in fairy tales." Dale looked around making sure they were really alone.

Ella prepared herself to run, but Dale grabbed her arm before she could start. "Ever after, Ella, ever after," Dale said coldly.

Ella looked into his eyes, then saw the Dark Watcher reform beside Dale. Ella's eyes widened as the thing, whatever it was, stood beside Dale and stared. Dale smiled as he watched the fear in her eyes, but then seeming to feel the presence, he turned towards the Watcher.

Dale looked up at the dark shape looming over him. He dropped Ella's arm. The Watcher shifted and it looked as if it bent down towards him. Dale took a step back and went over the cliff. Ella covered her ears in a vain attempt to block out the sound of his scream as he fell. When it ended Ella uncovered her ears.

There was a shout from the tree line. Ella looked over and watched as the young park ranger ran towards her. The Watcher rose up and glanced gently down at Ella then faded away as the ranger reached her.

"Are you OK," the young man asked.

"My husband," Ella looked over at the cliff.

The ranger walked over and peered down onto the rocks below, then shook his head. He turned back to Ella. "What was he doing?" The ranger asked.

"I think he was going to kill me," Ella said as her tears began to fall. "He tracked me here. Why? Why are you here?"

"I thought I should check on you again. You really weren't in any condition to drive. And when I got here, I saw another empty car in the lot." He shrugged. "What happened? I saw the end of your confrontation. It looked like he just backed himself off the cliff." The ranger looked into Ella's face as she tried to wipe away some of her tears.

"He saw the Watcher," Ella explained. "It frightened him."

"But all they do is watch."

"I guess Dale didn't know that," Ella responded weakly.

"Yeah, I suppose not." The ranger then put his arm around Ella then helped her back towards the tree line. As they walked, he pulled out his radio and called for the sheriff. "There's been an accident here at the vista point. Yeah, a man went over the cliff…"

Ella's eyes darted through the shadows of the trees. Even though she couldn't see anything, she thought she could feel eyes watching her as they walked away.

THE MEDAN

by Stephen Patmore

"What I'm about to tell ya, my friend, will take hold of ya, haunt every corner of ya mind and never again let go," Captain Antonio 'Chappy' Conti says to the newly appointed Trawler Man and Head Chef of The Natalia, Thad Newnham. Ice cubes chime their frozen song as he sips his rum and listens to the story the hoary Captain has to tell, wondering if he has bluing anchor tattoos on the thick forearms beneath his tatty old fish and fuel stinking roll neck.

The ember glow of his cigarette bounces along as Chappy speaks, sending up Morse Code spirals of blue smoke that fog his grey bristled face. The perfect storyteller's atmosphere.

"What I'm about to tell ya, young man, is the gods' honest truth," croaks the Captain. "No word of a lie."

"Hogwash!" Ash Denby scoffs and waves a dismissive hand at the old sea dog. "Don't you go listenin' to it, kid, 'tis just an urban legend. A seafarer's version of one anyhow." He turns to

Chappy. "I've heard this story more times than I've had a hot girl in a cold bed, Cap. Don't go sending this lad high-tailing outta here like all the others."

Through the toxic smoke, Chappy glares at his First Mate. "The story of the SS Ourang Medan is no 'Hogwash', ya motherless snide." His thin yellow teeth bare as they bite down on the end of his cigarette, "You mind that lip of yar's, Denby. One'a these days it'll get caught up in a trawl net, it hangs so fecking low, ma boy."

Plucking the shrinking cigarette from his lips, Chappy stubs it out with authority into the heavy glass ashtray already full and teeming with bent over, yellow ended butts; dead soldiers half-buried in ashy earth.

"Never mind that heathen," he sneers, chucking a thumb at the straight-backed Denby to his left, "wasn't given the privilege of a decent upbringing, this one. Mother's a hoor. Father ain't never been around to teach him right."

Wood squeals as Denby shoves his chair back and stands. "You're a son of a hoor yourself, you cantankerous wop." he says shoving the table forward. Glasses clink, swilling the liqueur inside like captured pieces of ocean. Their brown waves crash silently against icy rocks. A few glasses fall over and spill their miniature seas across the tabletop. As he storms past, Denby stops and leans into Thad, "… do yourself a favour, kid, don't get caught up in this old bastard's story. It'll be no good for you," he says, before heading for the bar and pulling up a stool. He plonks himself down and signals to the wiry lady, busy cleaning glasses, behind the bar.

"Don't mind him," Chappy says, "he'll be fine and dandy after a good soaking of the dark stuff. Won't ya, ya mewling little slag?"

"Fuck you, Chappy," says Denby, leaning into his fresh drink.

"Now, where was I?" Chappy rolls his eyes up as if the answer lays somewhere on the inside of his skull.

"The Orange Medal?" Questions Thad.

"Medan," Chappy corrects with a click of his fingers. "The bloody Ourang Medan, of course," and he slams his thick palm onto the table. The spilt alcohol runs and drips onto the floor. Any glasses remaining upright quiver.

"There's a universe of mystery clouding that old steamer, ma boy." He says, "But unlike all the heard-a-million-times-over ghost ship anecdotes the sea is so slick and filthy with, this one's as real and irremovable as the fish stink on me fecking fingers." Shoving two fingers with nails bitten to the quick and ingrained with filth under his nostrils, he sniffs deep, "Argh!" and continues.

"She weren't no freighter like they say she was. I fecking well see her with me own two peepers." he points two grimy fingers at his cloudy sunken eyes and Thad wonders if all the Captains' years staring at the ocean have taken its toll.

"She be a steamer, no doubt. Big bitch too. Some say she went missing around 1940. I can't say otherwise on that, but what I can tell ya is that February 3rd, 1948, was exactly when me and the crew of the Silver Star found her.

"I was Chief Navigator back then, guiding us through the Strait of Malacca, when we received a distress call. Oddest fecking thing, I tell ya. And to this very day, I can still hear it as clear as all them years ago. Basic. S-O-S at first. Simple as that.

"But then this onslaught of gibberish none of us could make out followed. Even our de-coders were scratching their flaky fecking scalps when suddenly, the message sort of… found itself again, forming words we all understood.

W.e.f.l.o.a.t. W.e.f.l.o.a.t. W.e.f.l.o.a.t.

"*No shit ya floating*, I remember thinking, *ya on a fecking boat*. Am I right or am I right?"

Thad nods.

"Morse Code don't have no tone of life, no audible difference between one dot or dash to the next, right?" Chappy doesn't wait for Thad to nod again, "I can't explain it, and I know no other man there that day could either, but every one of us on deck heard a voice between that static, and its eerily defined clarity stole everyone's breath when it said, *All officers including Captain, dead in chartroom and on bridge. Probably whole crew dead.* Turning us into a control room of… I don't know… fecking mute idiots?

"After a minute, the Random tap-tapping nonsense started up again; no words this time, just pointless clicks-and-clacks as if a kid found the Morse key and was thwacking the damn thing, playing out some old-time nursery rhyme they'd had swimming through their head since the age of titty milk and diapers. And then, nothing. Not even that familiar crisp rustling of static. Just complete silence, as if the whole thing had lost power. The rapid heartbeat of the Silver Stars engine humming away, thankfully, underplayed that silence.

"We stood looking at the radio like it was gonna somehow show us all the fecking answers we wanted. My skin rippled with shivers. My spine prickled with a poison ivy heat as the tension in that silent control room grew electric; invisible lightning filling the air around us like we were all standing in the middle of one'a them electricity ball things. What'd they call them?" Chappy clicks his fingers.

"Tesla Sphere," Thad says, almost surprised at hearing his own voice.

"That's it. Knew you were a smart one, boy." A knowing smile creeps across his weathered lips for just a second.

"I almost shit me britches right there and then when the radio crackled to life again with two words that froze the blood of every man there.

I die.

"Can ya fecking believe that? *I die!*

"Right then's when we were hit with these screeching, piercing metal-on-metal screams; a wall of noise that crept its way into every inch of space inside ya head and hammered away at ya brain. Real far back, hiding deep inside those static screams was the echo of laughter. Human fecking laughter with a guttural rumble that got louder and louder until I thought me brain was gonna pop like an overfilled balloon. Right at the cusp, as the pain seared through me, was when the radio blew. Nothing too dramatic. Just a little *pfft*. And thick white smoke came pouring from the speaker grills. No message ever came through that radio again."

"Shit…" says Thad, "… D'you find the signals transmission point?"

Chappy opens a brown leather tobacco pouch, starts rolling another cigarette and nods as he licks and seals the paper. The look in his eye - as Chappy himself might say - is *as serious as having the shits at sea.* He lifts the cigarette to his lips, flicks his lighter open and rolls the flint wheel under his thumb, creating sparks that jump like burning lemmings into the air, lighting up the Captain's face in a puckish orange glow. His eyebrows raise in shadowed oddity as light flickers across his cheekbones, sucking away their fullness and twisting him into a gaunt spectacle of the man he was, changing him from hardened sea dog to a withered dying old man with the deep-set look of a cancer patient nearing the end.

Chappy draws the flame to the end of his cigarette and takes a deep lung full of the sweet poison. The dry tobacco crackles. Like radio static. Briefly,

Thad thinks he hears some sort of ethereal cackling coming from somewhere within it. Chappy smiles with the corner of his mouth.

"We locked the signal's location to a rough estimation somewhere Southeast of the Marshall Islands." He says, dropping his smile, "But an expanse of open water four hundred square nautical miles wide - give or take - with Micronesia off to the West and the Wake Islands to the North, made one hell of a big fecking shot in the dark. But we were men used to pissing in the shadows and, even in rough seas, still able to hit the middle of the bowl with no trouble. So, you could say we were damn near confident we would find her eventually.

"For over nine weeks, we searched. Rotating shifts to maintain a constant watch. The sun, bouncing off the Pacific like it was the world's largest fecking diamond, had this crazed intensity that I have never seen in all my years out there. And eventually, eight crew members were laid out blind to it.

"Nights weren't no better either. When the ocean turned tarry and black, something even blacker was held within it. I can't say what exactly, but it felt like looking into the heart of madness itself. Three crew members lost their lives to that madness; all three jumping headfirst into its gaping maw without a single word or sound uttered. These weren't no rookies with knocking knees and beards full'a puke, but real experienced sailors. Men who had long earned their sea legs. But something got into their heads and broke each one as easy as China plates at a fecking Greek wedding.

"The crew stopped sleeping. Tension was bubbling over. Everyone was on edge and the urge to quit and call it a day was getting stronger. But hearing that another trawler received the same garbled messages kept us pushing on. No fecking way was we going home with our cocks all shrivelled and let those snide sons-a-bitches slip in and solve the mystery we'd been working our arses off to solve.

"Then, one night - a warm, heavy storm was brewing deep in the waves - a scream from starboard pierced through the air… MEDAN!!" Chappy screams and Thad's arse cheeks lift a full three inches from his seat as the prickly heat of embarrassment creeps along his hairline. Ash Denby looks over his shoulder and rolls his eyes before going back to his drink.

"Sorry about that," Chappy says, "I gets carried away with me'self sometimes."

He hears Denby mutter, "No shit," and smiles.

"So, did you find her, then?" asks Thad, shuffling his arse cheeks back to a comfortable position.

"You fecking bet we did," Chappy says, victoriously. "Bitch drifted straight towards us out of the shadows. Her deck was blacker than the eyes of the devil himself. Just as spiteful looking, too. At first it was hard to focus on her as if a piece of the world had been removed, a section of it cut out and placed elsewhere, like some puzzle piece destined to be lost forever."

The lights inside the bar strobe, the bulbs overhead hiss with a surge of electricity and crackle with static pops. With a gramophone thinness, Thad hears a voice somewhere close behind him repeat two words.

I die. I die. I die. I die.

He looks around for the acknowledgement that someone else heard it too, but he gets none. The wiry woman behind the bar is polishing a pint glass with a dirty rust coloured cloth whilst singing softly to herself. Thad doesn't recognise the tune, but it must be some old sea shanty because this is a bar made *for* sailors *by* sailors and is clearly responsible for the birth of at least one or two rowdy, swaying, drunken tunes in its lifetime. Ash Dendy still sits stooped over in a huff, mumbling into his glass of rum. A couple dance by the Jukebox. The woman, too drunk to move her legs, lets her partner hold up her limp body as her toes drag lifelessly across the floorboards. The poorly lit booths surrounding them hide the people sitting there behind shadows. No acknowledgement for Thad exists, and he can't help but wonder if he has finally gone mad like his father. Has the prefrontal cortex of his brain been infected with the same tumour, and now, at this very moment, was choosing to break him down piece by piece, dragging him slowly into a world of hallucinatory fuckery? Shit, even if it was, would he have the cognition to know it?

Opposite, Chappy sits frozen in place, as lifeless as a hunk of granite. His elbows resting on the table, a cigarette paper, filled with loose dry tobacco, rests between his fingers mid-roll in front of his chin, ready to be licked closed. His eyes are wide. Thin black hair-like strands writhe about inside them, wrapping themselves around his corneas, while the grin on his face, like the rest of him, is held in suspension. A disturbed sneer lays bare every one of his yellow nicotine-stained teeth and the soft blackening gums that house them. A muscle twitches beneath the frayed paper-thin skin of his cheek. The rest of him stays solid and as stiff as a ship's mast.

"IIIIIIIIIII DIEEEEEEEE!" comes a scream that rattles Thad's eardrums. His hair wafts forward at the force of invisible breath, and the smell of deep decay and salty seawater follows. Every muscle in his body clenches, his eyes squint half-closed and his teeth bite together, making his jaw crunch and ache. The lights overhead surge. Their bulbs, pushed to their max, glow brighter, thrumming and throbbing before slowly dimming back down to barroom luminosity as everything settles back to normality.

"That's when I knew," Chappy speaks again as if he never stopped. He licks his cigarette paper and tucks the tobacco in. No grin, no swirling strands of madness encircling his eyeballs.

"That's when I knew we'd stumbled upon real trouble". He lights the end of his cigarette. The ember pulses orange and black, and with each pulse, a small amount of life is given back to it, whilst simultaneously taking the same from Chappy with every inward breath.

"We hitched up on her port side…"

Thad finds it increasingly difficult to concentrate. If Chappy sees the fear manifesting inside of him, he never lets on to it.

"… and surveyed what we could from the deck of the Silver Star.

"The Medan, boy, did she creak a good'n. Constantly grumbling away to herself, she was. Our crew were nervous, having the heft of that big old girl looming over us with her eerie starkness darkening every inch of us. Ye could feel her inside somehow, reaching in, searching ya inner depths, but for what exactly, I still, to this day, can't say. She just clouded ya mind, dulled ya senses, and made ya drunk from looking up at her. No life existed up there. I didn't need to board her to know that. The stale and peppery scent of abandonment was rich in the air.

"The Captain decided to wait out the night. *We'll board her come first light* he said, *when visibility is on our side.* I s'pose there was no real point getting all that way, losing all that we had, to just storm in with blindfolds, right? Damn right, we deserved to lay eyes on every fecking inch of that bitch. So, the Captain assigned a skeleton crew of himself, the Bosun and Bosuns' Mate, plus six deckhands to keep watch through the night whilst everyone else was told to rest up for the big day ahead.

"I woke up as groggy as a hoor after a good earner, to the hum of frantic voices - *what time is it? Where's the Captain?* When I opened the deck hatch, the twinkling of Carina softly glistened in an onyx sky. Night? Still? Six hours of sleep, and the sun wasn't even peeking over the horizon yet. No sign. Not even a slither. And worst of all, there was no sign of it showing up anytime soon. It made no sense.

"The entire crew searched, but the Captain and the night watch couldn't be found. After an hour we come to figure one of two things: they either boarded the giant tethered to our port side or, like so many before them, had thrown themselves silently into the black mouth of madness. The former was the lesser of the two evils, so for the sake of our fragile minds, we settled on that."

Chappy knocks back his rum and yells at the bar lady for another.

"You want another, Son…" he asks pointing at Thad's still full glass, "… or you planning on nursing that one back to life?"

"Oh yeah, please," Thad says, "but what happened next?" He lifts the glass to take a sip. The smell of the liqueur inside stings the back of his nostrils and leaves a faint aroma of engine oil and mould clinging to the tiny hairs inside. He moves the glass away from his face, disgusted. Looking closely, he sees the brown liquid has a fatty, clotting grease consistency that moves like unset jelly.

"I'm just getting to that." says Chappy, "Everything alright, Boy?" His tooth baring grin slowly creeps in again. "Drink up and let me show ya". His gums, now completely visible, are blacker than disease. Those thin fibrous black strands wrap themselves around his eyeballs again, stitching through the pulpy soft lenses like cotton thread sutures. Thad's stomach clenches, and the feeling of madness grows between each retching constriction.

Chappy's hand raises, palm facing up, onto the bottom of Thad's glass and eases it towards Thad's mouth, pressing it against his lips. The voices of a hundred men can be heard echoing thinly from inside; a garbled, frantic message hidden deep amongst static. Chappy's hand presses harder, pushing the glass past Thad's lips and into his teeth with a fragile '*tink*'. The pressure becomes unbearable. Anymore and the glass will shatter into a thousand crystal splinters and slice through the soft plump flesh of Thad's lips. He parts his teeth, and with his eyes closed in a grimace, gulps back the viscous, rancid liquid. But Chappy refuses to let go until every drop is gone. Only then does Thad feel the heaviness against the bottom of the tumbler slacken. He drops the glass down onto the table and hears it bounce once and then burst into a million bright twinkles like stars falling from the sky in slow motion. His eyes shoot open. The table is gone. No longer is he sitting in the bar made *by* sailors *for* sailors. There's no Chappy, flashing his yellow gravestone teeth. No ghostly eyeball hairs. No drunk woman caressing the dancefloor with dead feet, and no Ash Denby, cautiously peering over his shoulder. Instead, all Thad can see is a helm control panel, cast in lifeless black and draped in dreadlocks of slick snotty seaweed. Behind it, a small set of windows are smeared with thick green algae. Every wall is crusted over with layers of jagged barnacles. The floor, thick with a sheet of greying dust.

Static blares out from the control panel in bursts of hissing crackles. Thad scuffles away from it, trying to escape the sound clawing at his mind, and kicks up a cloud of mushroom-coloured dust. Particles swirl up to orbit his body in lazy gyrations before settling onto his hair, on his skin and his clothes. Brushing it from his head, he moves a trembling hand to lift the receiver and places it against his ear. The static crackles away to silence, and with a faraway resonance, a voice hisses quietly. Thad's ear turns a waxy white as he presses the receiver harder against it, trying to hear the voice lost inside the storm.

"It hasss you now, my friend. You have become forever lossst." Air rushes around inside the earpiece like a storm swelling.

"RUN!" it suddenly roars, "RUN NOW." Thad drops the phone and lunges for the algae-filmed door beside him with cat-like agility. The receiver swings on its curled cord behind him, knocking with a cheap plastic *thunk!* each time, it bounces against the side of the control panel.

The handle to the door won't budge. Thad places his left hand on top of his right and heaves down on it with everything he has. But still, nothing.

A low swishing sound comes from somewhere behind him, like the sound of sandpaper abrading timber. He looks over his shoulder. Grey dust, shimmering in the dead air like particles of diamonds caught in the reflection of a fairground mirror, swirls up as he continues prying at the handle. The dust grows thicker, taller, forming a familiar outline. Features become more apparent, more defined, as more swirling bodies materialise, one after the other, until there are an entire army of dust men, too many to count, all with their mouths contorted jawbreakingly wide. Sickly screaming faces with thin hair-like strands floating around their newly formed mushroom colour eyes, stitching themselves in. The soldiers raise their arms above their heads, palms facing out toward Thad, and one by one, pant in quick sharp inhalations, become a single chorus chanting in hyperventilating whispers.

Unable to look at the screaming faces any longer, Thad turns away and tries the door again. His heart pounds so hard in his chest that he can hear it above the wheezing gasps from behind him. Muscles tear in his shoulders, his wrists are on the verge of snapping like kindling, blood vessels pop, bleeding red clouds across his eyes, and his neck ripples with ropes of thick tendons and bulging blue veins, and still, the door is stuck. Thad is stuck. His heart beats. His blood pumps. A hand slapping down hard on his shoulder is the last thing Thad Newnham feels before he implodes into a frenetically revolving funnel of a million grey fungal particles. His skin. His bones. His organs. His muscle. His tissue. Gone.

The screaming soldier statues fall back into their sandy revolutions, twisting tightly in the space they were born in. Tens of pirouetting cones drift languid feather flotations towards the floor, until, eventually, they each find their peaceful resting place.

From dust to dust.

One small cyclone continues turning in on itself for a little longer than the rest. When it finally settles, Thad Newnham is no more.

The room is still.

Static crackles.

*****

"What I'm about to tell ya, my friend, will take hold of ya, haunt every corner of ya fecking mind and never again let go." says Captain Antonio 'Chappy' Conti, to the newly appointed Trawler Man and Head Chef of the Natalia, Carlos LaGuardo.

The End

THE HAUNTED CURTAINS

by Ziaul Moid Khan

The day my mother was diagnosed with blood cancer, I cried well past midnight. In fact, all members at our home were woebegone, but showed a brave face. Father took a week-long casual leave from his Central Reserve Police Force duty at Delhi Metro. Nidhi, my sister, was sleeping beside me on the other bed. All members managed themselves somehow, but alas I was inconsolable.

All die one day and everyone knows it quite well, but Dr. Garg's statement, my Mom was in the second stage of this deadly disease and could hardly live a couple of months, sort of devastated me. I did not want her to die. My mind was not ready for it.

I'd never encountered such a gloomy atmosphere in my life before. None seemed to have any words of compassion to share with me. Speechless, I cried nonstop tears for hours. Still, none thought of wiping the wet salt from my cheeks. It was understandable: all loved my Mom and felt more or less the same sorrow for her when they came to know about her approaching death.

I recalled: a man named Ashok in my neighborhood had shot himself in the temple. Almost the entire village had gathered around their house as the news spread of his suicide. I could not dare to visit, despite all my other family members would rush to his house. Though they came back repenting, for Ashok's head after the fatal blow was in a gruesome state. Beggars description, you know.

I was happy for not going to his house, but very sad for his death. They speculated: he'd taken this dire step for a girl whom he loved, perhaps passionately, and she did not reciprocate. I always feared dead bodies and visiting funerals or mourning. And now my own mother was nearing death. I could not swallow this fact. The hard, harsh reality.

Lying prostrate on my bed, my face sunk in my pillow, my loose heavy breasts brushing against the cushion and my tears all running down my cheeks bedewing the pillow beneath, I felt helpless, hopeless, and loss of all positivity. I never wanted to lose my Mom—not at any cost. Come what may. The diagnosis giving mom only a few months to live stirred my latent emotions. My heart simply didn't accept this reality. Truth's bitter like a gourd, after all. But sometimes, or more often than not, truth is unacceptable.

I reckoned something was wrong in the report, some computer error or the doctor just miscalculated her illness. *She cannot die*, my heart said, *she cannot leave us when none of us siblings are mature and independent enough to survive in the cruel human world.*

No siblings in the family were children, true. The plan we all had to finish college was true, too, but Mom would not be here to help us. Nidhi was doing masters in Chemistry and brother, Dushyant, doing the first semester of B.Tech and I, a student of B.Sc. first year. Mom had said: "Shalu, you should be a cardiac surgeon." And I too wanted to crack the pre-med exam, but suddenly this cancer thing plagued all my dreams and shattered them like anything. I was lost in these thoughts; when I encountered something weird that night which I did not anticipate. The time was one a.m.

*****

First, I thought it to be just a fleeting self-doubt, but upon close observation, I sensed I was not wrong. The curtains suspended at the French window in my bedroom suddenly animated and moved like the pendulum of a wall-clock. It was a February night, so the ceiling fan was off and the window panes tightly shut, dismissing any possibility of the backstreet winds that could violate the peace of my bedroom. I saw the floral green blinds violently fluttering like the enormous wings of a raven, first right then left and then right again.

I sat up bolt-straight and gazed at them up-and-down, fixedly, trying to comprehend if it was at all possible. The faint neon light from the street bulb, penetrating the crevices of the window, fell onto the side of my cotton stuffed pillow. Rummaging around on the bedside study-table, I found the switch of my table lamp and the next moment the mercury vapor light illuminated the room.

The blinds were dead-still as if they'd never animated. *It's a mirage or an illusion,* I said to myself, turning off the light again and letting my head sink in the pillow's soft comfort for a nap. After that a few moments passed in peace, and then the fluttering sounds of the curtains returned, startling my very fundamentals. Every hair of my skin seemed to have sensed the bizarre, the paranormal. They stood at their ends. Horror knows no logic, no math.

All my rationale ran riot in the present condition. For a moment, I forgot my mother's cancer and beheld the strange night happening. Adapting my eyes to the darkness, I saw or I think I saw a face or rather a portion of a face: a woman, middle aged, with unkempt hair and eyes bloodshot, her hands with their long fingers and even longer nails clutched the blinds tightly. And it was she who was in fact shaking the curtains crazily.

As I screeched from the utmost core of my throat, Nidhi woke from her dreams and jumped off hers into my bed. She shook me terribly like the woman was shaking the blinds.

"SHALU…SHALU…SHALU," she said hysterically. "COME…COME…TO YOUR SENSES!"

I pointed to the curtains as she turned on the light. But they were drawn with all civility.

"What the hell's there?" she questioned with her voice shivering like someone exposed to extreme winter cold.

"Those curtains…those cur…," I muttered, still infected with bad fright.

"Yes, they're curtains," she said, trying hard to pacify me. "Then what?"

"They were fluttering," I said, still shivering and striving to figure out if it was real or my hallucination.

"You must have had a nightmare, kid," said Nidhi grimly. "See, they're OK, perfectly fine."

Then there was knocking on the door, a persistent rapping followed by a familiar voice.

"Nidhi…Shalu…open the door!" It was Daddy with Dushyant standing just behind him. They must have heard the screeches and hurried to the door. Opening the latch, Nidhi explained everything to them in almost wasting no time and they were kind of indecisive to believe it or not. Finally, Nidhi let them in to discuss further in this matter. Clueless, I was still looking at the curtains with apparent disbelief.

*****

None believed me. It was sheer madness they thought. Sort of an illusion, I must have imagined: my own brainchild. But I knew I saw it happen, whether one bought this story or not.

"Shalu," said Daddy, sitting beside and caressing my head affectionately, "you seem to have a bad impact on your mind. If need be, we'll seek a psychiatrist's counseling."

I was sane and not at all abnormal. Still, I said nothing. All other members in the family were clueless about the incident. The door opened again and this time it was Mom who frisked into the room. She said sitting beside me that she had heard the ruckus. Though Mom looked apprehensive but did not say much, only tried to assuage me by caressing my head. My eyes were still glued to the curtains, which seemed innocent but now were challenging my rationality. It was hard for me to justify a point in this abstract matter.

After half an hour or so, all left for their respective rooms, leaving me and Nidhi. She took hold of both my hands and said, "It's all OK. Now sleep, Shalu. We'll talk in the morning. So, no more discussion about it."

*****

Morning found me cheerful. Last night's ordeal was done away. And I was somewhat feeling relaxed. In some secret vault of my heart, I thought it to be my own brainchild. Thinking that I would not freak-out again, I got normal, but Mom's terrible disease was still so nightmarish I could not forget it, at all. And so, I devoted some time to her care during the day.

At twilight after supper, I went back to my bedroom. It was a starry night and the full moon's beams were easing through the curtains' gaps. Nidhi was watching T.V. in the drawing room. Dushyant and Daddy were with Mom in the master bedroom. I was getting ready to read my book on pharmacology. For convenience, I took two pillows, reclined them against the French window with the blinds down and supported my back against the windowsill. With it I immersed myself into learning. Of course, I wanted to score good marks in the examination. That was a priority.

I was striving to comprehend how drugs are chemicals of low molecular masses which interact with macromolecular targets and produce a biological response; when there suddenly appeared from nowhere a wet crimson mark right in the center of the page I was reading. With a shivering into my spine, I touched it with my forefingers and brought it close to my eyes. It was blood. I wiped my nose with my left hand. It was not bleeding. I double checked my hands; they too were not wounded. But the little blood splatter shone clear and glaring.

I was frozen to my place as the curtains suddenly revived and fluttered like the wings of a dying bird after a road accident. I looked up and could not believe my eyes: there was the *face*— the same *woman's face*, agonized with lip-cut and bruises all over her bloody countenance, eyes bulging out from the sockets and besmeared with horror.

Before I screeched my mightiest pitch, one more drop of thick blood fell from the corner of her lower lip. I saw it come like a ball in the game of cricket reaching in slow motion before hitting the wickets. The blood drop fell across the page, dismantling all my doubts.

This time the rescue team did not have to seek much explanation though, as they saw themselves: the two sizable drops of thick human blood, fresh without clotting. The sentence that the drops had almost covered read: *Most of the drugs used as medicines are potential poisons, if taken in doses higher than those recommended by the physician.* Amid hysterical screeches, I pointed to the curtains, which were still like dead limbs. The agonized woman's face was gone as if it might have never appeared from the curtains. Like it was a conspiracy to falsify my justification.

That night, Nidhi slept in my bed with me like a mother sleeps with her child.

But as I slept, I saw her—the woman—in my dream. Or it was a horror flick. This time I saw her completely. Not just the face: her whole body, unclothed, every inch of it. Not a thread was there to cover it. She stood dead-silent beside my bed. Gazing, with fuming wrath, straight into my eyes, and holding with her left hand the window curtains. Her sagging breast was smeared with fresh dark blood. Her belly, bulging out as if with seven months' pregnancy. And the bushes of black curly hair between her thighs were too nightmarish to talk about. She was a typical ghost: death-pale, fresh from the coffin, and haunting an innocent girl, me.

Then I heard a ringing. The ear-piercing chimes. Startled, I awoke. It was my 5am alarm bell. The early morning sunrays were making a light gold pattern over the window blinds.

*****

Psychiatrist Priya Jhajhariya's cabin displayed more about her personal accomplishments than abnormal psychology. From her scouting days to her casual meeting with Dr. Aruna Broota, almost everything was on the walls with citations including her honeymoon pictures, not in fact the bedroom ones, though. Daddy brought me to her for consultation against my willingness.

She seemed fit for a fashion show, ready for a catwalk or to give away her autographs. Shehnaz Hussain's entire latest makeup products seemed to have been used to partially hide her original appearance. And the thing never crossed my mind that she could at all be helpful in my case. I did not know why, but she could not impress me.

The room shone bright with a pink glow like it's there in casinos shown in *James Bond* flicks. It gave an apparent impression of tappers; instead, it was the effect of the fancy lights in the ceiling. The royal armchair Dr. Jhajhariya sat in gave an impression she did not wish to lose even a single client. No book on clinical psychology I could spot around. Either this branch of science needed more exposition, or she just needed some more exposure to learning.

I took the first chair from the left of her Chinese table and slumped in.

"Kumari Shalu, have you ever been to a counseling session before?" she said, taking a notepad in her hands, her baby-pink-nail-paint reflecting in the fancy lights giving an aura of acrylic nails. Though they were real, I thought.

"Not at all," I said casually, trying to look calm.

"You claim to have seen a woman's face peeping out of the blinds in your bedroom," she said, emphasizing on the word *Claim*.

"I'm not *claiming*. I actually saw it," I said, defending myself.

"But you simultaneously say, the lights were turned off."

"Precisely."

"How come you see a face when there is pitch dark in the room," she said, staring at me like a novice crime investigator.

"If you know, doctor," I said, re-adjusting in my chair, "after a while, eyes adapt themselves to darkness."

"Of course, they do," she conceded, "but not so much that one could tell facial expressions, blood and all that, I mean."

"But the second time I saw *her*, the light was on," I cut a solid point across, "and the blood drops…"

"Anyway," she continued, "do you sleep well?"

"Not anymore, now."

"When did the abnormality…I mean…the problem begin?"

"A fortnight before, just after our shifting to this new house," I replied.

"Shalu," she said, swiveling the chair a little to her left, "do you've an idea about Obsessive Compulsive Neurosis?"

"How do I?"

"It's a complication in which the subject is bound to do or think something, irrationally, again and again, due to depression or anxiety or both. Your mother is the case in point."

I didn't respond, just looked through her as if she did not exist.

Around a dozen more stupid questions she asked. The counseling took half an hour to finish. Then she sent me out and called Daddy in.

Later, on our way home, Daddy told me: the counselor thought my paroxysm was a critical case of somnambulism and hypochondria caused by Mom's illness. She had suggested I needed to come to her clinic for a few more sittings. Apart from it, Dr. Jhajhariya prescribed some antidepressant drugs, too.

I was adamant I would not visit her again, forget about taking the pills. All the same, I was pleased she did not straight away surmise me a schizophrenic and recommend an asylum, the worst possibility.

*****

Next night's nightmare was no different except that the woman was not unclothed. She seemed to be gazing out, and not gazing right into my eyes like she was doing the previous night. Still, her hands clasped the curtains tightly on both sides. I could not see the woman's breasts, but only the back of her and noticed a blood trail emanating from the neck and dripping off the center of her bum.

She wore a violet top, sleeveless and showing fairly from the sides her armpits and the remnants of the recently removed hair. What made her horrendous was her blood-smeared-body that otherwise was pale like it did not have blood in the veins.

Then I heard weird sounds: as if somebody was retching at a distance. Not this woman, but someone else. The sounds then changed into violent coughing, persistent and too loud to be ignored. I woke up. The woman disappeared. And I found Nidhi, still in deep sleep.

Unhooking the latch, I reached out like a sleepwalker coming back to their senses, as I came to realize my Mom was throwing up. She spewed blood with half-digested cauliflower she'd had for supper. I was sorry, being paranoid; I almost forgot the cancer that gripped her. But now the glaring truth was bare in front of me, again.

I took Mom's head in my lap and caressed it affectionately. It consoled her. Daddy and Dushyant too reached there, by now. For a moment I forgot the bloody ghost. Her eyes welled up and from the corners of them tears started rolling down, bedewing her cheeks and touching the sides of my hands. Death seemed to be approaching her every moment. And we could not do anything.

*****

I wanted to tell Nidhi my last night's nightmare, but due to Mom's illness I remained tight-lipped, for I didn't wish to enhance our family's complications. Daddy was already passing through a bad patch. So, I thought it better not to raise this matter at the moment.

Next night, I slept with a bit more fear for reasons unknown to me. In my dream *she* was there again. Reclined on me from my bedpost. Blood dripped from the corners of her lips and taking a course to her chin it was falling on and wetting my abdomen. I could feel its weird coldness. Its thickness. Its living vitality. Now it was going down my thighs. I could feel it in my lower abdomen, the area every spinster wants to offer only to her husband or lover or both. I could feel the numbness, a tickle, as if the blood was oozing out of my own body.

Suddenly I came to realize if I didn't sit up, she'd lie down upon me and pierce her four incisors into my neck like *Dracula* did to his chosen victims. Now, more and more blood was flowing from my V-part. Stirred, I woke up, panting breathless and found myself bleeding, profusely. OH MY GOD! I GOT MY PERIODS!

*****

Dr. Garg declared Mom needed the change of her entire blood periodically: every third or fourth month (if she would live that long). For it, we were at Yashoda Cancer Institute, Ghaziabad. To transfuse four units of blood, we needed to donate the same pints in return. That was the standard process in almost every hospital in our vicinity or in all the medical facilities in India, I guessed.

Nidhi, Dushyant and I gave each one unit of blood, but nevertheless we needed one pint more. Daddy was weak enough physically, his hemoglobin level was so low, we were against his donating a pint. Dushyant suggested the name of his physics' teacher, Rana Sir. He was a Good Samaritan and would not refuse to donate, my brother thought so.

And he was right. Rana reached the hospital's cancer wing in no time and our big trouble was solved quickly. Though I knew beforehand that he would agree to donate, for I once cherished a sweet relationship with him that nobody knew about. Yes, we had come close and passed some memorable moments in each other's arms.

And there evolved a romantic relationship we'd enjoyed before we split up, for no other reason than that we could not get married. In India, live-in is still considered a sin. And getting married to your sweetheart is equal to conquering Mount Everest. Thus, all options were closed and we better decided to close our chapter.

Momentarily though, Mom now sparkled some color from her cheeks after the transfusion, yet her poor health still reflected from her face. She would have to stay now in the facility for the first chemotherapy. Meanwhile, she suffered a great hair-loss, leaving her bald. Even if the treatment was successful, it'd take a long while to heal and get back her hair.

*****

The day Mom's chemotherapy was scheduled, I stayed at home for my exam preparation; while all others went to the sanatorium. I was sure I'd have no problem at all during the day. I made a cup of tea and boiled two eggs for breakfast. As I finished it, I immediately launched myself into hard-study mode and didn't bother about the Ghost. Until then *she'd* never paid me a visit in broad daylight. Ghosts seem to have their own self-made protocols, one of which is not to venture out in the daylight. Nights, somehow, are more convenient for them. They simply love the solitude of night. They too want peace. Good. God. But I was mistaken today. Every rule carries an exception, too.

It was a late sultry summer and as the day progressed, the blasting sun outside could be felt inside the house, too. I pulled the curtains on the French window to keep the room cool and soothing and free from the glaring sun outside. I reached my wardrobe and took out some clothes fit to beat the summer heat.

Pulled over an opaque floral blouse that revealed a fair chunk of my bosom, but I was comfortable in it. Without a bra my orbs looked bigger, heavier than they should, and my nipples protruded.

Strange but true: *breasts are the only part of a woman she both wants to show and hide at the same time. On the one hand they like to pull over deep neckline that sufficiently show their cleavage, but on the other they hardly like any peeping Toms around.* I sat down on my bed again. For a while, I read the book sitting crossed legs, but then shifted my posture. Lay on my back putting a pillow under my head and held the book in front of my eyes.

For quite some time, it was very comforting, but then I felt my eyes getting heavier with every passing second. A strange drowsiness began to possess me. Then my eyes shut. I tried to reopen them. They opened for a couple of seconds and then I could no longer keep them like that. My book fell onto my chest and I crossed to oblivion.

Unlike a common sleep, it was a queer intoxication: an abyss that could only be created by heroin or marijuana, none of which I ever took in my life. Soon I came to realize I was not alone— the specter stood beside me. Her hands held my paperback and she was peering into it, while mine were clasping my pillow tightly.

Then I stood up ramrod as if under some ghoulish influence, started stripping off my clothes one by one: my floral blouse that left me topless, my breasts hanging loose like two succulent mangoes, off was my mini skirt and then my milk white G-strings, too. The ghost looked at me with a grin, picked up my clothes from the bedpost and wore them piece by piece. The tables were turned. She took my place and I, hers.

Now, she was there reading my book, while I stood naked beside the French window clutching the curtains, my long hair hanging loose, my heavy breast sagging and my cleavage dripping with blood: crimson, fresh and wet enough to be precisely felt. We — God knows why— exchanged our positions. And then she called out my name shifting her gaze from the book and focusing it on me: "SHA LU…S H A L U…S H A L U…KID…SHALU!"

There I stood on my bed shivering, dripping with fresh, warm blood. And then there was a sound slap right across my face and the room's dimensions changed. The specter vanished from the view and the bedside where she lay was unoccupied. Instead, Nidhi now stood facing me and shaking me like hell by the shoulders. I came back to my senses. No blood dripping, instead it was my sweat. I realized the electricity supply was gone, so the room was blazing with heat. And my whole body was perspiring.

"Have you gone nuts, Shalu?" said Nidhi, forcing me down to sit on the bed. "Put on your clothes…hurry up. Thank God! It was me who came to your room, first."

I was, naturally, very embarrassed. Had there been Daddy or Dushyant in place of Nidhi, what'd have been my impression?

*****

Mom's growing illness reached a chronic condition: the third stage. And the first chemo was in fact not very helpful. Doctors at the facility said, *Mom needed a second chemo immediately.* Daddy mortgaged Mom's gold jewelry for the sake of her better treatment. We were financially devastated. This time, Naveen, mom's half-brother and a friend of his did the blood donation for transfusion. Two more units of blood we bought by paying some extra bucks. We were ready to go any length to save Mom anyhow. Still, we had but little hope.

Before Mom on her stretcher was carried into the Operation Theater, I hugged her tightly and cried. I feared to let her go, lest she should not come back, *alive*. I did not know why, but it felt as if I embraced the haunting ghost from my room and not my Mom. I shivered at the very thought and cried more and more. Daddy signed, as the standard process, the undertaking papers for full responsibility, in case of an untoward happening with Mom during the therapy. He remained strong, carrying a storm inside his mind. Nidhi and Dushyant were woebegone, teary eyed and looking flustered.

After a while, the bulb on the top of OT's glass door turned red and that was an indication the therapy was underway, *now*. The blinds were pulled over and we couldn't have the inside view. We waited out impatiently. Daddy had been off to the medicos to buy post therapy medicines. We sat in the iron chairs fixed to the floor facing the O.T.

Nidhi on my right and Dushyant on the left, while I sat in the center. None of us took breakfast today. My stomach churned but it was pointless to demand food under the circumstances. And I knew my siblings too must have been facing the same condition.

But we were more concerned about Mom's illness than anything else at the moment.

After half an hour or so, Daddy appeared with two packets in his right hand: the first one contained Mom's drugs and the other one having disposable paper-cups and a transparent polythene containing tea. Plus, a packet of glucose biscuits was a welcome relief. He served tea to all three of us and then poured into the fourth cup for himself. At that moment, the glass door made a creepy sound before it flung open and there appeared a nurse with a green scarf neatly tied to her Eiffel Tower bun. Approaching us she handed a slip to Daddy after having verified his relation with the patient.

Some injections were required. Daddy gave her the polybag containing medicines he'd brought and immediately left without finishing his tea. My eyes were glued to the door. The curtains at the glass door revived my fear from those hung at my bedroom window. For a moment it seemed the spirit stood there too, holding them with both her hands. I jerked my head in exasperation and the tea from my paper-cup sprinkled over my sky-blue blouse. Startled, I glanced at the glass door and felt relieved: The Bloody Ghost was not there. Both Dushyant and Nidhi were staring at me with questioning eyes.

*****

And then came out the bad news—Mom died. "The second chemo could not be successful," the oncologist said. I lost my wits and screeched hysterically the way I had when I observed the macabre specter in my bedroom the first time. My siblings too joined me in mourning. A few medical students walked past us making grim, sad faces. Death makes its own environment: gloomy and dreadful. The whole graveyard shifts to a place where someone dies.

Some paperwork was done and the body was handed over to us. Daddy was busy making some phone calls, while we clamored into the back of the ambulance after Mom's body was settled inside by the ward boys in green uniforms. Daddy took his seat beside the driver as he drove us home with our dear Mom, in fact only the last remains of hers.

Cancer killed her eventually or was it something else? The siren of the ambulance was very unsettling. And I saw: the window curtains, inside the death vehicle behind the seat where Mom lay, fluttered violently. I knew it was because the outside wind was getting inside through the windowpane which was slid aside. Still, I didn't dare to have a second look, for it seemed the specter sat beside Mom's head. I was baffled. It was like my soul was *possessed*. Was I *cursed*?

As we reached there, we found our house filled with varieties of people: black, white, long, short, and stout, including women, children, the rich and the poor. People came from all walks of life to pay their last tributes. Most of the respect to a person is usually given after their death. The funeral preparation was already underway.

Death is the mockery of human life. Everybody seems to finish up the business once someone dies. A dead body is sooner than later to be disposed of. People get stale, stunk after their death. But I feared the ghost woman was still there sitting beside Mom's cadaver. And in my heart of hearts, I wanted Mom to be cremated at the earliest. So, when they took her away to be burnt to ashes, I took a deep sigh of relief. Because then only I could have a look around with no peril of spotting the murdered woman. She was not there. Gone to the crematorium with mom, perhaps.

*****

"I'm sorry for your mother," said Mrs. Nehra, our immediate neighbor, and looked sideways before coming close to my face. "A word's no longer yours as soon as it slips off the tongue," she whispered. "The only favor I want from you is, I should not be dragged into this matter, in case you raise the alarm."

Mrs. Nehra was a typical, well informed, soap opera sort of woman. She knew her neighborhood to a level where other women in the colony were bound to envy her. She could give sermons over divorces, elopements, split-cases, lost jobs, miscarriages, and teenage love affairs that happened in the entire vicinity. She could easily update the local radio broadcasting station. It was, though, a mystery how she got to know these facts. But I was sure she must have some sound knowledge about the house we had rented recently.

"Your name won't surface anywhere, Auntie," I said undertone. "I just wish to know what the hell's wrong with this house or with my bedroom in particular. Or is there a connection between my nightmares and mom's death?"

"Connection I don't know but horrible," she said, "very horrible things happened in this house. Poor Kamini! Misfortune fell on her side."

"Who was Kamini?" I barked. "And what the hell does she have to do with me?"

"The lady who lived in this house before you," said Mrs Nehra, still looking apprehensively here and there. "She lived and died in this house…or…was murdered to be more accurate."

"Murdered? Who killed her by the way?"

"That I don't know," Mrs. Nehra said, trying to hide the truth. But her eyes told she knew it.

"Please Auntie, tell me! Don't cloud the mystery," I implored. "You know everything. I mean, almost everything."

She came closer.

"My name should not be dragged into this matter." She repeated her restraint.

"I swear, I would never tell a soul that you told this to me," I said. "Now tell me who killed her."

"Rajesh Kashyap, her own husband." Mrs.Nehra dropped the bomb.

"What?" I said, aghast. "Why will a husband murder his own wife?"

"Extra marital relations, you know!"

"Who was the cheating spouse: husband or wife?"

"Husband," she said. "Kamini was only trying to win back him."

"By the way, though it's none of my business," I said, trying to hide my fondness in this matter, "who was the woman responsible for this woman's murder?"

"The witch who ruined Kamini's world was her distant relative," said Mrs. Nehra. "A Shalu Verma."

The last words thundered into my ears like a bolt from the blue. A sudden realization dawned upon me: *The girl responsible for the murder of this woman was my namesake. Could it be the reason the dead woman was haunting me every night?* My fear from the ghoul was now shifting to sympathy for the poor woman. But my hair rose in dread on their ends over my whole body.

Irony. It was me who was being dragged into this matter.

*****

Thirteen days had passed since Mom died. As a mark of respect, her headshot was framed, garlanded, and put onto the wall, suspended from a peg in the prayer room. There was an unending chain of relatives who visited our house, meanwhile. Some of them stayed for a couple of days, some paid a passing visit only. All through this while my room too remained well occupied.

It was good, because the Ghost of Kamini did not appear for quite some time, at least as grossly and shamelessly as she would. *Ghosts too have their protocols*; this realization began to settle in me. But I wanted to get rid of the bloody curtains in my room. So, I stripped them off the French window and shoved them into the washing machine.

It was only then, I spotted — there were deep crimson marks over the windowsill. I took a dusting cloth, drenched it in water and wiped the window frame particularly where the sill was tarnished with dried blood. The bloody stains were too rough to be removed easily. I wondered if Kamini still kept a vigil over my frame-cleaning-business. Just to check, I looked over my left shoulder. Nobody was there. I resumed my work, though without much success.

So, I reached over my room cabinet and withdrew a plastic bottle, the label read: *Vanish Liquid Stain Cleaner, ₹62 only.* The spray refreshed the blood. It felt like it fell over there just moments before. I made a picture of Kamini's murder in my mind, but then shook the feeling off my head. I used the cloth rag to remove the stains but could do so partially. It was a hard nut to crack.

And it was then, I heard a bone chilling, cold voice behind me: "What are you doing, Shalu?"

The dusting cloth and the stain cleaner slipped off my hands and fell to the marble floor. But my squeal stopped midway as I spotted Rana standing very close to me.

"Damn! You terrified me," I said, recovering my breath.

"Are you a chick? Scared so easily?" he said and gave a forced smile. "I thought you to be a brave girl."

"Yes, once I was, but now a slight exertion can stir me."

"Your Mom's death must have a severe impression on you," he said. "I can understand. All you need is rest."

"All I need is some *Ojha*," I said. "Because it's *something else* that is haunting me day and night."

"Something *else*?" he said with curiosity in his tone. "And why do you need an exorcist, by the way?"

"Have a seat, I'll tell you," I said, offering him my room chair.

I narrated my predicament, only holding back Mrs. Nehra's identity, for I'd given her my word.

*****

Rana listened to me with rapt attention, occasionally nodding, and frowning with awe and queer expressions writ large over his countenance. When I was finished, he said coldly: "One more solution is possible to rectify this case."

I looked at him with questioning eyes, Nidhi beside me.

"And what is that?" I asked with cold interest.

"Meditation. And in your case: A séance meditation."

"How?" Nidhi blurted out. But Rana didn't seem to have noticed her and continued.

"Shalu, I'll assist you to do séance meditation and call *her*," he said, eyes focused in some vacuum. "It'll strengthen you to fight against the dark forces. It's a *therapy* I've practiced hard for years in Haridwar. And it'll help you too, I'm dead sure."

"When are we doing it?"

"Tonight," he said, rising from his chair, "provided that you want to get rid of this ghost issue."

Nidhi and I agreed.

Daddy was in New Delhi, back to his duty at Metro Station. And convincing Dushyant was not that difficult a task. A planned encounter with the Ghost of Kamini was henceforth scheduled.

*****

Early that night, Nidhi spread four floor-mats in my room. On the first one, Rana took his position sitting crossed legs. I sat just opposite, facing him. On his right was Nidhi. While Dushyant sat on his left. The doors were closed. The blinds were back on the French window after having been washed and ironed. Despite the presence of all these people, I still wondered if Kamini would be back to frighten me as I shut my eyes at Rana's cold command.

"Shalu, am I audible to you?" he said in his familiar, cold but husky voice.

"Yes," I said, putting both my hands in my lap.

"Fine. Are your eyes shut?"

"Yes." His own eyes must have been closed. Or he would not ask such a question.

"Let your whole body feel relaxed."

"OK"

"Feel your mind is a vacuum. No tension. No anxiety. No fear. No past. No future. Just the present moment and that's — pure and blissful."

I didn't respond this time. But tried to assume what was suggested.

"Remember some good moments of your life," he said.

I remembered my Mom giving me a shower, while I was a young girl, so young that I could not even pronounce Mom's and Dad's names properly.

"Recollect some more memories." He continued.

I did. I saw Rana and me, huddled together in bed without clothes. He was holding my tits and I was giggling like a fairy. Then those arousal moments were there — unforgettable. Sex isn't a sin. Still, it's almost banned in the entire world and considered a taboo that cannot be removed by any stain cleaner.

"How's it?" he asked.

"Beautiful."

"Now come to some difficult level: Try to recall some mathematical equation which you found hard to solve."

Suddenly, I found myself in seventh grade. Precisely, thirteen years old and at my puberty age. Now I looked like a girl, for my breasts just started getting a round shape. And I recently noticed my pubic hair and the occasional itching in that area. Mr. Rajendra Yadav, our school math teacher was there in the classroom, teaching us Algebra. The blackboard was filled with some equation, where X was unknown and I was trying hard to figure out what the hell he was trying to prove.

Have you got it? Mr. Yadav said after having filled the entire blackboard with his zigzag writing. All the other students replied in unison *Yes, sir;* but I said *No, sir.* He explained the entire equation again, but it didn't reach my head. He did it thrice; still I could not figure it out. Eventually, he gave up and said, *Come later to my office; I'll explain it to you, there.*

And I precisely recalled how I met Mr. Yadav in his office after school hours that day. As I took permission and went in, he gazed at me fixedly, perhaps at my chest which had taken a round shape in the past few weeks. It seemed he was in a different mood now.

"Remove your glasses," he said as I grasped the situation. He left his chair and came around the table.

Took off my spectacles and passed them to the oak table. No Algebra though he taught me there, just pulled me to his office sofa and kissed right onto my moist lips.

I felt his spiky beard with half gray hair against the surface of the soft skin of my face. It was my first kiss, a dirty one, a forced kiss rather. I could not say *no* to it, but I knew I was against it. I was underage. Was it child abuse? It was like two generations were meeting *forcibly*. Hell, both my relations were with my teachers. Was it a double coincidence or my fate or both? His eyes tore through me, his fingers did the rest.

My math was no good, but I knew quite well what he was doing was not *Algebra.* The creep was only satisfying his lust with his wooden office door shut, though not bolted; probably he knew no one would come. All had gone home except me and him. Eventually, he laid me on his office couch and in a nutshell did everything he could.

Sometimes we cannot stand against the wrong. I too couldn't object to Mr. Yadav's exertion. He saw my everything, and I could not say *no* to him. Thus, in the next few minutes he explored me totally and made me forget—*the bloody Algebra.*

Forty minutes later when I came back home that afternoon, my stomach ached. I regretted I gave away something precious to a wrong man. Rather I was robbed of something I should have safeguarded.

*****

I started with Rana's fresh command: "Now think of this bedroom. You are alone. Visit your present realities and nightmares, too. It's high time."

"OK!" I said. Still my mind drifted back as I realized my past was no less haunted than present with Mom's recent death and the bloody curtains.

And then I saw *her* again, drenched in blood, naked, loose hair all over her face, sagging breasts, and *she* was holding the *curtains*. One more thing, Kamini did not have eyes, just the pupils, peeping through the hair covered face.

"HELL, SHE IS HERE!" I shouted.

"COMMAND HER!" said Rana in a high-pitched voice this time.

"WHAT?"

"QUESTION HER. ASK HER WHAT SHE WANTS."

I didn't need to ask anything, though.

She spoke: *You ruined my family. I'll ruin yours. Fucking Bitch, you lured my husband and provoked him to kill me and my dear unborn child. Oh, dear, dear child!*

All heard it this time. The voice was loud and clear, but weirdly it was emerging from no other source than *my own lips*. With a changed voice, I was suddenly: a split personality.

"Now reveal your true identity," Rana said, "and command her to leave you."

"I have nothing to do with your fucking family," I yelled in *my* voice. "NOR DO I KNOW YOUR BLOODY HUSBAND."

You're Shalu. You instigated Rajesh to kill me, so that you could live in his arms for good, she thundered.

"GODDAMIT..! I'M NOT THE SHALU YOU'RE LOOKING FOR. I'M DIFFERENT. JUST A NAMESAKE. WE CAME HERE ONLY THIS MONTH. I DON'T KNOW ANY RAJESH."

There was silence for a few moments. Kamini in me spoke again: *I don't believe you. And why should I?*

"You don't have an option, *Kamini*," I said, this time in a soft tone. "And now leave me alone. Don't chase me like HELL. Just go away from my life."

And, if I don't go? The ghost bargained.

I was not sure what to say this time.

Rana came to my rescue. "Threaten her to go away!"

"THEN I'LL BURN YOU TO ASHES. JUST GET LOST FROM MY LIFE."

Where should I go? This is my house. I shall live here alone. She insisted.

"This is none of my business. Go to Hell," I said. "This was once your house. Now it's mine. You'll have to go."

No response. Just creepy crying sobs of the ghost. She was melting.

"And why the bloody hell, do you keep holding these curtains? Don't you've any other business?" I almost scolded her, only realizing later how offensive were my words.

Moments passed in silence when her voice escaped my lips again: *You don't know what excruciating pain I felt when he fed me those bloody pills that rinsed my guts and oozed my blood from my nostrils and mouth. I held FOR SUPPORT these curtains and called him for help, but he was so cruel looking at me as if he was waiting for my death.*

"You go or I burn you, bloody fool!" I said in a cold voice, imitating Rana. Though I wasn't sure how I could burn her. But the trick worked.

Please don't burn me! Don't burn me! I'll go! I'll go! She said and sobbed.

"Then get lost from this house immediately, right now," I commanded.

With a change of tone, she began to laugh like they do in horror movies: *I'LL GO, BUT THE TUMOR IN YOU WILL KILL YOU.*

"TUMOR?" I was taken aback.

Yes, the malignant tumor. Do you think your chest's recent extra growth is without a reason? The truth is: the way your mother died, so will you.

I felt drained of all energy. My mouth was choked. My head felt heavy. The entire house seemed to spin around.

*****

I opened my eyes. And then suddenly there was a terrible dust storm somewhere outside. The ghostly winds roared like hell. The bedroom door was flung open. The electricity supply was gone. The windowpanes shattered and the glass pieces scattered all around. The blinds fluttered like they did the first time I'd experienced the paranormal presence. The gusts of wind suddenly filled the bedroom and shook the entire interior. The curtains were pulled off forcibly from the pegs by the tornado and before we could comprehend anything, they just moved mysteriously out into the backstreet through the shattered, battered French window.

After a couple of horrible minutes, the blasts of the winds stopped as suddenly as they'd started. The tenseness of the eerie environment was shifted to calm and composed condition.

"Kamini is gone. For good, I'm sure," Rana said with finality looking at the bare window.

The only light available in the house now was from the blood moon out in the sky. Nidhi and Dushyant were still glued to the fallen shards of glass. I stood up from the floor-mat still looking at the missing curtains that hung at the window just moments before. Then I left for the prayer room with my eyes burning like hell.

There, I found Mom's framed picture on the floor, its glass scattered all around me in innumerable pieces. I sank to where Mom's battered snapshot lay and heard my own sobs as I came to realize: I was crying. The resurrected *ghost of Algebra* seemed less painful now. My breasts ached severely. The entire house was spinning around. The floor beneath my feet was collapsing, giving way to rubble and debris.

And then there was some severe itching felt in my throat followed by a violent cough. Tiny droplets of spit came from my mouth and scattered across my hands. Something dark came into view among the salivating particles. A close observation showed what it was: a blot of blood. Was it a death warrant?

The demarcation line between life, death, and faith suddenly seemed merged, intermixed. I felt more devasted than vulnerable. Life's as painful as death. I only realized that tonight. At the sound of footsteps, I looked up. Rana, Dushyant, and Nidhi stood surrounding me, probably trying to figure out the right words to pacify me. But no words could do so. Words have their own limitations.

"End"

SAN ESQUELETO

by Ross Baxter

Father Juan Porta waited patiently in the rundown arrivals shed of the small rural airport which served the town of Concepción, deep in the dusty grasslands of central Paraguay. Few commercial flights landed there, and the one he was waiting for, inbound from the capital, Asunción, was already an hour late. He was happy to wait, passing the time chatting to one of his many elderly parishioners, who sat waiting for her son to arrive.

Another thirty minutes passed before the part-time airport admin clerk, another member of his church, sauntered past to open the begrimed glass door out to the ancient asphalt apron where the plane would halt. The faint whine of distant engines increased, and the small aircraft finally bounced down the potholed runway and turned towards the building. A single door opened as soon as both propellers ceased spinning, and four tired passengers climbed gladly out.

Father Juan spotted his quarry straight away; a younger priest dressed in a well-pressed and tailored cassock, looking like he had just stepped out from the centre pages of *The Catholic Post*. His spotless attire was in stark contrast to Father Juan's well-worn black shirt, creased trousers and yellowing clerical collar. Juan stood and walked wearily over to the door to greet him.

The younger priest was last of the small gaggle of passengers reaching the dilapidated arrivals shed. Father Juan know them all, and shook hands with them as they walked past.

"Father Juan Porta?" asked the smartly dressed priest as he gingerly stepped inside.

Juan nodded. "Welcome to Concepción."

The new arrival gave a lukewarm smile and half-hearted handshake, making little effort to hide his disdain at the grim airport building, and the slightly dishevelled priest who met him. "I am Father Esteban López-Istúriz Echeverría, of the Vatican's Institute of Consecrated Life."

"Welcome," repeated Juan. "I trust you had a good journey from Rome?"

"Not really," replied Father Esteban flatly.

"Well, let's get you to our church," smiled Juan, leading the way out of the shed to the dusty road beyond.

A single taxi waited, an ancient, battered Ford with a broken rear window taped up with thick plastic sheeting. On seeing the priests, the driver jumped out and rushed to help Father Esteban with his suitcase.

"Thanks for waiting, Luis," said Juan to the driver.

The driver carefully placed the large case in the trunk, littered with rubbish and old newspapers. Juan held the creaking rear door open for his colleague, who frowned disparaging at the ripped vinyl seat before gingerly climbing in.

On the third attempt the asthmatic engine finally started, and the taxi trundled onto the dirt track which served as the main road to the airport. Juan attempted some small talk with the uncommunicative Vatican priest, but eventually gave up and instead watched the colourful but poor barrios of Concepción pass by the windows. Shortly after, the taxi squealed noisily to a stop outside the white-painted Church of María Auxiliadora.

Father Esteban looked at the ancient meter and pulled a crisp bank note from the pocket of his pressed cassock to offer to the driver.

"No, father," said the driver in surprise. "No charge."

Father Esteban looked at Juan. "You have an account with the driver?"

"Something like that," replied the local priest cryptically, nodding his thanks to the driver. "What do you think of our beautiful church?"

Father Esteban looked up at the modest church, and then along the quite street at the handful dilapidated shops and poorly maintained houses. "It looks fit for purpose."

Juan led his colleague up the short flight of steps towards the arched entrance of the building. He barged the creaking door open with his shoulder and stepped inside to the coolness of the open nave. Two elderly black-clad women sat stooped alone on separate polished wooden pews, both deep in contemplation, or possibly asleep. Neither looked up as the two men walked down the aisle and through a door near the ornate alter to the back of the church into what passed as Father Juan's office.

"Can I offer you a drink, father?" asked Juan, beckoning Esteban to take a seat.

Father Esteban sat and shook his head. "As you know, I'm visiting a number of parishes in central Paraguay. For the last two days I've been in the capital, Asunción, talking with the Archbishop, who has given me a free reign whilst I'm in Paraguay. I leave tomorrow morning, which is when the next plane out is."

Juan nodded. "I'm sure you'll enjoy your stay with us. We've two interesting museums, and the Paraguay River is great for fishing this time of the year."

"I'm not here to enjoy myself, as you well know," said the younger man curtly. "I'm here to investigate why the false folk icon, Saint Death, is still so popular in a region where ninety percent of the population profess to be practicing Catholics!"

Juan nodded again, this time more sagely. "Here he is better known as San Esqueleto, rather than San la Muerte."

Father Esteban's face reddened. "Saint Skeleton or Saint Death, either way it's the same false icon! And yet the priests seem to take no action, happy to let devotions continue. My mission is to establish the extent of the issue, and make recommendations to Vatican hierarchy about how we stamp it out."

"Of course," Juan conceded. "I've been the Priest at this church for over thirty-five years, and am well aware of the beliefs my parishioners."

"But still you've not tackled the issue, and San Esqueleto continues to have tenure her!" Father Esteban challenged.

This time it was the older priest whose face reddened. "As you said yourself, ninety percent of the population in central Paraguay are practicing Catholics. How does that compare with Rome, or your home town in Spain? We must be doing something right to keep the faith here, whilst it is in such rapid decline across the rest of the world!"

Esteban regarded the old priest in surprise; as a Vatican-based official he was quite unaccustomed to ever being challenged. "The issue is that the Church cannot be seen to condone folk tales and idolatry. Make no mistake, the Papal Authorities will read my report and will take any necessary action!"

"Well, I'll help you as much as I can," sighed Juan.

"Good," said Esteban. "I wish to concentrate on the role you, and the Church, has in stamping out San Esqueleto in this parish. I wish to take an early supper, then you can accompany me around the town to see the extent of the issue."

"Of course," said Juan, stoically. "I'll show you to your room, then I'll cook us something up."

"You have to cook?" Esteban questioned in surprise.

"Central Paraguay is a long way from the Vatican and Europe," replied Juan tiredly. "Very little money or support finds its way here, and we're left to our own devices to do the best we can."

*****

Despite Juan's best culinary efforts, Father Esteban seemed disappointed with the meal of grilled chicken and pasta. Even the wine, a good bottle which he had been saving, did not seem to satisfy his visitor. After Juan cleared away the dishes, they both stepped out into the early evening dusk, the air thick with the smell of fresh cinnamon churros wafting over from the carts of street vendors.

"So," began Father Esteban, "how many shrines are there to San Esqueleto in Concepción?"

Juan frowned. "Most altars are kept in the houses of devotees and are private. I have no idea how many of those there would be."

"What about public shrines?" pushed Father Esteban.

"Three. One by the river piers, put up by the fishermen. One in the garden at the rear of the

Regional Hospital, and a small one in the park by the Regimiento da Caballeria base."

"Take me to the nearest," Esteban ordered.

"That will be the one at the hospital," said Juan, moving to the right past the churro seller, who immediately handed over of the deep fried pastries to him.

Juan took the pastry and nodded his thanks, offering it to Esteban. "These really are good."

Esteban shook his head, so Juan proceeded to eat it as he walked.

"You didn't pay for it," remarked Esteban. "Just like you didn't pay for the taxi."

Juan shrugged. "That's how things work around here. The town is poor, and people can show their support for the church without giving money."

"That sounds dubious," muttered Esteban, wrinkling his nose.

Juan did not reply, concentrating instead on the steaming churro and traversing the uneven pavement. They walked on in silence, passing the closing shops and colourful barrios on the route to the hospital. After a short distance, Juan led Father Esteban down a side street behind the main hospital building, and entered a small public garden hidden behind a whitewashed brick wall.

"This is the garden of remembrance for the hospital," said Juan in a low voice. "It's where relatives and friends can contemplate or grieve."

"It looks a mess," muttered Father Esteban, eyeing the jumble of plastic flowers, faded photographs, and deflated balloons which littered the area.

"The shrine to San Esqueleto is by the rear wall," said Juan, leading the way towards an altar lit with candles and surrounded by a multitude of offerings.

Esteban looked at the shrine in disgust, his eyes roving down from the carved wooden figure of a black skeleton wrapped in a monk's tunic, the eyeless skull peering out from beneath a dark cowl. A number of fat church candles illuminated the multitude of offerings, which ranged from unopened bottles of premium spirits to a selection of high-end mobile phones.

"Look at this!" Esteban exclaimed "That's the new iPhone! There are thousands of dollars' worth of items just laying here. Why no-one has taken any?"

"These are the offerings to San Esqueleto, made by those wishing for a miracle for loved ones in the hospital. No one would be callous enough, or brave enough, to steal them."

"It's disgraceful that people trust and make offerings to a false icon. Why don't you tear this altar down?" Esteban challenged hotly.

"As I keep telling you, San Esqueleto is a folk saint, worshipped here alongside the true saints of the Catholic Church. Both exist together now as they have since the Jesuit missionaries brought Christianity to the native Guaraní Indians four hundred years ago. This makes the church stronger in central Paraguay, which is why people don't turn away from Christ here like they are doing across the rest of the Catholic world."

"Rubbish!" hissed the Vatican priest. "This is heresy!"

"No," Juan vainly continued. "To believers, San Esqueleto exists within the context of the Catholic faith. Offerings are given in exchange for favours relating to restoring love, health, and fortune, to protect worshipers from witchcraft, and to grant good luck. You should think of San Esqueleto as a local saint, not as an evil adversary."

Esteban grabbed Juan's shoulders and shook him. "How dare you say such things! Your refusal to act is a betrayal of the holy vows you took when you became a priest. You're not fit to serve the Lord!"

"Let's just take a minute," pleaded Juan. "Let me try and show you this in context of the people who live here."

"I'm going back to the church to make my report on Concepción, and the role you are playing in this heresy. We'll let the Vatican be the judge!"

Juan watched sadly as Esteban stormed out of the garden. Instead of following, he walked in the opposite direction, towards a bar on the corner of the street opposite the hospital. Inside, the bar was crowded, all tables occupied and with customers standing by the bar chatting happily.

"Father Juan!" called the owner from behind the bar. "What a pleasure!"

Juan nodded. "Can we talk?"

The owner, a small middle-aged rotund man, beckoned the priest through the crowded bar towards a door set into the far wall. Patrons nodded or happily greeted Juan as he passed, many warmly shaking his hand. The door led to an office, and the owner closed the door behind them.

"What can I do for you, Father?" asked the owner, pointing towards a seat.

"I'm afraid San Esqueleto needs an offering," replied Juan.

The smile left the bar owners face.

"Only a small offering," assured the priest. "It will be worth all the luck you got which led to you own this place, which seems to be doing really well."

"Of course," said the bar owner gravely. "I understand. What do you want me to do?"

Juan looked around the office. He took one of the clean tablecloths drying on a rack in the corner of the office and placed a magazine on the desk by the chair. He then beckoned the bar owner to sit at the desk.

"This will be quick," promised the priest. "Place your left hand on the magazine and spread your fingers."

The bar owner complied nervously, his hand shaking. Juan took a switchblade knife from his jacket pocket and opened it. Grasping the man's wrist firmly with his left hand, Juan pressed hard at the base of the bar owner's little finger with the wickedly sharp knife. The blade sliced through the skin and crunched easily through bone and cartilage at the knuckle. Wincing with pain, the bar owner closed his eyes but did not cry out.

"Done," said Juan, pocketing the finger and passing the table cloth over to the bar owner. "Wrap your hand in this to stop the blood. You'll need stitches, get someone to take you over to the hospital."

"Yes, Father," mumbled the bar owner through clenched teeth.

"Your debt is paid, my son," said Juan, slipping out through the office door and closing it behind him.

Outside the bar, the street was busy with patrons. He nodded to those he knew and slipped down a nearby alley in the direction of the church. His love for the town and its people had grown over his thirty-five years of service as Concepción's only priest, for which he felt justifiably proud.

On reaching the church he first walked around to the rear, seeing that the light in the guest room was on, and guessing that Father Esteban was busy writing his report for his Vatican masters. He opened up the back door and slipped into the cool interior of the building, not bothering to turn on the lights as he knew the layout so well. At the end of the gloomy corridor he unlocked the door to the basement and entered, carefully locking it behind him. Turning on the lights, he moved down the stairs to the chill cellar, a place which once served as a crypt but now was used for storage. Christmas and Easter decorations sat piled alongside parish records and cleaning equipment, boxes of bibles and miscellaneous junk accumulated over the decades. The subterranean cellar had a faint odour of damp and a strong smell of disinfectant. At the far end he carefully unlocked twin padlocks securing a low black wooden door, re-enforced with thick steel banding and heavy bolts. He crossed himself, then opened the heavy door, which creaked on ancient weighty hinges.

Inside was darkness. He took a candle from a small alcove just inside and lit it. The flickering light dimly showed a small vault of four whitewashed stone walls, a stone ceiling and flagstone floor. In the centre sat a raised rectangular altar, roughly carved from a single block of local limestone, with weathered engravings along each side depicting scenes of ancient Guaraní peoples. On it, partially wrapped in an archaic rough cloth habit, holed and decaying, lay a skeleton, it's bones blackened with age. Like the various wooden carvings throughout the region, the skeleton carried a heavy scythe, but unlike the other shrines, this skeleton was real.

The priest crossed himself, then withdrew the bloody finger from his pocket. He wiped the raw end of the finger across the skeleton's dark teeth, leaving a wet smear on the thick coating of dried blood. Finally, after throwing the severed digit on the large pile of assorted bones at the base of the altar, Juan bowed to San Esqueleto and retreated from the grim vault.

*****

After refusing breakfast, Father Esteban remained stubbornly silent during the taxi ride to the tiny airport. The battered Ford stopped by the dusty shed which served as both the airport's arrivals and departure hall, and the two priests stepped out into the morning sunshine.

"For the last time, I beg you not to damn the church in central Paraguay. The people and traditions here should be respected, not deplored," pleaded Juan.

Father Esteban ignored him, walking away through the deserted shed out to the grass airfield where the only aircraft of the day stood. The pilot beckoned him to climb aboard the empty plane, then returned to help the single airfield employee who struggled to disconnect the refuelling line from the small portable fuel bowser. After much cursing, they finally managed to disconnect the pipe, which dropped spilling fuel over the stony ground. Hurriedly, they pushed the bowser away, dragging the refuelling line behind then. After a short distance, the steel coupling at the end of the pipe struck a piece of flint, and the resultant spark ignited the spilt fuel. With shouts of panic the two men fled, and orange flame lept up to the wing. The resulting explosion knocked both off their feet and broke the only intact window of the shed. A huge fireball engulfed the twin-engine plane, and the single passenger trapped inside.

Even at a distance, Father Juan felt the intense heat. He crossed himself, then got back inside the taxi to return to his beloved church and saint.

UNWELCOME GUESTS

by Phillip T. Stephens

Matt Trübe nudged the refrigerator open with his elbow because his arms cradled a carefully crafted stack of casserole dishes, Tupperware, and half-empty take out cartons. As he guided the leftovers to the shelf he'd cleared before the mourners arrived, a jar of stone ground mustard tumbled from the top shelf onto his bad ankle.

His leg buckled and he listed to the left. The stack of take-out and Tupperware tumbled from their places on top of his sister's green bean and ground beef casserole dish. The food burst from the containers, splattering his pants, his shoes, and the floor he'd mopped only this morning. Wincing with pain, he kneeled to recover any salvageable food and a four-pack of Guiness Draught stout fell from the top shelf and hit his head. The cans hit the floor, puncturing one and spewing foam everywhere.

Matt slipped to the floor and massaged his scalp. All that effort and the refrigerator looked as though Gracie were still with him, making a mess of everything. He waited for the throbbing in his skull to subside and rose to clean the mess.

After he'd dropped the soaking paper towels in the trash, he returned his attention to the refrigerator. Nothing was as he'd left it this morning: the egg carton had overturned, the lid on the raspberry jam jar was loose, and the milk lay on its side draining into the vegetable bin. It must have been Gracie's sister, Hope, after her fourth glass of port from the bottle he'd hidden over the stove thinking she couldn't reach it. She bumped into half the furniture and spilled the port on the rest. Why not the refrigerator too?

(A full liquor bar in the living room and Hope had to find the hundred-dollar bottle of Sandeman's he bought Gracie for her last birthday.)

Matt salvaged what food he could, scrubbed the refrigerator top to bottom, labeled the new containers and arranged the food with casseroles on the bottom shelf, meats and vegetables on the middle, and salads on the top. With the last item stocked, he rang Gracie's brother—his drinking buddy, Cole.

"You won't believe the condition I found my refrigerator in."

"Still blaming Gracie? Jesus, Matt, you buried her this afternoon."

Matt held his iPhone away from his ear. Now that Gracie was gone, he didn't want to make Cole his new argument partner. After a few seconds he suggested they have drinks on the weekend.

*****

Matt planned to hard boil eggs for breakfast, but when he opened the refrigerator, the Tupperware tumbled from the shelves and onto his feet. Frozen solid.

Couldn't blame Gracie (or Hope) for this one.

Later that day, Matt returned to the refrigerator only to discover the Tupperware lids peeled off with the contents spilled and mold growing from the lidless jars. He slammed the door in disgust. He dined out for the rest of the week.

During his forty-year marriage to Gracie, he lost track of how often he'd open the door only to watch a bottle or jar tumble to the floor. Each time he'd close the containers, rearrange the shelves and stack everything neatly, discarding any suspicious blue fruits, and pushing everything back from the shelf's edge so it wouldn't spill accidentally.

Two days later, he'd open the door and a pickle or lime juice jar would plunge past his fingers, shatter on the floor and spray his shoes with glass shards and brine. Or a frozen casserole would dive from the freezer door like an Olympic athlete and finish with a ten-point high-impact touch down on his toe.

Gracie, God rest her, swore by her late mother's Bible that she put every item exactly where he'd left it. He would rip open the door, point to the disarray and she'd shake her head. "Can't imagine what happened."

And now, it seemed, neither could he.

*****

While sitting at the Four Seasons bar, sipping Coronas and dipping tortilla chips into pasty, lukewarm queso, Matt rambled for twenty minutes about refrigerator entropy. He thought at first that Cole's amusement reflected his storytelling skills, but halfway to the bottom of the queso, he realized Cole was laughing at him.

He tapped the lip of his bottle and raised two fingers to order another round. "Okay, Cole, what's the joke?"

Cole titled his bottle and drained the last half-inch of beer. "Gracie never told you about the unerwünschtergast, did she?"

The bartender dropped two fresh ones in front of them and swept away their empties.

"The whatgast? Is this another German fairy tale?"

Cole scooped a mountain of cheese onto a chip and held his free hand underneath to stop the drip. "Don't knock the old stories, Matt. Your family's fifth generation, but Gracie and I were raised on a farm outside of Osterheide."

Matt pictured his thumb and forefinger pinching. Yada, yada, yada. He'd heard it all. Rising before dawn, eating lamb fries for breakfast, milking cows with raw bare fingers in 20-degree weather, ghosts in the parlor and goblins in the barns. You can take the kids out of the country, but you can't take the country out of the kids.…

Cole licked his fingers then wiped them on a red paper napkin. "Gracie would never tell you because you look down your nose at the country ways, but she left the jars open to pacify the unerwünschtergast."

"I repeat. The whatgast?"

"A gremlin, but a particular kind of gremlin. In the old country there's *der Maschinenteufel,* which is what Americans think of when they picture gremlins.

Creatures that mess with machines. Or there's *der böser Geist*, or bad ghost. And of course, the *Poltergeist*."

Cole paused, lowered his head, and whispered. "But in our province, there's the *unerwünschtergast*, or *unerwünschtergäste*, but it's not a ghost so much as a demon. An uninvited visitor that moves into your house and can only be appeased by leaving out uncovered food as an offering. Our parents had a family of them. One of them hitched a ride with Gracie when we immigrated."

Matt tapped his wedding ring against his bottle. "Just because your people dream of moving back to the dark ages, doesn't mean there are any dark ages waiting for you to return."

Cole shrugged and dipped his chip into salsa, then the salsa-dripping chip into the queso. "My advice? Feed the beast and live in peace."

*****

Peaceful co-existence with a fairy tale? A fairy tale he'd never heard of before this week? Matt decided the best way to dispose of (or disprove) a folk tale was with total thermonuclear war.

He woke the next morning hung over and ready for combat. Not even bothering to dress, he heated a cup of water, added Starbucks powdered coffee, and tackled the kitchen like an All-Star linebacker tackles a junior varsity tailback.

First, he emptied and scrubbed the refrigerator. Then locked it. He stocked the shelves with canned goods, dried goods and tinned milk. This wasn't just war; it was a siege. If he had to live on canned tuna, saltines, and instant Starbucks for a month, so be it. He wasn't unlocking that refrigerator until he saw the unerwünschtergast's footprints pointing in the direction of Germany.

That evening, exhausted, he celebrated with a 007 marathon on cable and a bottle of warm Budweiser. If the Brits could drink warm beer then, by God, so could he.

After two swallows, he dumped it down the drain and retired to the bedroom to watch. The Brits must have trained their taste buds to ignore a total lack of flavor.

When he swaggered barefoot into the kitchen the next morning, chest thrust forward with the confidence of certain victory, he sliced his toe and hopped to the sink for a paper towel to stop the bleeding. Once he'd wrapped the wounded toe with a two-inch thick Brawny bandage, he hobbled back to the entrance to see what he'd stepped on.

He followed the blood trail to the trash can where, in the middle of the floor and covered with blood, rested the peeled metal lid from a Starkist can, finger ring half-attached. The rest of the floor was littered with macaroni, yellow cheese powder, corn flakes, powdered coffee, broken saltines, shredded tuna, shredded sardines, mounds of deviled ham with tiny footprints imprinted, fig bars, fig bar wrappers, port puddles and pools of evaporated milk, shredded paper labels, shredded cardboard and glass shards from the hundred dollar bottle of Sandeman's vintage port he gave Gracie for her birthday and that her sister had almost polished off after the funeral.

Someone knocked at the door. Shave and a haircut. Cole's knock.

He hopped to the door and, sure enough, Cole stood on his porch with a cup of take-out coffee in each hand and a bag of donuts stashed beneath his arm pit.

Cole marched to the kitchen and whistled. A long gliding whistle, three octaves down, like riding a slide to the bottom of a canyon. He wrapped Matt's fingers around one of the coffees. "I figured you'd try something. Lock him out of the refrigerator?"

Matt's toe throbbed like the head of a tympani during a grand finale. "The chains and padlock gave it away?"

"You're lucky he didn't rip apart the refrigerator to get to what's inside."

Matt stood on one foot to take the pressure off his toe. The blood had already soaked through his makeshift Brawny wrap. "There's nothing in the refrigerator."

Cole nodded knowingly. The "I told you so" nod. That smug nod people make to demonstrate their vastly superior storehouse of wisdom. "That explains why your kitchen looks like a dozen greyhounds ripped up your garbage."

He put the donuts on the stove and rested his hip against the door handle. "You can't rid the house of an infestation, buddy. The unerwünschtergast mates for life. You can make peace with him or the mischief and mayhem will escalate until you're a feeble octogenarian puttering about with house shoes and a walker. "

Cole reached into the bag and passed Matt a fresh, pink frosting with sprinkles Homer donut. "I'd eat these now because unerwünschtergasts swarm to frosted cakes like sharks to a thrashing swimmer."

They polished off all six donuts in the living room while reading the CNN headlines on Matt's muted TV. Cole devoted the entire visit to unerwünschtergast arcana. Once he started to recycle the lore, Matt checked his watch several times, and Cole finally got the message.

As soon as he closed the front door, Matt began to strategize his next campaign.

*****

Six weeks later, Matt finally admitted he was standing next to Custer at Little Big Horn with one bullet remaining. He'd loaded Gracie's china (what remained of it), home appliances, cutlery, their furniture, television and stereo, contents of their closet, any of their possessions that weren't fixed to the walls or foundation into a U-Haul and moved them to storage. All that remained were a sleeping bag, camp chair, camp stove and cooler for beer which he kept on the porch outside.

During that time, he'd moved everything from the kitchen to his study only to discover the unerwünschtergast had trashed his study, including his financial records and receipts for his tax filings. The battle of the utility closet followed within days, an utter rout that resulted in his water heater being reduced to scrap metal, boiler shrapnel embedded in the walls and a carpet so thoroughly soaked he had to hire a professional carpet cleaner.

The final battle of the kitchen ended with the shelves ripped from the cupboards, the cupboards ripped from the walls, the tiles ripped from the floor, the refrigerator's inner wall in the living room and the coolant soaked into the carpet. The carpet cleaner told him it would be cheaper to rip it out and lay a new one. Then he added, "but if you're going to party like this, I'd rip the carpet out and finish the concrete underneath with sealant."

The battle of the bathroom cost him a sink, the picture window the sink was thrown through, a toilet that he had to replace because he couldn't extract the plunger from the flange, half a dozen sections of pipe removed at random from the water network and an entire wall which was broken into sheet rock chunks and scattered through the house.

With every clash the unerwünschtergast seized more territory until Matt had retreated into his bedroom and barred the door with bungee cords. He crawled through the bedroom window to enter and leave the house and brought nothing edible onto the property. He drove to the shopping center to eat until the unerwünschtergast stole his tool kit, disassembled his Outback and tossed the parts into the creek behind the house.

As of this morning, nothing remained in his house beside the walls and concrete floor. He'd stripped every surviving fixture from their anchors and hauled them to storage. And now he sat with his butt on the bedroom floor, back to the wall and pump shotgun in his lap.

Matt had been a pacifist since he first protested the Vietnam War in college. He refused to hunt with his buddies and had never owned a gun. Not until he picked up a Hatfield semiautomatic shotgun at Academy Surplus the day before.

He didn't even know semiautomatic shotguns existed until he walked into the store. He'd planned to buy a handgun, but since he still hadn't seen his nemesis, he decided to try shock and awe. Better a wide field of fire than the need to aim at a moving target.

He leaned his head against the wall and pasted his eyes to the door.

Maybe if he'd served during the War—instead of being lucky enough to turn 18 the year after they ended the draft—he'd have known how to keep watch, but after thirty minutes his eyes were closed and his head collapsed onto his shoulder. His snores would wake Gracie in the middle of the night, but they never bothered him.

*****

He woke in the early morning. Woken by a sound like mice scrambling behind the baseboards. The moon had risen outside the southeastern window, the only light in the room, and not much light at that. He slipped his finger through the trigger guard but couldn't see anything in the room's deep shadows.

More scrabbling, this time overhead. Across the ceiling? He scanned the seams, but the room was even darker overhead. He draped the shotgun over his knee, hoping to catch the beast, if only for an instant, in his sights.

The scurrying started once more, this time faster and in his direction. He raised the shotgun and fired at the ceiling. A scream filled the room. Before the blast stopped ringing in his ears, claws ripped at his scalp, earlobes, and eyelids. In a panic he lifted the barrel above his head and yanked the trigger. The scream boomeranged away, a Doppler effect, like a police siren speeding away from the house.

He touched his ear and lifted his fingers into the moonlight. Covered with blood, but his blood or the creature's? Matt reloaded and raised the barrel toward the ceiling, straining to catch any sound to signal the next assault. Five minutes, ten minutes, half an hour and then, from straight in front of him but lower, on the floor, the sound of claws on concrete.

Matt swept the room with shot, one round after another until he heard a fat splat. He fired straight ahead, six times but still the creature rushed him, leaping and landing on his chest.

The unerwünschtergast stepped onto Matt's shoulders, drool and blood pummeling his head. Fat, sticky drops that ran down his forehead and into his eyes. For a brief second moonlight framed his assailant. Leather like skin dropped from the bones. Barely taller than two feet, the creature resembled a wingless pterosaur, all bones and leather, fingers covered with scales and curled talons extended from the tips.

In a frenzy, the unerwünschtergast ripped his clothing and sliced his skin. Its eyes were glowing bright yellow, and spines sprouted like porcupine's quills from its back. Matt threw his arms before his face and shuddered, preparing for the end.

Instead, the unerwünschtergast leaned toward his ear, growled, "egoistischer idiot,"[1] and vanished into the night.

Six Months Later

Matt's insurance denied his claim. His policy didn't cover mythical creatures. So, he took out a second mortgage to cover the damages.

The remodelers finished in record time, and Cole took a week off work to help Matt return his possessions from storage. Matt even splurged and built a smoker and grill in his backyard. Then he added a gazebo so he could watch the sun rise and set before the blistering summer months set in.

With his life back in balance, Matt fell back into his pillows and listened to Mantovani until he fell asleep. He dreamed of a refrigerator filled with fresh food, thick steaks and cold beer. He dreamed of a professional espresso maker steaming milk untended. He dreamed of rainbows penetrating the windows and fairies stocking shelves. He dreamed of tiny feet skittering across the ceiling and a floor shuddering under heavy feet. He dreamed of drool dripping like a fountain across his face.

But it wasn't a dream. He pulled his protesting eyelids apart. The sun had risen and brought with it his unerwünschtergast, who perched on his chest next to a second who was three-times larger. The second one gripped Matt's cheeks with his talons and snarled, "Hast du wirklich gedacht, du könntest meinen Sohn schikanieren?"[2]

Translations:
1 Selfish Jerk
2 Did you really think you could bully my son?

THE HOWLING

by Andreas Hort

"Take this."

I stared at the rifle in Petr's hands. "Are you serious?"

The look in his eyes told me that he was. "I know what I saw," he said for the hundredth time in the last two weeks. Now that the police had given up the search for Mr. Novotny, I supposed Petr saw no other option but to find him on his own.

Well, not entirely on his own.

I sighed and took the rifle. I hadn't held one in years, and it was heavier than I'd expected. Petr handed me two boxes of bullets, and I stowed them away in the pocket of my winter jacket. He shut the trunk of his car, his own rifle propped against his shoulder.

We stood side by side, breathing in the icy needles of the November air and breathing out steam as we gazed at the forest in front of us. On this dark, moonless night, the narrow gaps between the trees were not so much shadows as black holes. The leaves, yellow during the day and brown at night, shuddered and whispered before the wind slid under our winter jackets and bit into our skins.

We hissed and shivered, rifles in our hands and headlamps on our heads, and I couldn't help but think that we were idiots.

"We could go back to Prague." I heard Petr's sigh of frustration. "Watch the new *Conjuring*, hit the clubs. Linda could call her Vietnamese friend."

"Filip, if you wanna go, go." He looked at me, and his expression reminded me of the beggar I'd seen on the Charles Bridge a few days ago; the tortured look of a human being in a constant state of pain. "I gotta do this. I gotta save Dad. And if I'm too late, I gotta make sure no one else goes through the same thing." He saw me open my mouth. "And it *wasn't* a fucking boar. I *know* what I saw."

I nodded. "I'm going with you, man. You're my friend."

The tension in his face melted away.

"But," I said, "you and your dad came here to hunt boars. So, there *are* boars around here. Right?"

"Yeah."

"You know I only hunted once, right? And that was, like, two years ago. I have no clue what to do if we get attacked by boars."

"Just watch our six."

He released the safety on his rifle and lowered the barrel toward the ground; I followed suit.

I waited for him to start toward the trees, but he stood still, studying them, and the blackness between them. I prayed for him to change his mind. To say, Let's go to your place, let's stop by the convenience store, buy salty snacks, watch *The Conjuring 3*. Hell, if he suggested rewatching *Halloween Kills*, I'd have taken it. Still less of an ordeal than what we were doing.

I almost jumped at the sound of his voice. "If you hear it howling, don't answer."

He was looking at me, and I was taken aback by the wideness of his eyes and paleness of his face. His expression was a mix of fear and determination. He looked insane.

"Yeah," I said. "I know the fairy tales."

Don't answer the howler's call, or he'll tear you to pieces.

He swallowed. "My dad answered the howl. Then it took him. Next scream I heard was his own."

"Yeah. You told me." More than once.

"Just… don't answer."

"I won't."

He turned his face forward and switched on his headlamp. The yellow beam broke through the barrier of blackness, illuminating the first several feet beyond the edge of the forest and revealing more trees, more bushes, and more blackness.

Petr started toward the forest.

I turned on my own headlamp and followed him.

Before we passed by the first trees, a sound of cracking wood echoed in the distance.

Forest sounds, I thought. *Deer, birds, foxes, not boars.*

We let the forest swallow us. A twig snapped somewhere to my right, somewhere close.

Not a boar.

We walked on, me keeping an eye on our six, and soon, we were the ones snapping twigs as we tripped and stumbled, unable to watch the shadows around us and our step at the same time. I wondered if our noise could attract boars.

More twigs snapped, not under our boots, in the distance, first from the right, then from the left.

Shit, I thought. *Why am I here and not with Linda? Why the hell am I here?*

"It's a nocturnal animal," Petr had said the day before, after he'd asked me to come with him and I'd asked him why we had to go at night. "Well, a nocturnal thing, anyway."

Anger bubbled in my stomach, some of it directed at Petr for dragging me into this, most of it at myself for letting him. Yet I knew I'd do it all over again.

From ahead of us came a howl.

We froze. We listened. Not being an experienced woodsman, I couldn't be sure, but-

"Sounds like a fox, right?"

Petr nodded. "Yeah. Almost."

Before I could ask him what he meant, he started forward again, and I noticed a slight change in direction; as if he was following the sound.

Minutes later, the howl came again, closer this time. I understood Petr's remark; the sound was too deep for a fox. If it *was* a fox, it was a big one.

Or maybe you just don't know shit about foxes and how deep their barking is, I thought, which was technically true, but I'd heard a fox bark in the wild once, and I saw videos on the internet. I knew the sound.

And the more I thought about the howl, whose source we were nearing, the more I was confident it wasn't a fox.

But not a howler, of course it's not a howler.

"It's the same sound like last time," Petr said, and something in his voice told me he didn't mean the sound we'd heard minutes before. He picked up the pace, and I tried to keep up with him, and we were both stumbling and tripping and making so much *noise*, so much that it was impossible for anything in the forest not to know we were here, right *here*, come and get us, boars and howlers.

The howl came yet again, louder than ever, as if bellowed from a few feet ahead of us. We jumped and raised our rifles, trembling in our hands, my heart jackhammering as the echo of the howl slithered over us like a swarm of snakes.

We studied the trunks and bushes and the blackness behind them, watching for movement. There was none. Leaves rustled, twigs snapped, our breaths quivered.

I whispered, "Let's go back."

Petr whispered, "Don't answer the howl."

We jumped again when a howl—no, a scream, a man's scream—came from the right.

"Dad?"

I looked at Petr, and his large eyes rolled to me. His voice was high-pitched, as if not his at all. "It sounded like Dad."

I shook my head. "It wasn't."

"How do you know?"

I didn't, not really.

You can probably guess what happened next. I sensed it coming deep in my gut. I think some part of Petr knew, too, but he just couldn't help himself.

The scream came again and it *did* sound like Mr. Novotny, and Petr answered. "Dad! It's Petr! Where are you?"

Leaves whispered, and the icy claws of the wind scraped our faces and necks.

In the corner of my eye, a large frame materialized out of the blackness, pouncing on Petr and knocking him to the ground. A guttural growl reverberated through the air, not the sound of a boar, more like a bear, but there were no bears in the Czech Republic. The creature was much larger than Petr, and it looked *almost* like a person, only covered in what I suspected was hair.

The creature stood up, not like a bear, like a man, a seven-foot-tall, broad-shouldered man, and it reached for Petr with one hand, grabbed his jacket, and dragged him toward the bushes. Petr, who had dropped his rifle somewhere, fought with his bare hands, screaming, but the large creature barely slowed its stride.

I pointed my rifle at its back, my finger bent against the trigger, but my hands were shaking, and my aim skipped between the creature and Petr's face.

In my mind, I saw myself squeezing the trigger and Petr's face exploding in a mist of red.

I didn't squeeze the trigger.

Petr stared at me, his terrified, desperate eyes even larger than before, and I thought they'd pop out at any second. "Shoot, Filip! Shoot!"

I didn't. I couldn't, not without risking his life.

I couldn't move, either. I tried, but the sight of the large humanoid manhandling Petr like a doll with one hand (the other one was free to grab me and were those claws?) filled my feet with cement. I watched as the creature dragged Petr, screaming and wide-eyed and reaching for me, into the bushes. Then I knew for sure those *were* claws, because I heard wet crunching and tearing and chewing, and Petr's screams turned hoarse, then gargling and wet, then dead. The only remaining sound was the whisper of leaves shaking in the wind.

A warm sensation spread around my groin, streaming down my inner thighs and sticking the rough fabric of my jeans to my skin.

The scream came again. A man's scream. Petr's scream.

He's not dead, I thought. *I can save him,* I thought. *Move,* I thought, and I forced my feet to take a step forward, then another, and another.

I opened my mouth to call out to Petr, to assure him I was coming, but-

Don't answer the howl.

I pressed my lips into a tight line and started toward the bushes—then I froze again. One of the bushes wasn't a bush at all; it was a man. Or an animal, or both. What I'd suspected to be hair were leaves and twigs, bound together and covering the creature like a rudimentary version of a ghillie suit. The creature hunched behind a bush, its black eyes watching me from a hairy face, and its mouth, blood-framed and wet and full of fangs, gaped in an O.

Petr's screams came out of that mouth. I could see the creature's throat working, the muscles flexing and relaxing.

I almost screamed myself, but I swallowed it, hard, until my throat felt sore.

I raised my rifle, pointing the muzzle at the howler. The weapon still trembled in my hands, but Petr wasn't in the way anymore.

Only what if the shot didn't kill him? What if it made him mad?

What if he saw the crack of the rifle as the answer to his howl?

I decided not to shoot him unless he attacked me first. Keeping the muzzle trained on him, I began inching backwards. The howler watched me, screaming in Petr's voice, crouching behind the bushes.

I kept backing away, bumping into tree trunks and branches and shrubs, but I stepped slowly, careful not to trip and end up on my back with my stomach exposed.

I was shivering. The wetness in my pants had gone from cold to icy. Petr's screams reverberated off every corner of my mind, forming an image of his terrified face, his bulging eyes staring at me, pleading, before he was dragged into the bushes and torn to pieces.

I could be next.

Groaning, I kept inching backwards, one shivering step after another.

The howler followed. Cautiously, keeping distance; staying behind bushes and trunks. Watching me. Screaming Petr's screams.

Screaming in my friend's voice, he followed me through the forest to its very edge. I retreated past the last trees, stepping into an open meadow.

The howler's mouth snapped shut. Petr's voice died, again. The howler's black eyes were fixed on me as he melted into the shadows and I saw him no more. As if he'd never been there in the first place.

Shivering and groaning, my groin and inner thighs burning, I shambled along the forest edge, keeping a twenty-foot distance from the trees, until I found Petr's car. It was locked. I didn't remember him locking it, but I guess he did, at some point.

I walked back to Prague on foot, the rifle slung over my shoulder, just in case.

I had time to think. Hours.

Going to the police was a given, but what would I tell them? The truth? No one believed Petr. Most people thought he was crazy. Part of me had thought it, too, before I *saw*.

Still, it *was* the truth. They had to know. Everyone has to know what happens if they go into the forest. Especially at night, because the howler is a nocturnal thing.

I went to the police station and told them what had happened.

They looked at me like I was crazy.

Still, they searched the forest. They never found Petr. They never found his dad, either. I wonder how many people they never found in the forest.

I didn't tell anyone else about the howler, not for a few weeks. Not until, one night, while Linda was staying over, my own scream tore me out of one of my nightmares. For the hundredth time, Linda asked me about them. I started crying. Linda kept pushing, saying opening up about things might help me come to terms with the loss.

Finally, I told her what had happened.

She looked at me like I was crazy.

A few days later, she left me. Since then, I suppose the need to spread the truth, to hear "I believe you," has been growing inside me like a green, poisonous bubble. I guess I'm hoping that telling you the truth will burst it before it grows too big and suffocates me from the inside.

So now I told you what happened.

I'm sure you think I'm crazy.

The cops do. Linda does. I told them the same thing I'm going to tell you. I *know* what I saw.

-END-

<u>SWINE</u>

by Garry Engkent

She was eating him vigorously. Out in the open, well, in a back alleyway where only certain citizens live out their lives. From all indications, this person didn't mind it.

She looked at the intruder, me, for a moment, perhaps wondering about my purpose and intent. I stood still, to show I was no threat to her or to her actions. She continued eating his open stomach. She was sloppy and hungry. She gorged on his innards. She would have chewed on the heart, lungs, and stomach but they were underneath the chest. Hard to get at. Need to crunch through the ribs first.

No sense of decorum or etiquette. She grunted with satisfaction. What a pig!

Actually, she was humongous for a pig.

This sow was hogging into my territory, my turf, and I resent an animal taking over my feeding grounds.

I am Gregory Laine (call me "Gory"), a zombie with an appetite for human flesh and human blood.

Occasionally, I go slumming. Sometimes unwashed flesh and rough skin add flavour and contrast to the well-groomed, perfumed, and painted socialites whom I generally consume.

The sow oinked at me. I responded: "Oink, oink to you, too."

"You need to work on your swine sounds," the pig critiqued. Seeing my expression, she continued, "Why are you surprised that I speak English? You're a zombie and I am a gilt, sounds better than sow. And we both eat human beings."

"Educated." I pointed out. "Intelligent. Bold. Should I start calling you a name from literature and cartoons: Porky Pig, Miss Piggy, Wilbur, Napoleon?"

"Don't mock me, Mister Zombie!"

"So, what do I call you then?"

"Porchetta will do for now."

"I'm Gory."

"Okay, we're on a first name basis." The statement hung there for a resolution or a question. "What now?"

Porchetta had this wicked, mischievous gleam in her eyes. She was going to leave the sloppy seconds for me. She burped as if to signal that she had had a great meal, crème-de-la-crème in a back-alley way. Good enough for a swine equals good enough for a zombie slumming in this part of town.

"I left the heart for you," she said with a piggish grin. "You don't have one."

"Let's not waste time trading one-liner insults. Let's be civil." Actually, I do have a newly regenerated thumper inside my chest.

"Swine civil, or zombie civil?" Porchetta asked sweetly.

"I used to be human."

Porchetta sniffed in my direction. The odour came from behind me. It was a mixture of deodorant, body sweat, and bad breath with a goodly smack of alcohol. I turned. Oh, another used-to-be human. A were-she-wolf. And a hungry one at that!

She was quite attractive. Most monsters in human form have to be appealing and alluring in order to draw in their intended prey. Like me, this were-she-wolf was slumming. The only one in generic form was Porchetta, and she started running away on all fours. All three of us did not truly belong to this area, but here we were.

"Out of my way, zombie!"

"No." I felt protective of the pig. Porchetta had shown a wry sense of swinish hospitality in offering to join in with her meal. Sure, she slighted me. How else were we to get to know one another?

"Do you know who I am?" The were-she-wolf was still mostly in human form. She stood about three feet from me. We were eyeballing one another: who is first to blink? Instinctively, I sensed she was changing shape.

"No."

Zombies do not transform physically. Werewolves do. I could see subtle bodily transformations. Hair began to grow out of every pore in her body: most noticeably on face, neck, arms, and legs. Her hands grew paw-like with thick, long claws, ready to rip my throat. A wolfish jaw and mouth pushed forwards. Razor-sharp teeth became very, very evident. She was strong, she was powerful. More than Nature's wolf.

All this took less than fifteen seconds. She attacked savagely. Superheroes would most likely attack their opponent. Others martial artists would probably side-step or leap up in the air. Then counterattack. I dropped to the garbage-littered pavement. The were-she-wolf went over me. And hurried after Porchetta.

I pursued the wolf.

Horror movies consistently present zombies as slow, leg-dragging corpses always banded together as they pursued their frightened, female victims in high-heels. Surprise, surprise. I broke the stereotype when I rose from the dead five years ago. I can run. And fairly fast, though I must admit now, not as swift as the were-she-wolf. She caught up to my piggy.

"Stop! Stop!"

I did not expect this. I was quite surprised. The were-she-wolf stopped her attack on Porchetta. She still held the pig so Porchetta could not escape, but she wasn't about to end the swine's life for an immediate meal.

"Why is this sow important to you, zombie?" The were-she-wolf's voice sounded rough, less feminine in her creature form.

"She can talk," I said. "Intelligent. Witty."

"I am hungry."

"There's a half-eaten corpse a block or two back. All yours to enjoy."

"I prefer fresh kill, zombie. You and the sow eat anything that's dead."

I was about to object, but this was not the time to debate about food choices. I was saving Porchetta with whom I inexplicably felt an attachment. The were-she-wolf knew this and I could sense her delight in having me witness the slaughter.

"Please."

She laughed heartily but without mirth. This little piggy was going to die and be devoured right in front of me. I could do very little about it. One bite from her enlarged, wolfish incisors would go deep into Porchetta's throat. She would start bleeding profusely. Then the were-she-wolf would turn on me as my gilt lies dying.

Without warning, they came from the back and the left-side of the were-she-wolf. One instrument snapped off the monster's canines almost at the gum line. Looked like a bolt from an ancient crossbow. Before the were-she-wolf could scream in pain, another blow smashed her skull. It didn't kill her, but she released Porchetta. Our common enemy turned to face her attackers. Two sows, seemingly with workable limbs—and three fingers instead of hooves—were holding weapons. They were also on their hind legs. Upright.

"Next time," the were-she-wolf cried out in weakened bravado. She ran past me. For a brief moment, I saw that dirty, "I-will-get-you-too" look in her eyes at me. I was a marked zombie along with three little pigs.

"My gratitude," said Porchetta. She smiled weakly at her two rescuing compatriots. Her friends stare at me with suspicion, distrust, and wariness. They were also ready for action. To them, I was yet an undetermined stranger.

When Porchetta recovered sufficiently, she introduced me to her two saviours. Penelope and Portia, the twins. I could not tell them apart, but Porchetta could. Their wariness lessened but they did not let their guard down.

I picked up the were-she-wolf's enlarged canines. Souvenir. If we should meet again, I might return these razor-sharp, pointy ivories to her. I wondered whether she would regrow them. If the dead can become resurrected, if pigs could talk, then were-she-wolves should be able to reproduce a new set of teeth in no time.

"You should come with us," Porchetta invited. "The sun rises in about an hour. Bad time to be seen with a half-eaten corpse and three warrior pigs."

I could not get the folk tale about the three little pigs and the wolf out of my head. The nice, revised version has the three pigs alive in the end, and the original, cautionary story has only one piggy alive. But the big, bad wolf dies in both versions.

The three ladies travelled on all fours, and they knew the back alleys, to use an overused cliché, like the back of the hand.

When we stopped, I was out of breath and far from familiarity of place. This was their hideout. An abandoned warehouse somewhere in the industrial section of the city. (Have you ever tried to crawl through holes made through chain-linked fences or gaps between wooden ones? I struggled with every one of those unforgiving hollows. I felt every part of my zombie body being scraped.)

Amused, Porchetta looked at me. "Welcome to the house of brick." It was, in truth, an inner-city tent city. Blocks of clustered makeshift homes for the homeless.

This place had become a stye for them. From what I could tell, they had been here for a while. They seemed comfortable and familiar in their hideaway. I found it mildly foreign as their place intermingled with a tent neighbourhood of the homeless, the down-and-outs, and people with drug problems. The air reeked and I wished for a filtered mask. But I was polite and suffered silently.

"What happened to the houses of straw and wood?"

I could sense differing emotions from the triplet. Penelope and Portia were silent. Porchetta gave me the low-down.

The grandmother of Porchetta, Penelope and Portia produced a litter of 250 piglets which were shipped to a facility, the "institute for Abnormal Scientific Knowledge (iASK)" for experimentation. The scientists there separated the sows and the boars early. Experiments were done. Many piglets did not survive. The three gilts were third generation and had things done to them inside the womb. By six months after birth, the litter started showing signs of mental growth as well as physical changes. Their skulls enlarged to accommodate brain size; their limbs took on an almost human quality. The researchers noted these transformations and intensified their studies. Penelope said that she could sense the pain and suffering the institute's scientists inflicted on her siblings. Porchetta, Penelope, and Portia survived the first, second, and third wave of experiments done to them. Without the knowledge of the researchers and scientists, these three pigs developed mental skills: language, logic, cognition, reading.

Six months ago, the three escaped from the institute. Now on the run and being hunted by that were-she-wolf we encountered earlier. She also belonged to iASK, my old *alma mater* of evil deeds and more-than-evil researchers.

"I didn't know iASK did research on *sus scrofa domesticus*."

"You don't need the fancy Latin term, Gory," said Penelope flatly, "we're used to being called domesticated pigs, sows, and swine."

"Why would you ever think that the institute is only interested in zombies?" Portia asked. "Rather narcissistic of you."

Okay, I was put in my place.

I never stopped to think of the bigger picture. In my past, I had engaged with wicked humans, cannibals, and vampires that came from iASK. Recently, this anonymous were-she-wolf. Her target were the pigs, not me. So she merely dismissed my gallantry as a minor obstacle. She was not informed of my notorious existence and value to iASK. But once she reported back, she would.

"You girls need to leave immediately." I informed. "She and other iASK agents are probably scouring the city right now."

There was no argument from the three pigs. They said nothing because they could communicate telepathically.

"Will you come with us, Gory?" Porchetta asked.

"Thanks, but I think we should go our separate ways. This *loup-garou* can track us by smell."

Porchetta, Penelope, and Portia made faces. But it is true. Every living (even dead, like me) thing gives off odour. Some as pungent as spring flowers; some as muted as a grain of sand. Our different scent defines and differentiates us. Now the were-she-wolf and her minions would have to decide whom to hunt. Odds are that it would be me. That might give the piggies a chance to run away from the big, bad wolf.

"Till we meet again."

The three pigs went off in three different directions out of tent city. I took my time leaving to draw attention to myself. And hopefully away from the piggies.

She did not look like the movie version of the werewolf. She did not even look like the hirsute *loup-garou* with pointy ears and a savage snout sporting sharp fangs that chased Porchetta and got slammed by Penelope and Portia. She had long, flaming red hair coming down past her shoulder blades. Her bounteous breasts had a hard time being contained in her revealing blouse. Long legs there for staring at, and a face like chiseled ivory forces the spectator to be spellbound with awe. She was smiling, with a new set of sexy white teeth, against crimson, luscious lips.

She was waiting for me.

"Gregory Laine, zombie defender of the swine," the transformed were-bitch-wolf acknowledged. "Had I but known at our previous meeting."

Her name was a made-up nomenclature: Amber MaSoeur. It sounded fake. It didn't fit her, but that was what she offered up to identify her as a human being. She probably had more transforming powers than that of changing into her lupus form; moreover, she probably read my file and understood that I had a weakness for bodacious, erotic women. She was playing on that aspect now.

"Returning your fangs, Amber." I handed her the set of teeth from last evening's encounter. "But I see you have regenerated a new set."

"Where are my three little pigs, Laine?"

"Who knows."

"I could have you taken back to the institute right now."

"You mean the grey panel truck parked two cars down, and the three groups with tasers, stun guns, and steel nets a shout away?"

Amber MaSoeur smiled appreciatively. "Am I that crude and obvious?"

This iASK special agent would have had others chasing after the three piggies as we traded barbs and witticisms here. This could be a delaying tactic to keep me preoccupied and inattentive to other matters.

"What do you want, Amber?"

"You and the three pigs. In that order."

"Nice meeting you." I turned and started walking across the street. The three bands of agents came out from their hidden positions. They were dressed like cops from tactical units: helmets, armor, heavily armed, and topped off with shields. Then they stopped.

Amber MaSoeur signaled them to desist. They disappeared, as if by magic, back into the woodworks of a busy intersection of the city.

This was too easy. Too obvious. This little piece of theatre was distraction, to get me off balance. But for what?

With my zombie sensitivity to smells and scents, I detected pheromones strongly emanating from Amber MaSoeur, my were-she-wolf. So, no rough stuff, like tasers and guns. Rather, it would be sexual seduction. For me, it would be bestiality; for her, it would be necrophilia. What a thought! We quickly found an expensive hotel and charged it to iASK.

Were-she-wolf and zombie fucked like crazy in their human forms. Well, I could not transform into another physical being. She tried to control her conversion: at times her hirsute, animal nature grappled with her silky-smooth human skin. One moment she would be sprouting thick wolfish hair; next, she would be velvety as anything about her torso, breasts, pubic zone and length of legs. Throughout our multiple bouts of sexual exertion, we kept going until one of us cried, "Enough!" So we held on to the duel of sex: battlefield in the bed. Nobody wanted to lose; nobody called for a draw.

"You're better at it dead than my other lovers who are alive." Amber MaSoeur complimented. "We could be a team. A real fucking dynamic duo."

"You work for iASK. Dealing with the institute is like being in a pit of vipers, tarantulas, and all things deadly." I said flatly. "One day, they will turn on you too."

"They need me."

"iASK still needs me for organ transplants. I said no. They keep sending people like you to retrieve me."

"Dr. Morteus is willing to stop engaging you…"

"I thought Dr. Jim is CEO."

Amber smiled knowingly. "Dr. Jim retired from iASK. I believe you had something to do with his decision."

"Yeah, I took out his eyeballs and testicles, roasted them over an open fire, and ate them like toasted marshmallows."

The were-she-wolf giggled. "Really?!"

I was getting to like her.

"Enough about my exploits. What's your proposition?"

I could tell she already had a scheme. The sex was to soften me up and to suggest more such rewards to come after the completion of the assignment.

"Help me capture the sows."

"What's so important with Porchetta, Penelope, and Portia?"

"Telekinesis. Transferable to offspring genetically. Adaptation physically to human form. Ability to speak. High intelligence at birth. Three together creates a triple threat. iASK needs to do more research. For the benefit of mankind."

I have had dealings with iASK. I am unique in that I can regenerate my internal organs *ex nihilo* after removing them entirely. All it takes is about three months for maturity. I need to consume human blood and flesh. Yes, only human blood and flesh. The institute harvested me repeatedly over the years and profited immensely. They were not kind or considerate. I eventually escaped but am continually harried by their agents.

"Gory, these three little pigs are dangerous, diabolical and destructive. Not only to iASK but the World."

She was serious. I had to laugh in her face. Come on, I was taught the tale of the three little pigs and the big, bad wolf, the house of straw, of wood, and of brick. iASK's deal was a pig in a poke. The wolf didn't win. The piggies were the good guys—gals.

Surprisingly, she did not stop me from walking out on her. I did a quick check on my person and clothing to see whether she planted electronic bugs. I looked around for human shadows that followed me. There was none. I took that as a sign that she or iASK had better surveillance about. For an hour, I walked around lackadaisically to confound and confuse them. Gotta make them work for their pay.

"Looking for a good time, cutie?" Portia found me.

Where pigs can go, zombies have a hard time, really hard time. We went through long, narrow alleyways, down past the grates into the sewer system, and trekked in knee high slush and flotsam. I tried not to use my sense of smell and I breathed through my mouth. I gagged when in the shadow I saw Portia stopped to snack. And people think cannibalism is bad!

This section of the sewer system is quite long because we spent at least five hours under there. I was bent over, and clingy stuff raked over my head and shoulders. I was real happy when we went up the grate and into the open air of regular smog and smells. Even for a zombie, I felt self-conscious of how I looked with sewage dripping thickly down my shirt and pants. I need a long, perfumed bath.

But that was not to be.

"Zombie lover," she said, "you stink!"

Poor Portia was trapped in a large steel net and was shrieking loudly. The iASK agents handled her roughly treating her like a common animal, not an intelligent being. I myself was in no position to help as nets dropped and immobilized my movements. Amber MaSoeur looked satisfied.

My whole posture and demeanour shouted out the question: "How?" I was clean of tracking devices. I eluded my iASK shadows.

"I am Amber MaSoeur," she exclaimed triumphantly. "Werewolf supreme!"

Of course, I carry her scent; she knows mine intimately. Her senses are animalistic heightened to extremes help from the institute for Abnormal Scientific Knowledge. The were-she-wolf could smell me even through shit, slime, and underground concrete easily. No wonder she didn't need iASK agents to shadow me.

"The institute wants all of you home." She added, with the sound of regret: "We could've made a dynamic duo, lover-zombie!"

Portia loudly grunted.

And copiously vomited.

And in a diarrhetic way shat.

At her captors.

What came out from both ends was similar: it was brown, gooey, stinky, sticky, voluminous. When attached to skin or clothing, the mess stayed stuck. What came out from her multiple teats was worse: the milky white liquid burned flesh and skin. It started to melt the mesh of plastic and steel. Easily.

Her captors began to scream from the pain more than from the smell. Those who got sprayed in the face started sizzling, bubbles formed on the skin and burst, eyeballs popped, hands clawing at the face blistered quickly. They all writhed like the exaggerated TV walking dead.

I felt myself released from the iASK net. Amber had her own problems to contend with than to mock me. She was fighting off the afflicted agents, who blindly tried to grab at anything with the hope of ending their suffering. No sympathy from me, amigo!

"Gory," Portia called, "this way!"

For a three hundred pounder, Portia could move fast. Much faster than in that restrictive culvert. Five long blocks away, we were met by Porchetta and Penelope. These two had expropriated a cargo van. It took two of them to drive. Porchetta at the wheel, and Penelope at the brakes and accelerator. They communicated by telepathy.

"You drive," Porchetta threw me the keys.

We drove to another hideout in the suburbs. It was indistinguishable from the other middle-class constructions in the area, except for minor alterations and address. I parked in the garage. This way, nosy neighbours and home-surveillance videos would not capture the oddity of three pigs residing in their neighbourhood.

"You two should have helped me hurt them," Portia commented in English for my benefit.

"Don't worry. Penelope and I have a plan," Porchetta said nebulously. "We'll make them think twice before coming at us again. Anyway, we have some time to do this properly. They are still in disarray from this attack."

"Hold it," I almost shouted. "You mean to say Portia's and my incident an hour ago was arranged? A trap for iASK?"

The three sows smiled surreptitiously.

Porchetta looked patiently at me as if I were a schoolboy needing a lesson in life. "Do you know that in America alone, over 100 million pigs are slaughtered each year? More than all your human holocausts put together in the last two centuries of warfare, famine and disease? Gory, I have told you earlier that iASK has over 500 of our kind in their laboratories for experimentation and genetic mutilation. Just in that facility! We have heard their collective shrieks day and night without relief. Our brothers and sisters are being tortured. Because of our extended powers, we can hear them still. Dying in pain. Crying out for mercy."

"But…" I was about to say that pigs were food for human consumption, that they were animals bred to be made into chops, roasts, ribs, bacon, sausages, and lard. I closed my mouth.

"Would you permit this unending slaughter, this holocaust, if pigs were human?"

I didn't like where this was going. These are super-smart swine genetically improved by nature and technologically enhanced by iASK scientific research. I am intelligent but not like these three piggies. (I hesitate now to frame them as diminutive "piggies" when each weighed about 250-300 pounds. I'm only 180.) They are not lovable, cartoon characters. They are not wonderfully drawn children's book characters. They are out for revenge, for their sense of justice, for sheer chaos.

"So, what are you going to do?" I asked.

Penelope answered: "We would like to know which side you are on, Gory."

Portia gave a small, swinish smile. "You slept with, fucked, the were-bitch-wolf, Amber MaSoeur. She has strong ties with iASK. You still visit the institute. Don't deny it. I heard it all."

"Haven't gone to iASK for awhile."

iASK and I were no longer in good terms or in good working relations ever since I killed three of their CEOs since my escape. The institute still has standing orders to hunt me down. That isn't a badge of honour; it is a burden that I as the zombie must carry. In short, I have no love for those in charge and for those who work for them. Except, I confess, I was developing a soft spot for Amber MaSoeur.

"Gory, we need a person like you," Porchetta said. "You possess certain physical and mental talents that we lack. But we must know that you are totally committed to us, to our group. We need to know we can trust you completely, without a momentary doubt in our minds."

"If I join, what am I getting into?"

"Complete destruction of iASK. Interested?"

Three pigs and a zombie against one of the biggest, most evil, most influential research institute in the world. An institute that has money, power and all the resources. Suicide mission. Who could resist?

Me. Gory Laine.

I am a miraculously resurrected corpse, not an imbecile. I have watched a lot of TV serials and movies with the basic concept of David versus Goliath, one little guy or a band of misfits fighting the Mafia, the KGB, the government, the super-rich but evil patriarchs and win. In real life, the little guy gets crushed a lot more times that doing the crushing. I am tired of fairy tales.

"I'll take a pass on this one," I responded.

Portia whipped out a weapon and shot me. A very powerful taser that immobilized my entire body and nervous system. I may have even blacked out momentarily.

When I regained consciousness, I was hogtied. The three pigs took no chances. Steel mesh wrapped around my body, pinning me in place. I did not recognize my surroundings. Obviously, I was not in an urban alleyway anymore. How long was I out?

Hey, gang, our zombie's up.

I felt different. The three porkers looked at me expectantly. They were wondering about me, about my condition. I could hear their conversation even though their mouths were not moving. Immediately, I knew what they had done. They opened me up, took out my organs, and sewed me back. One of my secret zombie abilities that came when I lack internal organs is limited telepathy. I can hear active thoughts of others within a certain distance but cannot access passive memory. Porchetta, Penelope, and Portia were less than three feet from the bed where I was chained.

Let's see how he can help our plan without his innards, thought Penelope to the other two.

It takes about two or three months for him to regenerate a full set of mature organs. From the files on him, this Gory Laine can function somewhat normally. His main concern now is to satisfy his thirst and hunger for human flesh and blood. Porchetta informed. *Especially human blood that is immediately absorbed into his body without going through the process of digestion.*

We should have killed him when we had him immobilized, Portia interjected. *He will be problematical for us.*

We need him, Porchetta said. She had a quick thought and that was enough clue for me to realize I was back somewhere in the depths of iASK.

Somehow undetected, they got inside. That was some feat to have three pigs evade motion-sensor cameras, infra-red light, laser alarms, human guards, and a hundred other devices designed to stop infiltrators and unauthorized movement. More phenomenal, they had to lug my dead weight. Once in, they could perform surgery on a zombie without attracting attention.

"Are you hungry, Gory?" Penelope asked.

I was. All of sudden feeling ravenous. What's the saying about empty stomachs?

Good! Portia nodded.

"Can you move?" Penelope inquired. "Perhaps, a unit of AB positive will help." She pointed to the container and the plastic straw. I snatched it. I drank. I was still very, very hungry.

The three sows looked at one another with understanding. I was the pawn in this game against iASK without knowing the plan or the objective. I was in it whether I liked it or not, whether I knew what I was supposed to do or not, whether I would survive or not.

"Good hunting, Gory!"

I slipped off the operating table, steadied my legs, and put on my clothes. I could smell fresh, human meat just around the corner from this room. I am a zombie, and I do what I do best as a zombie.

The woman in the iASK uniform saw me, and froze. I am a poster boy of sorts at iASK. Everyone down to the maintenance workers recognizes me. I smiled. Hungrily. The first bite was heaven. Soft flesh. Spurt of hot blood into my mouth. I felt refreshed. Comforted. Regenerating. I drained her within minutes. I would have chewed off a few juicy parts of her body, inner and outer, but I remembered I had nothing inside mine. No stomach to digest, no intestines to transfer flesh into nutrient, energy. Those pieces would just sit inside me, waiting to rot, giving me methane to burp and to fart.

But I still needed more nutrients to recover, to rebuild. The three "little" sows did a number on me. And I knew why.

To use me as a distraction. A disruption. A wrecking crew of one. Killing and eating the help would certainly annoy all employees at iASK. Security would enact a number of measures to stop me and to keep the facility safe. Porchetta, Penelope, and Portia would have free hand to do what they deliberately did not want me to know.

There are proper times for rational thought. Unfortunately, not at this moment. The three gifted piggies did something to make me voraciously hungry, more so than my normal desire to eat after being organ-emptied. After draining my first victim, I needed more. So I followed my zombie instincts.

"INTRUDER ALERT! INTRUDER ALERT!" the loudspeakers barked. A second later loud alarm with flashing red lights came on. "Seventh level. Seventh level. All doors and elevators locked down." Standard lighting went off.

Those who could not get to safety were drained of blood. One pretty morsel made me regret not having my stomach. She would have been a delicious piece. Am I sorry that she gave her life to iASK? No.

Working for such a malevolent institute has its downside. You can die. Die horribly.

By now, iASK security would be marshalling various units, armed to the teeth, to confront me. In the past, I had gone through this routine. Unless the institute had changed each floor's layout, I knew some secret spots.

Energized with fresh blood coursing through me, I leaped up and pulled down the ventilation cover. I jumped again and pulled myself into the aluminum ventilation tube.

The the ducts were dark and noisy. Every little sound I made seemed to be an explosion. Climbing up the ducting exhausted me. Thank goodness for the cool air; my sweat drenched me from head to toe. On the fourth floor, I broke through the vent cover and dropped down into an office. It was empty. Of course, that didn't matter much because I would have killed and drained whomever I found there. Climbing vents makes for thirsty and hungry work.

I poked my head out the office door. The alarm bells and warnings were still sounding strong. Red lights strobed as they do in ambulances and police cruisers. There was nobody in the corridors. Should I chance it to the stairwell?

"Well, hello lover," Amber MaSoeur chimed.

Even in this gigantic, multi-leveled building, I should have known the were-she-wolf would search me out. I was going to ask how but I knew. She had done it earlier this same night. Going through the ventilation tubes, my sweaty smell merely directed her my position. Only the stairs had delayed her hunt, since all elevators went out of commission.

Although we seemed to be calm and collected, we both took up stances for sudden combat. Amber was having a hard time containing her human appearance. The werewolf elements kept popping out. In her animal form, she could not speak, and she wanted to talk more than to attack. Yet, something in her was forcing the transition maybe the result of iASK's tinkering.

"The three pigs are doing a lot of dangerous damage on the eighth sub-floor," Amber mentioned.

"Good."

"I need your help to stop them," the were-she-wolf said firmly.

"Why should I help iASK?" I retorted.

I had no love for iASK. I had very bad experiences with the institute, over the years. I was glad that other mistreated beings took up the call for the destruction of its research and experimentation. More power to these women! Maybe I should join them to destroy some of the facilities.

"Because what these sows are doing will have very awful effects on innocent people. It isn't just about the institute, Gory. If you don't, you will be accessory to genocide."

"A bit overly melodramatic."

"Porchetta, Penelope, and Portia are not ordinary. Genetic modification has given them intelligence, telepathy, and ruthlessness. After destroying iASK, they will do a lot more harm."

"Aren't we all wired up somehow by the iASK?"

Suddenly, something flashed in my brain. Where the hell were all the security people? With this danger alarm blasting this long, they should have been in every corridor, on every floor, armed to the teeth. On this floor, there was just us: zombie and she-wolf. Something was wrong.

I could not help but ask out loud, "Where's security, Amber?"

A flash in her eye told me that she just became aware of the discrepancy. And then the alarm blasts stopped, the flashing red lights ceased turning. Normal lighting and elevator service came back on. To state the obvious: something's wrong.

"Gory," Amber shouted, "take the stairs now! Gas is coming up the vents!"

She was moving towards the door to the stairwell, and that action was good enough for me to follow. "Hold your breath. Gas is seeping through." I wasn't worried: I don't have a new pair of mature lungs yet.

Gravity helped as we raced downward on the stairwell towards the position of the three pigs. They were separate though. Amber MaSoeur smelled Portia in the computer section. Portia was distracted by the banks of computers and particularly the screens. There were about fifty wide screens covering all the floors. Each screen was divided into different areas of surveillance.

Portia sensed our intrusion. She jumped out of the way as Amber pounced, now fully transformed into werewolf. Her shredded clothes clung to her in fragments. Portia rolled away on the linoleum floor, simultaneously drawing a taser, and shot Amber. In the midst of an attack, pain wracked through Amber's body. But the shock did not stop her. The were-she-wolf tore away one of Portia's eyes.

The pig squealed. In pain. In frustration. But she was determined to do more harm to someone I have affection for. I was caught in the middle: Portia or Amber.

Pig or wolf.

Help the sow that would destroy a goodly portion of iASK and its evil designs, or save the enhanced demon lover who is devoted to iASK?

It was easy.

With great difficulty, I hefted the 280 pounder away from the controls and away from doing more damage to my were-she-wolf. Sow blood pouring from her missing eye splashed onto my shirt and pants. Blood made the linoleum floor wet and slippery. Portia got the message that she should run away.

Amber MaSoeur shook off the last of the taser effect. Her jowls pulled tightly back in anger. Not pissed by the sow's escape but that I permitted the pig to escape. She could no longer trust me.

She ran after Portia. I followed. My were-she-wolf disappeared, so I took to the bloody trail that

Portia left as she fled. If both were going down the stairwell, so was I. I felt responsible for both women.

Before I hit the next level, I heard a horrendous shriek. Banging against walls. I picked up my pace. Amber had caught up with Portia. The were-she-wolf eviscerated the sow. Blood and guts decorated the landing and the half-opened door. One piggy gone. Amber took a moment to replenish herself, devouring the pig's vicera. Her feral features eyed me as she feasted.

She sniffed the air. And immediately shifted to attack mode. She dropped a half-eaten kidney from her mouth and turned to the stairwell door half a flight down. She faced and waited for Penelope to make her move.

Unlike Portia, Penelope was more lithe, more muscled, more energetic physically. Her snout showed sharp tiger-like fangs; her front hooves curled into vulture talons. She stood ready to rake through hide. To draw blood. To kill her sister's murderer.

Amber slipped on Portia's blood. She went down, and Penelope was on top of the wolf. The sow raked the wolf's back with her clawed hands. Amber shrieked in pain and attempted to fling the pig off. Penelope's claws held on tightly. The werewolf thrashed in vain attempts to shake off her opponent. Then she collapsed onto the bloody floor.

Amber MaSoeur's wolfish form was receding. Her thick animal hairs disappeared, and human epidermis returned. Her snout receded to jaw and luscious lips. She bled profusely from her wounds.

Penelope raised a taloned arm, prepared for the coupe de gras. Amber was in human form. Naked. Vulnerable. I leaped at the murderous pig. Her killing appendage missed Amber, slicing herself instead. The sow screamed. For a moment, she froze, then she ran down the stairwell.

"Poison," the were-she-wolf revealed. "Extra potent from iASK. Released through her nails." With that, Amber MaSoeur, my were-she-wolf lover, died.

I needed consolation. I needed vengeance. I chased after Penelope with thoughts of murder.

Porchetta greeted me when I reached Penelope. I stopped short of slamming into her. Penelope was on the floor a few feet away, twitching all four limbs and snout. The poison from her nails had grazed her stomach; it was enough to do her in. Racing down to meet Porchetta didn't help slow things to her benefit. She was suffering horrifically. Dying noises. Then, no more sound, no more movements. A dead pig.

Porchetta focused her attention on me. Anger still surged through my body. I felt good because I had a hand in Penelope wounding herself in the stomach and causing her to suffer and die. Revenge for killing Amber.

"Why do you persist on helping iASK when they have done you so much hurt?"

"Do you realize there are hundreds of innocent people on the upper floors now gassed to death? People with spouses, children…"

"If they work at the institute for Abnormal Scientific Knowledge, they are not innocent. Guilty, guilty, guilty! They are accomplices to physical, psychological, and spiritual slaughter. They have had a hand in utmost heinous crimes against humanity and the animal kingdom, Gory!"

I understood very well and sympathized with Porchetta's sentiment and anger. iASK had done very bad things to me. Somehow, the trio gassing all the human occupants in the facility seemed very wrong and drew comparison to Auschwitz and Birkenau extermination camps. Their dead bodies all over the floor, on their desks, in the labs and board rooms.

"Do you realize, Gory," Porchetta pointed out, "that everyday in America, over 1 million pigs are slaughtered? Of the 250 pigs used in iASK study and research."

I was about to retort something glib about food for hungry people, but I shut up.

"I'm third generation experiment in these labs, my treacherous zombie friend. They have done things to my mother, mother's mother, and me in the womb, after birth and beyond. You know, I can keep more than half the information in these data banks in my head and call up anything in an instant. I speak five languages and understand a dozen more. My kind can communicate telepathically for some distance. We can even transmute temporarily as you have witnessed a few occasions."

My own telepathic abilities were waning. Okay, gone. Theoretically, I should be hearing Porchetta's thoughts. I should have heard Amber's before she died, or Penelope's or even Portia's. I drew nothing. Did Porchetta have the ability to block me, or quelch my ability? What did these pigs do to me in that operating theatre? They weren't just removing organs. Probably, like iASK, these sows were planting or had imbedded electronics into me to serve their purposes.

"What did you do to me on that slab, Porchetta?" I asked nervously.

If a pig could smile, Porchetta was smiling. Her whole snout, eyes, cheeks, and eyes brightened up. She appeared, for a second, physically human.

"Gory," Porchetta confessed, "Penelope and Portia wanted you dead. Portia knew what to do to make you die permanently. I had a soft spot for you, and I rule the roost! We changed your metabolic regulators. You can reproduce your missing organs at a much faster rate now."

That's why my telepathic ability diminished! "Am I supposed to be grateful?"

"You'll love the other enhancements." She was having the time of her life.

Why does every genius, hot-shot scientist want to fuck with my innards? Just because I am the second person to be resurrected from the dead shouldn't make me a target. Now, even swine are at it!

"What did you do, Porchetta?" I was concerned. Even if my zombie face didn't show unease, my voice did.

"I need you to do something for me, zombie man," she said quietly.

Sounded ominous, even to a soulless creature like me, accustomed to dread and evil.

"What is it you want?" I said resignedly. "Kill somebody?"

"A rescue, actually." Porchetta outlined the assignment. I was to go to Level 11 and retrieve seven young sows from the special experiment sector. Bring all seven to her.

"Why these seven? Are they dwarves?" I asked cheekily.

"They are all pregnant. With 12 each in incubation."

Okay, I could understand that. Killing the unborn is morally troublesome, even for swine. But I sensed there was more to this rescue. Porchetta could be so pigheaded.

I expected trouble at Level 11 due to previous experience at iASK and personal paranoia. But there none surfaced. All the personnel lay sprawled about in death. What kept the seven sows alive was where they were penned up. The delivery system of air was different. Thick windows separated the living and the dead. Another pig on the examining table wasn't so lucky and died with the humans.

Herding seven sows required patience and dedication. With a kick, you could get three or four to move to the direct you wanted, but the others separately went on their own. And when you mustered those to your will, the original group decided to wander. I wished I could talk swine.

Out of exasperation, I shouted: "Stop, come this way!"

"Why didn't you say so?" came the reply from three pigs. They had a smarmy smile on their snouts.

These were not ordinary, domesticated barnyard pigs. I felt like an idiot, of course they were all genetically modified.

"Follow me! Porchetta is waiting!" They didn't even ask who Porchetta was; they knew. And I knew this little quarter hour distraction was orchestrated by my favourite piggy. These gilts were telepathically attuned to her.

So, the drift of seven swollen sows followed me, the zombie, into the elevator. It got crowded. We rode up in strained silence. Once the door opened, Porchetta was there to greet her brood. Yes, the seven were her children.

"Say hello to your human-zombie donor, girls!" Porchetta announced. And seven pregnant pigs turned to me.

I should have known! If I hadn't been transformed into a human-eating zombie, I would have loved chomping on a Porchetta pork chop or set of ribs at this moment. She made me a progenitor of half-zombie pigs! If my guess is correct, each pregnant sow has twelve fetuses and there are seven sows. I fathered a litter of 84 super-intelligent, telepathic swine.

"They won't all be giving birth for another few weeks," Porchetta informed me. "I want you to get them to a safe place, actually several safe places, before iASK regroups and rounds my children up. Will you do that, Gory?"

Parenthood. I had a stake in this. I could say no. I could just walk away. No, I couldn't. More zombie than human, I still retained certain traits engrained into me. I felt responsible; I had responsibilities that were tossed unwanted upon me. Maybe I hated iASK and this could be my contributing twist to their soulless corporation.

"Okay."

Porchetta's smile was divine, motherly, radiant. Maybe I wasn't seeing right, but Porchetta seemed to have transmuted into a human face. I blinked, and she was a sow again.

"Why can't you join your family?"

"Rearguard, Gory, rearguard." Porchetta chided. She handed me a print-out copy of the locations for her brood, then thrashed the computer completely.

I put the seven sows into an iASK van and completed my assignment. No complications: the seven sisters were very agreeable, didn't make a fuss or a mess in the vehicle, and said "Please" and "Thank you" politely. I told them I would come see their brood when they have delivered. After all, I had a stake in it.

Now I can add to my zombie resume: swineherd-parent. Maybe I will change the classic fable of "the three pigs and the werewolf" to "the zombie and the seven sows".

"THE VILLAGE OF CARROWMORE"

by Kevin Michael Clarke

In my long-passed youth, I used to visit Lacken in County Mayo, Ireland. We made the same pilgrimage every summer school holidays. My mother Mary, my good self, and my two sisters used to travel there by boat train. The train part was fine, but the boat part was horrific. It mostly entailed being pitched up and down all night in the Irish Sea, vomiting everywhere and feeling absolutely at death`s door. Our father, Kenneth, stayed at home in Leeds as the breadwinner. What a merciful relief that must have been to him. We used to stay for eight weeks at a farm owned by my Uncle Willy and Aunt Ellen. Looking back, they must have dreaded our visit, four kids from the grimy backstreets of Leeds. To make it even worse, they had no children of their own.

Today, fifty years later, I was here on a more sombre mission. Inside my suitcase were the remains of my cremated mother, making her last visit to her beloved homeland. My journey took me the same route as years gone by, though it is much faster and modern now. I got off the train in Ballina and made my way to my pre booked hotel. The hotel stood by the River Moy and was as beautiful as I remember. I ate a late dinner and spent a rather restless night. I dreamt of our visits all those years ago, and the relations I loved, now almost all gone. The visions whirled around, bits and pieces of different events and times, spinning around like jumbled clothes in a spin dryer.

The next morning, I made my way down to Killala by taxi. I had arranged to meet my mother`s only living sibling, my uncle Jerome. I knocked on his door and at length he appeared. He peered at me with his bloodshot whisky eyes, a frail old man who time had done no favours. He had never married, and the house was as ramshackle as I remembered, a hovel frozen in time. We exchanged greetings of a sort, and then he spoke. "What brings you here after all this time"?

I opened my suitcase and showed him the ashes of his older sister.

My mother had died twelve months previously. I sent him a letter to that effect, but he seemed to have no knowledge of the death at all. He was horror struck, and stared at the urn as though the Devil himself was inside it. At length after a stiff whisky, I asked him if he would like to accompany me to scatter the ashes, but I got no answer.

I told him that my mother often spoke of an old, neglected graveyard, near the old abbey of Saint Silas. He told me that no one went up there anymore. He added that the graves were so ancient, only moss-covered mounds remained, with the odd stone poking through like the teeth of an old crone.

My mother, Mary Hoban, had often told me of this old graveyard. She always said that she wanted her ashes scattered there, to be near her long gone ancestors. I never questioned her over it, but I found it strange that she did not want to be buried with the rest of the Hoban family at Rathfran.

Jerome muttered "Don`t go there, it is a bad place".

I needed him to show me where the cemetery was, and I arranged to meet him the following afternoon. Tomorrow would be Midsummers Eve, and on that date my mother had told me to scatter her ashes as the sun went down over Lacken Strand. She told me it was the most beautiful memory of her childhood. With that in mind, tomorrow I would do my painful, yet joyous duty. Once again, Jerome, the harbinger of doom, warned me again, "stay away from the abbey and Carrowmore". More garbled oaths and superstitious mutterings followed, but I paid no heed.

Day dawned on Midsummers Eve, a gloriously sunny day. The sky was full of ice crystal clouds, like the plume of a pheasant's tail. I sat outside my hotel and closed my eyes. My mind was flooded with the memories of my summer days spent here roaming the hills and windswept beaches with my siblings. I thought of all our loved ones long gone, and now my mother would now rest among them forever. It was a far cry from our home in the industrial grime of Leeds, with its smoke and filth.

There was no sentiment from me about my upbringing, although our parents did the best they could for us. The streets of Hunslet and Holbeck were filled with disease, poverty, and early death, and it was there I grew up. Our forebears came to Leeds through necessity, my mother included. Grim as it was you could work and eat. My mother was heartbroken when she walked out of Leeds railway station for the first time in 1947. She said it was foggy and everything was grey and filthy, but she stayed and reared me and my siblings. It was for that reason alone that she decided her ashes would rest forever in her beloved homeland, with its beauty and deep ancient sorrow and anger.

I left the hotel by cab and travelled down to Killala. The day was still dazzling bright, and the air was filled with seabirds, screaming in the wind. The clouds were lower now, with mare's tails that resembled the kites I flew in my youth. I paid the driver and strolled towards Jerome's house. I was taken aback, when I saw him suddenly open his door and march off down the road. He walked with an easy gait, as though the years had melted from his sparse frame.

I shouted loudly, but he paid me no heed, and then he vanished into the suns glare. The shock made me feel faint. *How could this be?* I was totally shocked.

The front door of his house was still open, so I decided to enter and await his return. I entered, my eyes struggling in the gloom. At length I pulled back the grimy curtains, the dust dancing in the sunlight. Turning away from the window, I suddenly tripped over something. Looking down I saw it was a person, taking in a short breath I turned the body over, it was my uncle Jerome. His face was contorted in absolute terror, his eyes bulging out.

What could this mean? I was terrified. I sat there for over an hour; my legs would not move. All of a sudden, I remembered with horror, a story my mother told me when I was young. I had seen the Fetch. The Fetch, according to folklore, was a spectral apparition who appeared to people who he wanted to die, I had seen the Fetch. To add to the fear, he looked exactly like his selected prey, and once his eyes met yours, your life was over. Panic stricken I ran out of the house and sat on a bench in Jerome`s garden. *Had the Fetch seen me?*

My mind was blank, but if the Fetch had seen me, I would be dead also. I once again recoiled in fear, I had left my mother`s ashes in the house. What was I to do and who could I tell? The only option was to tell the guards that I had found him like this. To relate the true tale would have seen me sent to the madhouse. I went back to the house for the ashes and sat beside my dead uncle. If I called the authorities, I would never meet my deadline at the abbey. All her life my mother had told me to never forget her last wishes, but I felt paralysed. There and then I was filled with resolve. I had promised my mother and I intended to keep that promise come what may.

With a heavy heart, I left Jerome and headed for the graveyard at Saint Silas Abbey in the gathering gloom. I felt guilty at leaving him, but I knew no one could have seen me at his remote house. I stumbled on and arrived at Lacken and made my way down to the Strand. I should have checked the tide; the river was now three feet deep. At length, with the ashes hoisted above my head, I waded across. The air was still, and the only sounds I heard were the crash of the waves and a lone mournful curlew. The sea seemed to breathe in and out for me, as though pulling me along.

It was now eleven o` clock. The clouds were blood red and purple in the last throes of the day. Darkness was approaching, but I could see the abbey. Perched high up a steep hill, it was as I remembered. It stood brooding in the twilight, derelict, and with an air of sadness about it, its flock long gone. Tired and wet I reached the abbey and quickly found the ancient graveyard.

With a heavy heart I scattered my mother`s ashes and said a silent prayer, my duty done. In the distance I heard a church bell chime twelve. The sound resonated through the air in equidistant shockwaves, as each toll of the bell struck. I gathered myself together and set off back on the lonely path to Killala.

Suddenly, I could hear violins playing in perfect harmony. I stopped still and heard them again. My mother had often told me that she would go listen to the gypsies when they camped down the lane, near Fog Hill. That was long ago in the distant past, who could be here, at the abbey in the dead of night? I advanced towards the music, and just when I thought I had found its source, it would dance on the breeze to another location. The music was accompanied by sinister giggling and whispering, as though I was being toyed with. I spun around and around, completely disorientated, the music growing louder and more manic, and then suddenly it stopped.

Terrified and totally lost, I began to try and find the path back to Killala and my dead uncle Jerome. Stumbling along in the dark and falling everywhere, I decided to stop and rest.

All at once it was daylight, and I could hear people's voices. They spoke in an unknown dialect, and I could not understand it with my English upbringing. Dumbfounded, I walked towards the sound.

I came out into a clearing and beheld the most pitiful sight, I, or any other human being had ever seen. It was a village of mud huts and squalor. The inhabitants were walking skeletons, their eyes sunk into their skulls. Their faces were black, and blood came from their sunken, pitiful eyes. This was the Black Fever. It was transmitted by skin lice. When they slept, this was passed on from one to another, as the filthy lice crawled over their emaciated bodies. Those who could walk were dressed in rags, and dead people littered the ground. The living carried on with their wretched existence, oblivious to the horror at their feet.

After a while, I noticed that they totally ignored me. I was invisible to them. I walked around the village like a ghost. The children ate grass and weeds, or anything they could forage. The few animals they had were in the same pitiful state, with no flesh on them to support a meal. It was a scene of absolute horror, Hell itself would have been no worse for these poor emaciated creatures. Where was I, what was happening to me, was I dead? At length I stumbled over something in the grass and looked down. The ground was covered in partly covered bones. They were scattered all around, some of the bones had rags wrapped around them, the remnants of shrouds. The people did not have the strength to dig a proper grave.

My uncle Jerome warned me not to venture here, but I, in my natural stubbornness, had ignored him. Then it struck me, this was a famine village, the like of which I had read about in history books. No book could describe this desolate scene. Death followed in their footsteps every second of every day. I sat there numb with fear and helplessness, invisible to all, and having no idea in which realm of existence I belonged.

I must have slept with sheer exhaustion. When I awoke, I could hear the sound of the sea and the waves crashing. The famine village had vanished along with those tormented starving people, or so I thought.   The wind grew in strength and surf filled the air, leaving the taste of salt on my lips. The sun had risen, and here I stood, but how could I tell anyone of my terrible experience.

I found a path, and through the haze I could see figures dancing on the rocks. They appeared to be women collecting seaweed for food.   How these walking skeletons had the strength to do this astounded me. When the waves crashed in, the women would dash back to shore, when the waves ebbed the women would dash forward and grab the seaweed. I watched this dance of death, invisible, alongside several children who could barely stand. One of them turned towards me. She looked like my mother, Mary, when she was a child. Her clothes were not rags like the other children wore, but they were old fashioned. I stared in disbelieve at her face, as she stood and smiled at me. I could not take this spectral vision in. I ran towards her, her arms opened to embrace me. We were nearly united, when I tripped and fell headlong into the sea.

I must have struck my head on something, for when I awoke, I was lying on Lacken Strand. In the distance, I could hear the sound of a car engine. A short time later, a range rover stopped, 200 yards away, on the Foghill side of the river. My uncle Jerome and a guard stepped out of it. They hastened towards me.

"I thought you were dead", he shouted. He looked at me like I was a mad man, and in reality, I nearly was.

The guard wandered around the beach, saying nothing. At length he spoke, "you were lucky someone pulled you out of the water, or you would have surely perished."

All around me were the footprints of young children. They must have dragged me from the sea and gone back to their never-ending accursed life.

The guard said, "I wonder why they just left you and said nothing?"

I recovered my senses and told Jerome and the guard, that I would wander back to Killala. I sat and watched Jerome and the guard walk back to the car.

Suddenly, a third person appeared and walked by their side. They marched on and faded into the early morning sunshine. I shielded my eyes and saw the range rover was still there. I ran towards it and noticed the guard on the floor, Jerome and the third person had gone. The Fetch had claimed another victim. *How was I to explain all this?*

I must have passed out and I awoke in a hospital. "Welcome back to the living" a voice said. "You must have suffered some kind of breakdown."

I have been in here for six months. The guards had found me in the sand dunes, demented. They also told me a guard had gone missing on the same day and he was never found.

Eventually, I regained my strength and was discharged from the asylum. Jerome had gone for ever, and his house was more or less derelict. What a tale to tell, and a tale which I could never tell a mortal soul. I collected my possessions from the hotel and called a taxi to take me back to Foghill. I had resolved myself to take one last look at this eerie place.

I gathered my senses and turned towards the abbey. Something caught my eye on the rocks. It was a little girl waving forlornly to me. Her black hair blew in the wind, and without warning the apparition vanished. Tears filled my eyes and I prayed to God almighty, that it was not my mother, banished forever in the lost famine village of Carrowmore. Looking back across the river I could see a faint figure, and I ran and ran.

<u>LAST NIGHT IN RUE CHILDEBRET</u>

by Sergio 'ente per ente' PALUMBO

edited by Michele DUTCHER

The gates of Guillotière Cemetery in the city of Lyon had been closed at 5 p.m. and since that moment on, of course, no one had been inside. Or better, no one should have been.

Pre-dusk had quickly come and gone, with the sky endowed with many colors such as orangish and reddish shades, and then the darkest part of the evening, until it was replaced by full darkness.

Robèrt Meunier, wrapped in his burnt umber overcoat and his warm charcoal-colored trousers, had only a small flashlight with him, and he tried to avoid switching it on until the right moment. The 70-year-old graying man didn't want to attract too much attention before the proper time came.

Now, the dark branches of the sunless trees swayed because of a soft wind that blew along the hidden paths, past the cavernous-like entrances of the family tombs on both sides, making him unsettled and full of distressing thoughts. The plants and stone structures that prevented the flowers and the graves from being reached from the sun rays during the day, now looked like deadly arms and fingers that played a dusky music along with the overwhelming night and its mysteries which were kept hidden in its hug. These were the seeds of fear and wonder that the man had already started to sense inside, and his location obviously contributed to such feeling of uneasiness more and more as minutes went by.

Suddenly, the thought that this was also the place where the famous Lumière Brothers' Tomb was located made him uncomfortable. This might look like a ghostly scene which would have been perfect for a black and white horror film, but surely his frightening surroundings weren't the thing the man preferred to think of or remember at present.

Lyon's largest and most ancient cemetery, that happened to be the site where he was strolling now, had been built in 1822, and though there was a newer portion of a later period, completed in 1854 to address the shortage of burial spaces in the city, this area in the *La Guillotière* neighborhood was characterized by long paths surrounded by trees and old stone tombs that dated back two centuries. Robèrt knew this very well, as he had researched the graveyard before coming here, but he was having second thoughts. Perhaps he should have decided to stay at home for the night…

These were the grounds where the remains of dead citizens had been buried or otherwise interred, and there were so many of them. After all, the aged man reminded himself of one of the best phrases that he had once written in an old article of his, when he was still working as a journalist: '*Men had always been affected by an unbeatable epidemic that left no choice but to accept: death!*'. Some of those graves had headstones engraved with a name, date of birth and death and other biographical data, set up over the place of burial. Usually, the more writing and symbols visible on the headstone, the more expensive it was.

Robèrt Meunier wondered why he had picked out a night with a full moon to stay here, unnoticed, after closing time. His worried mind wondered if it had been a bad thing to entertain his growing interest in those newspaper's articles, the few ones he had downloaded on his outdated smartphone over the course of the last two days which reported strange unexplainable cases of grave diggings that seemed to have happened during the last two years in this town.

He still thought like a journalist, though long retired, and he felt he needed to get a first-hand account and experience about what he had read previously, if he really wanted to discover anything more about what was going on. Provided that something real was behind those reports, and not just the written words of a promoter or an aspiring newsman, of course. Which wouldn't be too surprising in this field that frequently resulted in the dumping of fake information and fanciful blogs, as Robèrt knew very well.

'So, are you starting to believe the stories about unearthly presences that come back from the afterlife to pay visits to us from time to time?' the man asked himself, in silence, as he stared in a tumultuous state of mind at the tombs around him. He noticed that the statues that surrounded him were slightly enlivened by the moonlight that filtered through the partly overcast sky. Undoubtedly, he had no belief in the undead and such, and he had come here to discover the real truth behind all those recent strange cases. 'Keep your mind busy and focus on other things,' Robèrt forced himself to think. Everything else he could turn his apprehensions to, of course, but the present dark scenery was most welcomed.

Then, he heard noises coming from somewhere in the darkness, and the strange sounds were nearby. Or so they seemed to be, coming from the other side of the path he was walking now. Once those sounds disappeared, however, he tried to pretend they had never happened. But he knew he had heard something, and that thinking differently was the wrong thing to do and was certainly unhelpful.

Contrary to what Robèrt wanted to do, he forced himself onwards in spite of his trepidations. And so, the short man moved in the direction he believed those noises had come, while wrapping his overcoat tighter around him, as if he hoped it might protect him from whatever he might find. He kept walking though he considered at times that he really didn't know what he was doing, and what might happen.

Then his blue eyes saw something, under the brilliance of his flashlight. He increased the area enlightened by it and there he saw two bodies! Or, at least, parts of them. Actually, some portions of those corpses seemed to have disappeared, or have been removed. Incomprehensibly, they looked as if they had been gnawed on, however incredible that might be.

As the man approached, the bodies appeared to him to be the remains of recently deceased people. From what he could ascertain given the moderate amount of light given off by his flashlight, there was still some dry blood on their clothes and hair. But this didn't make it understandable. Plus, the dim light gave everything a macabre hue. Why had they been moved away from their graves? And who on earth had done so?

Then the man heard the growl in a subdued tone, he turned his head, widening his eyes to focus through the darkness of the night. What he spotted made him forget about his purpose in coming and about everything he knew pertaining to what he believed about the dead.

The sight of the tall hairy creature with glowing eyes, fiercely standing just a few feet from where he stood, made him speechless. And the wide fanged jaws that were atop of its considerable height, openly dripping to the ground portions of meat, or better human skin and entrails, almost drove him mad at once.

*****

At night, even in the chill air of March, Robèrt Meunier insisted on cranking the air conditioner all the way up. His usual temperature always did run a couple of degrees higher than others liked, but maybe it was simply the air of Lyon that made him desire a cooler climate. After all, he lived in Val de Saire, Normandy, though he wasn't born in that area of France. Up there the strong winds and the cold weather ruled over the rainy surroundings for many months during the year.

The man had received, as a bequeathal from a next of kin, his one bedroom apartment in a loft in the French city of Lyon, in Rue Childebret. He only stayed in Lyon a few days a year, to rest and spend some time here. He could say he loved that place, because this was France's second largest city, and he loved that *rue* because it was a link – a passage, if you will - from the River Rhone to the River Saone. You could view both of them from a window of the top floor of a building situated in the middle of the street, while looking down at the people who were strolling around. Moreover, just a few steps away stood the well-known restored Carolingian church dating from 1107.

The man had been retired for five years and was now in his 70s. He always took the time to stay in this city when he could, both to thoroughly check if everything was okay in the house - as it would otherwise remain unoccupied for too long - and to enjoy a break that usually lasted about a month. There were many places to visit here. In the city stood those ancient ruins of the past, the two *Théâtres Romains*. Every time he visited Lyon he also loved to visit the *Musée de la Civilisation Gallo-Romaine* whose underground had a collection of statues, coins, and inscriptions evoking Lyon's Roman past.

After all, he had to find something to do now that he was retired.

Having been a journalist most of his life, for three different newspapers, and having a comfortable pension – that was something his younger colleagues couldn't be certain to collect eventually under the present circumstances, and the downturn in the economy recently - he thought that appreciating art and visiting the monuments he had long been writing about was the perfect thing to do to fill his free days and have a great time.

The man usually closed out the day, before deciding to go to bed, with his head bent over the pages of a magazine with a glass of Bénédictine. The famous French herbal liquor with its typical sweetness could be found at his side in the sitting room full of old cushions covered in antique embroidery. He thought about the delicious entrées that would be waiting for him tomorrow at lunch at his beloved restaurant situated nearby, made of 'andouillette', a whitish sausage of pork with wine and the renowned Lyon's own quenelles. His nightly ritual always proved restful enough to let him fall asleep in his bedroom later on.

The next morning Robèrt got dressed, took his *petit déjeuner* then exited the apartment. He walked down the stairs, remembering how scary the entryway to the building had appeared to him the first time he was here, years ago, but he also knew that it was part of the pleasing seduction of the place.

He spent part of the morning busy shopping between Place Bellecour and Rue d'Auvergne before getting to his favorite French restaurant, which served single dishes and other meals he liked. It was there, when he was already sipping his wine and looking at the news on his smartphone, that he noticed something strange and unusual. There happened to be a short piece about some unexplainable occurrences that had been discovered in one of the local cemeteries, inside the Guillotière Cemetery to be more precise.

According to the article, it seemed that some unknown gravediggers had opened the tombs of recently deceased persons, a few weeks ago, but nothing had been taken. Those who had first come there were shocked as thieves plundering graves wasn't a common occurrence. On the other hand, though no personal objects or other decorations had disappeared, two corpses had been reported with some parts of the body missing, and this made it all the stranger.

As nothing valuable had been removed, and the only evidence was missing body parts taken away, or eaten, there were suppositions that perhaps some wolves coming from the heart of the Monts du Massif, were to blame. These mountains lie less than 30 kilometers from the city, and wolves might have covered that ground at night as such animals were said to do at times, so maybe they had entered the cemetery in search of food. This was a possibility, as wolves had been spotted in that area that was full of marked trails and beautiful lakes in the recent years, with breathtaking views of the Alps. However, it was a very rare thing that they would dare to enter a large city like this, even if they needed food. The French newsman whose article he was studying and whose name he hadn't previously heard had said that this might be a case involving bloody societies, whose members included individuals who still believed in dark sorcery. Groups of people who came at night to unearth human remains and turn to some unholy rituals of old. All this was nonsense, the man thought.

The occurrence of the graves being opened had happened during a night when the full moon was out. And the peculiarity of the place where the events had occurred – if the reports were true - and the nighttime made it all much scarier. The man immediately started drawing his own conclusions. This seemed to be one of those curious news items you could find near the end of the worst newspapers. He remembered that when still he was at work, they called such paranormal reports 'portnawak', that meant rubbish, and the younger newsmen who wrote about them as 'benêt', or doofus.

Then, the consideration that such news had appeared just two days before the next Full Moon in the area made Robèrt imagine that it was meant to attract younger readers or the fans of mysteries, those who followed such bloody and dark reports and loved to zone out. These articles were merely curiosities for the airy-fairy types.

Robèrt didn't look for that kind of short piece in newspapers. He had just downloaded it by chance onto his smartphone and started to gloat while eating his lunch, tasting the excellent cuisine of the place. After his last glass of wine, probably because of his blood alcohol content, his curiosity was piqued.. He still wasn't certain about those events, but he promised that, once he had gotten back home, and after taking a nap, *why not?* He would start a thorough investigation over the internet to look at previous reports of such a thing. That was, of course, if there were other similar reports about this.

*****

It took him about three hours to recover from the alcohol he had drunk with his lunch, though he spent that time in his sitting room, abstractedly watching the large TV screen until he fell asleep for half-an-hour or so. But when he awoke again, that thought, and his memory of that strange article, resurfaced and started agitating his mind again. So, he switched on his computer and began his search.

Time went by very quickly. The afternoon soon became evening until it was almost entirely dark outside his window. Robèrt considered some strange things he had found in his internet searches until night came. What interested him was that he found online other short articles by different people on blogs, and even in two small newspapers, detailing such activities. There were articles about unknown graverobbers, which had occurred in burial grounds of other towns, especially in Montbrison, in Serrières and even in Pérouges. These additional reports attracted his attention more and more.

He was born in Pérouges, a fortified hilltop village of medieval houses that was not far from Lyon, a place well-known to be originally the home of immigrants from the Italian city of Perugia. His birth town had been used, not surprisingly, as the setting for historical TV fiction or films on occasion.

So, it seemed that the same group, or other groups behaving the same way, were doing regrettable things around the country. The question, of course, was: why? And who were they, anyway?

The man could almost envision before his eyes a scene of individuals wearing dark clothes sitting on the tombs. Maybe the groups were made up of stupid teens drinking cheap beer when it turned dark at night. Perhaps before cracking the tombs open, they would pinch their nostrils together because of the smell of the decay that came out of the inside. He wondered how somebody might want to do so just for fun, or for some evil ritualistic ends he certainly couldn't comprehend, nor approve of. 'Damn, what could those teenagers be thinking? This is nonsense!' This was what he said to himself at the top of his voice that sounded angrier every time he repeated it. Honestly, he didn't care about whoever might hear him, be it his neighbor or someone who was going down the stairs outside his floor at that moment. But he also considered that it was possible, given the hour of the night, that most of the tenants were asleep.

Robèrt certainly didn't know what to think about it all. But, as with all the other times he had read about a possible promising case, or a recount that might have something real behind it, he knew he wouldn't be able to sleep peacefully until he investigated it. His smell for the big story, as a former journalist, had never failed him before. Maybe there were even worse things than those he had discovered so far.

That same evening, after having studied the info on many sites online, and having discovered what he now knew, he looked exhausted. His eyes studied the sitting room he was in, furnished with a mixture of original features and contemporary touches, and looked at the woodwork painted on the old chairs and on the walls near the window. He liked this style, though it hadn't been him who had endowed this house with such decorations that had survived half a century without scratches. The home was exactly as he had found it when he had accepted the bequeathal, except for a few minor personal changes.

The mystery at the cemeteries attracted him, and he couldn't remove it from his mind. The man would like to know much more about it; so to leave no stone unturned, in a manner of speaking, he decided that if he wanted to investigate it all, he might have to go there, and see things for himself.

Well, what the hell...why not? He came to this conclusion as the only thing that really mattered in this all was to know the truth. He wanted to reveal who the real culprits of such actions might be. And if, in order to get to know the truth, he had to break some rules and take some chances, he had to try, and go see for himself. What else had his working life as a journalist taught him, after all?

It seemed as if his retired life had become routine, with his mind focused only on his sofa and tomorrow's lunch. Perhaps he would enjoy escaping from the drudgery, at least for a while. Maybe there was something else he needed to do, some way he could be active again, like he used to be.

So, eventually, an elated Robèrt made up his mind. He would see things for himself the next night! Just when the Full Moon was visible over the city. What could be better than going there to find the truth for himself?

For now, he would try to get some sleep and tomorrow he would discover if those articles were true!

*****

Guillotière Cemetery was the name of two adjacent cemeteries in Lyon that were reputed to contain around 40,000 tombs. The old cemetery was situated just north of the new one, and the two were separated by Avenue Berthelot and the railroad tracks. The new cemetery had been organized in concentric circles and was the largest in the city itself.

As the aged man kept walking, he passed the Franco-Prussian War Monument, in the new cemetery, and saw the graves that were present in that park-like setting. Different from many others in the country, this urban cemetery had never fallen into disrepair and had never become overgrown, as it had never lacked endowments to fund care of the grounds.

Eventually everybody emptied out of the area at closing time, and the gates were closed. What he had to do was simply keep himself hidden and wait to be certain that his figure couldn't be spotted by the few individuals tasked with the assignment of guarding the place. After half an hour, he was certain no one was there but him.

As the sunset had come and night had wrapped almost everything in it, insomuch that it was difficult to see where he put his feet on the ground and only a pale light of the Moon in the sky granted some brilliance, the man regretted deciding to come here, staying inside the cemetery when everyone else had left. Then his mind started filling-up with many - *too many* - terrible fears that deepened his suspicion about the place. Every corner now appeared to be a possible threat or a connecting point to the afterlife. He began to believe that some unearthly being, or creature, would come out of the ground at any time to attack him. It was impossible to think otherwise given the late hour, and the lugubrious site he was in now. It took him some time before he could really fight his way through that feeling and come to terms with his decision to be here at the present time, exactly on this day. As he regained his strength, he slowly forced himself to walk and he had to do that more than once along the way to prevent himself from running to the exit as fast as he could.

"Oh, I made the right decision to come here," he considered in silence, making fun of himself, "for I feel steeped in calmness and content…"

In the wide pocket of his overcoat, he touched the small video recorder he had brought along with him. The man was unaccustomed to such devices that used Night Vision, as he had always been a man who wrote sitting somewhere, and not the man who took footage in the field, but he had tested it a few times while at home, from his window. That gizmo didn't seem to be too difficult to use, and he wanted to get images of the faces of any individuals who might be wandering the cemetery tonight, practicing their unholy activities.

Not that he really thought he might be so lucky that night to discover something. In a way, the image of himself being home again, safe and sound, the sooner the better, didn't appear to him to be such a bad way to spend his time after all. The fearsome sensations he had felt since darkness had fallen had prodded his memory, and he remembered that even as a rebellious teenager he had never dared to stay inside a cemetery at night. No, he had never done anything like that before.

It was exactly at that moment when it happened!

The noises, the things brought into light by the brilliance of his flashlight, the pair of bodies of recently deceased people on the ground, and the growl coming from the tall hairy creature.

*****

The hairy monster towered over the man, an impending landfall from a mountain that was about to cover the silent ground below the slope. He dropped the small video recorder on the ground and didn't try to pick it back up, nor did finding it cross his mind. Glad that he still held the flashlight in his hand, he was surprised that he hadn't fainted because of the unexplainable sight!

Then, the creature growled again, turning its large, fierce face towards him. It lunged at Robèrt, knocking him onto the cold pathway, his feet sprawled in the vegetation and the lost recorder thrown somewhere in the darkness. The monster straddled him, its bristly hairy skin touching his clothes, and the beasts girth pressed down on him. His eyes watched apprehensively as the creature got back on its large rear legs and stood still.

Then, unbelievably, it not only growled fiercely, the creature surprisingly spoke, "You're a man. You're still a living being." Its words rumbled in a low and unearthly voice. "You shouldn't be here, not now, not yet. This place is for the dead. And for me."

Robèrt would have tried to say something, to open his mouth, even to scream, but he found he was entirely unable to do so as his eyes stared, locked on that unbelievable thing.

"The Full Moon is in the sky, and I need to feed again. I have turned into what you see, and I don't have a choice. You shouldn't be here, not yet," the monster added in its chilling tone of voice.

"What?" the aged man was probably the more surprised as he discovered he was able again to be breathing a sound. "What are you? Why? Why did you say not yet?"

"You are man. I am a *loublin!*"

"What?"

"A *loublin.* Haven't you ever heard tales about me? Don't you listen to the legends of old? I was turned into a werewolf after a hunting trip in the woods, long ago. I was late reaching my dear friends outside of the boundary of the forest. I got lost. And then I was assaulted by that creature, the werewolf… Before that day, I too was only a man just like you, a science student. I didn't know anything about such mythical beings, nor that they might be real in this world! But one of those turned me into something else, and since then my life had become very different."

Robèrt kept listening to the words that came out of that face in the shape of a large wolf's snout, which was much bigger than a common wolf's indeed. "A man?Like me, you say?"

"From that night I started feeling the need for meat, and blood. Not just the blood and skin of other animals, but that of humans. I came to require those bodies and I also had to eat them if I wanted to satisfy my deep hunger. I couldn't resist, at first, but I was ashamed by my cruel actions very soon as I saw my victims lying on the paths of the woods I chose as my hideout during those first years."

"Your victims…" the man let his voice out in a scared way.

"So, even if my body under the light of a Full Moon was turned into that of a bloody werewolf, my mind was still human, and I could still reason as a man, at least for the most part. I regretted what I had done during my first months of my new condition. So, I decided to follow another course of action, I had to! Here in France people have a name for creatures like me, they call us the *loublin,* fabled werewolves that are said to frequent cemeteries. And here I come, from time to time, entering this wide cemetery, or others in a few cities nearby, under the drive of my nose, walking along the graves until eventually I discover the smell of the recently deceased humans, because their remains are what I need to appease my foul and evil hunger. As I want to do, I only feed on the bodies that have recently been buried, the dead that have left the world of the living beings just a few days before Full Moon and still attract me. These corpses fill my stomach and make me be strong and able to survive until the next month."

The powerless Robèrt was wide-eyed, still keeping silent.

"I had to get used to the stench from decomposing corpses, and that wasn't easy for a long time, but the fact was that I couldn't be affected by the bacteria or the viruses which usually came from decomposing human bodies, that can cause disease and illnesses to most living creatures," the werewolf explained in his very low tone, and then fell silent for a moment. "In a way, I'm not completely alive, but not-yet dead."

Robèrt almost couldn't believe what he had been told, but the reality of that creature, of what he appeared to be, and what he was doing, was before his own eyes, and it couldn't be refuted. This was a fact. Although unbelievable in his mind, this was really happening here and now! What could he do about it now?

He remembered he was not armed, and the only object that might be used as an insignificant weapon was his flashlight, which was endowed with high-impact plastic body. But that certainly wouldn't be of any real help against a fierce tall creature like that. The man didn't know if it was because of his desperation, terror, or just raw adrenaline, but his mind kept considering every detail around. His thoughts kept racing, trying to find any way he could get out of there alive. Then, something made him become aware of a particularity of what the monster had previously told him, and he addressed the unearthly creature. "So, you are not going to attack me? You only feed on corpses of men who are already dead?"

"No, never again on a living being, I made a promise to myself," the other uttered. "But I also have the gift of a farseer, which is a part of my power. I have been able to tell the future since the moment I was turned into the angry werewolf I am now. Therefore, I knew that somebody would come here tonight, under the light of the Moon. But I couldn't know who, or why. Anyway, I also knew that the man who would be here before me tonight would die because of an unexpected heart attack. That man must be you! So, not yet, but soon. I can't feed on you while you are still alive, but in a very short time you will be dead and then I'll eat your body. This can't be changed. Frequently I made use of this ability to find juicy meals. This power is great, and useful. The trail of incoming blood of the next death that appears in my visions has always been easy for me to follow."

The aged man couldn't really believe that what he was listening to, those horrible words and their stark reality froze his blood.

"It's about time. The moment is almost upon us. So, you're going to be a corpse soon, and I'll be able to feed on you without breaking my promise to never harm a living being again," the monster added as he stood before the fearful, scared stiff, former journalist who had just discovered that he was going to die that night, in a few minutes. The man had begun to believe that he wouldn't be killed by that unearthly creature, as he had just been afraid of until a moment ago, but he would die tonight, anyway. It left him speechless and astounded.

Then, it happened. Exactly as the monster had told him. The man felt the oppressive inability of the heart in his chest to continuously cope with its workload of pumping blood to the rest of the body. At first, his massive heart failure affected the left side of his body. An undiagnosed coronary artery disease, complicated by pulmonary hypertension could no longer deal with the unexpected stress of the night. He felt the effects of his heart's failure especially in his legs and ankles. His intestinal tract became congested, causing discomfort, and then released its contents into his pants. Other painful symptoms followed. But those didn't last long.

The clouds moved and the Full Moon showed its own face, just a short sliver, only a sort of hint. There was the last light that reached his features, the disappearing brilliance on his eyes before the time came, and then he completely fell on one side to the ground, lifeless. Immediately after, the body at full length began being fiercely pierced, deeply cut, and tasted.

And the werewolf got a bit of the meat caught between its teeth of course…

SI-TEH-CAH

by DJ Tyrer

Long ago, long before the outsiders had come from beyond the ocean, the cave had been on the shore of a vast primordial lake. Later still, it came to overlook the bed of a much-smaller lake that only occasionally filled with brackish water. Now, it looked down upon a dusty desert landscape, the waters seeming less and less likely to return to fill the basin, however briefly.

Today, where legend said rafts woven out of sedge had once floated, an old camper van sat on the salt-speckled ground, and nearby, a man preparing a barbecue as he swigged beer from a bottle taken from a bucket of ice, his wife and children sitting in the shade of an awning.

The old Paiute shook his head as he watched them from his vantage point, near to the cave entrance. They didn't belong here, not in this place, not even in what they termed the State of Nevada. They didn't understand the danger.

Then again, neither did his people, and they knew the old tales. Only, they believed them to belong to the past, hadn't seen what he had seen.

Country and Western music drifted up to him from the camper van as he recalled his youth. He shivered, despite the heat. When he had been just a young Paiute, listening to the stories his grandfather told of the Si-teh-cah, he had felt sorry for the ancient men described as red-headed giants, their stature and ferocity seeming to grow each time his grandfather recounted the tales.

Yes, legend said the Si-teh-cah had been cannibals, but it also said they had lived on their rafts of sedge out on the lake to avoid his warlike ancestors, that the ancient Paiute had hunted them down until they cornered the last few in this cave and had used fire to suffocate them.

As a child, he felt bad about that, the way they had lived in fear of his kind and the callous manner his ancestors had killed them. He had shuddered at the thought of them choking in the darkness. Really, was it that different to what his people had suffered in his grandfather's youth?

For all the heroism the stories purported to celebrate, his child-self had identified the Si-teh-cah as victims and he had felt guilt.

Now, he knew better.

The old Paiute looked down at the campers. The barbecue ready, the man was serving up hamburgers and hot-dogs to his wife and kids.

Why had he come here, chosen this spot?

The fool! No, not a fool – it was ignorance, not stupidity that led him to endanger his family.

The same ignorance that had cost the old Paiute his brother…

He still recalled that day, six decades earlier, with perfect clarity.

It had been the day his brother died and the day he learnt just how ignorant they had been.

A day very much like this, hot with a bright sun shining down upon the valley, a heat haze shimmering across the long-empty lakebed like sparkling waters.

He and his brother had ranged far from home, drawn by the old legends, carrying simple, childish bows with which to re-enact the deeds of their ancestors.

They had ranged across the basin, the air shimmering with heat, and then, it had ceased to be haze.

The old Paiute could scarcely believe it now, but he knew what he had seen, the sudden appearance of waters swirling about them, the engulfing terror as it rose above their heads in an instant and their feet lost contact with the lakebed.

Not the onrushing of waters, though, but a sudden appearance from nowhere, neither from the heavens, nor from beneath the ground, nor from any compass direction. The water had just appeared, surrounding them, swamping them before they could react.

The terror was fresh, the water rushing into his lungs, the burning, choking sensation…

He had kicked for the surface, then, the shore, driven by a desperate urge that drove all thoughts from his mind. Pulling himself from the water, he glanced back and saw that his brother was struggling, floundering. Nearby was a raft, but he saw no more as he collapsed, gasping and coughing, a paralysed ball of panic spewing salty water.

Finally, when he pushed himself up from the ground and looked back, he saw the raft reach his brother and the people upon it, tall with cascading locks of flaming-red hair, drag him aboard. For a moment, he had felt relief, imagined his brother rescued, but then he had been forced to watch, impotent, what they did to him once they had him in their grasp. Brutal and swift, staining the waters of the lake red, the speed of the act was their only mercy.

Then, he had watched them feast.

He had fled, run far into the mountains, become lost for days, before he finally found his way home.

Nobody had believed him, the waters having vanished and his brother's remains with them, by the time he was able to lead them there. They had said they must have become lost in the desert, that he must have become addled by the sun.

Indeed, he had scarcely believed himself.

But, he had returned regularly, seeking first answers and, then, revenge. More than once, he had seen the haze turn to water and the red-haired brutes out of legend upon their reeds of sedge. He had ceased to feel any guilt for what his ancestors had done.

He knew that when the haze changed to water and there were victims for them to take, the Si-teh-cah would come. It was as inevitable as the sunrise.

They would come today, he was certain.

He sat and watched.

Yes, this was it. The haze was changing, the rippling shimmer becoming something more solid, becoming water.

This was it.

He could have shouted a warning, he knew, but didn't care. He wasn't here as a saviour, but as an avenger. Besides, would they have heard his cry, heeded it?

Shrugging, he stood and readied his rifle as water surrounded and submerged the camper van.

He could see the family, startled and scared, struggling in the water.

He could see a raft of sedge approaching.

Yes, this was it.

The old Paiute didn't know if the Si-teh-cah were men drawn to the present from their own time, beings who lived in some parallel world tangential to his own, or if they were the spirits of the men his ancestors had long ago slain, somehow given physical form once more. It didn't matter. All he cared was that he owed his brother vengeance.

If it happened to help the campers, so be it.

He took aim and fired.

One of the red-haired figures stiffened and fell into the water, then another, and another.

Long ago, he had been impotent, had watched as his brother's blood turned the lake water's red, but not now. Not today. Today, the stain belonged to them, not innocents.

The last of the Si-teh-cah fell from the raft into the shimmering waters, then, a moment later, there was no water, merely the ripple of a heat haze, and four dazed and confused tourists lying sprawled upon the ground, a mist of steam rising from their damp clothing.

They would have a story to tell or a hefty therapy bill. The old Paiute didn't care. He had done what he had come to do. He would tell no story, merely offer up a prayer of thanks to the spirits that his aim had been true.

Quickly, he slung his rifle and collected up the ejected brass, then disappeared away from the dry lakebed into the desolate mountains. At last, he was at peace, his life's work complete.

Now, he could rest.

Ends

THE WINGED ONES

by Russell Hemmell

The nightclub was hosted in a deconsecrated church, and it was decadent and luxurious at the same time, black velvet all over the sitting area and stroboscopic lights of a thousand colours fluttering to the music vibe. The perfect venue for Leonora's personal Halloween celebrations.

A far cry from places of the same kind elsewhere in the world, she decided, strolling across the nave, eyes slowly adjusting to the penumbra. After all, in 2187, up-class entertainment venues were nested either inside sky-reaching, glimmering 300-odd-story towers or deep down the subterranean cities several hundred metres underground. If the reason was to protect patrons from the nasty weather or keeping the poor crowd out, Leonora couldn't tell.

But the world was not Rome.

In Italy, the past and the present seemed to live side by side without solution of continuity, and the future seemed to come always as an uninvited guest. Part of its undying charm. The hell with the weather, too: in Rome, it was better than most of the world cities anyway.

That night, however, Leonora didn't pay attention to those extravagant surroundings, the exquisite orange pumpkin *décor,* the alluring waitresses in their bat-winged robes. Something weirder had grabbed her attention as soon as she'd walked in. A woman, every inch as refined and snobbish as Leonora was. No Halloween costume for that one, either.

The woman sported a long red robe, diamond earrings, and an insulting smile on her face. She'd taken her place beside Leonora, asking questions with a palpable lack of interest in Leonora's replies.

Life had taught Leonora there were two reasons for such behaviours: one, people didn't care about the questions in the first place. Two, they already knew the answers.

"I'm out of that world. I'm surprised anybody still recognises me after so many years," Leonora said, bluntly. She didn't add *and so far away from that scene;* there was no need to state the obvious. Bloody expensive it might well be, a half-empty nightclub, in Rome or otherwise, was not what she was used to. After all, she was Leonora Saveri-Devereux, not a common model.

"Is it so?" the woman said, her long eyelashes fluttering like butterfly wings. Not beautiful in a classical way, the stranger, but outrageously sensual, with irises so black that it was impossible to separate the pupil from the rest. "Do you miss that life?"

"No." The truth. No matter if she'd been in the modelling world for eight years, the job had always been a means for Leonora in getting what she really wanted: study archaeology in the World's top colleges. A rather uncommon subject, granted. An expensive one, too, until the moment her research had started paying enough to sustain her lifestyle.

Leonora's specific field of expertise was a difficult one to pursue. She was a scholar of Death and the Underworld, in all its iconographic forms, cultures and times. Her all-time favourites were Japan and Korea, but she'd recently developed a passion for the Mediterranean. The weather played a role, of course. Ancient civilisations in both places, but she could do without radiation and snowstorms every other day.

That's why she had eventually settled down in Rome, Italy. What better place for history than a city alive since three thousand years and counting? "Look, Miss…"

"Axel."

"Axel." Leonora drank her champagne and poured more, sneering. "You mean Axelle."

"I like Axel more." The woman's eyes were glittering like obsidian stones. "You don't really care about gender, do you?"

She'd been probably one of Leonora's fans once upon a time. How else could she be privy to all those details, otherwise?

"I'm not sure what you've approached me for, Axel-Axelle, but you're wasting your time."

"I don't think so." Her precious, carmine gown opened when she crossed her long legs, revealing a sleek skin almost luminescent in the semi-darkness. Sex, that was her game. Axel was a hooker, although a peculiar one.

"I'm not going to pay for that." Leonora laughed, unsure if feeling amused or insulted, certainly intrigued. "It'd be the other way around, if any."

"Oh, you're mistaken. Sex is out of question here," Axel laughed, too. "I'm a partner better to avoid."

An original pick-up line. Leonora's curiosity perked. "There are no bad lays, only careless lays.

Nothing dedication and good advice can't fix. Take the word of an expert here."

Leonora was not pretending. In her modelling years she'd started counting them into triple digits, helped by the fact she didn't discriminate in terms of gender, age and race. Once her new life had begun, however, she had become more selective, not because she'd grown more tasteful but because she'd less time for playing.

Axel snickered, shaking her head. "You got it wrong."

"So why I have the strong feeling you want to offer me something?"

"Because you're smart, and that's what is going to happen."

Leonora emptied her glass. "I've already told you: I'm out of that world."

"You're very much in the one I'm willing to bring you into."

Axel took out her holoplate and a tiny 3D image materialised in front of their eyes.

"Do you know this place?" she asked with a smirk on her face, waving her hand in front of the view while pouring yet more bubbling liquid into their glasses.

"You must be kidding, right? If you know all these things about me, you also know that's a question you shouldn't ask. Just because I have legs that go from here to London doesn't mean I'm turtle crap at what I do." There was more a hint of acidity in her voice, but Leonora didn't bother. "This is the Etruscan necropolis in Cerveteri, not far away from Rome. That's it, a city of the dead."

"I knew you wouldn't disappoint me. Would you follow me there?"

"That's a good place to celebrate Halloween, I'll give you that."

"Forget celebrations. It is for that offer you were talking about. A job."

"In an ancient cemetery in the middle of the night? You do know how to pick a venue for an interview, Lady Axel."

Axel's eyes narrowed, and a glint of irony lit them up. "Are you scared, maybe?"

Leonora could, in theory. But she was not. Tricks or treats.

*****

The Etruscan burial ground was located on top

of a hill north to Cerveteri.

Leonora had never been there, but she knew what to expect, like any archaeologist worthy of their name. It was an architectonic wonder, well preserved and eerily charming even for people that didn't share her obsession for death.

It had not taken long to get there with Axel's state-of-the-art aerial transport, and now, in the silence of the night, they were walking across an avenue, among thousands of tombs in close succession. From *Via Sepolcrale Principale* to the minor streets of the dead city, the entire metropolis consisted in circular tumuli and spherical lines of perfect symmetry. Narrow, debris-ridden tombs, and noble hypogeums made Cerveteri precious and morbid at the same time.

They strolled along the Fenced Area of the plateau that hosted the Tomb of Reliefs.

Leonora had so far only seen photos of what was considered one of the masterpieces of funeral art of all times. She stopped in front of the sarcophagus, mouth agape and stars in her eyes.

"This tomb is just marvelous." She came closer, examining the monument with expert eyes. Its extraordinary decorations and reliefs in stucco represented objects of everyday use in amazing details, mixed with the demonic images of the Etruscan pantheon, gorgeous and terrifying at the same time.

A feast for the eye and the earth of the beholder.

"It's my favourite, too. I've been living here for a long time," Axel said, touching Leonora's hand for just a moment.

Gelid fingers. Sleeker-than-alabaster skin.

Leonora didn't hide her skepticism. Not only was it illegal, it was unlikely. Axel was rich and sophisticated, not a homeless beggar. "Here. How long, exactly?"

"A few centuries."

"Is that so? And the custodians?"

"They don't see me. I go out only at night." She smiled. "Daylight annoys me."

"I see, like a vampire." Leonora laughed. "I had a lot of weird Halloween nights in my life, but this beats it all."

Axel sat on the marble base that supported the sarcophagus, offering again to Leonora's eyes a glimpse of her magnificent legs. "Would it appeal to you if I were one?"

"Nah. Not really, no. Sharing your dark gift

with me would a waste of time." Her hands waved, conveying an ill-disguised contempt. "I don't appreciate those white-washed suckers, or anything that can be fought off by waving a garlic head."

"Eternal life nonetheless." Axel sneered, while her eyes challenged Leonora to say the contrary.

"Eternal life is more of a temptation. But you're not a vampire, right?"

"Vampires don't exist, not the ones that drink blood, at least. My job proposal still stands, though."

"Which I still fail to grasp."

Axel stood up and tilted her head, as if she were to persuade a recalcitrant child. "Given your specialty area, I thought you would've guessed straight away. Look around."

Leonora turned her head around, eyes staring at the necropolis. "Maybe I lack imagination. What you want me to be, an undertaker?"

"But with a fancier name, and a long and honoured tradition."

Axel pointed at a winged figure on one of the tombs nearby. There was a young woman engraved on the stone, kneeling beside a dying man and helping him to get into a chariot. She was bare-chested, wearing a hunter's dress. She had flowers in her hands. On the side of her body, she carried a sword, and on the ground at her feet there was a torch and a scroll. Large, featherily wings springing from her shoulders were displayed in all their majesty.

"Do you recognize her?"

"Is Twenty Questions in a Graveyard your idea of fun, Axel? That winged girl has many names, some of them funny. In other cultures, she was even a man."

"But this one is a winner, you'd agree with me. And what she carries…"

Axel's mouth curved in what looked like a grin but with a wicked light in her eyes.

"The asphodels. Of course. Not so popular nowadays as they were in the past. People prefer lilies now. Idiots. Lilies are equally white, but not that gorgeous, let alone everlasting."

"I'm glad you cherish the Etruscans, too," she said, her lithe hands playing with mane of her long hair. In the dim, orange light of the monuments' nocturnal illumination, Leonora found the strange woman even more sensual but also scary.

"I find their culture fascinating, especially in the conception of the afterlife." Axel's grin became an open smile. "They took many of their underworld's references from the Greeks, these flowers included."

"Not everything. This goddess of the *Inferi,* as they say in Italy, is their own creation," I said, admiring the bas-relief that looked almost alive under my stare. "She's the Etruscan psychopomp. A winged one. She accompanies men and women to the realm of the dead, whereas the Greeks had that young scoundrel of Hermes. Puny, little wings at his feet only."

"Her name is Vanth. And she's as beautiful as you are." Axel's voice was charming, but there was also something ominous in that suave tone. "I'd like you to do the same, Leonora."

"Bringing you white flowers?"

"Reaping souls and taking them to the underworld. For me."

*****

After a visit to the external circles of the necropolis, they'd headed toward Cerveteri's inner core, where the best-preserved architecture was located.

And there they'd stayed, sitting on a raised platform at the centre of one of town's main tombs. They'd entered the rectangular chamber through a steep, descending stairway, surrounded by oblong niches carved in the tufa walls. Leonora knew what they were for: places to put the dead bodies, a few of them big enough to host two people together. No mummies were there though, she noticed with disappointment. However, she could still admire sombre reliefs of demonic deities all around, some well-known like Kerberos, others more mysterious, like the one with a fish-tail holding a serpent.

"This one looks from the Middle East," Leonora said, not really waiting for an answer.

"She's Sumerian. The iconography came to the Etruscan through the Phoenicians, to which they were related."

"This theory has never been proved though."

Axel smiled one of her mischievous smiles. "You can trust me on these things, Leonora."

"Trust. What an interesting word." After these hours with Axel, in a situation that had become stranger every minute more, Leonora had only one question left, even though a crucial one: if Axel truly was what she pretended to be, what she needed a mortal for? "Here's another one: Logic. What you said defies any logic."

"Not really," Axel said. "Think about it. It's

2187. Nobody dies any longer."

Leonora burst into a laugher. "It's a lie. A blatant lie, too. How many people were slaughtered in China's last civil war? Millions of people. And let's consider this last century. Atomic bombs were only minor inconveniences compared to the rest."

"Ah, but you have just said it, Leonora; the 22nd century is different from any other in the history of humanity. Before that, everybody was dying, *en masse*, no matter their age or kind. Now? Only people that can't afford technology for long-term preservation pass away." She sighed in a theatrical way, but Leonora felt part of Axel's grief was real. "I can offer you precise figures, should you want them."

"Maybe later." Leonora scratched her head. "A few million in cryo-storage here and there and rich countries with whiz-type healthcare are still a drop in the ocean."

"But a golden drop."

"Oh, now this. I thought Death was the only God who did not discriminating between creatures."

Axel's eyes were like a dark abyss from the depth of the universe, black holes in their own right. "Up to a certain point. But when you start getting only the poor, the destitute and the ones who have no choice but dying, it's the creatures who discriminate. It doesn't look right, don't you think?" Leonora noticed for the first time a sort of dark red flame burning in those eyes, of a famished demon eager to devour souls.

"If you are what you pretend to be, you eventually get them all in your realm."

"It's not just snobbery, mine," Axel added, with a pensive tone. "It's the *eventually* that's unhealthy. And dangerous, too. This planet is exploding. You have even started to colonize the subterranean levels, now that the surface is crammed, and outer space is not a viable option, yet. Your resources are on the verge of collapse." She pointed at the ground, where marbled tiles separated our level from the terrain. "Humans need to keep dying at a certain, steady pace, for all the rest of the living things on Earth to be safe and survive."

Who Leonora was to argue with basic truth? And even if that were an excuse, she wouldn't have blamed Axel in any case. Leonora shared the same cult for beauty, too. "All jobs come with a paycheck. What do I earn in exchange? It must be worth the hassle."

"Freedom from my embrace, for as long as you desire it. And proximity, too, so that you can continue enjoying my company."

So unreal. So alluring. So, so tempting. Tipsy or not, that was all Leonora could think. "Tell me something. Are there many of them, your psychopomps, or whatever you call them?"

"My Winged Ones. A few, yes. Carefully selected among billions of people."

"Why me?"

"Haven't you dedicated to me all your life, Leonora?" Axel smiled her most charming smile. "Even Death fancies admirers."

*****

Leonora walks along the main street of Sorrento, in what is known to be one of the most beautiful little towns of the Mediterranean. Here and there the aroma of squeezed lemons mixes to the smell of the salted sea and the mountain breeze, one in particular: that Mount Vesuvius her employer always found so enticing.

She can relate: it's more than two decades she's chosen the Amalfi Coast as a dwelling. She's never regretted it. Not a lot of climate change-related mayhem here, if one excludes tropical storms in summer and sticky blood-sucking insects. The weather is still fair the way it's been for a few thousand years and before, a shining sun and a sky that reflect on the dark blue sea. The occasional rain takes nothing out of enchantment of the place.

And it's not just the weather.

This place has some unique perks, delicious food first. Fresh fish from the marine depths and mineral white wine from the hills nearby still manage to fill me with delight.

Leonora bites a luscious pomegranate, indulging on the red seeds as a modern Persephone. She got a better deal than the maiden-goddess: she can stay around for the whole year. She's just to be careful not to get outside in the middle of day, keen as she is to maintain her skin white and silky the way she likes it. She misses at times sunshine in summer, but down here it's definitively too fierce for her pale complexion. She's to wait until wintertime when daylight is gentler and lasts only a few hours.

Not a problem, Leonora can wait. Time flows in a different way for her, now, like an eternal present without clouds or creases. Were she not watching the news, she could easily forget in which year she lives.

Beauty and comforts aside, there's one thing that makes Sorrento and its hinterland the best place on Earth. The quality of the people Leonora is able to source here exceeds her most optimistic expectations, to the point she doesn't even venture more than a few kilometres away from the town.

What for? What she finds here satisfies all the job requirements she has, so to speak, while giving her the opportunity for exquisite encounters when she desires a different and more sensual kind of appeasement.

Like the one right now in front of her, on another Halloween night.

A young woman stunning by any standard.

Even the skeleton face she's painted on features can't hide how beautiful she is. About twenty years old, her look tells Leonora she's a model, as Leonora was so many years ago, in another country, another life, another time. Still recent enough for her to remember which pickup line works best with these people difficult to hook and even more challenging to persuade.

She sits in front of Leonora, gleaming smile and peach-soft skin, with that naivety that only youth and beauty can bring. Leonora reads in the polished mirror of the girl's clear green eyes an existential sadness and an *ennui* that smothers all *joie de vivre*.

Leonora orders champagne, while her hand reaches out to caress the girl's sleek wrist.

"Who are you?" the girl asks, shivering under Leonora's touch. "You're wearing no costume."

"I don't need one."

Leonora's voice is suave, but she knows the girl finds it more threatening than reassuring. An intended, subtle threat, which adds to the charm Leonora exercises on her. Leonora opens her overcoat for the girl's eyes only, showing off the expensive outfit she wears, seeing the girl's eyes following the line of the vertiginous cleavage of her dress.

Desire sparkles up for a brief moment in those grief-ridden pupils, while she devours with her gaze Leonora's breast.

"Do you want me?" The girl asks, voice that trembles but face suddenly alive.

"I do."

Leonora takes the girl's wrist, brushing with a slight kiss the vein that pulses. "But not for myself. Not just." Her lips bites delicately the girl's forefinger. "I'll help you to get to whom you're really after. Come with me."

"Where?"

"We're going for a stroll on Sorrento's breath-taking view on the bay. High cliffs tumbling down to the dark blue sea. Moonlight that washes the seashore in silver. A tapestry of stars for lovers and sprites."

Leonora doesn't add *where the attraction of the void might prove too strong for troubled souls like yours*. She doesn't need to. The girl will be quicker than others to grab the opportunity for a plunge in the void, eager and ready.

She already is.

"Who are you?" The girl asks with wide-open eyes, tightening the grip on Leonora's arm while following her outside the bar.

Leonora smiles, serene as ever. "Vanth, The Winged One."

END

Liked These Stories?

Don't forget to read the other
<u>From The Yonder</u> volumes

And other releases from
War Monkey Publications

Online at:
www.warmonkeypublications.com